D0846226

THE
HIGH KING'S
GOLDEN TONGUE

The High King's Golden Tongue
Tales of the High Court 1
By Megan Derr

Published by Less Than Three Press LLC

All rights reserved. No part of this book may be used or reproduced in any manner without written permission of the publisher, except for the purpose of reviews.

Edited by Samantha M. Derr
Cover designed by John Coulthart
http://www.johncoulthart.com/
Map designed by Raelynn Marie
http://becausethatswhatido.tumblr.com/

This book is a work of fiction and all names, characters, places, and incidents are fictional or used fictitiously. Any resemblance to actual people, places, or events is coincidental.

First Edition November 2015
Copyright © 2015 by Megan Derr
Printed in the United States of America

Digital ISBN 9781620046234
Print ISBN 9781620046241

To all the talented tongues in the world

Special Thanks to Fehu for the original prompt that inspired the tale

THE
HIGH KING'S
GOLDEN TONGUE

TALES OF THE HIGH COURT 1

MEGAN DERR

CHAPTER ONE

Allen had never been so terrified in his life. That he was thoroughly trained in the courtly manners of nine nations and had practiced ruthlessly for life in the High Court for the past two years did nothing to assuage his fit of nerves.

He smoothed his hands down the front of his jacket. Normally his clothes made him feel better, gave him armor to rely upon when all else failed. The new jacket was dark gold and embroidered with amber and pearls, had a subtle rose and feather pattern in the fabric. It fell to mid-shin, as latest fashion dictated, slit up the sides to his hips and cut so that the white pants beneath showed well, flaring slightly where they were tucked into high, glossy brown boots. Lace-trimmed cuffs fell to just past his wrists, longer than he cared for but also a dictate of fashion. But though he admired the clothes, had felt confident as he put them on, at present they brought him no comfort.

Reaching up, he lightly touched his hair. He hadn't brought his own servants, so he'd been anxious that he wouldn't be able to see it arranged properly, but a palace chamber servant had swept it up in an elaborate twist of several braids, secured with jeweled pins and clips. It had taken her well over an hour, but Allen had been immensely pleased with the results. He had always been particularly proud of his hair, but at present even that failed to bolster him.

Nor did all the beautiful jewelry he wore, the

crowning piece a diadem of sapphires and yellow diamonds gifted to him by his parents. One thing to be told, over and over again, that he had been chosen as High King Sarrica's new consort. Quite another to be minutes away from meeting the man he had been preparing to marry for the past two years.

What if, despite all the preparations, the High King did not want to marry him? It was, unfortunately, a possible outcome. Everyone knew High King Sarrica had been madly in love with his late husband, High Consort Nyle, who had been well-known and greatly liked despite the fact that he'd left the empire as a child and hadn't returned until he was sixteen. Sarrica himself was a fierce soldier; stories of his deeds in battle were still told, over and over, usually right alongside rumors that he would never marry any but another soldier.

Which couldn't be true, or Allen wouldn't be there. He'd been specifically chosen because he wasn't a soldier, because he was meant to complement the High King's strengths and abilities. Allen's battleground was the court. His weapons were words and other people. He was precisely what the High King needed, or so he'd been told by those who had prepared him for the role. Their words had been echoed by his mother, who was rarely wrong. Who'd fought so fiercely to see Allen was chosen, had been so proud when he had been—happier even than Allen, it had seemed at the time. If he'd thought her relentless with his training when he was young, it did not compare to his High Consort training.

Allen had been thoroughly trained in law, diplomacy, court manners, and the traditions of every kingdom in the Harken Empire. He spoke fourteen languages and also knew three dead ones. Further training ensured he could dance, sing, ride, and even host many religious ceremonies if necessary. He had been crafted since birth to rule a kingdom, and more recently molded to rule an empire.

All he had left to do was meet the High King and formalize the tentative engagement. Surely after everything he had done to reach this point, accomplishing that one tiny goal would be a simple matter. Nodding, he abandoned the mirror where he'd been fretting over his clothes and returned to the sofa, pouring himself a cup of tea—and promptly abandoned it as his anxiety-knotted stomach rebelled at the smell.

Striding over to the bookcase against the far wall, he browsed the offerings, somewhat heartened to see so many languages crammed onto one shelf. Most surprising was the row all the way at the bottom, dusty tomes written in Pemfrost, Lumor, and Charm: dead languages, all of them. His mother had taught him Pemfrost, but she'd had to pay heavily for the tutors who taught him Lumor and Charm.

He pulled out a volume on the history of Gearth written in Pemfrost. Most of it was grossly inaccurate, amusing at best, horrifying at worst, but working through the dense language kept him occupied—so occupied he startled when the door opened and someone cleared their throat.

Allen snapped the book shut and shoved it back into place, then rose, dusting off his clothes and adjusting his lace cuffs. "Beg pardon."

"Your Highness, His Majesty will see you now."

Anxiety came rushing back like a storm-tossed wave. "Thank you." Allen followed the servant from the waiting room and across the hall, through the enormous, gilded double doors that led into what was, apparently, the *lesser* receiving hall.

He was long used to the lavishness of his parents' palace, but even that was dwarfed by the grandeur of Harkenesten Palace. The lesser receiving hall was beautifully done, with gold and scarlet walls and carpet, a rainbow of stained glass across the tops of the walls and nearly all of the ceiling. It was breathtaking and, as much as he hated to admit it, very good at intimidating.

Firmly pushing back all unsettled feelings, Allen focused on the man at the far end of the hall.

Well. On a purely physical level, he would have no problems keeping the marriage bed warm should Sarrica ever indicate he wanted such a thing. That was a relief. One thing to be like his cousin, who simply did not care for sex. Another thing entirely to hate a spouse so much that sex and affection must be found elsewhere. He'd seen what that could do to a marriage firsthand, courtesy of his aunt and uncle, and his brother Chass and his wife, and he dreaded sharing their fate. He did not expect the kind of romance his parents enjoyed, but he wanted a happy marriage.

Allen had expected Sarrica to be handsome, or striking perhaps. He had not expected Sarrica to be beautiful. Or so big. Sarrica would tower over him exactly like Allen's brothers, and those shoulders were broad enough that he probably wore armor like it was linen. He had olive skin, and dark brown hair that had the faintest hints of red where the sun struck it, and an extremely close-cropped beard Allen wanted to stroke. Even the scar on his forehead, the two cutting across his left cheek, did not distract from his stunning features. His eyes were the softest moss green... and currently glaring at Allen as though he was guilty of some unforgivable crime.

He ran quickly over all that he had done since entering the hall, and then since arriving at the palace, but couldn't pinpoint anything he had done wrong. Court etiquette had been some of his easier lessons growing up, and he'd practiced and practiced until he was sick of it. He'd done everything correctly, he was certain of it.

Allen counted slowly in his head, matching his steps so he did not accidentally start walking too fast as he made his way steadily down the hall. When he reached the base of the dais he knelt and bowed his head, hands splayed on the floor on either side of him for balance. He waited for Sarrica to greet him, but the heavy silence stretched on, as troubling as the glare he sensed Sarrica was still casting him.

There was no doubt he had completed the first step of their meeting perfectly. His manners were impeccable, his skill absolute. If his mother were there, she would have been proud. He was dressed properly, had acted properly; his only aberration was to arrive alone, and that break in tradition was a good rather than bad. He had journeyed alone to Harken as a show of absolute trust and faith. The majority of his belongings would not arrive for a couple of months. The bodyguards who'd escorted him had already left the palace and would begin the journey home in the next day or so. He had put himself completely at the mercy of the High King.

"Rise," Sarrica finally said.

Lifting his head, Allen rose smoothly, letting his arms fall to rest easy at his sides. "It's an honor to at last make your acquaintance, Your Majesty. I bring you humble greetings and gratitude from the House of Gaulden. Blessings of the Pantheon be upon you." Oh, thank the Pantheon, he had not stuttered or stumbled over a single word. If it had been at all appropriate, he would have smiled.

Sarrica did not appear to be impressed. If anything, he seemed even less impressed than he had already been. The dread filling Allen's stomach began to spread through the rest of him, and sweat prickled at the back of his neck.

"I was informed today that a candidate for High Consort had arrived. I took that to mean that I would be presented with someone who was of use to me. You do not look like a soldier, however," Sarrica said. "Indeed, you look like someone has yet again accidentally let the songbirds loose. All feathers and pretty song, little prince. Is there anything of substance to you?"

Only two and a half decades of training allowed Allen to retain a calm he no longer felt. "With greatest respect, Your Majesty, if I lacked substance or usefulness I would not have been selected as a potential consort."

"Hmm," Sarrica replied and started to say something more when the man beside him bent to speak in his ear. The man was slightly taller than Sarrica, with a tight, lean build that wore armor with ease. He had dark olive skin and hair cropped too close to his head for the color to be clear—dark brown or black, possibly. He was smooth shaven, with pale gray eyes and a nose that looked to have been broken more than once. Sarrica was thirty-seven years old, and the man speaking to him seemed to be about that, perhaps a little older.

He must be High Commander Lesto Arseni, who controlled the Harken Imperial Army and was in charge of coordinating with the twenty-odd mercenary bands that supplemented the army. His brother, Rene Arseni, was Captain of the Three-headed Dragons, one of the most famous mercenary bands in the empire.

Lesto and Rene were also the older and younger brothers, respectively, of Nyle Arseni, Sarrica's late husband, dead now for the past four years. They were a powerful military family of Harken and held one of the oldest titles, the Duchy of Fathoms Deep, which had given its name to the mercenaries that had first formed there. Their bloodline hailed from the days when Harken was only a minor kingdom struggling not to be crushed by Tricemore and Cartha. The Harkenos and Arseni families shared a long history, a bond that had grown even stronger when Sarrica and Nyle had married.

Lesto met his gaze, the faintest smile flitting across it, chased by a bare nod. Reassurance? Allen tried to take heart and not let despondency get the better of him, but it had never been such a difficult struggle. Not even when two of his brothers had whipped him so badly he'd been unable to attend his own birthday festivities had he been as miserable as he was in that very moment, so immediately rejected and all but called worthless by the most powerful man in the empire—the man he was meant to marry.

Sarrica made a dismissive motion, and Lesto stepped back, a tight frown on his face. These men wore so much emotion on their faces, it left Allen dumbfounded. His tutors would leave his knuckles black and blue for revealing his thoughts and feelings so carelessly.

Pantheon, he hoped he was controlling his expressions as well as he knew how, because revealing anything would not help him in the slightest. He tried not to tense as Sarrica finally looked at him again. "I do not suppose you are more of a soldier than you appear?"

"No, Majesty. My talents lie elsewhere." Allen's heart sank even further. Whatever frayed thread of hope had been left snapped and fell away.

"Where, pray tell? I am an empire at war. I have no need of simpering fools who sit around court all day spinning lies and stabbing one another in the back over frivolous matters. I need someone who understands how battlefields work and the best way to move armies. You do not seem capable of even holding a sword."

Allen tried to gather his thoughts, which had been shattered to pieces right alongside his pride and confidence. Movement caught his eye, and he flicked a glance at Lesto, caught him staring at Sarrica with the barest pinched, pained look on his face before it was smoothed away.

The dread coursing through him hardened into an awful, terrible realization that all of a sudden seemed obvious in retrospect: Sarrica knew nothing about him. Two years of correspondence and training, two *fucking* years of preparation, and instead of arriving to *finalize* matters, Allen was a complete stranger to the man he was meant to be marrying. No one had told Sarrica that he had been tentatively bound to a diplomat rather than a soldier. Or warned Allen that they'd left the High King clueless.

Tamping down on anger, Allen carefully chose his words and said, "No, Your Majesty, I am not a soldier. My skills lie in language, diplomacy, law—"

"Your skills are of no use to me," Sarrica cut in. "You are—" He broke off as Lesto's hand clamped on his shoulder, and he bent to once more whisper in Sarrica's ear. Sarrica scowled and twisted to glare at Lesto, muttering something in reply. Allen could not make out anything they said, but there was no mistaking the anger on Lesto's face when he replied. Finally Sarrica snarled and turned back to Allen. "You are dismissed for now, until such time as I decide whether or not I want to continue this discussion."

It did not require Allen's level of training to note the way those last words had been dragged out of him by force. "Yes, Your Majesty. Thank you for your time, my best to you and yours." Allen swept him an elegant bow, then rose, turned, and left the hall as calmly as he arrived.

It took every scrap of training he possessed to ignore the tittering, the whispering, the fluttering fans lifted to poorly hide derisive looks and mocking commentary.

Arrived to marry the High King, and he had been thrown out of court in less than fifteen minutes. He had waited *hours* to be received, though he should have been seen immediately. He'd been derided, mocked, and dismissed out of hand. Worst of all, not once throughout the entire audience had Sarrica used his name.

Numbness overtook him as he reached the hall and a servant appeared to lead him to his rooms. Training alone recalled him to thank the woman, retain his decorum until he was well and truly alone.

Even then he could not bring himself to unbend, let go—what if another servant arrived abruptly? What if he was recalled to court? If he lost control of himself now, gave in to the anger and hurt, he would have trouble tucking it all away again in time. Then Sarrica would think even less of him, for what good was a master of the court who could not control himself?

Of course, proper control of a situation required having all necessary information. Like being informed that Sarrica knew nothing about him. The entire situation might have played out differently if anyone had warned him that he was going to come as a bit of a surprise to Sarrica.

Instead, the lack of information had guaranteed the whole thing was a disaster. He almost wished he could track down the bastards responsible for withholding the information and do something truly heinous. What, he wasn't sure, but there would be a great deal of suffering involved.

Allen strode over to the table where a carafe of wine and a single glass had been set out and drained an entire glass in several quick, greedy swallows. It was too sweet, a gold wine Allen knew to be favored in Harken. He had been drinking it with increasing frequency so as to become accustomed to the practices of his husband and the high court, but right then he would cheerfully cut off his hair for a glass of the dark, dry violets favored in Gaulden.

He would give quite literally anything for a familiar face, for some comfort of home. Anything to make him feel less alone. Traveling by himself had been a carefully calculated move, but it was the sort of move that succeeded beautifully or failed miserably. And it most certainly had not succeeded.

Sitting down at the table, he poured a fresh glass of wine and took a healthy swallow before slumping in his seat, appearances be damned, and stared morosely out the window a few paces away. Despite all the languages he knew, Allen could not find words adequate to describe how he felt. If tears had not been beaten out of him at a young age he would have been a sobbing mess. Years of preparation for nothing. Sent to Harken to become the second most powerful man in the empire and he'd been thrown out of court like a child. If not for Commander Lesto, he suspected he would already be on his way home.

How in the Pantheon was he going to explain his abysmal failure to his mother? Explaining it to the rest of his family would be bad enough. His brother Larren would be disappointed, his brothers Chass and Manda would be sneering know-it-alls who claimed not to be surprised. His father would be crushed, and his dame heartbroken for him. His mother was by far the worst, though. All he could see was her disappointment, the way she would lift her chin higher, fold her hands, and be every stitch the stately queen because it had been she who taught him to hide his emotions, and she would not falter even in the face of such a devastating blow.

There had to be something he could do. Lesto had convinced Sarrica to simply leave him hanging about court, awaiting a possible second chance. There was no telling how much time he had before Sarrica completely lost patience and sent him packing, but surely he had at least a few days. That was enough time to manage something to impress Sarrica. To prove his worth. He was a silver tongue, for Pantheon's sake. A silver tongue who far outstripped most since the standard was two to four languages, and he knew far more than that.

Patience would be the key. Sarrica was not a man whose mind changed in a moment, that much was clear if he was so stubbornly set on having a soldier, and only a soldier, for a spouse.

Allen took another sip of wine, weighing his options. That he'd been thrown out of court was going to be an impediment. Nobody would willingly spend time with a man mocked and derided by the High King. He chafed at the idea of working slowly, circling carefully, picking and feeling step by incremental step—but wars were most often won not by those who hit the hardest, but by those who could endure the longest.

Sarrica had struck a brutal blow, but Allen would wager a kingdom he had superior staying power.

Another key to war was knowing the lay of the land, and he would not learn that remaining in his chambers. Finishing his second glass of wine, Allen headed into the bedroom and stripped out of his formal court clothes. Standing in front of the wardrobe, he considered his options.

After several minutes, he settled on dark green pants, black boots, and a long, heavy jacket of dark blue, with an under robe of green and gold. The jacket fell to his ankles, fastened down the front with gold buttons. It was slit in four places, all the way to his hips, to display the under robe. The cuffs were long, but thankfully did not get in the way of his hands as had the formal jacket.

Unbinding his hair, he combed it out before tying the long, dark blond strands back with a green and gold striped ribbon. Jewelry he eschewed, save for gold hoops for his ears and his Gaulden royal signet.

A signet he had hoped to have replaced that day with an engagement ring, surrendering his ties to Gaulden and giving his loyalty wholly to Harken. Sarrica should have also given him a welcome banquet to introduce him to the High Court and make him a part of it. In return, Allen's own gift would have been to contribute to the court by way of sponsoring some event or project or hosting a lavish ball or banquet.

His mother had posed several ideas, but Allen had latched onto some of the ideas posed by his dame. They were more social leaning and light-hearted than his mother favored, but Allen had always liked his dame's light-heartedness. Envied it, even. There was no time for such things when he was working so hard to rule a kingdom—an empire. His dame, Eila, youngest sister of his father, had given up her life back in her homeland to join his parents in Gaulden, had agreed to be dame to them and bear the children his mother sired. Afterward, Eila had been free to return home but had chosen to stay in Gaulden, a bright, cheerful counterpoint to an otherwise serious-minded family.

Together with her, Allen had made an entire list of possible sponsorships, determined to do something that would make a real difference and tie in to his own abilities. Something with language or law, two professions that always needed more support than they ever received.

Perhaps he could find a way to still do that. He ran the risk of overstepping himself, acting presumptuously, but only if he failed. If whatever he chose to do succeeded nobody would mind, and Sarrica might be willing to give him a chance.

Abandoning his rooms, Allen wended his way through the halls, attempting to memorize the layout as he went, determined to have no need of a servant in order to get around the enormous palace. His determination faltered, however, when he immediately lost himself trying to get to the gardens he had caught a glimpse of hours before. Twenty minutes of wandering did not get him unlost, unfortunately, and he finally conceded defeat when he found himself in a gallery. He sat on a bench padded with dark violet cushions, and glumly studied the rather dull, if technically sound, landscape before him.

A Delfastien artist, if he was not mistaken, though he only knew art just well enough not to embarrass himself in general conversation. Delfastien artists tended to favor heavy blues and purples, and it was currently the trend to show a heavy hand on the brushstrokes. Allen much preferred the works where it was nigh impossible to see any sign of brushstrokes at all.

He pulled out his pocket watch to check the time and sighed to see so much of the day was already gone and nothing even remotely positive had been achieved. Perhaps he should give up his wandering for the day and return to his rooms on the chance an invitation to dinner was extended.

On the other hand, given the way Sarrica had treated him, that only Lesto's interference had kept Allen in the palace, dinner was highly unlikely. Best to keep wandering about the palace like an imbecile until it all started to become familiar.

Which would not happen if he continued sitting. Allen stood and shook out the heavy folds of his jacket, fussed with his cuffs, turned—

And paused when he heard a voice, sharp and angry, speaking in clumsy, stilted Tricemorien. Another voice replied in fluent Tricemorien, but it was cut off by the angry voice, which was cut off by another angry voice speaking some horrible mish-mash of Harken and Tricemorien. Occasionally he caught slips of Selemean, one voice native, another moderately fluent.

Allen followed the voices until he located a discreet doorway tucked behind what looked like a flat wall until one was right up on it. A cluster of five servants stood together arguing, arms flying, faces flushed, occasionally remembering to keep their voices down but more often than not failing. He could not even sort out what the argument was about, there was so much disorder to the conversation. That was easy enough to fix. Allen brought his hands together in a sharp, ringing clap.

The servants all jumped, looked at him, and blanched. The one who seemed to be in charge darted forward and nearly fell over in his haste to bow. Speaking Harken, he said, "Your Highness, I apologize that we have disturbed you."

"You have not disturbed me," Allen said. "However, I am concerned." He repeated the words in Tricemorien and Selemean. They all gaped at him. Were silver tongues so peculiar a thing in the palace? Surely not. Allen directed his attention to the man who had spoken to him. "What is your name and position?" he asked in Harken.

"Remis Thatching, Your Highness. I'm Head Footman of the West Wing." He raised an arm to gesture about them.

"Who are your comrades?"

"Marta, Joffre, Fen, and Carnac, Your Highness. All recently hired."

"They have not a single language in common?"

Remis shook his head. "No, Your Highness. Servants come and go from all over the Empire. We try to teach them Harken, but..." He shrugged.

Allen nodded in understanding. Of all the languages in the kingdom, Harken and Mestan were the most difficult to learn, especially the formal versions used in court—and the informal versions weren't all that easy to begin with. Harken was also an extremely dense language, and that it was the language of the High Court did it no favors. "Harken isn't a practical choice, but we'll address that in a moment. What is the problem here?"

"The rooms aren't being cleaned properly, and if we mess up one more day we are going to be thrown out, every one of us. The dusting hasn't been done, the rugs need to be taken out and shaken, and the incense and candles replaced. Never mind the usual sweeping, polishing, so on and so forth. I can get them to partially clean some of the rooms, but... It's a mess, Your Highness, though it is not *your* mess."

"Nonsense," Allen replied, beckoning all of them closer. "If the problem is communication, it is a problem for a silver tongue." He turned to the two that seemed to speak Tricemorien. *"Tell me the problem."*

"We don't know the problem," said the woman. *"We try to clean what he says, go where he says, but all we get is yelled at and told we are going to be terminated today if we do not do it correctly. Only we do it all correctly and just get screamed at more."*

"I see," Allen replied. *"I will sort it out. Do you speak Selemean at all?"*

The man beside her, Fen, regarded him warily. *"Passably, Your Highness. We lived not too far from the border with Selemea; we speak it enough to go to market."*

Allen smiled and nodded, then turned to the two men who had been speaking Selemean, switching to that language. *"What is the problem?"* Their explanation matched with everything the others had said. Allen turned back to Remis. "Do you speak anything other than Harken with passable skill?"

"No, Your Highness. I've lived here all my life. I speak some Tricemorien, but nothing I would take to market."

"Would you be willing to learn another language?"

Remis looked confused but nodded. "Yes, Your Highness."

"Good. Is this problem common in Harkenesten Palace?"

"Does the moon come out at night?" Remis asked wryly, then flinched and bowed low. "Apologies, Your Highness. I did not mean to be so rude."

Allen shook his head. "I'll pay it no mind this time. You answered my question clearly, which is all anyone can ask. You may rise. I will relay your instructions to this group, and they can convey them on to anyone who needs to know. After that, you and I will speak further."

"Yes, Your Highness."

Turning back to the other servants, Allen quickly laid out their duties first in Tricemorien, then Selemean. When they all acknowledged they understood, he dismissed them, smiling when they bowed and thanked him. After they had gone, he turned back to Remis. "Who is in charge of the staff and ensuring they are capable of understanding each other? Who instructs them when they come to Harkenesten Palace but cannot speak Harken?"

"You would need to speak with the Seneschal, Your Highness. He does the hiring and assigning. Generally he tries to group people together according to language, but it gets to be impossible after a point. The Chamberlain may be worth speaking with as well."

Such a gross lack of effective communication was puzzling, to say the least. But it was not something to be discussed at length with a servant. It wasn't really his place to be discussing the matter with anyone, not yet. It was a problem he might be able to help fix, however, and he had been hoping for a way to prove himself... Well, at the very least it couldn't hurt to ask if he could help. Reaching into a pocket of his jacket Allen extracted one of his calling cards. "If you would please explain tonight's incident to the Seneschal and inform him that I respectfully request to discuss the matter further with him, I would be most grateful. He may call upon me in my suite, or send a note as to where I should meet him. He might invite the Chamberlain, or a suitable representative from that office, to attend the interview as well. Any further questions, he should feel free to contact me directly."

"Yes, Your Highness." Remis tucked the card away and bowed. "I thank you most humbly for your assistance. There are never enough silver tongues to go around this place: the soldiers steal them as fast as they arrive. Can't remember the last one as good as you. I can't tell which of those three you speak natively."

Allen's mouth curved. "My native language is Gaulden. Good evening, Mr. Remis. If there are any further troubles with which I can assist, I am happy to help."

"Good evening, Your Highness." Remis bowed and remained that way as Allen left the gallery.

The palace bells were just ringing the eighth hour of the evening when he finally found his rooms again. He opened the door, immediately glanced at the table by the door where messages were left... and tried not to feel disheartened that no invitation to dinner had been left.

His wine had been refilled in his absence, at least. He had been in Harken twelve hours and all he had accomplished was sorting out a minor tiff amongst secondary staff. His mother would be weeping into her sleeve.

Striding into his bed room and over to the chest the servants had placed at the foot of his bed, following his instructions to leave its unpacking to him, he unlocked it and threw back the lid. He had left most of his belongings behind in Gaulden, determined to throw himself into his new life in every way.

But he'd not been able to part with some of his favorite books, or even wait for them to arrive with the rest of his belongings. The books were mostly collections of folktales, legends, and particularly famous historical moments. He had brought twenty volumes, all old and well-maintained but requiring regular care as well as proper storage. It should have been a simple enough matter to request they be stored in the palace library—if he was the High Consort.

Since he was, apparently, just a songbird, he would either have to keep the books in his trunk or beg a favor of the Master Librarian. A task for another day, though he was half-tempted to address it immediately since he would rather do anything than stay tucked away alone in his suite.

Carrying his chosen book to the table, Allen poured a fresh glass of wine and settled in. He opened the book to his favorite story, a silly tale of a silver tongue in disguise joining the army against his father's wishes. To a boy stuck inside studying at least fourteen hours almost every single day, the story had always held strong appeal. Tales of heroes were always tales of soldiers. Every once in a while the story went to a dashing, sword-swinging crown prince. Sometimes a wise wizard. No one ever told tales of brave and daring silver tongues. If they appeared in stories at all it was simply as side notes to help the hero along.

The sound of knocking made him startle, splash wine over his hand. Huffing at himself, he pulled out a kerchief and mopped up the mess as he called, "Come in." A servant stepped inside and bowed. Nervous anticipation sped up the beating of Allen's heart.

"Your Highness, Seneschal Pallman extends a humble invitation to join him in his quarters for dinner, though he of course understands if Your Highness is otherwise occupied with matters far more important. If dinner is not to your preference, he says that he will be happy to call upon you tomorrow at the hour most convenient for Your Highness."

It was certainly better than eating alone. "I would be honored to accept such a gracious invitation to dinner, and I appreciate the Seneschal's generosity on such short notice. When I should arrive?"

"Entirely at your leisure, Your Highness. He says if you prefer to come with me now, he has a wine that might appeal to you and is happy to share it while dinner is prepared. He has also invited the Chamberlain to dine as per your request."

Allen wondered what the High King would say if he knew his servants were kinder and more gracious than he had proven to be. "I'll come now, then." He closed his book and set it on his bed, abandoning the used handkerchief as well and retrieving a new one from his bureau before following the servant.

She led him through unfamiliar halls to a wing of the palace decorated in a much darker, more somber manner than the others he had visited that day. The West Wing, if he recalled Remis' words correctly, which had been all green, gold, and cream with the occasional splashes of blue and teal. Whatever wing he was in currently, it was all purples and reds, dark woods, accents of silver. His parents' palace was fairly uniform in design, but Harkenesten Palace was so enormous he could see where harmonizing it in full would be an insurmountable task.

The servant stopped at the end of a narrow, dim-lit hallway and rapped on a door carved with the griffon of the High King clutching a bundle of flowers, representing the nine kingdoms of the Harken Empire: Harken, Tricemore, Selemea, Delfaste, Rilen, Gaulden, Mesta, Gearth, and Outland.

"Seneschal, His Royal Highness Prince Allen Telmis."

"Thank you, Kara. If you will be kind enough to fetch our dear Chamberlain, after that you are free for the evening."

"Yes, Seneschal." She bowed to him, gave a deeper bow to Allen, and departed, closing the door quietly behind her.

"Your Highness, I am honored to have you for

dinner," Seneschal Pallman said, rising from the chair where he had been sitting—one of two, along with a small sofa, clustered around a small, low table, arranged in front of the large fireplace. On the opposite end of the room was an enormous desk, a wall of bookshelves behind it, though few books and many other items occupied them. The office was of the same dark wood that filled the rest of the wing, and there were only two small windows, but lamps and brightly colored tapestries and paintings lent light to the space.

Pallman was a handsome, dignified looking man. He had pale skin, red hair liberally touched with gray, pale gray eyes, and heavy lines cut into his face. Despite the gray and the wrinkles, he did not seem all that old—not more than mid-forties. "Thank you for indulging me despite the short notice. I received your note, and am most sorry that your early impression of us must convey a sense of disarray." He clapped his hands. "I am getting ahead of myself, though, Your Highness. My apologies. I promised a wine that would please you and I shall deliver. Sit where you like, of course."

Allen took the sofa, suspecting the chairs were a longstanding tradition of Pallman and the 'dear Chamberlain'.

"My late wife, Pantheon welcome her, was from Gaulden. She would drink the wines favored here, but she never loved them." He picked up a carafe resting on the desk and carried it over to the circle of chairs and sofa, along with three glasses.

Homesickness washed over Allen, hurting like a fresh wound, when he saw the familiar purple-red color of Coresta wine, the most famous wine in

Gaulden, unique to the Coresta Valley where it was made. Gaulden pulled in obscene sums every year on the taxes levied on wine exports. "You were correct, that is a happy sight. My thanks, Seneschal."

Pallman made a dismissive noise. "Seyn is my name, and Master Seyn will do fine, Your Highness. We—" He broke off as a knock came at the door, bid the knocker enter, and rose as a large, striking woman stepped into the room, purple robes shimmering in the fire and lamplight. She reminded Allen fleetingly of his Delfastien tutor, with dark brown-black skin and hair dyed purple at the ends before being coiled up into an elegant arrangement he would never be able to duplicate. She was so big around his arms would not meet if he wrapped them around her. His Delfastien tutor had been the only one to hug him, bring him sweets, or teach him how to do something more than speak her language. The only one he had missed when she'd gone.

He rose as she bowed to him. "You must be the Chamberlain."

"Yes, Your Highness. My name is Anesta Demray."

"An honor to make your acquaintance, Lady Demray." They all took their seats, and Seyn poured wine, handing Allen's glass over first before offering the second glass to Anesta.

Seyn took a generous swallow from his own glass before saying, "I was just about to tell His Highness that many of us were positively mad with excitement today to hear that he was chosen as a candidate for High Consort."

Allen froze with the glass at his lips, taking a hasty sip before lowering the glass and saying, "Were you? I am pleased, of course, but I did not know the announcement would provoke such a reaction."

Seyn and Anesta shared a look, then turned back to him. Anesta replied, "Perhaps we speak out of turn, Your Highness, but we heard you are quite the accomplished silver tongue, and there are not many of those at your level. Master Seyn shared with me your message from the footman, so you've already had a taste of the problems we have here at Harkenesten Palace. I promise it *was* only a taste—the problems created by language gaps and barriers grow every day. Pantheon bless His Holy Majesty, he is busy with war and other matters of state, but... Well, it will be nice to know that someone in court understands other problems and may help us address them. I apologize, Your Highness, if my words are too brazen."

"Brazen? Perhaps. But I respect honesty, and that unfortunately compels me to admit what you clearly do not know: His Majesty was not pleased with me and dismissed me from court only a few hours ago. I am sorry to prove a disappointment so immediately." He took a sip of wine, fought an urge to drain the damned glass. Appearances mattered, and he was already leaning precariously over the line of propriety.

They both seemed to slump in their seats, though their expressions did not reveal as much as they could have. Allen refused to be a complete disappointment when there had apparently been hopes pinned upon him. "That being said, I would like to help howsoever I am able. That is why I requested to see you tomorrow. I appreciate you were willing to see me immediately."

"You are the gracious one, Your Highness, I assure you. If you've already thoughts upon the matter, by all means share them."

Taking another swallow of wine, Allen set his glass

on the table and folded his hands in his lap. "You may have already attempted my suggestion, which is this: stop teaching the servants Harken. It's a difficult language, requiring at least five years of focused study just to take to market. Impractical in a place where turnover is high and communication is already scattered at best. I recommend using Selemean as the main language for servants and that you require only primary servants to know Harken. You should have staff aplenty who already know Selemean, which will help speed the learning of it, and you may even be able to find people in the city willing to act as tutors for a time. Every person in Harken is given an hour a day to devote to prayer, and that hour can be given to study instead. Encourage staff to use that hour to focus on language for at least the next six months, and I promise that should be sufficient time to ease many of your difficulties."

"Harken is the language the High King wants to be the common language," Seyn replied.

"Harken is the language of the court and all primary staff will know it. No one cares below that, as you well know. It cannot hurt to experiment, and I will happily provide the funds to see the project started if that will help settle the matter." It was not as though he had anything else to do with his gift money, or even his personal funds, until he had a place in court. Hopefully Sarrica would be too busy to note that he was overstepping until too late.

Anesta and Seyn had another silent conversation. After a few minutes, they nodded to each other then turned and gave him a half-bow. "As you say, Your Highness. It shames me to admit that it is not something I thought to try before. All my plans have revolved around trying to teach Harken, but it never takes. We will try your suggestions."

"Calculate the necessary funding, and I will see it is given to you," Allen replied and raised his glass to them before draining it.

Anesta smiled and refilled it for him. "Your Highness—"

The door slammed open, making them all jump. A fierce-looking man strode into the room, jangling with every step, and turned toward the desk. "Seyn—" He broke off as he realized the desk was vacant, and turned, poised to speak again. He paused when he saw Allen, eyes flicking to the marks on the shoulder of his jacket. "Your Highness, I'm sorry to interrupt. Master Seyn, is there anyone is this damnable palace that can speak Outlander? I need them *now*, or it will—"

"I can speak Outlander," Allen said, standing. "Take me where I am needed."

The man did not look as though he quite believed Allen, but he only nodded and spun sharply on his heel, storming from the room with the same loud jangle with which he'd arrived. Allen turned to Seyn. "Thank you very much. I hope to speak with you again soon. My apologies for the abrupt departure." He hastened after the soldier, stifling a sigh because at least this man seemed to *need* to hurry, unlike Allen's brothers who only walked quickly because they knew he could not keep up.

Allen followed him through another maze of hallways until they were suddenly outside, the air cold, the sky so clear the stars looked like sharp-edged bits of glass. Voices milled about him, speaking at least half a dozen languages. Torches and small fires lit for the guards on duty to keep warm provided the only light, dark and flickering, casting strange shadows that lent an eerie quality to everything. Allen caught snatches of words: blood, battle, mercenaries, dragons, ambush. He ignored them, focused on keeping pace with the stranger.

Until they came to an abrupt halt in front of a cluster of men, all dressed in the same black tunics and leather armor as the man Allen had followed. They were sweaty, bloody, rank with recent battle. They parted in front of Allen and the man, the word Captain floating on the air.

Their tunics bore a crest of a three-headed dragon... So this was very likely Commander Lesto's brother, Captain Rene Arseni of the Three-headed Dragons. The resemblance seemed obvious now that he was paying attention. Rene was a younger, rougher-edged, yet also prettier version of his brother, hair long enough to note it was black and prone to curls.

Someone moaned, and Allen turned his attention to the bloody, battered man lying on the dark stones of whatever pavilion they were in. He had the gold-brown skin and brown hair common to the Outlands, but that wasn't Outlander he was speaking. Allen knelt beside him, trying to ignore the blood that covered the man's robes. Pantheon, he was used to blood, but there was so much of it. The man was clearly dying.

Allen wrapped an arm behind the man to help him sit up slightly. Holding one of his trembling, bloody hands, Allen said, *"I am sorry for your pain."*

"It was—"

"What does he say?" Rene demanded.

Allen's head snapped up and he met Rene's eyes as he said coldly, "Be quiet." Not waiting for Rene's reply, he looked back down. *"Tell me what we need to know."*

"The Swan wrecked off the coast of Yryma, and Benta took all the survivors prisoner. There were Carthians among the Bentans. I managed to get away, but they got me at the base of the mountains. Thank the Dragons for me. Tell my family I love them."

"Rest in the arms of the Mother Ocean, brother." Allen held him until he went still, then set him back on the ground. He stared at the man's ears, which were bare, but showed several holes in each where he'd removed all the piercings in his ears, and there signs of others over the rest of his face. Piercings, especially earrings, were an important part of Farlander culture. As were the tattoos Allen could see hints of on his arms and the base of his throat. He should be in Farland, not dead in the heart of Harken.

Breathe in, breathe out. Emotion had no place in court. He would not fall apart in front of a group of damned soldiers. When he was certain he had himself under control, Allen rose to his feet and looked at Rene. "He is a survivor of a ship called *The Swan*. It wrecked somewhere off the coast of Yryma, and the survivors were taken prisoner by Benta. He managed to escape, but the Carthians caught up to him at the base of the mountains. He said there were Carthians mixed in with the Bentans."

"Damn," Rene muttered, raking a hand through his hair and sighing. He nodded as he looked up again. "Thank you, Prince—uh."

"Allen. I hope I was of some use. Do we know his name?"

Rene shook his head. "No, but it will be figured out. There aren't that many Outlanders on military vessels."

"Farlander," Allen corrected.

Staring at him blankly, Rene said, "What?"

Allen's mouth tightened. The man was dead, had died to bring them important information. Couldn't they at least bother to get that one detail about him right? "He wasn't from Outland. He's from the Farland Islands, the South Star Island, if I had to guess, though his accent was hard to determine. I am guessing he was pressed into service to pay off debts, or because he looked at someone wrong. That's how the Islanders usually wind up as... what is the charming term soldiers use? Ah, yes. Easy targets."

Rene opened his mouth, but immediately closed it again and stared pensively at Allen.

"They all sound the same," someone else muttered.

Allen knew that was fair enough. Knew how hard it was to tell the difference between Outlander and Farlander without training. But Pantheon damn them all, the man had died in his arms. They could *care where he was really from.* Not even trying to fight his temper, just letting it consume him, Allen drew himself up and said coolly, "They only look and sound and feel the same to those who do not care enough to note the differences. The next time you think 'they all sound the same' put yourself in that man's place and imagine how your loved ones would feel if your body was lost because Tricemorien and Carthian 'always sound the same' and they shipped you to Tricemore instead of Cartha."

"How did you know I'm Carthian?" the man demanded.

"Your speech is stilted, and you speak too flatly,

like someone accustomed to the tonal languages of Cartha and overcompensating. You use pronouns with ease, which faded out of frequent use in Tricemorien well over a century ago, but which Carthian retains. Among other things."

"Silver tongues," Rene said, shaking his head again. "Thank you again for your assistance, Your Highness. I will ensure that the Farlander is returned to his proper home. Goodnight." He turned and strode off, his sword belt and spurs jangling, the sound echoing off the stone walls surrounding the courtyard.

Allen wondered if anyone would be willing to show him back to his rooms, but the scowling faces not quite looking at him seemed a definite no.

"Your Highness..."

He turned and saw that Seyn had followed them. "Seneschal, my apologies again for leaving you so abruptly. I hate to abandon dinner, but I think perhaps our conversation is best resumed on the morrow."

"Of course. I'll have someone show you to your rooms if you like. Um... might I ask... how many languages do you know, Your Highness? I was impressed already that you were fluent in Harken, Tricemorien, Selemean, and of course Gaulden. You also know Outlander, Farlander, and Carthian?"

Allen stifled a sigh because his sudden need to be left alone was not anyone's fault, and they should not have to endure his temper. But he was long past ready for the day to be at an end. "I speak fourteen languages. If you will pardon me, it is time I call this night ended. Goodnight to you all."

"Of course." Seyn motioned to a servant, who hastened forward and bowed.

Managing a thank you, Allen followed him,

ignoring the whispers that chased him inside, trying not to think about how it felt to hold a man as he died. When he finally reached his bedroom, Allen stripped off his bloody jacket, sat on the edge of his bed, and cried.

CHAPTER TWO

Sarrica wished his head would stop hurting for one damned hour. Goddess grant him mercy, just one hour of relief was all he needed.

He looked up when the door to his private inner office opened, beckoning Lesto and Rene to enter. "Did you manage to learn anything from the sailor before he died?"

"A little, thanks to your feisty little silver tongue."

"My what?" Sarrica motioned impatiently when Rene started to answer the question, though the startled, curious look that overtook Lesto's face almost gave him pause. "What did he say?"

"*The Swan* wrecked off the coast of Yryma and Benta took the survivors prisoner. There were Carthian soldiers cooperating with the Bentans."

Sarrica slammed a fist on his desk. "Damn it. If they bothered to capture a bunch of sailors, they must know one of them is much more than he seems. If they figure out they have Prince Morant, that is the end of Korlow, and Benta will be in a position to challenge Harken outright."

"Especially if they've managed to gain the cooperation of Cartha," Lesto said from where he leaned against the wall opposite Sarrica's desk, arms folded across his lean chest. "Korlow's loyalty and Cartha's apathy were all that kept Benta in check. Korlow isn't strong enough to hold out."

"They will be if we can still figure out a way to put

Morant back on his throne. Benta can't do a damned thing in the face of a rightful heir," Sarrica said. "With Korlow shored up, Fyr Dane and Vemeteria will turn on Benta, and after that we can start to oust Benta from the rest of the northern continent." He leaned back in his seat, smacking his desk lightly with the flats of his hands. "Ideally, anyway. If only saying it were enough to make it true."

Rene shook his head. "I would not want to be the man with that kind of power."

Sarrica smiled briefly.

"The council won't like it," Lesto said, and they both turned to look at him.

"If I was concerned with the council's opinion on a matter about which they are not fit to opine, I would have told them of the scheme in the first place. Espionage is not the council's purview. As to hearing we may have to prepare for war... If that comes as a surprise to them, they are greater fools than I had already believed." Sarrica scrubbed at his beard, noting absently it needed a trim. "We need to get into Benta and get Prince Morant back out—or confirm that he, and therefore Korlow, is lost. I can prepare the council for war in the meantime, but I would much rather infiltrate Benta and end this war with far fewer casualties."

"The Dragons can handle it," Rene said. "We've done that kind of work before. It wasn't with Benta, I admit, but we're here, fully recovered from our last mission, and no new orders have been given. We can be ready to leave in three days."

Sarrica's mouth tightened as he stared at Rene and Lesto, who looked so much like Nyle that some days it still hurt to look at them. In the days immediately following Nyle's death he hadn't been able to be in the same room with them for very long. Rene and Lesto were five years apart; Nyle had been younger than Lesto by two years, older than Rene by three, and had considered himself the easily missed middle child, especially since he hadn't returned to the empire until he was sixteen, and he and Sarrica hadn't properly met until Nyle was eighteen. It had taken Sarrica a long time to convince Nyle that it really was him whom Sarrica loved.

And he honored his Nyle's memory by sending his brothers into battle again and again. "Do it," he said quietly.

Rene nodded and left, as quick to come and go as ever, as if he was afraid he would be trapped if he held still too long. Lesto swore, shot Sarrica a look that was tired-angry-understanding all at once, and chased after Rene.

The office was silent in their wake. Sarrica hated silence. He also hated not eating; the fact he could not remember when he last had eaten certainly explained part of his foul mood and probably his headache. A glance at the clock confirmed what he had vaguely noted earlier: dinner had long since come and gone. He could not recall the last time he had been able to attend a public dinner. Which was unfortunate, because though the dinners were exhausting and he had no real talent for the talking and mincing that went along with them, they were occasionally useful for accomplishing some small matter that otherwise would require hours of tedious meetings, court hearings, or summoning people to his office to issue orders or threats. The best way to convince someone to listen, Nyle had always said, was to ply them with food and drink and music. They had both hated giving up the battlefields and fortresses to return to the palace and settle into court life, but Nyle had been better at handling it—at first, anyway. But Sarrica did not feel like further ruining his mood by dwelling on things that no longer mattered.

A mood that would never improve if he did not eat and his head did not stop hurting. Which reminded him of the other reason he had hoped to attend dinner that night: Prince Allen Telmis. The poor timing of his arrival, and the surprise that he was not the soldier Sarrica had requested, had not been Prince Allen's fault. He could not be expected to be aware of all that was happening when Sarrica could barely keep up with it himself.

Perhaps it was for the best he had been such a bastard to Prince Allen. Sarrica had conceded to a second marriage, but with the stipulation that the candidate be someone who could help him—an experienced soldier who could also endure court life, someone strong and capable and who understood it would be a partnership of state and nothing more. Prince Allen had a cold demeanor, but he'd also been soft and pretty, and meticulously dressed, practically dripping with jewels. He had looked like a songbird in need of careful handling and plenty of attention.

Sarrica had no time for such nonsense, or the aggravation that inevitably came from such persons when they did not receive the attention they required. He had an empire to run, small wars to stop—or at least keep manageable—and a much larger war to prevent. He did not have time to hold the hand of a pretty little prince from...

Where did Prince Allen hail from? Sarrica thought

over the brief encounter in court, but all he remembered of the man was his beauty and cool demeanor. He had spoken Harken like a native, but that pale, gold-toned skin wasn't common in Harken or the immediately surrounding kingdoms. Whatever. It hardly mattered when he was just going to send the man scurrying off back home, no matter what Lesto said or threatened.

He scrubbed a hand over his face, tried to wake himself up because there was still quite a bit of work to do even discounting the new problem with *The Swan*. In addition to everything else, he was going to have to work out what exactly he was going to say to the council so that they could begin to quietly prepare for full war without alarming everyone. He also needed to make certain they took long enough that the Three-headed Dragons had time to accomplish their mission.

The door to his office opened, and Sarrica looked up, sighing when Lesto stepped in, closed the door, and locked it before striding across the room to join Sarrica at his desk. "I'm sorry," Sarrica said.

Lesto shook his head. "We all have our duties, and Rene is an adult; he can make his own stupid decisions. I'm more annoyed with him for always wanting to run into every fire that sparks to life. I wish I could figure out, once and for all, what he is always running *from*."

Sarrica was at least sixty percent certain Rene was running from Lord Tara, but he had promised not to say anything. "I want Fathoms Deep ready to move on a moment. At this point we must assume that everything is going to go wrong."

"Fathoms Deep is always ready to move on a moment," Lesto replied. "Dinner should be waiting in your suite by now. Everything is locked up for the night."

"Then let's go have dinner," Sarrica said and locked his desk and cabinet. Slipping the steel ring that held all his keys back onto its loop on his belt, he followed Lesto across the room to a hidden door built into the wall, concealed by a profusion of paintings, statues, and plants. Lesto lit a small torch, leading the way through the dark maze of secret passages that connected the main rooms of the High King: offices, bedchamber, solar, and a secret escape route. They connected to a few other places as well, but Sarrica and Lesto seldom used those passages.

Lesto paused as they reached one of the intersections, casting Sarrica a look that, even in the dark, was clearly sly and faintly amused. "I learned something interesting from Rene."

"Oh?" Sarrica asked and slipped by him, more interested in food than gossip.

Following him, Lesto replied, "Apparently when he went in search of a silver tongue he could not find one. He finally went to demand Seyn locate him one, but a pretty prince speaking with Seyn and Lady Anesta said that he could speak Outlander. Except when he was finished speaking with our poor, dead sailor he revealed the man was actually from Farland. In the span of a few minutes, he snapped at Rene to shut up, reprimanded the imperial army for its longstanding bad habit of pressing Farlanders into service, and implied Rene and his men were halfwits for not being able to tell the difference between Outlander and Farlander—and after only listening to a few short words, was able to identify the Carthian defector in Rene's group."

Sarrica stopped, half-turned, and scowled. "What is the point of this tale? That there is a talented but rude silver tongue on the premises? Hardly new. Silver tongues all think they're special for speaking multiple languages and scoff at those of us who cannot. As though I have time to sit around studying all day and talking just for the sake of talking." His scowl turned into a glare when Lesto laughed. "What?"

"Sarrica, the silver tongue who helped them was your fiancé, the man you threw out of court today after humiliating him in just about every way possible. If not for him we would not know anything because silver tongues who bother to learn Farlander are few and far between."

"I hadn't realized he was a silver tongue," Sarrica said. "He spoke perfect Harken; I thought he must know it natively."

"He's from Gaulden. Did you bother to read or listen to anything we've said about him, Sarrica? I know you have little interest in the marriage, Sarrica, but this man would be good for you—at least so far as running the empire goes." Lesto grinned briefly. "As to what other uses you put him to, well, that is between you and him, but I would not let something that pretty go to waste."

Sarrica turned away, angry and sad and tired. How could Lesto speak so easily of him fucking someone else when it was his own brother that Sarrica had loved? Still loved, even if he was painfully aware he must move on.

"Nyle would want you to move on, you know."

"I'm not discussing this right now, Lesto. I just want to eat, visit my children, and see if I can't make some order of the mess at my feet."

Lesto sighed but nodded. "Don't forget to sleep."

As if he ever did much of that. He hadn't slept more than four to five hours at a time since Nyle had died. Some nights, he didn't sleep at all. Sarrica had the feeling he was in for another one of those sleepless nights.

At least it allowed him to get more work done.

His private chambers, as they stepped out of the hidden door behind the bureau in the bedroom, were redolent with the fragrant spices of dinner, sharp and pungent with an undercurrent of sweet. Ignoring the waiting meal, he passed quickly through the suite to the door that led to the hallway, then down the hall to the door all the way at the end. It was the safest location in the private imperial wing, and in addition to the battle-trained nanny who attended his children, a man and a woman from Fathoms Deep guarded the door.

He nodded to them as he pulled out his key ring and unlocked the door, returning the ring to his belt as he slipped inside. The front chamber was dark, but pale yellow light spilled from the door across the way. Pushing the half-closed door open, Sarrica nodded to the nanny, Emilia. "How are they?" he asked quietly.

She smiled and closed her book. "Just fine, Your Majesty. Sad of course they could not see you, but they understand."

Sarrica stifled a sigh, approached the beds, and stared down at his children, soft and fragile looking in sleep. They looked so much like Nyle, looking at them left Sarrica feeling happy and sad and lonely. Nyle hadn't enjoyed pregnancy, found it even more confining than palace life, but he'd been adamantly against finding a woman to be their dame.

Old anger tried to rise up, but Sarrica guiltily shoved it down. Whatever had happened, whatever had been said, Nyle was dead and Sarrica would give anything to have him back. Kneeling by the bed on the right, he brushed soft, dark curls from his daughter's forehead. Bellen was six, and though she looked like Nyle, Sarrica was already seeing far too much of his own temper in her. She opened her eyes, smiled, then went right back to sleep.

Turning to the other bed, Sarrica smiled fondly at Nyla, a perfect miniature of Sarrica at five years old, face currently smooshed into a bedraggled stuffed purple dragon. Kissing the top of his head, Sarrica nodded to Emilia and left as quietly as he had come.

He yawned as he stepped into his own chambers, half-wishing he could skip dinner and crawl into bed, whether he managed to sleep or not.

His suite consisted of six rooms: a receiving room, the only room where visitors were permitted, a dining room he rarely used, a private sitting room that also usually went neglected, two bedrooms, and an empty, neglected room that had once been a library. Nyle had ordered it emptied, the books relocated to the imperial library... And had gotten too busy, and then been far too dead, to oversee its renovation as his private gallery.

Sarrica sat down and poured wine while Lesto filled their plates, ate rice and lamb in a creamy mint sauce while he read over the stack of reports and correspondence left him for him by one of his five secretaries. "Where am I supposed to find the time to attend the Festival of Harmony?" he asked. "How did I forget that was occurring in nine months?"

"You forgot—constantly *forget*—because you hate

it and don't want to think about it," Lesto replied and swallowed a small bite of meat, chasing it with wine. "As to the first question, if you do not want to attend yourself, you could, oh, I don't know, get married and foist the duty upon the spouse specifically chosen for his ability to *skillfully and happily handle such matters*. Though good luck getting him to marry you after the way you treated him in court."

Sarrica made a face. "I was going to apologize tomorrow."

"I should think so," Lesto replied. "Did you even really look at him?"

"I had other things on my mind," Sarrica snapped, grabbing up his cup of wine and draining it. "I did notice he is the exact opposite of what I said I needed and would accept in a spouse. What good is he to me and the kingdom if he cannot hold a sword, never mind manage wars?"

Lesto poured him more wine, and from the look on his face, Sarrica suspected he should be grateful that Lesto didn't dump it on his head. "Managing your wars is my job, and quite frankly this country does not lack for soldiers. We have soldiers by the cartful. If all this warring ever comes to an end there will be a lot of soldiers with skills no longer needed. Training people up to go die on a battlefield is not, at the end of the day, all that hard. It should be, and I will not say training a good soldier is an easy thing, but we do not lack for them. What we lack, increasingly, are the soldiers of peace time."

"Soldiers of peace time?" Sarrica glowered. "What is that supposed to mean?"

"What do you think it means?" Lesto asked. "I know you detest the ponce and frippery of court, but those songbirds, as you like to call them, are essential to running an empire."

Sarrica huffed. "I hate the double speak and machinations, the way deceit and cruelty are treated like chess, the way the lords and ladies trusted to keep my people safe and happy instead use them as pawns to best each other."

"The fact you cannot see there is good in it only further attests to how poorly you play the games of court yourself."

Sarrica set his cup down before he gave into a childish urge throw it. Shoving back from the table, he stood up and began to pace about the room. "I had this argument with Nyle more times than I care to count. I know very well that I am grossly lacking in any ability to contend with the intricacies of court."

Lesto groaned, and looked about two minutes away from pitching something at Sarrica's head. "So why won't you see that you need a spouse who excels at such things? Surely even you can concede there is logic in that."

"I suppose you're not wrong," Sarrica replied, pausing at the wide balcony to stare out at the night. There were pinpoints of light from torches, slightly larger ones from visible fires. "But how would I be able to trust someone who enjoys these petty, vindictive games and is more aware than most that I cannot play them?" Because he *had* looked at his potential consort, whatever he had claimed otherwise. He had seen a beautiful man dressed with calculated care and no real expression on his face. A man as cold as he was soft, a man who no doubt negotiated the political pond of Gaulden with ease and would adapt easily to the more treacherous waters of the High Court. But how was Sarrica supposed to trust someone like that? Nevermind *like* the damned man, and he really did not want to marry somebody he could not get along with.

"Not all politicians are untrustworthy," Lesto said quietly. "You know that. Skills are skills; the same way tools are tools. How they are used defines the user, not the tools."

Sarrica sighed. "I'm too tired and busy to deal with this right now."

"You will always be too busy and too tired to discuss moving on and marrying a man who might be good for you—and good for the empire. He was not picked on a whim, you know. The court has searched for years for a spouse for you, and Prince Allen was chosen only after extensive investigation and deliberation. He has been training specifically for the role for the past two years, and if given half a chance he would excel in that role." Lesto ran a hand over his hair, refilled his cup, and promptly drained it. "You need to put aside old grudges and insecurities and act like a high king. Learn something about your affianced, make certain your apology is a good one, and have the sense to marry him before some other noble or visiting dignitary snatches him up."

"I will try," Sarrica replied. "Though I am already suspicious that apparently he was conversing with my Seneschal and Chamberlain in private. How does he even know them? He's not been in Harken a day. What need would he have to hold audience with anyone?"

Lesto made a face. "Do not make an issue out of something that very likely is completely innocuous. If I was a young man who had trained all my life to be a powerful scion of the court and two years preparing to be High Consort only to be thrown out of court by my husband-to-be within minutes of being presented, I would find something to do that might put me in his good graces, and that is probably what he's doing. Sarrica, you are my dearest friend, but right now I am finding it increasingly difficult not to punch you in the face."

Sighing, Sarrica replied, "I concede I would deserve it, all right? I'll figure something out and try to make nice with the pretty little prince from Gaulden."

"Well at least you noticed he's pretty," Lesto replied, finishing his wine before standing up. "I will leave you to what remains of your night. Try to spend it resting instead of brooding. Practice that apology you owe. He likes books, or so I've been told, not that you deserve the help."

Sarrica grunted and gave Lesto a brief hug. "Get some rest yourself, halfwit. Like you aren't going to return to your room and brood about Rene."

"Shut up." Lesto clapped his shoulders, smiling briefly before he headed out.

Leaving Sarrica far too alone with silence and his own tangled thoughts. And his damned headache. He was tempted to take the powder that was all that ever helped, but it had the unfortunate side effect of putting him to sleep for several hours—hard sleep. The room could fill with the entire council shouting at him and he would not stir.

So he endured and drank all the vile teas shoved at him by well-meaning healers that never really helped past slightly dulling the edges. Which, to be fair, was better than nothing.

Returning to the table, he poured what remained of the wine into his cup. He carried it and his stack of papers into his bedroom, setting them on the table beside his bed before wandering into his dressing room to strip off his clothes and pull on a night robe. He settled into the reports and correspondence, making notes with a pencil as he went.

He huffed when he came to the bottom of the stack, a thick report tied along the edges with blue ribbon—a personal report. There was a note affixed to it: *Read it, because if you can't answer my questions in the morning you will regret it. L*

Why anyone thought Sarrica was in charge, he did not know. If any of the court knew how much hold Lesto had over him they would not constantly be frustrated at the lack of opportunity to approach Sarrica—they would be infuriated the High Commander was even more elusive.

Resigned, he opened the file to read over the tiresome details that said so much about a person and yet nothing at all. Lesto had not lied about Prince Allen's training. A prince of Gaulden, which of course meant his mother was Queen Marren, one of the finest diplomats in the Harken Empire. She had, despite her youth, managed to talk four kingdoms out of a brutal war that men with decades more experience had declared inevitable. She could have had her pick of kingdoms, but she had chosen to marry a minor prince of a small, forgettable kingdom and take him home to be her consort in Gaulden.

By the file notes, her youngest of four sons was the one crafted most in her image. A silver tongue, though there must be some mistake because it said he knew fourteen languages. Who had the time, never mind the ability, to learn fourteen languages? How did one learn to do anything else, shut away with books and tiresome tutors? It sounded like the very definition of misery. It did not sound like someone who would actually know how to move amongst people. Sarrica had yet to meet a scholar with that kind of skill who did not prefer to be as far away from large groups of people as possible unless there was an opportunity to bore them to death.

Twenty-eight years old. Not necessarily young, but young enough. Nine years younger than Sarrica, but it may as well be a lifetime. At twenty-eight Sarrica had already been married several years and gone to war more times than he could count. Twenty-eight was when he'd traded battlefield for palace because his father had been too sick to rule. He'd been thirty only a few months when his father had died, finally free of the illness that had wasted him over the course of five years. Finally able to join the wife he had never stopped missing.

Three years later, not two weeks after Sarrica's birthday, he'd received word his husband was dead, slain on the battlefield.

Sarrica had stupidly thought he would never have to know the pain of losing a spouse until he and Nyle were old and gray. Now they all wanted him to move on, build a new marriage, erase Nyle completely. By way of some milksop with a pretty face and a silver tongue.

He wasn't being fair. He should at least give Prince Allen a fair chance before casting judgment. If nothing else, Lesto would never support someone he knew Sarrica would definitely hate, even if he and the council had gone against *all* of Sarrica's requests on the matter.

All he could see was a young man with whom he had felt no immediate connection, who seemed to thrive on everything that Sarrica detested. He would never forget the way Nyle had burned right through him on first sighting, that low, hot feeling that had only grown stronger, fiercer, the more time they spent together. He had never wanted anyone but Nyle. He'd been twenty-one and Nyle just eighteen, but Sarrica had not been able to tear his eyes away. They'd married just two years later, and despite the doubts of the courts that it was youthful folly, all the disagreements and challenges, the marriage had held strong.

How was he supposed to go from a marriage like that to something that felt like a cold and empty imitation?

On the other hand, he would like his children to see more of him than he had ever seen of his own parents. He did not want to be a stranger to them, for them to know him better as a king than as a parent. Bad enough they were too young to remember the man who had given birth to them. Having a spouse who could share his burdens, take up those duties Sarrica had been neglecting... That was reasoning he could not continue to ignore, no matter how much he detested letting somebody take Nyle's place.

Their interests and duties would be so disparate, he doubted they would see each other much anyway.

Of course, it was all irrelevant if he could not make amends. Books, Lesto had said. Perhaps the Master Librarian could offer ideas. Sarrica would visit with his children for an hour then visit the library before heading to the office.

Decided on his plans for the morning, Sarrica finished his wine, set his papers aside, and snuffed the lamp by his bedside before settling down into bed and slowly falling into a restless sleep.

CHAPTER THREE

Allen fussed with the gold lace cuffs of his dark, wine-purple jacket, then made himself hold still. Every gesture, every movement, gave something away. He was not going to impress anyone if even the laziest servant in the palace would be able to tell he was nervous.

Not that it really mattered since he had already disappointed the only person he needed to impress, but that sort of thinking wouldn't accomplish anything. It was a new day. New opportunities awaited.

His first step was to secure a safe place to keep his books. A personal errand, but if he could accomplish a trivial task, he would feel a bit braver about the important ones.

The library was soothing in its quiet, familiar enough it twisted the ache of homesickness in his gut. Ignoring it, Allen ventured further into the enormous imperial library. The floor was covered in elaborate rugs; there were so many of them the dark green tiles beneath all but vanished entirely. The main room was spacious, echoing, with enormous columns leading up to a curved roof of wood and glass. Lamps, carefully covered in heavy glass, extended well away from the shelves on long metal arms, offering plenty of light to both the shelves and the four long columns of tables arrayed in the middle of the room.

Perhaps twenty or so people were scattered about

the tables, some conversing quietly, most bent over books with stacks of more at their elbows. A few were students, to judge by the papers piled with their books and the exhausted look to their faces that said they would rather be anywhere else in the world than bent over one more damned essay.

Allen could sympathize. His schooling had been entirely private tutoring, but he'd still spent many a night writing, writing, writing—and the following night rewriting, when his first attempts proved dissatisfactory.

Toward the end of the columns, rows of free standing shelves took up the floor, and beyond them he could just spy an archway that likely led to the archives and special collections. Tearing his eyes away, he glanced around the room again but spied not a single librarian. The servant who had brought him his breakfast that morning had told him the librarians wore brown and amber, though senior librarians often did not wear uniforms and instead wore gold quill pins on their lapels.

Likely they were busy or were settling in for the day and not yet on the floor. Allen wandered across the enormous room to the shelves that were designated as histories, pleased when he saw an entire set of shelves dedicated to volumes written in Pemfrost. How exciting. His mother's collection was not nearly so extensive. Pulling out the first on the shelf immediately before him, he opened it to the first page and began to read. Halfway through the second paragraph he snickered softly.

"Beg pardon, Your Highness..."

Allen looked up to see that two young women were watching him curiously. "My apologies, I did not mean to disturb you."

"You didn't, Your Highness," said the woman who had spoken. They both looked to be twenty or so years of age. The one who'd spoken had extremely dark skin; the other lighter, red-brown skin. To judge by their stylish clothes, they came from wealthy, probably titled families. "I was only curious, if you will pardon my interruption, as to what was so funny. I've never known those books to be amusing."

"No?" Allen asked. "Amusing is perhaps not the word, as to that, except in a wry, 'you've no idea what's about to happen to you' sort of way. Pemfrost used to be the most powerful nation on this continent, and their versions of history speak to their arrogance. This particular volume recounts the War of the Seven Roses, which they won, but about twenty years after this book was written the War of the Last Roses destroyed Pemfrost forever and divided it into what would eventually become Gaulden, Mesta, and Gearth—and a century later, Gearth split in two and so was born the Outlands. So to hear a history of Pemfrost speak so confidently of their strength only two decades before they are destroyed and all but their written language lost... Well, finding it amusing probably speaks to *my* arrogance, but so it goes."

"I never learned Pemfrost," the second, slightly shorter, woman said, a note of envy in her voice. "There's only a handful of tutors available to teach it, and they've got long waiting lists. My father is the Duke of Emberton-Heights, and I still could not manage to obtain lessons with any of them."

So this must be Lady Laria Amorlay, the Duke of Emberton-Height's youngest child. According to everything Allen had heard, she was being trained up to marry the ambassador of Nemrith and return home with him, help to foster relations between the Queendom of Nemrith and the Harken Empire. The Duke of Emberton-Heights was a powerful figure in court, and his holdings in Selemea were immense. He and Allen's mother had trained together when they were children, had briefly been considered to marry before their families had chosen different directions.

"I am certain that had I tried to hire one of them, I would have fared no better, royalty or not," Allen replied. "It was my mother who taught me Pemfrost, at night when we retired." He rarely ever saw his mother outside of official capacities or fleeting moments. Those nights where they had studied Pemfrost together... Even when he was so sick of studying he could cry, he had looked forward to those lessons. They had been a mother teaching a son, instead of a queen overseeing the training of a prince.

They shared a look, surprise rippling across their faces. "Beg pardon, Your Highness, but you must be Prince Allen of Gaulden?"

"Just so," Allen replied. "Lady Laria, I presume? I am afraid I do not know your companion."

Beaming that he knew her, Laria gestured to the woman beside her. "Lady Quell Devren, daughter of the Earl of Mark."

"A pleasure to meet you," Allen said and bowed his head slightly. The Earl of Mark was no one to trifle with. He had a long history of animosity with Emberton-Heights due to their current opposed opinions on war and various skirmishes, duels, and tragedies in their family histories. Interesting that their children were good friends.

Of Mark's children, Allen knew precious little. He

had four: a daughter set to follow in his footsteps, a son more interested in being in the war than turning profits from it, a wastrel of whom no one spoke, and Quell, who like most youngest children, was pushed into scholarly pursuits.

Interesting that Quell was spending time with Laria when their parents were known nemeses at court.

"How are you finding Harken, Your Highness?" Laria asked. "We were all hoping to meet you at dinner last night, but you must have been exhausted after traveling so far."

She had tact and could appear sincere with no effort. Allen smiled politely and nodded in agreement. "Quite tired, yes. The palace is beautiful, if still confusing. I did stumble across and enjoy the art gallery, briefly. Part of it, anyway."

Quell brightened at those words. "There is a new exhibit going up next month: a collection of Rilien tenth century ikons on loan from the Twelve Voices Monastery. Our friend Gorden Bells, his father helped my father arrange the loan." She rambled on about the exhibit, which seemed to relax Laria too, and Allen was more than happy to continue chatting with them. It was not as though he had anywhere to be until that afternoon.

"Your Majesty!"

Allen froze, turned his head toward the man who had spoken, then turned completely to see that, sure enough, Sarrica stood in the entryway, accompanied by two men who, for all their slight size and innocuous appearance, looked dangerous. Bodyguards. Allen had rarely needed them because he spent so much time in the palace. On those occasions where he had gone beyond that safety, it was usually in disguise so that he could better practice his conversational skills. He could count on one hand the times he had required bodyguards. If he were to become High Consort, they would become a near-constant in his life.

If Sarrica had cared about that possibility, he would have assigned Allen a bodyguard. That he had not bothered was just one more insult.

He watched as Sarrica looked idly around, offering a polite smile and half-bow when Sarrica noticed him, and quashed the frustration and disappointment that rose up when irritation flickered across Sarrica's face. "Pardon me," he said to his new acquaintances, acknowledging their bows with a nod before he crossed the room and bowed low to Sarrica. "Good Morning, Your Majesty."

"Good Morning, Prince Allen," Sarrica said. "What brings you to the library so early?" His gaze flicked briefly to the students. "First servants and now students? You make strange friends."

Allen stared back calmly, though he didn't feel anything close to calm. "I think the Chamberlain and Seneschal are a bit more than servants, Your Majesty. I was speaking to them about language, that being something of a passing interest of mine." Sarrica narrowed his eyes, but Allen only stared blandly back. "I spent half an hour speaking to them about language-related problems in the palace. This morning I've spent a few minutes chatting with students who admired my knowledge of Pemfrost. Nothing remotely untoward yet you accuse me of wrongdoing. Since when is familiarizing myself with my new home a crime?"

"It's not your new home quite yet," Sarrica replied. "With that sort of brazen familiarity I wonder all the more what games you're already playing."

Someone coughed discreetly, saving Allen from giving an injudicious reply. "Majesty..." A tall, thin, white-haired man who, by the markings on his expensive blue velvet jacket must be the Master Librarian, looked between them. "If you'll come to my office, Your Majesty, I will be more than happy to help you. Prince Allen, it is an honor to meet you. I've heard many wonderful things about you. Was there something with which one of my librarians could help you?"

Allen looked at Sarrica, whose face had closed off minus a tight look around the eyes that indicated frustration and impatience. So much for finding a home for his books. If he tried asking now, Sarrica would likely take issue with that too. Looking away, Allen smiled politely at the Master Librarian and shook his head. "No, I merely wanted to acquaint myself with the library, but thank you anyway. I bid you good day. Majesty." He bowed again to Sarrica and departed, forcing himself to keep to a civil pace only by counting slowly in his head and matching his steps.

When he found himself alone in a small hallway, he pulled out the note from Seyn that he had received that morning inviting him to lunch to finish discussing their plans. Allen had been looking forward to it. He was trying to *help*, and Sarrica thought he was scheming.

The man was determined to hate him. How in the name of the Pantheon had anyone managed to marry him and *stay* married to him? Everyone knew his marriage to Nyle had been a love match, but Allen could not fathom it. How did anyone fall in love with a man so... so damnably stubborn and willfully reprehensible? Sarrica had humiliated him, accused him of scheming based on the flimsiest of reasons, but not spared even a moment to ask him if he was all right.

Then again, why would he? Sarrica was an experienced soldier, as were all his friends. They had seen and held dead men any number of times. They would probably sneer and laugh at him for being so weak that he'd had to run off to hide in his room and cry. But even now thinking about it hurt. He hoped Rene had meant it when he said they would get the sailor home to Farland. Allen would rather endure another whipping than ever again watch a man bleed to death in his arms.

Tucking the note away again, he decided another session of 'explore the palace' was in order. Maybe he could meet some people of whom Sarrica would approve.

He was eternally grateful his mother wasn't there. Twenty-eight and he felt like he was fifteen and attending his first ball. The only thing that had gone well that night was the way he'd made fools of his brothers by flirting with the women they hadn't been able to talk to because they didn't speak Mestan. It had become one of his favorite methods of revenge.

Picking a hallway at random, he wandered through offices, sunrooms, meeting halls, at least three ballrooms that were being prepared for fetes that evening. People bowed and greeted him, a few paused to chat, and Allen filed away every name, mentally connecting them to the piles of information he had memorized as part of his high consort training.

Training that was likely to go to waste if he could not convince Sarrica to give him a chance. Damn it, he had been hand-picked to help Sarrica rule the Harken

Empire. Why was he wandering halls alone and aimless?

If Sarrica wanted a soldier so badly, they should have chosen Chass instead. Allen's second-eldest brother, he had several years ago taken over as Captain of the Penance Gate mercenaries, the largest, and some said most aggressive, of the mercenary bands that worked for the Empire. Allen had always believed the rumors of aggression easily. Chass was the one who had first dragged Allen out to teach him a 'real lesson'. Manda had later joined in, just as bitter about Allen's 'easy, lazy life'. One had become a mercenary, the other a spymaster. Allen had been surprised by neither decision.

Chass would make a far more suitable spouse for Sarrica, though the idea of Chass on a throne turned Allen's stomach.

The sound of a crowd drew him from his thoughts; Allen followed it until he came upon a set of open doors that led to an enormous balcony overlooking a vibrant lawn edged in colorful flowers. Currently the lawn was covered with tables and chairs, even a dance floor. The chatter was coming from the many servants bustling to arrange everything.

Off in one corner, a handful of musicians were tuning their instruments and practicing. An ache settled in Allen's chest, his breakfast roiling in his gut. It was precisely the sort of fete Sarrica should have had arranged to welcome him, introduce him properly to everyone. Pantheon, even the council could have arranged it. No one had done anything, however, because apparently everyone save him had known that Sarrica would throw a fit about the matter. Alone, rejected, *humiliated*... And self-pity would accomplish nothing, but he was completely at a loss as to what he should do.

Maybe he should invite himself to the garden party, or another event taking place that night. He'd already breached protocol by helping to sort out the language problems amongst the servants; he may as well keep going until he was told to stop. Everything would be much more difficult without Sarrica to help him learn who they wanted to avoid, where favor should be granted, and so forth, but it wouldn't be impossible. He was his mother's son, after all.

Seyn would probably know what parties he could invite himself to without rippling the waters overmuch, something else to speak to him about at lunch.

Allen watched the preparing of the garden party a few minutes more, enjoying the fresh air, letting it carry away his anger. If he kept getting angry he would only cause more problems. Sarrica seemed angry enough for three men, and he was welcome to it.

Leaving the balcony, he retraced his steps until he turned down a new hallway, wide and brightly lit by windows all along one side with mirrors matching them on the opposite wall. Halfway down it was a beautiful set of glass and wrought-iron double doors. A small gold placard beside the door said *Imperial Aviary. Ring bell for admittance.*

His mouth flattened. So he'd found the royal songbirds. The temptation to let them out was greater than he liked admitting, but childish behavior would not accomplish anything. Still he lingered, half-tempted to at least see the damned things he had been accused of resembling.

The sound of footsteps distracted him, and he

turned to see a man walking slowly up the hallway, his attention more on the letter in his hand than on his surroundings. He looked up, though, and then came to a brief stop before resuming walking at a faster pace. "You're Prince Allen!"

Coming to a stop in front of him, the man tipped into a beautiful bow. He had light olive skin, and his long, dark brown hair was woven into an intricate braid, tied off at the end with a jewel-threaded ribbon. His clothes were the very glass of fashion: a long, dark-green jacket embroidered with gold birds, silver vines and white flowers, and brown boots and breeches. Emerald and diamond flowers adorned his ears, the stems and leaves of them wrapping up the edges of his ears. Even holding still, he seemed to vibrate, unable to truly stop moving. "Your Highness, it's an honor to meet you. My father was the one to put your family— and you specifically—forward as a candidate. He pushed hard for it, and I've been looking forward to meeting you. I was meant to go with him when he went to meet you, but I had to return to our family estate to handle a problem with flooding in his place since *he* could scarcely cancel a trip to see you."

Blinking at the flood of words so freely and artlessly given, Allen quickly rifled through his store of knowledge. "You are Lord Grase's son. The Marquis Warrant, if I recall correctly?" The troublesome child of the Grase family, known for being shockingly honest and vibrant, flouting many a rule and tradition. Eccentric was the kindest word ever used. The man before him was not what Allen had been expecting. This man seemed... Allen wasn't quite sure. Different, to be sure.

Lord Grase beamed. "Yes, just so. Tara Grase, at

your service, Your Highness. I am about to have tea, would you care to join me?" He extended his arm.

Bemused by the exuberant, even somewhat overly familiar, behavior, Allen replied, "Tea sounds ideal, Lord Tara. Thank you."

"Thank *you*," Tara replied, smile widening when Allen took his arm. "I'm certain you've been asked a hundred times how you are liking the palace, so I shall not ask again. Have you met any of the other silver tongues? About a hundred are on permanent retainer to the palace, with another couple hundred who come and go on a daily basis. Practically all of them are stolen away by the imperial army and the mercenaries. Never enough to go around, that is for certain. Many of them eventually leave to settle into private work. Less stressful, they say." He winked and continued on with the light, easy chatter, never giving Allen a chance to do more than offer a nod or make some noise of agreement.

The chatter eased off, however, once they were settled at a small table in a tidy little sunroom in some part of the palace that Allen did not remotely recognize. Tara stirred a good deal of sugar into his tea, and his smile faded away entirely as he looked up. "Your Highness, I want to apologize for your poor reception yesterday."

"That's hardly your apology to make, and anyway, His Majesty was under no obligation to grant me an audience or accept me as his High Consort," Allen replied.

Tara made a face. "Everyone knows he is being a brat, and why, but that is no excuse."

Allen frowned. "I do not care to speak ill of him."

"You would be the only," Tara drawled.

"Everyone's favorite hobby is speaking ill of others, especially the High King and his stubborn ways. I wanted to assure you that, despite how the situation must seem, you are off to a promising start." He laughed when Allen did not reply. "You don't give away much, but I can still see you think me a liar. I promise! Did no one tell you about how he and High Consort Nyle met? My father has told me the tale many a time. They got into such a fight they had to be pulled apart. They did not speak to each other for nearly a month after, and then as little as possible. To hear my father tell it, High Consort Nyle thought the High King a spoiled, useless brat; and the High King though Nyle an arrogant bastard. I promise, anyone who annoys him greatly at the start winds up close to him later."

"That is heartening, thank you," Allen replied, though he did not believe a word of it. They hadn't fought. Sarrica thought him a useless songbird—and one already conspiring against him. Far cry from a potent clashing of what seemed personalities more alike than either party cared to admit. "You seem well-acquainted with the High King."

Tara smiled, but there was a sad note to it that he could not entirely hide. "I am well-acquainted with the Arseni family, or was, rather. They're a taciturn lot, generally, but loyal and even occasionally sweet."

Hmm. Lovers, if he had to guess. Rene or Lesto? If he had to guess again, he would say it was the lover who ended the affair, not Tara. His demeanor was all sadness, longing, not defensive anger or relief. "I encountered them both briefly. They have a presence."

"So tactful," Tara said with a laugh. "My parents

despair of my ever learning even a modicum of tact. I am well known around the palace for being a chatter-bird."

Allen permitted himself a wry smile, warming to Tara despite himself. He reminded Allen of his dame, Eila, vibrant and cheerful where everyone else was contained. He'd always envied her the ability to be so, when Allen had always been made to keep his barriers up, and it had become so habitual now he did not think he could ever be like Eila and Tara, even if he knew how. "Well, as I am apparently a songbird, perhaps we are well-suited."

"It sounds to me like we most certainly should be friends, Your Highness." Tara slapped the table with one hand then lifted his teacup in a toast.

"As you say," Allen said with a small smile. "So what do you do with your days, my new friend?" His only friend, if they actually became so. He had acquaintances and associates aplenty, and tutors he remained congenial with, but all his hours studying and training had left little time to forge friendships. None that had lasted, anyway. Somehow, they always drifted away. It was something his mother had promised would change once he was settled into Harken.

Taking a sip of tea, Tara set the cup back down and replied, "I manage the family affairs, and I am nearly finished with my law degrees. This time next year I can start sitting on the council as an observer, begin training to replace my father in another decade or so." His mouth curved in a small, playful grin. "Centuries, if he has any say in the matter. My father is very set in his ways. He will haggle with the Goddess of Death someday, mark my word."

Allen laughed, then ducked his head, taken by surprise.

"Oh, ho, he begins to crack." Tara grinned more widely and winked when Allen looked up. "I promise I shall not use your laughter against you. It's too difficult to prove in court."

"I suppose that is true," Allen said with a faint smile, lifting his tea to take a sip. "You must stay quite busy, with so much on your pile."

Tara shrugged. "I like to stay busy. Too much idleness leads to too much trouble and all that. I'm certain you'll be much busier before long. Silver tongues are hard to come by, and we've not had a sovereign with that skill in... three, four generations? Four, I think. Yes, four. How exciting that we'll have a silver tongue on the throne. From what I've heard you're talented enough to be a golden tongue." He waggled his eyebrows.

Allen shook his head, another smile twitching at his mouth. "Golden tongue, that is the most absurd thing I've ever heard." The term silver tongue came from the early days when the empire was little more than a bunch of scattered, bickering kingdoms and Harken only just beginning to grow in power, and silver was slowly becoming the monetary standard across the continent. Finding people who could speak two languages was an easy feat, but those who could speak three or more were rare—and it was even more difficult to find one who could be trusted to translate honestly. An honest linguist was worth their weight in silver, and in demand enough they could earn a sizeable fortune for their work. The term 'silver tongue' had stuck.

Gold, though, that was only used for jewelry and

the like. Come to that, it went along rather nicely with 'songbird'. At least Tara didn't say it like it was an insult. If Sarrica ever heard it, Allen had every faith it *would* become an insult.

"I think it has a certain ring to it," Tara said, but he shrugged the matter aside. "What are you about today, Your Highness?"

Allen took another sip of tea and set the cup down slowly. "I confess I do not know. I was attempting to familiarize myself with the palace, but it remains confusing. The library is beautiful, I saw that much, but..."

"I heard about that," Tara said, smiling sympathetically. "If it is any consolation, rumor has it His Majesty was most annoyed with himself. People are trying to figure out why he was in the library at all. We can count on one hand the number of times he has visited it. Until today, I would have bet my wardrobe that he did not know where it was." He drained his tea. "Would you like a tour, Your Highness?"

"That would be appreciated, thank you." Allen finished his own tea and stood with Tara. "If we are to be friends, I think formality may be dropped."

Tara smiled brightly, the happiest Allen had yet seen him. "Agreed. The court will be in a fit about that! Lord Chatter-bird already on a first name basis with the High Consort Presumptive."

"They should have been quicker to offer me tea," Allen replied and took the arm that Tara offered.

"Best place to start is at the beginning," Tara said as they left the sunroom and traveled halls that Allen did not recognize. He should not be surprised by that, but he had done so much wandering he thought something should have looked familiar by that point.

Eventually they came to the grand entrance, which he did thankfully remember. Hard to forget all the glass: colorful panes in the ceiling that formed a sunburst and a band of more stained glass all around the top edge of the ceiling. The sunburst in the ceiling matched exactly the sunburst mosaic on the floor, and all along the walls were dozens of paintings of the various kingdoms and important moments in the empire's history. Allen knew them all, just one more of the many things he had been made to learn in preparation for his role.

People milled all around them, many gawking openly, some more discreetly. "The Hall of the Sun," Tara proclaimed, extending one arm. "I hope you are impressed by the creativity in the naming because it's a running theme. Now, from here you can see the eight grand hallways, four leading to the compass wings: north, south, east, west. The four halls set between them are called the counter-compass wings collectively. Individually, they are called after their carpets: blue, red, green, yellow. I told you the creativity was overwhelming.

"Generally speaking, the compass wings are public domains. Galleries, gardens, ballrooms, meeting halls, library, so on and so forth. The counter-compass wings are the private domains intended for government, palace inhabitants, military..." He waved a hand in the air. "Just to keep things confusing, there is plenty of overlap, and even the High King probably gets lost upon occasion. Blue and green are where you will find most of the personal quarters. You are probably somewhere in the blue wing, close to the imperial suite, which is buried all the way at the end of it behind several locked doors and the finest, most hostile-looking guards that Fathoms Deep has to offer."

Fathoms Deep was the High King's private guard, serving as bodyguards and whatever else he required. They were personally led by Commander Lesto. They had once been a mercenary band but had turned to being private guards when Sarrica had resigned from military life to assume his imperial duties full time. Though technically surrendering their role as mercenaries made them regular army, they'd retained their private uniforms and everyone still called them Fathoms Deep.

"Now, down the red hall..." Tara trailed off as he turned, and the levity on his face died, replaced by resignation and a tightening around his mouth and eyes. Allen followed his gaze just as he registered a familiar jangle of spurs and sword belt.

"Prince Allen, Lord Tara," Captain Rene greeted as he reached them, bowing low.

"Captain." He waited until Rene rose to his full height before he asked, "Is there something I can do for you?" He did not miss the way Rene's eyes dipped briefly to where Allen still held Tara's arm.

"Your Highness, Lord Tara, I apologize for interrupting. You were of great help to us last night, Your Highness, and I find myself once more in need of your services if you would be gracious enough to lend them."

Tara snorted a soft laugh. "You must be anxious for help indeed, Captain, to speak so prettily."

Rene shot him a look, and Tara jerked slightly before he regained himself. Allen squeezed his arm gently. "I'm always happy to help, Captain, though I am surprised the Three-headed Dragons have no silver tongues of their own. Lead the way. Lord Tara, did you want to come?"

"I think Captain Rene is happier when I am out of sight," Tara replied. "Would you care to meet for lunch later, Your Highness? I can finish giving you the tour."

Allen let go of his arm. "I am meeting with the Seneschal and Chamberlain for lunch. I am certain they would not mind if you joined us, however. We can conclude the tour after?"

"As you say," Tara replied and swept another of his beautiful bows. "Until later, Your Highness." Turning neatly on his heel, he strode off.

Turning to Rene, Allen studied him briefly. "Given your relationship to His Majesty, I will likely be spending a great deal of time in your company. Lord Tara is proving to be my friend. Is there always going to be such strife between the two of you?"

Rene tore his eyes from where he had been watching Tara, and Allen caught anguish in them before he managed to bank it. "Time eases all ills, Your Highness. We know how to be civil when we must."

"Very well," Allen replied. "Lead on, Captain, and explain why you've need of me."

"This way, Your Highness." Turning to his left, Rene led Allen down the yellow hall, which Allen recognized—it was the same hall he'd used when escorted to a sitting room while awaiting his audience with Sarrica. "My men managed to hunt down the men who killed that sailor. Lesto told me you know Bentan, which is what they keep snarling at us. I know when I am being called a filthy cocksucker, but that's about it. His Majesty has twenty-seven silver tongues who know Bentan, but none of them is on the premises right now, or they are not in any condition to work."

Allen nodded, tried to ignore the dread and fear that settled in his chest, but could not quite keep himself from asking, "I trust none of these men are going to bleed out?"

Though he thought he kept his tone level, impersonal, something must have given him away because Rene came to an abrupt halt and rounded sharply to face him. He studied Allen intently. What did he see? A pathetic songbird to be made fun of later? "I apologize, Your Highness," Rene said quietly. "We should not have done that to you, not without more warning, or speaking with you after."

"I'm fine," Allen said sharply. "Lead me to these men we need to interrogate."

Rene hesitated, then gave a sharp nod and resumed walking, but this time he walked at Allen's side. Allen could feel the looks Rene kept casting him, but ignored them. He never should have spoken at all. The very last thing he needed was Rene running off to tell Sarrica that he could not handle one man's death.

Putting the matter aside until he could better deal with it, Allen focused on his Bentan, on his control—on proving that he was more than a useless songbird.

CHAPTER FOUR

Sarrica looked up as the door opened, relaxing when he saw Rene—and tensed all over again as Allen appeared behind him. Damn it. He should have known from the looks Lesto and Rene exchanged that they were up to something. "Took you long enough."

Rene rolled his eyes. "I was only gone a few minutes, and I brought back the best silver tongue money can buy, if I am to believe what my brother tells me." His smile had the distinct feel of threat to it.

But Rene didn't threaten half as well as Lesto, so Sarrica ignored it and focused on Allen. "Are you the best money can buy?" Allen stared coolly back. "I keep hearing incessantly about your talented tongue, but now is not the time to find out that you're a liar."

Allen replied in a sharp tone—and in words that Sarrica did not even remotely understand, though he recognized them as Bentan. He sounded precisely like every native Sarrica had ever heard, sharp and quick, even that little guttural thing at the end of some words that non-native speakers could never manage, or managed poorly. So he probably did have real ability.

Not that Sarrica was in the mood to admit it. "I cannot be impressed if I do not understand what you're saying."

"Where are the men we're questioning?" Allen asked.

"Through here," Lesto said before Sarrica could reply. "Your Bentan is perfect, or so close I can't tell otherwise."

If Allen was moved by the compliment, his face did not give it away. He did give Lesto a deep nod, however, as he said, "Thank you. It was one of the harder languages I learned, though not as difficult as Mestan and Harken. Or Pemfrost, come to that."

Pemfrost? He'd mentioned that in the library. Who in the Penance Realms had time to learn a language no one spoke? What a perfect waste of time. Sarrica said nothing as they left the front room where they had been waiting, traveled down a dark, bare hallway of brown stone walls and flickering sconces, to one of the dank holding rooms at the far end.

Six men were chained to the back wall; all of them had the bone-white skin common across most of Benta, their eyes so pale the color almost seemed translucent. Most had blue eyes, but one had green and another brown. It was Brown Eyes who seemed to be in charge, though none of them bore any markings to denote rank, or even that they were military—though that much was obvious from their behavior.

"Bentan mercenaries," Lesto said, giving them a wolfish smile as he walked toward the middle of the room and looked at each man. "Good ones, not great. The kind that will probably get the job done, and it's no big loss if they die doing it." He turned to Allen, beckoned him forward. "They do not seem to speak Harken, Tricemorien, or Carthian, which further testifies they are cheap mercenaries."

Allen's eyes were focused on the men, flicking rapidly between them. When Lesto stopped speaking, he looked at Sarrica, standing with Rene by the door. "They understand every single word you're saying."

"What?" Lesto demanded—and cried out as one of

the men abruptly burst forward and knocked him to the ground.

Sarrica moved as another one sprung, shoving Allen back, catching the arm that came flying and barely avoiding a knife to his face. He rammed a knee up into the man's groin, grabbed his hair as he doubled over, and drove the knee into his face.

Dropping him to the ground, Sarrica gestured sharply to Rene, who moved forward and killed the other prisoners. "Leave Brown Eyes," Sarrica said. Rene nodded, and Sarrica left him to finish his grisly task, turning to see that Lesto was all right. "Did they get your pretty face, Lesto?"

"What in the Twelve Realms of Penance did you think you were doing!" Lesto bellowed, shoving off the dead body lying atop him. He grimaced at all the blood that was covering him, ignored the hand Sarrica offered in favor of rolling to his feet himself, and yanked his dagger out of the dead man's stomach. Standing, he turned toward Sarrica again. "How many fucking times must I tell you to get out of the damned way?"

Sarrica glared. "What would you have me do? Stay still while they killed Prince Allen?" He looked toward Allen, who had moved to stand by the door. "Are you well?"

"I'm fine, Majesty, thank you for saving me." Allen's face was, as ever, expressionless, but his skin had gone practically bone-white, taking away the warm, barely-there gold tone to it. He also was not looking *away* from Sarrica, which betrayed his distressed state. Probably both from the attempt on his life and the five murders that had just taken place right in front of him.

Two more reasons Sarrica had wanted a *soldier* for a spouse. He had no desire to subject someone to the more brutal elements of his life, no desire to force terrible memories and nightmares on them. "How did you know they understood us?"

"They paid too much attention but were trying hard to look like they weren't paying attention," Allen said, the barest sliver of tremble to his voice that slowly smoothed away the more he spoke. "It's… rather hard to explain. It's something you begin to notice studying languages, studying *people*. The only thing more useful than being fluent in several languages is knowing that no one else in the room is aware of it. People get careless, and more importantly, cocky, when they think no one else understands what they're saying. There's a rush to it, a… smugness. That's what betrayed them." He looked away, stared at the floor for a moment, then back up, eyes skimming quickly over the bodies before focusing on Sarrica again. "How did they get free of their chains?"

Rene grunted, held up a slim bit of metal. "Lock-pick. Guards must have missed it searching them. They'd probably meant to all be free before we returned. Would have been easy enough to kill the guards, slip out through the sewage ways down here, and away they go."

"I am going to go yell at the guards," Lesto said. He leveled a finger at Sarrica. "Do not think I am done with you. Saving your betrothed is all well and good, but getting yourself killed sort of undermines the deed. Rene, make certain they stay out of further trouble."

"Commander," Rene drawled and gave his brother an elaborate bow, snickering at the crude gesture Lesto flipped him as he left. His levity faded as he looked at Allen and crossed the room to stand in front of him. "My apologies, Your Highness. I promised no men would die in front of you again."

"It's hardly your fault, Captain," Allen replied. "May as well begin as I am expected to go on."

Sarrica said nothing, only jerked his head at Rene that it was time they left. "We'll wait in the hall. I want the one still alive stripped and chained in a new room. We'll question him tomorrow, after he's had time to stew a bit."

Rene grunted, nodded, and got to work. Sarrica motioned for Allen to precede him out, and when they were in the hall, he gently pushed Allen against the wall, not liking the slow, careful way he walked. "Are you certain you're well?"

A hint of anger clouded Allen's face for the barest moment. Sarrica should probably not be pleased he had put it there, but it was nice to know the man felt things and could not always control his expressions. Gods knew how cold the man would be in bed.

Not that Sarrica was interested in bedding him. He had meant it when he said the union would be a matter of state alone. Someone that pretty, and political, probably preferred a multitude of lovers anyway. Why would he settle down with a man nine years his senior who had two children from a previous marriage?

"Quite well," Allen replied. "I am sorry I was not able to learn anything from them before it all went wrong."

Sarrica shrugged. "It is neither the first time nor the last we have lost prisoners before they could be made useful. There is one alive. Having lost all his men, and knowing full well Benta will leave him to rot, he can probably be coaxed into talking."

"I see." Allen looked away, down the hall, mouth a flat line.

Stifling a sigh, Sarrica pulled a flask from the wide sash wrapped around his hips. Uncapping it, he held it out. "Drink."

Allen looked at it warily before shifting his gaze to Sarrica. "Why?"

"Because watching men die, especially under Rene's brutal efficiency, is never pleasant."

Instead of taking it as he had expected, Allen drew back, anger once more flickering across his face—and his eyes practically blazing with it for a moment. "I know you see me as a songbird, Your Majesty, but I am not so frail of constitution I need liquor to soothe my nerves. As I am no longer needed here, I shall spare you enduring my presence any further. Good day to you, Your Majesty."

He strode off down the hall before Sarrica could reply, the long tail of his braid swinging back and forth across his back, glinting gold in the murky torchlight. Sarrica tore his eyes away as the door opened and Rene came out dragging Brown Eyes with him.

Rene looked down the hall to where Allen had just vanished through the door, then rounded on Sarrica. "What in the Twelve did you do this time, you sandbag?"

"I offered him a drink," Sarrica muttered. "He looked troubled."

Rene closed his eyes and said a few choice phrases that would get most men thrown in stocks. "Let me guess: you did it as rudely as was possible."

"I said it was never pleasant watching men die," Sarrica snapped. "He accused me of calling him frail and flounced off."

Snorting in amusement, Rene replied, "This all sounds so familiar. I would have thought going through this nonsense once would have made you a little bit better at it the second time around. How a man who so skillfully runs an empire cannot court a lover without bungling the matter is beyond me." He sighed when Brown Eyes gave a soft grunt. "Let me secure him before he wakes. You did a splendid job breaking his nose, by the way. That should make talking to him even more fun."

"Shut up." Sarrica sighed, leaned against the wall, and folded his arms across his chest, scowling as he watched Rene haul Brown Eyes down the hall to a different cell and vanish inside with him.

A few minutes later, a familiar jangling stride made him hang his head in despair before he looked up to see Lesto glaring at him hard enough Sarrica was impressed it did not strike him dead. Every time Lesto glared at him like that he was astonished he survived. "What in the Pantheon did you do to make him mad this time?"

"I offered him a drink!" Sarrica threw his hands up then raked them through his hair. "Pantheon knows I will not make *that* mistake again."

Rene laughed from behind him, clapping him on the back as he rejoined them. "Prisoner's locked up and naked, so there will be no more hiding lock picks. As to Prince Allen, you should have taken a swallow yourself before offering it to him and not said a single damned word."

"He asked. I said it was because watching men die wasn't pleasant. He took offense and stormed off. How many times must I explain it?"

The brothers shared a look but neither replied to his outburst. "Come on," Lesto said. "Let's return to your private chambers so I can clean up and change, and we can figure out how to make nice with the man you are determined to turn into an enemy. Rene, go after His Highness, see if you can calm him down. He seems to like you."

"He seemed to be getting on rather well with Lord Tara," Rene said, voice carefully light. He'd better be more careful, or Lesto was going to figure out his secret. "I found them in the great hall. Lord Tara was showing him around, I think. They seemed quite friendly; Prince Allen was smiling and everything." He made a face. "I am glad somebody can make him smile because you've been abysmal, and sadly, I've not been much better."

"What do you mean?" Sarrica asked.

Rene grimaced again. "I went to Seyn's office, encountered Allen there, and took him to the sailor. The man bled out in His Highness's arms. He gave no sign at the time that it bothered him, but in retrospect, I think he was struggling to hide it. Would explain why he was so quick to anger, and why he departed so quickly afterwards, according to my men. His Highness should have been at dinner, getting acquainted with the court, you know? Instead a man died in his arms. I would say we're all doing a fantastic job of convincing him to join this family." He clapped them both on the shoulder, then pushed between them to stride off down the hall, jangling and rattling the way Lesto had coming, the sound cutting off abruptly as the door closed firmly behind him.

Lesto slowly lowered his fingers from where they had been pinching the bridge of his nose while Rene told his story. "If Nyle was here he would cut off all our dicks."

If Nyle were there, they wouldn't be dealing with Allen at all. Sarrica kept his mouth shut and strode off in the opposite direction, bound for the secret passage in a storage closet that would lead back up to the main floors of the palace, and from there they could use another secret passage to return to his chambers, avoiding Lesto walking through the palace covered in blood. "I'm glad you're unhurt."

"I'm annoyed he got me by surprise, the stupid milk-skin bastard." Lesto smacked the wall with the flat of his hand, then pushed ahead of Sarrica and slipped into the closet, feeling along the wall until he found the catches. "Aha." The secret door swung open, the musty scent of a dark, enclosed space washing over them.

Lesto vanished into the dark and Sarrica followed, swinging the door shut behind him. "Do you think we'll get anything out of the remaining prisoner?"

"No," Lesto replied. "It was a slim chance, anyway. Far more telling that they were willing to try killing us when only two of them were free. Even with the element of surprise, they likely would have all died before being able to get to you." He huffed and came to a stop, turned around. "At least, that would have been the case had you stayed by the damned door as I am forever telling you to do."

Sarrica shrugged. "I cannot turn off my own training, Lesto. What should I have done, let them kill Prince Allen? He is not us, able to handle such an attack. They would have gutted him or snapped his neck before he understood what was happening."

"Perhaps, but I do not think he is as weak as you

believe."

"I don't think he's weak; I think he's not a soldier," Sarrica snapped.

"Semantics. If you do not stop wallowing in self-pity and give him an honest chance, you will come to regret it."

Sarrica scrubbed at his face, could feel the beginnings of a headache forming. "What in the gods' names does it matter? So I don't marry this one. There are plenty more."

"Yes, you're correct, it's perfectly harmless to cast aside a man who was specifically chosen and spent two years training to rule alongside you. That will not sour our relationship with Gaulden at all. It's not as though they are an important kingdom or anything." Lesto looked approximately three seconds away from punching him.

Well, he wasn't the only one who felt like smashing a fist into someone's face. "What confounds me is that Nyle's own brothers are the ones who keep pushing me to replace him, as though he never fucking mattered at all." Sarrica stormed past him, turning a sharp left at the end of the hall and taking the stairs there two at a time, up two flights until they reached the paler stones that indicated they were once more on ground level.

"Sarrica!" Lesto grabbed his arm, squeezed it tight at the elbow, forcing him to stop. "Sarrica!"

"What," Sarrica snarled, jerking his arm free.

"Stop," Lesto said. "Just stop. All of it. Stop getting angry. Stop pushing all of us away. Most of all, stop feeling guilty. It's not easy for any of us, but unlike you, Rene and I *talk about it*. We always knew this would happen. You're not replacing him, for Pantheon's sake.

No one ever could. It is time you moved on, and the whole empire knows you need help. There's only so much the rest of us can do. No one is asking you to fall in love with the man, but he will make a good consort if you would just give him the chance."

Sarrica sighed. "I am trying, I swear."

"Who are you fooling? Every time you look at him you find something else to complain about. The damnedest thing is that despite your treatment, he has already made an impressive start in charming your palace."

"How do you mean?"

Lesto grinned, pushing him aside to walk in front of him. "Let us get to your chambers, and I'll tell you what I've heard about your songbird."

Sarrica said nothing, simply followed behind him, down the hall to the secret door in his private parlor, quickly covering the short distance down the hall to his office, and from there through the secret passage that led upstairs to his chambers. "I swear I spend more of my time traveling through these dank tunnels than the actual halls of my palace."

"Would you rather travel through the crowded halls? That can be arranged." Lesto gave a toothy smile.

Sarrica made a face. "No, because 'arranged' means 'half a dozen bodyguards' and you know I hate that."

"Such a child." In Sarrica's rooms, Lesto quickly stripped out of his bloodied and torn leather armor and clothes, throwing them in a bin to be cleaned and repaired. He strode naked into Sarrica's dressing room, and Sarrica could hear him pulling down clothes and new armor from the back corner where spare sets were always kept for him.

Sarrica moved out into the main room and settled on the sofa, propping his feet on the low table in front of it, head falling to rest on the back of the sofa. He stared up at the ceiling, pale green with random loops and whirls of gold and white.

He still remembered, far too clearly, the number of times he and Nyle would sit there in the evening, shuffling papers back and forth as they continued to work, planning out meetings, banquets, festivals, and parades, interspersed with battle plans, supply requisitions, and juggling all the local and foreign dignitaries demanding their attention. It had taken him well over a year before he had been able to stand going to bed alone, and he'd barely been able to spend any time in his private chambers at all.

Much of that work Sarrica now shuffled down to the council to handle because with Nyle dead and war an ever-increasing problem, he did not have time for the rest of it. Had never cared for it anyway. No one and nothing, not even his late husband, had ever been able to make a formal banquet anything but interminable.

He lifted his head as he heard Lesto enter the room. "Respectable again?"

Lesto jerked the sleeves of his shirt down until they settled in place. "As respectable as I ever get. I'll call for lunch." He walked off before Sarrica could reply.

Making a face at his retreating form, Sarrica let his head fall back again, tried to focus on all the work that needed attending. Hopefully Lesto would order that brought to him along with the lunch. He still had the council meeting in two days to prepare for, and no matter how well he did prepare, it was going to be a long, brutal, exceptionally frustrating meeting.

Nyle had been much better at gauging how each of the twenty-seven members would react and planning accordingly. In four years of managing alone, Sarrica had proven to possess not even half the skill. If he did not have Lesto and his secretaries to help, the whole empire probably would have collapsed.

He had obviously not paid as much attention to his lessons as he'd thought, but normally it did not bother him so much. Perhaps he was simply getting old.

The sound of the door opening drew his attention, and Sarrica lifted his head, looked at Lesto in silent query. "What took so long?"

"I was speaking with the guards," Lesto said, mouth quirking as he took a seat in a chair opposite the sofa. "Gossip has already spread to the far reaches of the palace that your prince has become fast friends with Lord Tara, just like Rene said."

Sarrica scowled. "Why do I care if he is friends with Lord Tara? On a very short list of people I genuinely like, he is near the top of it. Even if he wasn't, Prince Allen hardly needs my approval of his friends, betrothed or not." The scowl faded into puzzlement. "Though as to that, why is he not spending time with the Gaulden set? Surely he must want to enjoy any bit of home he can find. Gaulden is almost as far from Harken as it is possible to get."

"As though he would purposely associate with people before he knew your opinions of them," Lesto replied with a sigh. "You may have no patience for politics, Sarrica, but Prince Allen... This is what he does. He knows all the rules, written and unwritten, all the exceptions and loopholes that go with them. If he is meant to be your spouse, he must know where you stand so that he can stand with you. He is probably only friends with Lord Tara because, well, it's Lord Tara. That man excels at flouting rules. Come now, Sarrica, you *know* all this. Why are you being so stubborn?"

He *hadn't* known that, not really. He and Nyle had tended to like and dislike the same people anyway. Sarrica had no patience—or ability—to use people like game pieces and secrets like special moves. People came to him for things or they didn't. When he wanted something, he requested it. "So he is waiting for me, even to the point of avoiding people from home, whom he must know if they were good enough to be sent here."

Lesto nodded. "Yes."

Despite himself, Sarrica was impressed. "Yet Lord Tara managed to reach him anyway." He smiled faintly, thinking of the boisterous lord that drove most of court mad and had managed to catch not just a Three-headed Dragon, but their elusive Captain.

Until whatever matter was currently keeping them apart, but Sarrica assumed it was only a matter of time before they stopped behaving like fools. "I suppose I should set the court upon him, if that is what he wants. Make it so."

"Yes, Majesty," Lesto drawled. "I'll speak to your secretaries when we return downstairs, have them arrange matters. It may behoove you to attend the dinner where introductions will be made."

"I never would have guessed."

"You would have tried to avoid it, though," Lesto said and stood as a knock came at the door.

A few minutes later he came back leading three servants who quickly arranged a meal on the same table where Sarrica and Lesto had eaten dinner the night before. Sarrica's stomach rumbled as the smells reached him—gold-tip, his favorite fish, redolent in herbs and butter. The green rice and thinly sliced vegetables that accompanied it were also amongst his favorites.

He sat down, thanked the servants as they poured wine and finished off a last few touches, eyeing Lesto suspiciously until they had departed. "Why are you trying to... oh, how do you and Rene say it? Oil me up, that's the one. It loses something in the translation."

"Yes, it sounds dirty in Harken," Lesto replied, spearing and eating a bit of fish before he said. "I'm not oiling you up for anything."

Sarrica took a sip of wine, casting him an unimpressed look over the rim. "Try again."

"I'm just trying to get you placated before the councilors arrive."

Sarrica choked on a bite of fish. When he had finished coughing, he drained his wine glass. "I hate you."

"You're going to hate them even more, and I'm the only one who will be able to physically remove them without catching trouble for it."

"Loathe, despise, and detest you," Sarrica said bitterly and put all his focus on his lunch so he was able to enjoy it before misery descended upon him in the form of whiny councilors.

Lesto snickered and settled into his own meal, and they were nearly done when there was a knock at the door—sharp, quick, the kind of knock that always meant something was wrong. Sarrica sighed and took a last sip of wine while Lesto went to get the door.

A soldier stepped inside, wearing the uniform of

the Fathoms Deep: a dark teal tunic emblazoned with a black skull over crossed swords, a compass rose in the right eye. "Commander, there's a bit of a mess going on in the west barracks, and I think you'd best come sort it out before your generals murder each other."

"If that is the way they are behaving, maybe I should let them," Lesto groused. He gestured sharply to three of the men standing guard in the hallway. "In here, guard His Majesty until my return. Make certain none of the councilors get too close, and if they try it, feel free to remind them of their place howsoever you see fit. Don't kill them, obviously, but you can scare them."

They saluted, and Lesto turned to Sarrica. "Behave or I swear to the Twelve that I will lock you in your closet."

"Yes, Majesty," Sarrica replied.

Lesto shot him a warning look before he turned and strode off, the haggard-looking messenger close on his heels, rapidly explaining the matter in full.

Sarrica nodded to the men who settled in his room—one at the door, one near the table, the other between Sarrica and the circle of sofa and chairs where the councilors would soon be sitting.

The knock he expected, however, never came. Instead, the door swung open and Rene strode in, jangling loudly with every step. "Lesto sent me. He says the rest of you are to report to him at the west barracks immediately and come ready for bloodshed."

The soldiers all looked to Sarrica and, at his nod, swiftly departed. Sarrica listened as the door was locked behind them. "What in the Pantheon is going on?"

"I don't really know. I followed after Prince Allen like Lesto ordered, but he wouldn't say much to me and clearly did not want me around. I was headed to the barracks when I crossed paths with Lesto. He wasn't very clear, just said something about one general being dead and a different murder provoking the whole mess. He said he would come as soon as he could to explain it all to you, but until then you are to remain here because all this chaos makes it easy for an assassin to slip in."

"Somebody needs to bring me work to do, or I'm going to start murdering people myself," Sarrica replied.

Rene grinned. "I told your pretty secretary to bring it."

"They're all pretty, according to everyone who wanders through my office," Sarrica groused. "I don't think noting the prettiness of my secretaries is going to help you get back into Lord Tara's good graces."

"I don't want back in his good graces," Rene said and dropped down onto the sofa.

Sarrica stole Lesto's wine glass and refilled it and his own, then carried them over to the sitting area and handed Lesto's to Rene. "I don't believe you."

"I can handle my own affairs." Rene scowled at the cup. "I hate gold wine." He drained the glass. "Aren't you busy enough mucking up your own affair before you can even begin it?"

"Obviously not. Why did you end matters? I was certain you two would be married by this time next year."

Rene made a rough noise, something between a snarl, a sob, and a bitter laugh. "He proposed. I said no."

"Why?" Sarrica asked again, voice soft, low.

"Nyle," Rene said with a sigh. "He tried and tried to settle down, but we all know he wasn't really happy; that's why he went right back to the front the moment he had recovered from giving birth to Nyla. Look where that landed him. None of the three of us has ever been good at settling down, and I don't want to repeat Nyle's mistakes—trying to be something I'm not, argument after argument, finally going back into the fight only to die and leave my family in pieces. Tara deserves better than that. Can you really argue with me?"

Sarrica shook his head, remembering every bitter fight that he preferred to forget about. Nyle had been by his side every step of the way, but he had not been able to leave behind his soldiering days the way Sarrica had. He had finally reassumed his military role, despite the misgivings of many... and six months later he'd been killed in one of his damned battles. Sometimes, especially on a really bad day, Sarrica still wanted to be angry, but what was the point in being angry with the dead? "When the secretary gets here, call for more wine."

Rene raised his empty glass. "Yes, Majesty."

Chapter Five

Allen headed off to his meeting with Seyn and the others with his temper firmly back under control but the anger still simmering low, waiting to come up bright and hot again. He had never cared for violence, having had entirely too much experience on the receiving end, but the next time Sarrica opened his stupid mouth and said something odious, Allen was going to punch his teeth out.

Knowing his luck, however, Sarrica would just catch his fist, or he'd miss entirely, and Sarrica and Lesto and Rene would all laugh at him and send him home.

Anger collapsed into misery. He *couldn't* go home. His mother would never look at him with anything but disappointment. His brothers would never stop humiliating and mocking him. Damn it, he had trained *his entire fucking life* for a role like this. Granted, he'd expected to marry a king or queen of a single kingdom. Nobody had anticipated his being approached for the role of High Consort. He was more than capable of doing it, though, and more than willing to keep learning and improving as he went.

If only he could get that through the head of the most infuriating person he had ever met. How was someone that obnoxious, that condescending, that *fussy*, the High King?

So Allen wasn't used to murder and death. He would learn to master his discomfort, but Gods above, wasn't he allowed a little bit of time? He hadn't learned to endure whippings in a single night, and murder seemed a bit of a step up from that. Step down? Whatever, it was worse.

He was losing his control. Bad enough he'd lost his temper in front of Sarrica. If he lost control completely, Sarrica would definitely never change his mind about the marriage. Allen sighed and looked around, spied a small hallway that appeared to be deserted, slipped down it a few paces, and saw a window seat just far enough in that he would not be visible unless someone came upon him.

Sitting down, he watched the people milling around outside. Soldiers, in several different kinds of uniforms. Bah. He was bloody tired of *soldiers.* Allen was well aware that it was practically a soldier's duty to hate the bureaucratic engine that ran the war machine, but that very same engine helped keep them alive, kept supplies moving, and often prevented more battles than any soldier bothered to realize. As though it was *easy* for his mother to order men to go die. They probably thought she signed papers after a quick glance before flitting off to another party.

They didn't see her spend hours preparing for balls and dinners where she worked herself to the bone coaxing funds, delicately negotiating the muck and mire that could have turned into more wars. They didn't see her quietly cry as she signed all the letters that must go out when soldiers died.

No, no, all hail the soldiers, who could never do anything wrong. Perish the thought. A poor, suffering soldier would never do anything as vindictive and cruel as drag their brother out of bed, tie him to a post, gag him, and whip him until he passed out.

Over and over and over again for the better part of six years.

Allen drew a deep breath, let it out slowly, focused on the ember of resentment that still burned. Resentment, ha. It was hate, pure and simple. He did not hate anyone the way he hated Chass and Manda. Thankfully he was unlikely to ever see Manda again since he was closely tied to Gaulden Palace and their mother's bidding. Of the two, Manda was by far the worst and he would gladly go the rest of his life with never seeing Manda again.

Chass... Allen would surrender all he possessed never to see Chass again, but hopefully when next they met Allen would be High Consort. Let Chass choke on *that*. Captain of the Penance Gate he may be, but that meant he answered to any order Allen gave him. If the bastard ever touched him again, Allen would be more than happy to order him locked up for the rest of his life.

Thinking about his brothers had the strange effect of calming him, at least externally. No tutor could have taught him better than they that the person who remained calm retained the power. If only he did not immediately lose his control the moment Sarrica stepped into the room.

Abandoning the window seat, he headed back the way he'd come and continued on toward Seyn's office.

"Prince Allen! There you are, thank the gods." Tara came behind him just as Allen started to turn, nearly knocking him over as he latched on. Letting go, he bent over double, heaving for breath. "You must come at once."

Allen nodded and immediately followed after him. "What's wrong?"

"Murder," Tara replied. "The whole thing is a right mess."

"Am I needed to translate?" Allen asked. "What murder?"

"No, no translation—but it's ugly, and right now you could do worse than stand at Sarrica's side and make it clear that you support him, even if..."

Murder. He was needed to show support. That could only mean Gaulden was involved, and not in a good way. Allen wanted to groan, swear, something. Instead he focused. "General Faharm is involved in this somehow that might put Gaulden at odds with the throne."

"General Faharm is dead, killed by General Vren."

Dead? Oh, no. People back home would be devastated. Allen pushed his own sorrow away; there would be time for that later. "Why?"

"Because it was a well-known secret that General Faharm and Lieutenant Bells were lovers. Bells was found dead a short time ago, and the entire matter exploded into a nasty fight between Faharm and Vren. I don't know the details of that, yet, but something happened. Faharm is dead, Vren is under arrest, and the Fathoms Deep are about to go on a murderous rampage."

"Fathoms Deep? Why?"

"Lieutenant Bells was Fathoms Deep."

"Bells... as in the Baron of Clay, that Bells?" They were a powerful trading family in Tricemore, which was nothing to sneer at, but they had little standing or power outside of that, if Allen recalled correctly.

"Yes, just so. I think he has a brother who works as a clerk here in the palace."

Allen nodded. "I see." His mind spun, trying to keep

up with all the information.

Fathoms Deep angry with the regular army, the regular army divided between those supporting Vren and those supporting Faharm. General Vren was from Mesta; relations between Mesta and Gaulden had been strained for the past two decades. There would be increased tensions between Gaulden and Mesta until the matter was resolved, and depending on how it went, the resolution might only make matters worse.

Not to mention the effect his presence could have on the whole matter. If he favored Gaulden, he would be accused of playing favorite to his homeland. If he favored Mesta, he would be regarded as betraying his homeland. Nevermind that as Sarrica's betrothed the only 'side' he took was that of the High Throne. He would have preferred an easier, less tragic and violent way to prove himself, but as he'd told Rene: Best to begin how he'd be expected to go on. Life wasn't going to get *easier* when—if—he became High Consort.

"Let us pass," Tara ordered as they reached the barracks courtyard. Men were slow to move at first, but as they registered Allen and the markings of a Prince upon his jacket, they parted hastily to let them pass.

Sarrica stood in the middle of the courtyard, two bodies draped in black cloth behind him. Lesto stood beside him, one hand held to his side, covered in blood, the fabric around it soaked in blood. He looked shaky, pale, but snarled every time the healers tried to approach him.

A few paces away, secured in manacles and held by two palace soldiers, General Vren looked pale and defeated, drying splashes of blood on her face and in her hair.

The sudden murmurs as people noted Allen drew Sarrica's head up with a sharp snap. His mouth flattened, but he said only, "Prince Allen, I assume you have heard about what happened to General Faharm. My condolences."

"Thank you, Your Majesty," Allen said quietly, looking at the blood drying on the stones, how Sarrica stood amidst it as though it were nothing more than dirt. "I came to lend my support and aid, should you have need of it." He silently bid the stubborn bastard to say yes.

Sarrica gave a sharp, short shake of his head. "Your Highness, there's no need to drag yourself into this matter, though of course your offer is appreciated."

Allen did not reply, simply turned on his heel and walked off. Whispers and exclamations of shock rose up behind him; he ignored them. If Sarrica wanted to dismiss him so callously—again—so be it. Allen could dismiss in his turn.

Once he was well away from the barracks, however, all his anger left him. Men were dead, and a prestigious general was likely to be executed over the matter. His personal tribulations could wait.

Though he was about to give up entirely and go home. This was *precisely* what he was meant to do, exactly the tangled, gnarled mess he was meant to sort out. Sarrica would not even give him a chance, would rather throw him away than swallow his pride for two minutes and make use of Allen's skills.

He stopped a footman on his way back to his suite and bid him tell Seyn that he was indisposed and would make up the canceled luncheon to him and his friends another day.

A day that would likely never come because he could not anticipate he would be there much longer. Better to sever the betrothal than continue to humiliate himself and his family by enduring rejection after rejection. Any royal family in the empire would be proud, even ecstatic, to have him.

The High King could find some precious damned soldier to wed precisely as he wanted, and Allen hoped they rotted. *Soldiers.*

"Allen!"

He stopped as he heard Tara's voice and turned around. "My apologies for abandoning you."

"Not at all," Tara said. "You cut him beautifully. Sarrica wanted to hit something; you should have seen his face. I don't think anyone has had the nerve to treat him that way since—well, since High Consort Nyle." He grinned. "I'm not the only one to have marked that, either."

"I see," Allen replied, though he did not really see at all. The very last thing likely to help him was everyone whispering about the noble, glorious, *perfect* soldier that Sarrica had loved.

He should not have surrendered to the impulse, his self-control should be much better than that. All he'd done was confirm to the whole of court that they were at odds. It was a weakness anyone with brains and ambition would be happy to exploit.

On the other hand, that concern was largely irrelevant since Sarrica obviously wasn't going to marry him now, even if there had been some lingering chance. Allen was not going to keep making nice with a man who had already decided to hate him. Allen had fought that battle with his brothers, he was not going to fight it with Sarrica. Foolish to, anyway, since Sarrica could punish not just Allen, but his entire family, if he was so inclined.

"Aw, don't look so glum." Tara nudged him gently. "He'll come around eventually. One day when they bury him, his tomb will be inscribed: *Here Lies High King Sarrica the Stubborn*.

Allen smiled fleetingly, and smiled a bit more when Tara gave a pleased grin.

"So what do you think of our dear High King when he is not being a mule-headed ninny?"

"He's an exceptional ruler," Allen replied. "By all accounts he was a good husband. Brilliant military tactician, well-liked. I thought we would get on well enough."

Tara made a soft noise, shook his head. "You sound like you're reading a report. What do you think of *him*?"

Allen thought of Sarrica, huge and beautiful and so devoted to his dead husband he would not consider a new one, no matter how useful it would be to have a consort to share the weight and take over all those duties that Sarrica despised. He thought of all the ways Sarrica had looked at him, treated him. He had come to serve a purpose, had worked so hard, but Sarrica didn't want him, wouldn't even give him a chance. "What I think doesn't matter. All of this resides on what *he* thinks, and he has made his opinion of me clear. I have gossiped like a soldier quite enough. If you will excuse me, I'd best be off to my room. I've matters to think upon."

"You don't—" Tara closed his mouth and shook his head again. Drawing them to a halt, he turned Allen to face him and gripped his arms. "Do not give up yet. I would not blame you at all for doing so, but I think the situation is not as bad as you think. Sarrica is stubborn and not very good at conveying the intentions behind his actions." He pursed his lips, head moving back and forth as he lost himself in whatever thoughts filled his head. "What if... What if a private meal could be arranged? Just the two of you? I think free of audiences and all the stress of court and duty, a more positive encounter might be managed. Certainly Sarrica would stand a better chance of behaving himself."

The idea had appeal, even if he still wanted mostly to dump Sarrica in the ocean. "Perhaps, but I do not see him agreeing to such a proposition."

Tara laughed. "No one would bother to ask him. First rule of dealing with the High King: go through Commander Lesto. I'll take care of everything. *You* choose something pretty to wear. If the man hasn't noticed you, he's even dumber than I thought, and believe me, my opinion of him is pretty low right now."

Despite himself, Allen smiled. "You are not the sort of friend I expected to make. People like you do not usually last long at court." Nor did they befriend people like Allen, the so-called predators of the court, while everyone else struggled not to be the prey they caught—people like Tara, bright and emotional and artless.

"People like me?" Tara narrowed his eyes, but his mouth twitched at one corner as he fought a smile. "That could mean any number of things. Which people like me?"

"Vibrant. Honest. Open."

Tara's cheeks flushed slightly. "You're a lot nicer than everyone else. That was part of the reason father suggested you, he said you weren't quite as icy as the rest of 'that lot' tended to be. Almost everyone else I know has tried to drum my unseemly behavior out me, but I won't have it. My father thinks he is winning the war by trying to negotiate a marriage with the Selemea royal family, but he is going to be disappointed in the end."

Allen's brows furrowed. "Selemea? But they're all married off except for Prince Bann and Princess Chey, and she is only twelve. It will be three more years before they can legally betroth her, and Prince Bann must marry for heirs. Which adoption could solve, but Selemea is too old-fashioned and rigid in their thinking for that."

"Heirs I can provide," Tara said wryly.

"Ah," Allen replied, mouth quirking. "Maybe they're unbending some of their rigid tradition after all. In that case you would make for an ideal spouse. Except I do not think you would do very well at court there. I learned much from that place, especially in regards to controlling my emotions, but it was... exhausting."

Tara snickered, squeezing his arms one last time before letting go. "Exhausting, yes, that's the most tactful adjective. Not that it matters, because I'm not marrying Prince Bann, but I'm letting my father enjoy thinking I will for the present. Now then, you return to your rooms, and I will go see about arranging that private meal. It will probably not happen for a day or so, but I'm sure you'll get the invitation tonight or tomorrow morning. Until later, Your Highness." Tara leaned up and kissed both his cheeks before darting off with a parting wave.

Everything seemed so much quieter with Tara gone, in a way Allen wasn't used to noting. If nothing else came of his journey to Harken, at least he had found a friend.

Mood somewhat improved, he returned to his rooms. A carafe of wine and a light luncheon had been left for him—as well as quite the stack of notes. Removing his heavy jacket and carefully draping it over the back of a chair, he settled at the table and ate while he slowly worked through the correspondence.

Most of it seemed to be notes from various persons in the palace welcoming him and inviting him to lunch or dinner should he ever be so inclined. Several mentioned large events where it would not be terribly out of place for him to attend, whether Sarrica had presented him formally or not. Polite, cautious, curious.

There was a more genuine welcome, a full letter, from the Gaulden ambassador, Lady Naurren. A pity Allen could not go and see her, especially now that there was the problem of two murders to solve, and Gaulden was right in the middle of it. Sarrica should have let him stay to assist, damn it. He'd spent his entire life watching his mother maintain a careful balance between Gaulden and Mesta; he would have known precisely what to say and do in the current circumstances.

Sarrica was not a fool, though, and he had plenty of other people to help him. Allen wasn't the only one trained, and he needed to control his arrogance before it controlled him. Damn it, though, he was *better* than most—that was why he'd been chosen.

He drained his wine and shoved all the correspondence aside. He needed exercise, to escape the suffocation of a lost cause, just for a little while. Regain his lost control before his private meal with

Sarrica—assuming, of course, that it happened at all.

Stripping off all of his clothes, he went to his wardrobe and pulled out something more nondescript, the kind of clothes he wore when he ventured out to practice his language skills without the distracting weight of intimidating bodyguards.

Breeches, boots, a plain white undershirt and a simple, thigh-length green tunic trimmed with blue and white flowers, and a light-weight, dark brown jacket. He bound his hair into a knot at the back of his neck and draped a dark green wrap over his shoulders, to pull up when the weather cooled or if it seemed he might be recognized. The only concession he made to his status was to remove his royal signet and tuck it away inside a hidden pocket in his jacket. A small purse of coins and he was ready.

Finding his way out of the palace proved simple enough, and it was easy to be overlooked in the throng of people coming and going in the public pavilion.

Harkenesten City was even busier than he recalled from his quick journey through on the day of his arrival. Just walking along he could hear snatches of conversation from nearly every language he knew, and a few he recognized but couldn't speak. The knots of tension in his shoulders and back eased as he walked, and for the first time since laying eyes on Sarrica and seeing only contempt on his face, Allen felt like he could breathe properly.

He headed first for the market, pausing at various stalls to haggle for sweets or trinkets, really for the chance to stretch his skills. The most common language seemed to be a mish-mash of Selemean and Harken, which was promising for his proposal that the palace staff be taught Selemean.

Tucking away a bag of cinnamon drops, Allen bid the candy seller good day. He popped a sweet in his mouth and slowly meandered away from the market and into the heart of the city.

It was hot, dusty, a cacophony of noise and movement: shops, messengers, pedestrians, horses, carriages, the occasional farmer with a heavy cart or leading along various fowl or occasionally hogs. The whole mess reminded him of home, as Gaulden was also a port city and relied heavily on international trade. A full fifth of Gaulden's wealth was in the export of wine and cider, with textiles making up more than a quarter.

The Harken Empire ran on taxes supplemented by other sources. It had run strong for two hundred and fifty-seven years. Benta was dead set on seeing it never reached two hundred and sixty, and there were plenty of countries that would be happy to pick up the broken pieces, but if the Empire was run by Sarrica's stupid, stubborn head, Allen could see why Harken was winning the fight.

He paused when he came to a bookshop, wavered a moment, then conceded defeat and went inside. It smelled like all bookshops: paper and ink and a bit like dusty vanilla. The man at the counter, sorting through stacks of books, smiled politely. "Merry afternoon, good sir." The words were Harken but spoken slowly, in a thick Mestan accent. Not surprising. Mesta was the strongest in the empire for knowledge, and all the best-made books came from there.

"Good day, bookseller. What does your shop have to offer by way of historical works?"

The man's face lit up. *"Good day, good day."* He quickly abandoned the counter and came to greet

Allen in more Mestan fashion, gripping both his hands and bowing slightly. Allen returned the bow, then let the old but spry man lead him through the crowded shop to where the history books were kept, rambling on and on about each one, often wandering off topic to mention other books in the shop.

In the end, Allen settled on a dozen books. He helped the old man, Pya, carry them all to the counter. *"Thank you for the help, bookseller. You have a marvelous shop."*

"You're too kind, sir. Half a sovereign altogether."

Allen laid two regals and a mark on the counter. *"If you could have a runner send them on to the palace for me, I would be most obliged. Have you a scrap of paper, pen, and wax I could borrow?"*

Pya's eyes had gone wide at the word 'palace', and he quickly pushed supplies across the counter. Smiling in thanks, Allen quickly wrote a note for the guards that the books were to be delivered to his chambers. Pulling out his ring, he dripped wax on the bottom of the note and pressed his seal into it. When the wax had dried, he set it on top of one of the stacks of books. *"Many thanks for your help, good bookseller. I hope the winds send you good fortune."*

"G-good day, Your Highness. May favorable winds always guide you."

Allen nodded in parting and slipped from the bookshop—and was nearly trampled as people rushed past him. His head knocked hard against the bookshop door. Grunting, he waited until it seemed safe, then stepped out into the street where people still seemed to be rushing madly. Fleeing, actually.

The sound of a whip striking skin, followed immediately by a scream, made him freeze. He snapped his head in the direction of it: the place from which everyone seemed to be fleeing. Who in the Pantheon was being whipped? The practice was almost completely illegal, permitted only under very specific circumstances, and it was considered reprehensible.

"Move!" he ordered when people continued to get in his way. He was not above pulling out his ring, but thankfully the tone of his voice seemed enough to convince people that moving was the wisest course of action.

At the end of the street was a small square with a public water fountain for those who did not have water piped directly to their homes. A young man had been roped to a pole where notices were hung, though currently it was bare.

An older man, huge and round and heavy, though clearly most of that bulk was muscle, angrily lashed the younger man, snarling in guttural Rilien. Ugly words that only fueled Allen's anger.

"Enough!" Allen bellowed.

The man with the whip paused, turned to glare at him. *"Stay out of business that does not concern you, gutterwaste."*

"You will regret those words," Allen replied. He stood in front of the man tied to the post. *"Put down your whip."*

"Make me." He let the whip fly.

Allen jerked his head to the side and raised his left arm, breathed out as the whip struck. At the same time he reached out with his right hand and grabbed the whip, held it fast just long enough to wrap a few lengths around his stinging left arm, walking toward the man as he did so.

The man's face went red as he tried uselessly to yank the whip back. *"Who the fuck do you think you are?"*

"I—"

"Whoever you are, you've just whipped Prince Allen Telmis of Gaulden, betrothed to his Imperial Majesty the High King," Rene's voice cut across the square, startling them both to a stop. He stepped in front of Allen, grabbed the whip, and sliced it apart with a dagger. Sheathing the dagger, Rene drew his sword. "Do you understand me? Do you speak Harken?" When the man nodded, he continued, "Tell me why I shouldn't slit your throat for daring to strike the High Consort Presumptive."

The man's face had drained of all the livid color it had held only a moment ago. He dropped to his knees and bowed his head low. "A hundred apologies, Your Highness."

Allen stepped up beside Rene, ignoring the scowl that earned him. "Someone cut that boy down."

Rene gestured sharply, and Allen saw three men in the uniform of the Three-headed Dragons. Two of them went to the post and cut the young man free, carefully helping him to his feet and holding him gingerly about the waist so as not to cause further harm to his injuries. "Take him to a healer, make certain somebody watches him until this is sorted out." He looked back at Allen. "Why am I not surprised you're a troublemaker?"

Ignoring that for the moment, Allen looked at the man still kneeling several paces away and asked in Rilien, *"Why were you whipping a man who is barely out of boyhood? What crime did he commit that merits such severe punishment?"*

"He is my apprentice, Your Highness, and he broke several valuable pieces in my shop. The discipline was more than fair."

"Pieces of what?"

"Glass, Your Highness. I own a glass shop. He broke work that took my blowers months to make, work I cannot easily or cheaply replace."

"How did he break them?"

"He fell asleep like the slattern he is," the man snarled. *"Fell asleep at his station, knocked his equipment over, and caused an avalanche across the entire shop!"*

Allen hummed thoughtfully as he turned to Rene. "I think his story is missing pertinent details. He claims the boy fell asleep at his work station, and it ultimately resulted in the breaking of several costly pieces of glass."

Rene grunted. "If he's anything like most masters, the apprentice was overworked. I'll set my men to track down city guards that will see the matter is handled fairly. Will that suffice, Your Highness?"

"I suppose it will have to, but whipping is a cowardly way to punish, and I will not treat lightly anyone I catch doing it. Especially repeat offenders." He looked at the glass shop owner and repeated the words in Rilien.

Gesturing sharply to his remaining man and issuing terse orders, Rene grabbed Allen's arm and hauled him away much as Allen's tutors had when they'd caught him in the halls chatting instead of at his desk where he should have been. Three times Allen tried to ask where they were going, but the glares and growl-like noises he got in reply before he could even finish the question finally forced his surrender on the matter.

He did not expect Rene to take him to a handsome, understated but clearly expensive city house. Like most of the houses on that well-paved street, it was made of dark gray stone trimmed in red-flecked pale gray stone. Rene's house—it must have been, given that he produced a key—was also covered in patches of green ivy with dark blue flowers. Inside, the house smelled like leather, metal, and some sort of flowery incense.

Rene dragged him inside to stand in a beautiful, colorful foyer. "Stay there." He turned around and slammed the door shut, locked it and stowed the key, then whipped back around and planted his hands on his hips. "What in all the Realms did you think you were doing!"

"I wanted to get out of the palace for a little while," Allen replied. "I didn't think it would do any harm to walk about the shops for a couple of hours. I certainly had no plans to embroil myself in a confrontation. I do not understand why you're so angry with me, my welfare is not your concern."

"If you were not royalty, Your Highness, I would tell you to shut up."

Allen's brows rose. "Perhaps I have misjudged, but that does not strike me as something that has ever stopped you."

Rene muttered something he did not entirely catch, then replied, "In that case, *shut up.* Do you know what kind of trouble would have come down on all of us if your body had turned up in a gutter? Of course you know! You're supposed to be marrying Sarrica because you're *not* as stupid as him."

"I was not trying to cause trouble, Captain. I

apologize. I only meant to take a walk about the city to clear my head, but I heard the whip and saw people running..."

Sighing, Rene jerked an arm to the archway to the left. "Come on, let me look at your arm while I medicate myself heavily with wine. Let us pray to every star in existence that this tale does not reach Sarrica and Lesto, and if it does, let us hope they laugh it off as a grossly exaggerated tale."

"I think you are overreacting, Captain, though I appreciate you do so at least partly on my behalf." He pulled away when Rene tried to take his arm. "It's fine, I promise you. At worst it will be bruised."

"I'm looking anyway, Your Highness, and if I must pin you to the ground to do it, I will. If you do not believe me, ask your fiancé about my threats sometime."

Allen's mouth flattened, but he said nothing, only discarded his jacket and pulled up his sleeve. "See? Only reddened, mildly tender. There will be a few bruises by morning, but nothing more. He was not hitting as hard as he could have, and my jacket took the brunt of it."

"Bah." Rene vanished into what was presumably a pantry and reappeared after a few minutes of clattering, banging, and swearing. He set down cheese, bread, olives, and a jug of wine. "It's not much, but I'm rarely home long enough to bother doing anything properly around here. Even when I am, I spend more time at the palace."

"So this is your home? I thought so at first, but it's so..."

"Empty? Spare?" Rene shrugged.

"Quiet, I was going to say."

"I use it when I need space." The last of Rene's anger faded off as he looked at Allen. "I guess you probably do need some of that yourself, eh, Your Highness?"

Allen nodded as he accepted the cup of wine Rene slid across to him with a quiet murmur of thanks. "I am grateful for your assistance, Captain. I am not generally so confrontational and had not entirely figured out what I was going to do next. I only wanted the whipping to stop." He finally looked up, but immediately looked away at the pensive, too-knowing look on Rene's face.

"I'm glad I was there. We heard the ruckus and went in search of the source. I was not prepared for what I saw. If you are trying to *scare* Sarrica into marrying you, I think you might be on to something. Don't do it anyway."

"I'm not going to marry a man against his will," Allen replied. He took another swallow of wine, frowning when that wound up emptying the cup. Had he drunk it so fast?

Rene grunted and refilled both their cups. "He'll come around."

"I no longer particularly care. Perhaps I should have said that I am not going to marry a man against his will, especially when he has done nothing but humiliate and insult me since my arrival. I refuse to subject myself to that sort of treatment every time he is in a snit about something, and it seems to me that where I am concerned the snit is permanent. There are plenty of other people I can marry, kingdoms I can assist, without being treated like a punishment."

"I think this is the most I've heard you talk, except perhaps to Lord Tara."

Allen raised a brow at the bitterness. "You two have quite the history, I sense."

"Not really. Ex-lovers always take time to settle back into being something else." Rene raked a hand through his hair and stared into his wine, looking as despondent as Allen felt.

So his theory had been correct. They would make a handsome pair, and Tara's family must have been thrilled to see him form a connection with the imperial family. "I'm sorry."

"Not yours to be sorry about, Highness, but thank you. Once my men have come by to tell me matters have been addressed to your satisfaction I'll take you back to the palace."

"I came to the city by myself, Captain, I can return the same."

"No," Rene said flatly. "You never should have been out here alone to begin with. Completely ignoring all the people who would love to hold the High Consort Presumptive hostage, there are plenty of others who will slit your belly simply to steal your boots. You are too well-trained and aware of your station not to know that."

Allen acknowledged the point by way of a judicious swallow of wine. "I think we should adjourn somewhere more comfortable than your kitchen table."

Rene snorted a laugh, refilled their cups, carrying the jug as he led the way out of the kitchen. "Are you propositioning me, Highness?"

Tempting. If not for the mess in which he was currently stuck, Allen would have been more than happy to flirt with Rene and coax him into bed. Soldiers might irritate him in the day to day of things, but men who had survived as long as Rene knew how to enjoy the moment and make the most of it. And Rene was hardly a strain on the eyes.

He was not Sarrica, but even if the marriage did somehow take place, Allen had no doubts on that point: Sarrica had no amorous interest in him whatsoever.

The despondence Allen had been fighting since the altercation in the prison cells finally bested him, crashing into him like the people outside the bookshop earlier. All he'd wanted was a reasonably happy marriage and to spend the rest of his life doing what he'd spent the first part training for. He was meant to be sitting at Sarrica's side, getting to know the high court, learning more of the duties he would be taking on, settling into his role.

He had also secretly hoped to be learning how Sarrica kissed, how he tasted, how he looked and felt when he came. Political marriage though it might be, he had still foolishly hoped there might be something more to it someday. He wasn't stupid enough to hope for a love match like some naïve fool, but he had hoped he and Sarrica would get along, even become good friends.

Among all his other belongings, he'd brought an entire chest of items and special clothing in anticipation of enjoying all the benefits of marriage... and his life married to Sarrica would instead either be spent in a cold bed, wishing for a lover he could trust, or settling for a string of bed warmers who never lasted long enough to be a threat.

He startled when a hand fell heavy on his shoulder and looked up. "Highness, are you all right? I do not think I have ever seen you so visibly upset. You did not look this distressed when you were facing down a man with a whip."

Allen laughed bitterly. "Whips I can handle." He took a healthy swallow of wine. "Being subjected to derision, humiliation, and abuse because I am not a soldier *again*—that I cannot take. Will not take." He drained the cup, then sat down on the large, wide settee that Rene had guided him to. "My apologies, Captain. If my mother were here she would strangle me for behaving so abhorrently."

"It's not abhorrent to be human," Rene said quietly. "You seem like you spend too much time alone."

"Perhaps. The only time I spend with others is in honing my skills. Lord Tara is the first person to be nice to me without any overt motive or because he was ordered. He is… refreshing."

"Yeah, he is," Rene said quietly before draining his own wine. "I brought you here to shake some sense into you, not…"

Allen smiled faintly. "Act abhorrently?"

Rene gave a soft laugh and dropped down next to him on the settee. He smelled like leather and wine, a hint of something earthy, smoky. Allen looked away before he started thinking or doing something stupid. "It's not abhorrent to be maudlin in my own home. Abhorrent was ending an affair I enjoyed because I got scared, but no matter how many times I go back over it all ending the affair seems the best solution. I am not the settling down type. No one in my family is."

"High Consort Nyle managed well enough."

He jumped when Rene gave a sharp bark of laughter, almost recoiling from the anger in it. "No, no he didn't. It doesn't matter now because he's dead, but he managed horribly." He lifted his cup and drained it, then fumbled for the jug and filled their cups once more, splashing a small bit on the white marble tiles and the green rug that partially covered them in front of the settee.

Allen stared at him, too worn or too drunk for the proper words to come. "I'm sorry."

Rene shrugged. "It's over, and time heals all wounds, or so I am told." He raised his cup and smiled crookedly. "To marriages that will never happen."

"To that I will drink," Allen replied and tapped his cup against Rene's before slowly drinking. His head spun, but he wondered how much of that was simply because he *wanted* it to spin. The last time he had gotten drunk he had been alone, and before that he had only gotten mildly drunk with Larren a couple of weeks after Larren had put an end to the whippings. *That* had been the last time he'd cried over the matter, and he cringed whenever he remembered it.

Since then, he had been too busy to do something so foolish.

He shivered when rough fingertips dragged lightly down the side of his face, turned, and blinked at Rene, licked wine from his lips.

Rene huffed a soft laugh. "Sarrica is a fool. He should already have you wedded and bedded."

"His loss," Allen replied and drank the last of his wine, bending over to set it on the floor—and nearly toppling, breath seizing, head spinning, and found himself staring at the ceiling, Rene hovering at his periphery, too close and too tempting. He turned and met Rene's gaze, sighing softly to see his own frustration and despair reflected.

Who moved first, he could never recall.

~~*

Allen looked up from the table where he sat nosing through Rene's papers, mouth tipping up at one corner when Rene grunted, opened his eyes, then closed them and went back to sleep.

For a soldier, he was remarkably determined to avoid the morning. Allen poured a fresh cup of tea, enjoying the late morning sunshine, the muffled noises of the city, and the illicitness of having been out of the palace for a day and night. Had anyone noticed his absence?

Perhaps whoever had delivered the papers to Rene's house and left them on the table for him would report that Allen had stayed the night there. Ideally without mentioning the details, but he had decided his actions; he would face the consequences of them.

Rene stirred again, and this time when Allen turned toward him he stared back with full awareness, grunted and shook his head. That was immediately followed by a wince.

"There's breakfast here, and festival tonic."

Rene grunted again but climbed off the settee and pulled on breeches and shirt with slow, awkward movements. Stumbling to the table, he dropped into the remaining empty seat and pulled the bottle of festival tonic toward him.

Really it was just cheap alcohol with other bits for flavor—the curse is the cure, as healers liked to say. Drinking it was a special form of torture, but it did work.

Allen bent his attention back to the papers he had decided to read, mostly out of boredom, partly out of genuine curiosity. Requisition forms, stamped with a seal of approval and orders as to when supplies would be picked up or where they should be delivered. A few places were marked as not cleared with a terse note that Rene knew better than to ask.

"I am relatively certain those papers are none of your business, Highness."

"I'm the High Consort Presumptive. Or should be. Everything pertaining to the empire is my business."

Rene rolled his eyes. "I see you slept well."

Allen smiled briefly. "I've certainly had worse nights. You must be planning quite the journey. Six sacks of sugar is not the sort of supply a company like yours typically requisitions—or purchases at all. It's too expensive. Unless it's going to be used for a very specific purpose."

"It's sugar," Rene said. "There is nothing special about sugar."

"Do not treat me like I'm stupid. My father tested me on international trade every other morning when I had breakfast with him and whoever else was dining with him that day. My dame tutored me personally on international law. Gaulden is not a master of trade because we're pretty. Sugar is only sold by three countries, and contracts with them are extremely hard to come by. That does not even begin to include shipping, storage, security, and taxes. When all is accounted for, one Harken-standard sack of Treya Mencee sugar can cost as much as a sovereign. The Harken Empire can easily afford that, and there aren't many other countries who can say the same.

"Benta, on the other hand, cannot afford sugar; they are too poor from decades of poor leadership and unsuccessful warring. Especially when you factor in that they are planning to go to war with Harken once they have secured everything north of the Cartha Mountains." He set down the papers. "If I were a mercenary team being sent into Benta, I would anticipate having to bribe my way through in several places. Currency is problematic for a number of reasons. Certain spices and other foodstuffs, however, would make excellent bribes—especially sugar."

Rene pressed his fingertips to his temples. "No one should be able to deduce that much just because my damned papers mention sugar."

"It's the details that save and destroy," Allen replied and picked up his tea. "I hope you have a silver tongue on your team equal to the task. Benta is hyper vigilant. If they sense you are Harken mercs they will cut your throats with relish."

"You do not need to tell me that." Rene scrubbed at his face and settled back in his chair. "No, I don't have a silver tongue yet. As you would know, silver tongues fluent in Bentan are more than a little difficult to come by. I told Sarrica I would be able to leave in three days, however, which is tomorrow. The timeline does not allow for the delays that would be required to wait for the return of a silver tongue qualified for the task."

Allen looked at the papers again, lips pressed together.

"No," Rene said. "Absolutely not. Sarrica would *kill me.* That's assuming Lesto didn't get to me first, which I hope not because Lesto's meaner."

"I am fairly certain we are both already dead anyway," Allen replied. Vanishing from the palace for a whole night and sleeping with Sarrica's brother-in-law was definitely *not* the way to prove himself a worthy consort. On the other hand, Sarrica could barely be bothered to use his name, and probably hadn't even yet noticed his absence.

Rene made a face and stole his tea, drained it, and handed the empty cup back. "It's not something to be repeated, I'm sure you agree, but if Sarrica even *dares* to get angry about this he won't like what I have to say to him in reply."

"And Tara?" Allen asked quietly.

Rene flinched, but in the end he just scrubbed his face again and replied, "I ended it. We've no longer any claim upon each other."

Allen let the matter drop. "You should hire me to be your silver tongue. I'm one of the best in Harken, and definitely one of very few who can speak Bentan as well as a native."

"And so modest."

"Modesty has nothing to do with facts." Allen refilled his teacup and held it firmly. "Sarrica will never give me a chance if I don't prove to him I'm just as good as his precious soldiers. You need a silver tongue."

"You don't have any experience in the kind of thing we're doing. You'd be a liability."

Allen scoffed. "That's a poor excuse, and we both know it. Precious few silver tongues have military training. Would any of the other qualified silver tongues be less of a liability?"

"That's irrelevant," Rene bit out. "None of them are a damned prince engaged to the High King. My answer is and will always be *no*."

"So what do you intend to do once you're in Benta?" Allen countered.

"Figure it out when we get there."

Allen folded his arms across his chest. "You need a

silver tongue. I need to prove to Sarrica that I'm fit to be High Consort."

"I think those scars on your back would do the job fine," Rene said quietly.

Allen stiffened, then dropped his arms, fumbled for his tea. "I thought I had gotten away with you not noticing."

"Woke up in the dead of night when my men came with the papers. They never crossed the threshold, though I suppose they could make assumptions given my state. I saw the scars on my way back. Who in the hells whipped you? If I'm not mistaken, they did it for *years*."

"It doesn't matter," Allen said. "Showing Sarrica my scars won't help anything. I want to be the silver tongue for the Three-headed Dragons. My Bentan has been well-honed by Bentan citizens who fled to Harken for refuge. My mother spared no expense on my training."

"I can't risk your life that way, Highness."

"You can't just throw away the lives of all your men."

Rene slammed a hand on the table. "I don't need you telling me that. You know nothing about it."

"I don't?" Allen demanded, slamming his own hands down and standing up to lean over the table. "I know exactly how badly silver tongues are needed. I know exactly how often the mercenary groups and regular army suffer without them. Of course I know! I have family scattered through them. My brother Larren is a General for the Gaulden Army and my brother Chass is Captain of the Penance Gate. I see problems with communication every single day, in military and civilian alike. I know how much people lose simply because they cannot speak to one another. Why do you think I have an education worth a kingdom? Entire households do not cost in a decade what my mother paid out in a year to see me properly trained. I know what I can do, and I know what will happen to you in Benta if you do not have a silver tongue. Take me. When we come back successful, maybe Sarrica will be more willing to listen to both of us."

Rene's head dropped to the table, where he beat it softly for a few seconds. "I am going to regret this," he said, the words muffled. Slowly sitting up, he said, "Your absence will be noted, and it's entirely possible one or both of us will be murdered upon our return."

"If we remove my things from my suite everyone will think I slunk off home. By the time they figure out that I didn't, it will be far too late to track me down. Why are we going to Benta?"

"To retrieve a man they kidnapped from that wrecked ship. It's vitally important we get him out. I'll tell you the details later. It should, in theory, be an easy in, easy out. The easier it should be, however, the harder it always is."

Allen nodded. "I understand."

"Do everything I say, Highness. Without question, without hesitation. Soldiers who don't follow orders get everyone killed."

"I know," Allen said. "I will listen, I promise. I want to help." He wanted to prove himself a worthy consort. Whatever his maudlin behavior in the night, come morning it had only made him more stubbornly determined to change Sarrica's mind. If he had to endure being a mercenary for a little while to prove that, he would. Assuming he didn't get himself killed first. "What do we do?"

"We figure out how to smuggle your belongings out of the palace," Rene said. "Thankfully my men will handle that, probably with a little too much relish. First, however, I want a bath. We're going to have to cut your hair; it'll draw too much attention the way it is."

Allen flinched but nodded in assent. He'd made his decision; he wouldn't balk over his hair no matter how much he hated the idea of losing it. Standing, he followed Rene out of the room.

Chapter Six

Sarrica almost threw his coffee across the room. "What do you mean he is *gone*?"

The servant who had delivered the news bowed again, hands white-knuckled where he clasped them against his stomach. "I beg your pardon, Your Majesty, but it is exactly as I've said: Prince Allen is gone. His suite is empty, he failed to keep appointments, and no one has seen him since the day before yesterday when he, uh, spoke with Your Majesty briefly in the barracks."

"Thank you," Sarrica replied, dismissing him with a sharp gesture. He ordered everyone else out of the room as well. When the office was empty, he leaned back in his seat, braced his elbows on his armrests, and pinched the bridge of his nose. He listened as Lesto approached the desk, could practically feel his disapproving glare. Looking up, he said, "I believe my fiancé has canceled our marriage."

"I believe you deserve it." Lesto folded his arms across his chest.

Sarrica grunted. "I meant to protect him."

"Which he might have realized if you had not—"

"Enough! I know." Sarrica stood, abandoning his desk in favor of pacing around the office. "I swear I only meant to spare him having to choose between me and his homeland before I had even formally introduced him. I was going to speak with him once I had sorted out that damned mess."

"Well done."

Sarrica cast him a look but did not argue. Lesto was only speaking the truth. "I want him found, if only to be absolutely certain he did leave of his own volition. I obviously do not know him, but it strikes me as out of character for him to leave without a word to anyone."

Lesto sighed and dropped his arms. "I agree. I've already put my men to work in the palace and the city."

"The city?" Sarrica paused at a window and stared at the bustling city in the distance, just visible over the roofs of the palace. He could not remember the last time he'd left the palace grounds. "I doubt that will turn up anything. Why would he go into the city?"

"Better to look and find nothing than do nothing and miss something."

"Fair point."

"What will you do when we find him?"

Sarrica shook his head. He had no idea. Every time he opened his mouth around Prince Allen he just made matters worse. Prince Allen had chosen to run away rather than continue enduring him. After giving Sarrica that cold cut in the barracks. Even through his frustration Sarrica had been impressed. Prince Allen might have more steel beneath that pretty façade than he'd surmised.

"I suggest you start with begging—and begging expensively," Lesto said, voice dry as dust.

The words elicited a reluctant smile. "I do not think throwing clothes and jewels at him will help anything, though actual begging might."

"To be fair he clearly likes clothes and jewels, but I agree, those won't suffice," Lesto replied. He leaned against Sarrica's desk, hands lightly gripping the edge. "As I believe I told you once before, books would go much further. As would arranging a ball or banquet to welcome him. Give him an engagement ring, and I would commission it now and order it done as quickly as possible. Prove that you want him here, that you're sorry you made him think otherwise."

Sarrica nodded, pushed away from the window, and strode back to the desk. "Get your ass off my trade agreements. Send my secretaries back in." He looked up as Lesto turned around. "Thank you, Lesto. I do appreciate that you never kill me the way you probably should and have not given up on me as you definitely should."

"I would either be hanged or ordered to run the empire in your place, and neither sounds terribly appealing," Lesto replied before turning and striding from the office.

A minute or so later, Sarrica's five secretaries returned and resumed their work, their assistants filtering back in more slowly. Sarrica beckoned his head secretary to his desk. "Myra, have the Master Jeweler brought to me. The Master Librarian as well."

Myra bowed and bustled off, calling to his assistants and sending them scurrying off with summons.

Sarrica sank back into his work: reports from various fronts, letters official and not from across the empire, trade negotiations to look over, and Pantheon knew what else. So much work, and the pile never seemed to go down. Never mind he would spend all afternoon trapped in meetings and court sessions. And one of his damned crippling headaches was just waiting for an excuse to tip from irritating to excruciating.

He swallowed, hit abruptly with memories he'd prefer stayed buried in the recesses of his mind. The dull ache that never really went away sharpened. He missed being able to look up and share an understanding smile with Nyle, who used to sit directly across from him, their secretaries on either side. He missed having someone to sneak away with to steal kisses in an empty room.

Stifling a sigh, he picked up the letter he was supposed to be reading over and focused. Jotting down a few notes, he called over one of his secretaries and began to dictate a reply, pausing occasionally for a sip of coffee. "...therefore we strongly advise..." He stopped as the door opened and the clerk who controlled the antechamber stepped inside and bowed.

"Your Majesty, Master Jeweler Smythe, Master Librarian Telor, and Master Gorden Bells are here to see you. I was also just brought word that the Gaulden delegates are delayed, but if Your Majesty will indulge them, they can meet with you at half past four."

That was some nerve. He glanced at Myra and Emerella, the secretaries who maintained his meeting schedules. Myra said, "Your Majesty and Commander Lesto are meeting with the Treya Mencee ambassador at four, and you've executioner's court right after that."

Sarrica nodded and turned to his clerk. "They will meet me at the original time granted them, or they will wait until tomorrow."

"Yes, Your Majesty. Who shall I send in first?"

"Is Lesto still here?"

"No, Your Majesty."

"Send in the jeweler, and the librarian after him. I'll meet with them in my private office. Inform me at once when Lesto returns; we'll speak with Bells then."

"Yes, Your Majesty." The clerk bowed and slipped away.

A moment later Smythe entered, and Sarrica motioned him into his private office. "Thank you for coming to see me so quickly."

"It is always an honor to serve, Your Majesty," Smythe replied, clasping his hands and resting them on top of his enormous stomach. He smiled. "How may I be of service?"

"I require a betrothal ring for Prince Allen. Something simple, elegant, and pretty." He drummed his fingers on the desk.

Smythe nodded. "Any particular gems, Majesty?"

"Hmm..." Sarrica looked at the wedding ring he still wore—should probably remove if he was going to be marrying someone else. He was just so accustomed to the weight of it. Peridot and yellow diamonds gleamed; Nyle had chosen the colors to match their eyes and because both stones were lucky. "Sapphires, possibly blue diamonds as well, so there are multiple shades. Whatever you feel is best to achieve that. Set in white gold, I think. I'd like the gems arranged in a gradient, if that can be arranged."

Beaming, Smythe bowed. "That can certainly be done, Your Majesty. I will come up with some designs for you and present them the day after tomorrow, if that is acceptable to Your Majesty."

"That's fine. Thank you." Smythe bowed and left, and a couple of minutes later, Telor entered the room. "Good day, Master Telor. I do not suppose you've learned anything since our last conversation?"

"Not much, Majesty, but a little bit. I expect I will know more in a week or so. I did happen to learn why Prince Allen might have actually been in the library the other morning."

"Oh?" Sarrica settled back in his chair, bracing his arms on the rests. He'd nearly forgotten the library incident amidst all the other disasters he had caused regarding Allen.

"I was speaking with the Viscount Mellir about some old family books he is having stored in the special vaults, and he asked laughingly if there was room for them with all the books that Prince Allen must have brought along."

Sarrica frowned. "What does that mean?"

"Apparently it is well known in Gaulden that Prince Allen is quite the book collector and has a number of rare and valuable tomes. I think perhaps he visited the library to ask me about storing them, which of course I would be happy to do..."

But Sarrica had driven Allen off before he could ask and probably made him feel as though he *couldn't* ask. Damn it.

An idea flickered through his mind but Sarrica recoiled from it. Prince Allen had run off. There was no guarantee he would return and agree to the marriage. Why should Sarrica destroy one of the last traces of Nyle for Prince Allen?

He could practically hear Lesto yelling at him.

Shoving down the sick, roiling guilt, he said, "I have a better idea: I would like you to coordinate with the palace architects and see about converting the room in my chambers back into a private library. You will know how best to prepare it for storing a valuable collection."

Telor's widened for a moment before he caught himself and smoothed his expression out. He bowed low. "Yes, Majesty."

"The moment you know what books he'd like to have added to the collection, see they are obtained and spare no expense. Use my personal funds, coordinate with my secretary Myra."

Bowing once more, Telor departed. A few minutes later, Sarrica sighed and returned to the main office. He worked for nearly three more hours, slogging through paperwork and enduring tiresome meetings, before Lesto finally returned. The thundercloud on his face was not promising. Sarrica quirked a brow at him. Lesto gave a single, sharp shake of his head. "Later. Let's speak with Bells, first."

Sarrica nodded and crooked two fingers at his clerk, hovering patiently in the doorway awaiting his command. At Sarrica's signal, he vanished into the antechamber and a moment later Master Gorden Bells stepped into the room. He was a slight, short, modestly handsome man with dark skin and black hair, pale eyes currently filled with shadows. Sarrica rose and Lesto led the way into the private office. Sarrica resumed his seat behind the desk; Lesto leaned against the corner at the front of the desk, on Sarrica's right. "Thank you for coming to see me, Master Bells. I am sorry for your loss."

"Thank you, Your Majesty." Bells bowed his head, hands clasped tightly in his lap. "I am willing to do whatever it takes to bring my brother's killer to justice." He hesitated, looked up, then back down at his hands. "Though I heard they had already arrested someone."

"Nothing has been proven," Lesto replied. "Did you

know your brother was having an affair with General Faharm?"

Bells nodded. "Yes, Commander. I told him it was unwise, but... well, that has rarely ever stopped the infatuated from doing exactly as they please."

"Very true," Lesto said. "Can you tell us anything about the relationship?"

"I know his comrades weren't happy. That many soldiers around the palace weren't happy. They thought it gave my brother an unfair advantage, special treatment. I cannot say if they were right, but I know my brother did well as a soldier." He shrugged. "He mentioned that some people were threatening to report them, but he didn't think they'd go through with it because who is stupid enough to incur the wrath of Fathoms Deep?" He looked at Lesto, bowed his head low. "Um. Begging your pardon, Commander. No offense intended."

Lesto shook his head. "None taken."

Sarrica almost felt bad for Fathoms Deep. That tone of voice, calm and steady and reasonable, was a death sentence. If Lesto did actually kill them all, it would be a mercy. Unfortunately for them, Lesto did not kill anyone unless he had no choice.

Not that Sarrica would stop Lesto if he did go for the kill. Fathoms Deep was essentially Sarrica's private army. Their gross misconduct reflected on him as much as on Lesto. He might just kill them himself.

Lesto asked, "Did your brother ever mention General Vren to you?"

"Only that she was especially disapproving of the relationship. He always said that if anyone was going to reveal the relationship to you, it would be her."

"Any problem between your brother and General

Faharm?"

"Just the stress of secrets and unhappy friends."

Lesto nodded. "Thank you, Master Bells. You've been most helpful. We will keep you apprised as much as possible. If you think of anything that might be useful, no matter how slight, let us know at once."

"Yes, Your Majesty, High Commander. Thank you."

When he had gone, Sarrica went to the door and ordered food and wine brought. Closing the door again, he sat down in Bell's vacated chair, resting his elbows on the armrests and letting his twined fingers dangle. "What's wrong, Lesto?"

"I'm not even sure where to begin," Lesto said with a sigh, rubbing a knuckle up and down the bridge of his nose. "Apparently all of Fathoms Deep is in sore need of a thrashing. Even in the wake of this whole mess nobody came forward to tell me any of what Bells just told us." He dropped his hand, balled it into a fist, and thumped his thigh. "I am going to put the entire damned unit on notice. They'll be suspended until I feel like acknowledging their existence again. I'll put enlisted to work in the dockyards, and the officers will be confined to quarters. They'll continue to guard you, but they're not going to enjoy that either. Unless you want me to do otherwise."

Sarrica smiled, sharp and hard. "I would just give the impression that I wanted heads removed, and you talked me out of it. That should keep everyone on their best behavior for at least a week, two if you keep up the scowling."

Lesto blew out a breath, glaring at the wall. "They'd better behave a good deal longer than that. But speaking of scowling, that brings me to our next problem."

Sarrica untangled his fingers to press the tips to his temples. "I really don't want to hear this, do I?"

"Not even a little."

"Wait for the wine, at least."

Unfortunately, the wine arrived only a moment later. Once it was poured and the servant gone, Sarrica drained half his glass, refilled it, and spun his hand for Lesto to carry on. "Get it over with."

"One of the men I sent into the city to search for Prince Allen thought to try the bookshops."

Sarrica frowned. "There must be countless."

"Yes, but he started with Market Street. He tried nine shops before coming up lucky in the tenth. The bookshop owner, a man from Mesta, was very happy to brag about the prince in his shop who spoke his language perfectly."

Sarrica hid an unexpected, fleeting smile in a swallow of wine. "Did he happen to know where Prince Allen went?"

"No, but he did provide a list of all the books His Highness bought and told us he left instructions that they were to be taken to the palace."

"He planned to return," Sarrica said, frowning. "So why didn't he? What happened to him? Do we know?"

"The bookshop clerk said he doesn't know where he went, past that there was a ruckus further up the street that had people fleeing, but His Highness went toward it. After that, the shopkeeper did not see him again."

Sarrica pinched the bridge of his nose. "That fool. What did he think he was doing? What fight did he get in the middle of?" Allen in a fight. Sarrica could not even imagine it. The man had steel in his spine, but he was no fighter. "What does any of this have to do with his disappearance and missing belongings?"

"The footman who delivered the books said the rooms were clearly occupied. That was in the evening, since the shopkeeper waited until the chaos had died down and stayed down to send someone to make the delivery."

"So sometime early yesterday, or late the previous night, Prince Allen had his belongings removed. After becoming embroiled in an altercation in the city? Why in the name of all that is holy am I only hearing about this now?"

Lesto kicked his ankle. "I know you're capable of patience. Let me tell the story."

"Tell it faster."

"You'll regret those words because it doesn't get better."

"Then hurry up and get it over with."

"My men went in search of the altercation, which wasn't hard to track as everyone in the pubs was still gleefully discussing it. I'm sure in another day or two it would have reached us."

Sarrica closed his eyes.

"The short version is thus: a glass merchant was whipping one of his shop apprentices in a public square. Prince Allen ordered him to stop, and when the man tried to whip Prince Allen, he grabbed hold of the whip and would not let go. Stories vary, but that's the popular one. Anyway, the man was about to assault His Highness when a soldier put a stop to the matter and informed the merchant of Prince Allen's identity. Prince Allen had the man arrested and rumors are going around that anyone caught whipping people will be disciplined by him personally."

Sarrica choked on a swallow of wine and hastily set

the cup aside as he coughed. "What?" he asked hoarsely. "Do I need to attempt to ban him from the city?" Not that he disagreed with the pronouncement—except for the personally part. Whipping was atrocious, and he'd started working to abolish the practice the moment he'd come of age. Many still resisted, and the practice had yet to be completely banned, but it was slowly falling by the wayside. If Allen had helped the matter further... "What does he mean personally?"

"I doubt he said it at all," Lesto said. "Though I do wonder what he actually said. I would love to hear the real version of the entire tale. Anyway, you haven't asked about the soldier who assisted him."

"I'm not sure I want to know."

"Rene."

"Of course," Sarrica said and retrieved his wine. "I still do not see what all of this has to do with Prince Allen going missing. Would you please come to the point?"

Lesto grinned, all teeth. "If I had to hear the whole of the tale one agonizing sentence at a time, so do you."

"Get on with it."

"Rene assisted him with the glass merchant, and there are witnesses who saw them walk off together, but no one knows where they went. I've sent men to search Rene's house since that seems the likeliest place for them to have gone."

Sarrica frowned. "They should have come straight back here."

"No, it was better for them to wait and return after everything quieted down."

"I'm going to kill him. Both of them. Everyone."

Sarrica set his wine back on the desk and scrubbed his face with one hand. "So do you think Allen is still at Rene's house? But why have his things taken there?"

Lesto let out a laugh that sounded cracked and broken. "You have not deduced it? I'm awaiting confirmation, but my guess is that while Allen's belongings are at Rene's house, Allen is not. Let me put it this way: two days ago your fiancé left the palace; yesterday Rene informed me he had found a silver tongue fluent in Bentan; they left this morning at dawn; Prince Allen is nowhere to be found."

Sarrica's mind went blank, a forever-stretching field of white nothing.

Then anger crashed through it, bright red and sharp-edged. "Prince Allen wouldn't. *Rene* wouldn't— he's not that stupid."

Lesto lifted one shoulder. "Perhaps a clever tongue persuaded him."

Something ugly and thorny coiled through Sarrica, something he preferred not to name because he shouldn't have been feeling it at all. "Shut up."

"I didn't mean it that way, Sarrica."

Sarrica gave him a look, and Lesto lifted his hands in concession and apology. Sarrica sighed. "It doesn't matter. Even if it were true, it's not my business. Damn it, he *can't* be with the Dragons. He's not trained to— he's not a bloody soldier."

"Silver tongues don't have to be trained, and mercs are retained because they regard rules as negotiable at best," Lesto said, folding his arms across his chest. "I've known plenty of mercs who simply kidnapped silver tongues when they could not hire one properly. Silver tongues are worth their weight in whatever they demand."

"Yes, but the silver tongue in question is not usually the High Consort Presumptive! They're not usually royalty at all unless they're accompanying a general or *you*. They do not fall in with mercs for a crucial covert mission where they could be taken hostage if not killed outright! We have to stop them."

Lesto shook his head.

"Do not tell me we can't." Sarrica surged to his feet.

Lesto stood with him, fisted a hand in Sarrica's jacket when he tried to head for the door. "We can't. I'm sorry, but we can't. They left an hour before dawn. They've been traveling twelve hours; they're well in the Cartha Mountains by now, and by the time we could reach them they'd be too far into the mountains to get him back without destroying the whole mission."

Sarrica jerked free, thumped a fist on the desk. "Why would Rene be so stupid?"

"I don't know," Lesto replied quietly, looking away, frowning at the floor for a long stretch of silence. Finally looking up again, he said, "Probably a few reasons. He's been depressed lately, but will not tell me why. I think he has, or had, a lover he's been keeping quiet..." He stopped, eyes narrowing as he starred at Sarrica, mouth tightening. "You stupid *bastard*."

Damn it. He'd always been shit at keeping anything from Lesto for very long. "That's not how you talk to your king."

"It's how I talk to my useless brother-in-law!"

Sarrica snatched up his wine, and fled to the other side of the desk. "I found out by accident, and he asked me to keep it secret. He ended it a little while ago, though he didn't want to."

"That fool," Lesto whispered, burying his hands in his hair, dragging them roughly through it. "He's not Nyle. He would settle down *fine*."

"Are you a mind reader?" Sarrica asked with a huff.

Lesto shrugged one shoulder. "Only observant, and none of you halfwits is difficult to read." He took the seat Sarrica had vacated. "The rest of you are so bloody stubborn and set on wallowing, someone has to pay attention and fix everything."

"I'm sorry."

Smiling faintly, Lesto said, "Save those words for your fiancé. He needs to hear them more than me, and I know how hard it is for you to say them."

Sarrica grimaced and drained his wine. "We need to stop them. I can't just let Prince Allen go into a situation where he will come to serious harm, and very likely die."

"We cannot risk the mission, and if we dare interrupt it we will only endanger everyone further. Best to let Rene take care of the matter. He's reckless enough to take Allen along but not stupid enough to let him get hurt."

"That is not something he can control."

Lesto shrugged again. "He will do the best he can, and it doesn't really matter. The situation is out of our control, and gods know we have enough problems of our own to deal with. If we do not figure out soon who murdered Lieutenant Bells we may have a riot on our hands. Never mind deciding what is to be done with General Vren. Damn it, I do not need Fathoms Deep and a swath of the imperial army in disarray right now."

"You need to rest, Lesto. You look like you haven't

slept in three days."

Impatiently waving the words aside, Lesto asked, "When do we meet with the Gaulden set? I'm sure they're frothing to have been kept waiting this long."

Sarrica heaved a sigh, finished his wine, and climbed to his feet. "Any moment now, I think, if we are not already late. After that, I am canceling the rest of my day, and we are retiring to my quarters. No arguing, I mean it."

"Yes, Majesty," Lesto said and strode ahead of him out of the room.

They walked in silence until they left the crowded hallways behind. Sarrica glanced at Lesto, grimaced at the expression on his face. "Don't ask. I don't have an answer for you."

"So what, when Gaulden asks where Prince Allen is you're just going to pretend not to hear them? You'd better come up with something better than that."

"Maybe we'll get lucky and they won't ask," Sarrica muttered, but even he wasn't actually foolish enough to think the Gaulden delegates would not ask about their prince—especially after witnessing Sarrica's dismissals and Allen's cutting reply.

If Sarrica didn't come up with a way to hide that Allen had run off to join the Three-headed Dragons in an extremely dangerous covert mission... "Are you certain we can't go get him and drag him back?"

"With greatest respect, Majesty," Lesto replied quietly, "what's more important: one potential consort, or the man we need alive to prevent a war we stand a good chance of losing?"

Sarrica didn't reply.

"His Highness probably knows better than us the ramifications of his actions," Lesto said. "We are going to have to trust him and Rene to handle themselves."

"I am beginning to appreciate why politicians spend all their time playing courtly games. At least it confines the trouble," Sarrica said. "Honestly, what sort of half-witted silver tongue goes stomping off on a covert mission that would make a hardened soldier hesitate?"

Lesto smiled faintly. "The same kind of silver tongue who faces down a man with a whip and wins, I'd imagine. The same kind of silver tongue who cuts the High King down without saying a single word." His smile widened into a smirking grin. "I hope he's stupid enough to marry you after all of this because suddenly I'm having a marvelous time."

"Stop talking or I'll have you put yourself in the stocks," Sarrica replied, giving him a light shove.

Lesto snorted and did not deign to reply further.

Their momentary levity faded off as they reached the large, dark red-brown double doors that led to Sarrica's preferred meeting hall. "I have no idea which is worse: saying that Prince Allen has gone missing and I have no idea where he is, or that I know precisely where he is."

"Tell the truth: he has gone to handle a delicate negotiation as he is the only silver tongue talented enough and trusted enough to do so."

Sarrica shot him a look. "I think we need to discuss what the word *truth* means."

"The lies they don't figure out." Lesto gestured to the guards when they reached the doors and strode through as they were pushed open.

Sarrica could practically feel the hostility wash over him as he stepped into the room. "Good people," he greeted and walked around the table to take his seat at the head of it, Lesto to his immediate left, the seat to his right vacant. How very useful it would have been to have Allen right then, but even Sarrica knew he had only himself to blame for Allen's absence.

Had it been so difficult between him and Nyle? Worse, probably, since younger nearly always meant stupider. He and Nyle had gotten into some truly impressive arguments; Sarrica had wound up wearing his dinner more than once.

"Thank you for seeing us, Your Majesty," one of the Gaulden delegates said stiffly. Lady Naurren, the ambassador of Gaulden and some distant cousin to the throne, the sort of tenuous connection that existed only if no one looked too closely at the official documents. Beside her was Lord Riddell and across from them were Lady Meyer and Lady Harmonia.

"You deserve to hear all we know and ask your questions," Sarrica replied. "I am sorry the time could not be moved. Unfortunately, my good folk, I have precious little to tell you. We are still investigating the matter."

Lady Naurren puffed up like an angry cat. "What is to investigate? It was perfectly clear to even a half-blind fool that General Vren is the murderer. We should not be discussing an investigation, Your Majesty, but an execution."

"Lady Naurren, you might want to tread more carefully in telling me what I should or should not be doing because you seem to be forgetting that those two men are dead because they were having an affair. Unless you want to try and justify to me why a Gaulden general thought it acceptable to fuck a lieutenant, be quiet."

She opened her mouth then snapped it shut again,

though Sarrica suspected her silence had more to do with the warning look Lady Harmonia cast her than anything else.

"As to your certainty that General Vren is to blame, that remains to be seen. Nobody saw the murder happen, only the aftermath, and any clues we might have gained from examining the location of the murder were thoroughly ruined by the fight. Both generals should have known better, even in their grief and rage, than to engage in a fight. Vren claims killing Faharm was an accident, and I am inclined to believe her until I am presented with evidence to the contra—"

"She's from *Mesta*," Lord Riddell hissed.

"So are a good many other people," Lesto said, regarding him coolly. "Just because you hate them does not mean they merit that hate. If you cannot be professional, my lord, why are you here? Queen Marren is no fool, and she would not send fools to represent her. If you are going to throw tantrums and make baseless accusations that could result in an innocent person's death, this meeting is over."

"We apologize, High King, High Commander," Lady Harmonia said quietly. "I hope you will understand that we are highly distressed and grief-stricken by this tragedy. Whatever General Faharm's poor choices and behavior, it did not warrant his death or that of his lover. They should have been punished fairly, not coldly murdered. This is not the first time in even recent history that Mestan soldiers have acted unjustly regarding our own." She cast him a reproving look. "In addition to that is the matter of Prince Allen. We did not know he had been chosen as your High Consort until his arrival in court, and we cannot even really speak with him."

Sarrica's mouth tightened. He leaned back in his seat, rested one hand on the table. "I wasn't aware it was your place to know such things before I chose to make you aware of them." They bowed their heads to acknowledge his point, murmuring apologies. "You will be able to speak with Prince Allen upon his return; currently he is doing me a favor."

"A favor? After—" Lady Harmonia stopped. "Beg pardon, Your Majesty, but I am somewhat surprised Prince Allen is doing you a favor."

"I suppose that's fair enough. There have been some… miscommunications. Prince Allen is an accomplished silver tongue, however, and I had a matter that required skill and trust. Who better than my High Consort Presumptive? Have you any further matters to address?"

They shook their heads. "No, Your Majesty."

"We will keep you apprised of the investigation as it develops," Sarrica said. "If you come by any information that may prove of use to us, please let us know at once. When is the mourning ceremony for General Faharm being held?"

"Tomorrow morning at dawn, Your Majesty."

Sarrica nodded. "I have a task for you, if you care to take it on after the mourning period has passed."

They frowned in puzzlement but bowed their heads. Lady Harmonia said, "We are happy to serve, Your Majesty."

"Prince Allen has not had the best of arrivals, and I concede much of that is my fault. Now he is away doing a favor for me, and I've no idea when the matter will be settled. When he returns, though, he merits a proper reception, and as you know him best, I thought you might like to arrange it. My funds will pay for it."

"Of course, Your Majesty," Lord Riddell replied, face brightening. "We'd be most honored."

Sarrica nodded and rose. The others rose with him and bowed. "Include Lord Tara in the matter as a favor to me. He and Prince Allen already seem to have become fast friends. I'm sure he would like to help." They looked slightly less enthusiastic at that but nodded. "Good. Thank you. My condolences once more on your loss, and my most abject apologies this tragedy occurred. I will find answers. Good day to you all."

"Majesty," they murmured.

Sarrica strode out, Lesto at his side. He blew out a long sigh. "That might have gone better."

Lesto cast him a look. "It could have gone much, much worse. I will be amused to see what His Highness thinks of your little lies regarding his absence."

"As long as he returns, I do not care much what he has to say," Sarrica replied. "Come, we are going to my chambers, and you are getting some damned rest whether you want it or not. I cannot flush a murderer from his hole by myself, and I refuse to visit the healing ward to keep you updated."

"And everyone claims I am the incessant nag," Lesto muttered. "I'm fine."

"You're as fine as I am even-tempered," Sarrica retorted. "One more word of complaint out of you and I'll see to it a three course meal is shoved down your gullet first."

Lesto fell silent and remained so as they walked through the palace, but Sarrica did not mistake it for a victory.

CHAPTER SEVEN

Allen ran a hand over his hair, cut for the sake of convenience and added precaution, since extremely long hair was almost always an affectation of the nobility. Only soft fuzz remained, strange to the touch, and he felt a bit confused every time he reached the back and his hand fell away. Nor had he realized just how warm all his hair had kept him. The mountain air was cold, and he had a sinking feeling there would be snow eventually. Harken wasn't even that far away. How could the weather change so drastically?

Laughter drew his attention, and he glanced across the camp to where several Dragons were huddled around a campfire, talking about their families, friends, previous missions. Allen had tried, the first couple of days, to talk to them, but what did he know about talking to soldiers? He was usually happiest when they were far away from him. It felt strange, even wrong, to be not just in their midst but essentially at their mercy. The feeling was mutual to judge by the way they seemed nervous around him. All his training in talking to people seemed to be of no use in a mercenary camp. Everyone seemed happier if he just stayed out of their way.

He looked away, ran a hand over his poor hair again, wishing he had thought to bring a book or something. Surely there was a book he could have studied to help make him better at being silver tongue to a group of mercs.

"It stops feeling odd eventually," said a gruff but friendly voice. A woman who'd introduced herself as Jac, who looked Mestan but sounded Outlander, sat down and handed over a beat up metal bowl filled with gruel drizzled with honey.

Jac smiled, scrubbing a hand over her own hair, which was only slightly longer than Allen's. "My hair was halfway down my back when I first joined up. I was immensely proud, thought it made me look like as fine as any court lady. Whined about cutting it, and Captain said I could keep it if I really wanted. Then this ugly bastard with a fondness for knives got a hold of me—" She mimed a fist grabbing her hair from behind. "Took me three months to heal up, and I haven't had it long since. Only thing I miss is being warm, which reminds me: I rustled up some stuff for you, High—err, Allen." Jac shook her head. "Speaking of things that feel strange. Anyway, Captain said you didn't have time to better prepare. Traded for it, told the others you'd write letters and such when there was time."

"I'm certainly more than happy to do that," Allen said, barely moving his bowl out of the way in time to avoid the items Jac dropped into his lap landing in the gruel instead. Setting the unappealing food aside, he examined his new belongings.

One was a rough cap, the close fitted kind he normally saw sailors wear. The other was a scarf of the same dark green and brown wool. They matched the clothes Rene had given him: dark brown trousers and long-sleeved shirt, itchy against his skin but warm, and a black tunic embroidered with a three-headed dragon. The only difference between his tunic and those of the others were the bands of white along the edges and the white star on his back marking him a civilian. The heavy cloak he carried, but was not yet wearing, was similarly marked. It was required by the world treaties regarding war that all civilians be clearly marked and were not to be harmed. Those very same treaties also tightly controlled what armies were allowed to do and how they should act. Harken and many other nations skirted many of the regulations by employing mercenary bands or similar such. The only rule most of them obeyed was that regarding civilians.

"Thank you," Allen said and pulled the cap over his head. Oh, that felt better already. He draped the scarf over his shoulder but did not yet wind it, instead picking up his gruel. He did not often think of himself as a spoiled brat, but right then he was painfully aware he was because he could think of a thousand things he would rather be eating. Anything that was not the bland-looking substance before him, though the honey lent a sweet smell.

He watched Jac, who drank her gruel with seeming relish, alternating it with bites of the dark brown bread she'd set between them on the log. "Be grateful someone rustled up some honey to add to it," she said when she saw Allen watching her. "It's the best we'll get for a long time since once we cross the river it's full dark."

"Full dark?"

"No fires, no light, no talking, no noise that isn't strictly necessary," Jac said. "Food is whatever you can carry and can eat quietly."

That sounded lovely. Allen looked again at his gruel. Well, it couldn't be worse than the bland broths the palace healers had made him drink whenever he fell ill. Or the last time his brothers had whipped him, and the wounds had been too severe to hide. The time he'd not been able to attend his own celebration, and Larren had put a swift, brutal end to the whippings. Nothing but tepid broth for days. He'd *hated* it.

Allen picked up his bowl and drank the gruel tentatively at first. Not as bad as he'd feared, and the honey did help. Drinking the rest more quickly, he soaked up what remained with bits of bread. By the time he'd finished, another soldier was coming with steaming metal cups that proved to contain strong, dark coffee.

"Thank you," Allen said, winding his scarf around his neck before accepting it.

The man hesitated, and Allen didn't miss the glower Jac gave him, the sharp jerk of her head that she quickly tried to hide by ducking it when she saw Allen looking. Had they been ordered to talk to him more or something? Huffing softly, the man asked, "So how *did* Captain manage to convince you to come along? Name's Regena. Don't think we've ever had your sort with us before, not unless carting you around was the mission, anyway."

Allen smiled tentatively. "I want to help and learn more about the military and mercenaries. It's hard to do that stuck in meeting halls and ballrooms."

"I'll take the ballrooms," Jac muttered before shoving a last bit of bread in her mouth.

"So you're from Gaulden, right? You must hate this weather," Regena said.

"Yes and yes. You sound like you hale from Delfaste, but close to the border with Tricemore."

"You're good," Regena said with quick grin. "Captain said you were, and he's not prone to exaggerating or lying about such things. That was impressive, what you did with that Farlander sailor."

Allen shrugged. "I'm glad I could help. I was sorry he died, and so far from home."

"Well, for what it's worth, we found friends of his in the palace. He's homebound by now, along with compensation to his family." He drained his coffee.

"That makes good hearing. Thank you for telling me," Allen replied. It *did* help, eased some of the sharpness from the still-painful memory. The man had died miserably, but at least he would rest in peace where he belonged.

Regena sat down on his other side, nudged Allen's shoulder with his own. "How did you learn Bentan, of all languages? That's a hard one."

"Not as hard as others I've learned," Allen replied. "I learned it through practice, practice, practice. When I could fool a dockworker into thinking I was native Bentan, my tutor considered me adequate. When I fooled a noblewoman who had fled her homeland, he considered me skilled."

Regena nodded. "Still think the Captain was a bit mad to bring you."

"He had little choice. I hope I do not hinder the mission. This is all very new to me."

"Stay back when we tell you and it should be well," Jac said. "Mission like this, there won't be much in the way of out and out battle."

Allen took another swallow of coffee, which didn't taste all that bad and definitely was helping to keep him warm. "How does it get so cold so quickly? What *does* a mission like this entail? Captain Rene was not able to tell me much before we were on our way, and he is a touch too busy to tell me more now."

"First stage is get through Cartha without getting killed. Technically we have a treaty that says we get safe passage through the mountains, but Cartha has practically never kept it. We suspect they've aligned with Benta, which means they're all the more likely to kill us. Avoiding them is mostly a matter of stealth and getting to the scouts before the scouts report us," Regena said. "Once we reach the border, we sneak past the walls, hopefully without too much trouble. From there we pretend to be merchants and work our way to the crown city by whatever means necessary."

"Bentamasura," Allen murmured. "I was tutored by nobles who fled Bentamasura during the Gilded Slaughter."

Jac and Regena both grimaced, and Jac said, "We weren't there, obviously, but the Three-headed Dragons of the time were. Only a handful made it out. They were barely able to get the Dragons back to full strength. Nobody is looking forward to going back, but we're good at what we do, and we were available to do it."

"We know Cartha better than anyone since a lot of our dirty work is here." Regena wolfed down the last of his own bread. "Anyway, I'm always happy to get one over on Benta and knock over any of them that get in our way. They've killed us plenty of times, for no reason other than that they could. And like I said, they almost destroyed the Dragons in the Gilded Slaughter. We owe them one." He switched briefly to Tricemorien. *"The body forgets, but the blood remembers."*

Allen nodded. *"The blood will be settled."*

Regena beamed, clapped him on the shoulder. "Welcome to the Three-headed Dragons, Silver Tongue. Though maybe Golden Tongue would be more fitting given you're so pretty and if you get hurt the price will be our heads." He winked and strode off, calling out to some soldiers on the far side of camp.

"I'm not a *golden* tongue. That doesn't even make sense," Allen muttered. Golden tongue sounded too much like songbird, and he was there to prove he wasn't one.

Jac coughed, grinned. "To be fair, you are meant to look pretty and sit on a throne."

"Will ordering you to be quiet get me anywhere?"

Laughing, Jac clapped him on the back, nearly sending him toppling from the log. "No. I only take orders from the Captain. Speaking of, I've gotten you a hat and scarf, but you're still lacking gloves so I had best go in search of those."

Allen hesitated, because he didn't want to get in the way or make anyone uncomfortable, but he was really tired of sitting alone and feeling out of place. "Can I come? If I am to wear the articles, it seems only fair that I do the asking. Or should I remain here out of the way?"

Jac stood and offered a hand. "You can come. They've been trying to leave you in peace for a bit to let you acclimate. Some of the group were placing bets as to whether or not you'd fuss about the food."

"Almost," Allen admitted.

"No more than the rest of us," Jac said with a smile. "Come on. I'll introduce you 'round." They headed toward the campfire in the middle of the small camp, where a cluster of five sat around it talking and laughing, cleaning weapons and armor.

One of them looked up at their approach, pulling a thin, faintly sweet-smelling cigarette from her mouth. "Ho, Silver Tongue and Brat."

"Who are you calling a brat, Street?"

She grinned, flipping the dagger in her hand and sliding it back into her belt as she stood. Holding out a hand, she said, "Don't listen to Jac, Silver Tongue. Name's Hedge." She pointed at the rest of the group, which consisted of two more women and two men. "Saral, Tynce, Wystie, and Broad. We're some of the Dragons' best swordsmen, and we all used to work with merchants, so we'll look and talk the part. Jac there is one of our sharpshooters. Regena is a sneaky little bastard, him and Trulia, that woman over there." She pointed across the camp to a tall, stocky woman with short, bright red hair. "You'll get to know the others as we go. There's fifteen of us in all, including you and the Captain. Small for us, but anything more would look strange for a private merchant company with just two wagons."

"Where are we getting the wagons?" Allen asked.

They all laughed and grinned. Hedge pointed a thumb over her shoulder to where Regena was talking to the soldiers he'd called out to earlier. "Regena, Trulia, and those two, Mixx and Handel, will handle it. That's what the sneaky ones are good for." She waggled her brows. "They get what we need; nobody asks questions."

"I see," Allen said, smiling ever so faintly. They seemed much more open than they had a couple of days ago; maybe it just took time. Or maybe they were only following orders. He'd prefer they talked to him because they wanted to, but he hadn't exactly tried hard himself. At least they *were* talking, anything was better than sitting alone. "Speaking of things needed, I am apparently in need of gloves to combat this wretched cold."

Hedge clucked, smirked. "Yeah, I bet your fancy

threads would look a might odd around here, Silver Tongue. I've got a spare set that should fit your pretty little hands. Heard you trade for letter writing and reading."

"Yes, gladly," Allen replied, but with a frown. "Though I'm surprised you're allowed to have letters and such, since the mission is so secret."

It was Jac who replied with a shrug. "It's not really secret now. It's just a matter of not getting caught. Cartha doesn't care who comes through their stupid mountains, just that they dare to at all. Once we reach Benta, we'll have to ditch everything, right down to our underclothes and swords, exchange it all for Bentan items. So bringing a few letters and books along doesn't hurt anything." She smiled sadly, gave another shrug, and Allen was reminded again of the sailor who'd died in his arms.

Hedge turned and knelt by the stump she'd been sitting on, rifled through a pack, and came up with a pair of gloves made of dark blue and gray wool. They were softer than everything else Allen wore, the kind that were fingerless but had a flap that could be pulled over his fingers if desired. Once he'd taken them, she held out a small book. "Would you be willing to read this to me? My husband sent it, but bless his heart, I'm not as good at reading as he thinks, though he's an excellent teacher."

Allen smiled and took it, flipped through the flimsy pages. It was a cheaper version of a book he possessed, the sort printed on scrap, bound in cardboard and waste fabric, and sold for bits by street vendors and bookshops in poorer districts. His volume had been written in Harken; this version was written in Rilien. "Poetry, and excellent poetry at that." He flipped through the book a few pages more and found one that had been marked with a personal note: *This one reminds me of us. All my love, Ereth.* Clearing his throat, Allen switched to Rilien and quietly recited the poem for her.

Hedge blinked rapidly when he'd finished, took the book, and clutched it close when he held it out. "That jerk. He knows not to make me cry when I'm out here. Thank you, High—Silver Tongue."

"Always an honor," Allen said softly.

"Me next!" said the man beside her, Wystie if Allen recalled correctly. "I've got a letter I wasn't able to find someone to read before we were sent out again. Do you know Gearthish, Silver Tongue?"

Allen nodded and accepted the letter as it was held out.

"Take my seat, Silver Tongue," Hedge offered. "I'm supposed to be joining the scouting party soon, anyway." She clapped him on the shoulder, bid the others farewell, and strode off.

Opening the letter, Allen skimmed through it—and the group burst into laughter as his jaw dropped. "Your wife and husband are quite, um, ardent. They miss you."

"I think they miss his cock," Jac said with a snigger. "Nobody misses his talking."

"They might miss his tongue all the same," Saral said, elbowing Wystie in the side, laughing when that got her shoved off the rock she'd been sitting on. "Tongue like that, should have known you'd need one of those Gearthish country marriages to keep you satisfied."

"Shove off," Wystie said cheerfully. "You don't have to read those bits, Silver Tongue."

Loud protests nearly drowned his words out, and Allen did not even attempt to speak until they'd quieted down. "I don't mind reading them. I was just not expecting it, though I suspect that was the goal."

Wystie grinned. "We're not a very civilized lot."

"Civilized can mean a lot of things," Allen replied. He cleared his throat and began to read the letter, including the lewd promises of what they planned to do to Wystie when he returned.

When he was done with that letter, another was handed to him, along with a cup of coffee laced liberally with what tasted like cheap cherry brandy. "Alcohol, now finally someone is trading something I care about." That got him a round of laughter, and he began reading, translating the Delfastien to Harken so everyone could understand it as he had with Wystie's letter.

He'd read two more when they were interrupted by Rene, whose stride sounded strange without the spurs he usually wore. "Pack up, get ready to move out. Scouts spotted Carthians lurking about. They haven't made a move yet so I'm hoping we've gone unnoticed. But better not to linger and find out. We're going to get over the river tonight, and hopefully to Shalmoor Pass within a few days."

"Yes, Captain," the group said, jocular, easy demeanors dropping away to be replaced by hard-eyed soldiers.

Allen rose slowly, watching them go before he turned to Rene. "Is there anything I can do, or should I just stay out of the way?"

"You can shadow Jac if you really want to learn the thrill of packing a saddlebag," Rene said with a grin. "Otherwise, stay here until we're ready to go." His grin faded to a softer smile. "You seemed to be getting along with my Dragons."

Allen shrugged. "I do not know I would presume that, but I am glad I could read letters and such for them. It's always refreshing to put my skills to a happy use."

"Quite." Rene clapped him on the shoulder, which was going to be thoroughly bruised by the end of the day if they all kept doing that, forgetting he didn't have their layers of armor and under armor to cushion the force of it.

Allen watched him go a moment then went to find Jac. Packing a saddlebag was exactly as exciting as Rene had implied, but there was some satisfaction in seeing his own meager belongings packed in amongst all the rest.

He would still rather be in a library or at a dining table smoothly talking his way through delicate negotiations, but at least out here he was proving he was not simply a songbird.

What did Sarrica think of his absence? Did he believe that Allen had slunk off home, as they'd tried to arrange? Or had he figured it out? Sarrica did not seem the sort to leave a matter alone until he was absolutely satisfied, and if they had investigated in the city at all, they'd probably heard of his altercation with the merchant.

He'd done such a good job of not thinking about Harken and Sarrica, but once the thoughts broke through it was hard to put them away again. Did Sarrica care? Would he use Allen's reckless behavior as grounds to get rid of him once and for all? Or would he be impressed and finally see Allen as more than a songbird? No matter what he did, no matter how

Sarrica saw him now or later, he would always be less than High Consort Nyle. Not that Allen wanted to be seen as better; he had no desire to overshadow Nyle.

But he wouldn't mind being seen for himself. Would like to be trusted and valued enough Sarrica counted him a friend, treated him with the same respect he showed Lesto and Rene.

Shaking away his scattered, meandering thoughts because they were making less and less sense even to him, he finished preparing his horse and mounted up, riding across camp to where Rene was talking with two of his people: a tall, slender, handsome woman and a pretty person too androgynous to mark one way or another. By the designating beads on their throat, a practice in Outland, that was the way they preferred it.

"Ready?" Rene asked, and when Allen nodded, lifted a hand and closed it in a fist. Around them the noise and bustle stilled, and the group headed out in silence, walking in a long line in pairs that were well-spaced out for a reason that eluded Allen. Something to do with fighting, likely.

After about an hour, they broke out of the trees, walking along a ledge with a steep drop to Allen's right. He closed his eyes then immediately opened them again because having them closed made it worse.

Jac shot him a look. "Scared of heights?"

"Apparently, when it comes to long drops off the sides of mountains," Allen replied.

Jac laughed. "We won't fall. Probably."

"You are not a nice person."

"Nope." Jac grinned as she lifted a hand and pointed.

Allen reluctantly followed it, and his brows rose

when he saw what Jac had indicated. An old, broken and crumbling fortress. "What is that? Some old Carthian stronghold?"

"One of ours, actually, there are dozens of them scattered through the mountains. It's too bad we're going in the wrong direction, you'd be able to see Fortress Amorlay. It's a couple days' ride northeast from here, but hasn't been abandoned that long so it's still in good shape."

"I see," Allen said quietly. Fortress Amorlay had been built back when the Cartha Mountains had belonged to Harken. But the many clans of Cartha had never tolerated being part of the Empire and caused so much trouble and proved to be so expensive that Sarrica's great-grandfather had granted them independence. Part of the treaty said that a portion of the mountains remained as part of Harken, watched over by the Duke of Amorlay.

The title no longer existed, though it was preserved in the surname of the Dukes of Emberton-Heights, because the Carthians had made sport of attacking the fortress, sneaking into it and slaughtering everyone inside. Between that and the sabotage constantly inflicted on supply wagons, the territory had been declared too dangerous and expensive to maintain and was abandoned in the days of Sarrica's grandfather.

It was a handsome fortress, partially carved from the mountain, the rest built up by cut stones weathered dark gray. "It's a shame we were unable to maintain Amorlay, it would probably be infinitely useful right about now."

Jac's smile returned. "First rule of this job is that nothing is ever easy, and if it seems like it's easy then you should be extra-wary. Anyway, I'm sure the council would tell you that it's not worth the cost to maintain a fortress just to make the lives of soldiers and mercenaries safer."

"They will not say such a thing to my face more than once, I assure you," Allen said. "What is this Shalmoor Pass we are bound for?"

"Most of the border between Cartha and Benta is heavily guarded, and the walls are practically insurmountable. They're roughly six men high, and rumor has it certain stretches have some nasty traps. Never run across them myself, but then again, we aren't stupid enough to try scaling the wall. We can't go by way of the official gates, obviously, so the only other way into Benta is by way of Shalmoor Pass, a narrow little strip in the mountains where it's plain impossible to maintain the wall. Too much snow and ice; the rock there is fragile and prone to breaking and sliding, and the whole place smells like somebody shoved a bundle of matches up a horse's ass." She grinned when Allen laughed. "Lots of hot springs, and the contrast of hot and cold, it's always steamy or misty or whatever. Dangerous, to put it mildly, to the point even Benta and Cartha don't bother guarding it much. They know it's a weakness, and still they let it protect itself."

"That sounds like it's going to be... interesting," Allen said. "It also sounds a bit overconfident on the part of Cartha and Benta, but I suppose they would know better than me."

Jac shrugged. "It's not like they have to worry about anyone but us, and we first have to get through Cartha to reach Benta. So they're not entirely mistaken in resting easy. But we're willing to take advantage of the weakness when necessary, though we try not to do it so much that they finally bother to guard it properly."

"Why not bring in engineers to topple the rock sufficiently to block the pass? I know that's been done other places." Allen frowned thoughtfully. "The Battle of Harken Castle, in fact."

All that got him was a blank stare.

"Is it called something else? I admit the books I read were a bit outdated. Harken was still just a territory, and the third Duke of Harken fell defending it. Harken Castle is long gone now, but some of it was repurposed to build the current palace."

Jac shrugged again. "History like that is for people that can read it."

"Fair enough. They brought down an old merchant's road by blowing the mountain on either side of it, left the Clans that were attacking unable to reach them except by way of more heavily guarded areas. That whole area has changed now, of course, but that was how they won the battle. Historians say that if Harken Castle had lost that battle, there would be no Harken today—possibly no Empire, though that is heavily contested."

"Does it really matter? It's not like anyone can go back and change it."

"No, but learning how things were done, or why they happened, can prevent such things from happening again. Or, alternately, I suppose, they can be reused to a similar end."

Jac grunted. "True enough, I guess we do much the same, though we don't tend to look back hundreds of years. I don't—" The words were cut off by a sharp, muffled thunk, followed by a scream of pain and a startled cry from Jac's horse.

Jac hit the ground with a grunt, further alarming the horses and people around them. Rene bellowed for a halt, rounded his own horse, and carefully threaded through the lineup—right as more arrows began to fall.

"Silver Tongue!" He registered Hedge's voice right before he was toppled from his horse and pressed to the ground, covered by Hedge's body. "Are you all right?"

Allen managed to nod, ignored all the aches that flared from being so roughly slammed to the ground. "I'm fine. You?"

Hedge grinned. "Stay down, keep close to the wall. Don't stand up until someone tells you, understand?"

"Yes."

"Good." Hedge rolled off him, stood, and raced off.

Allen looked around for Jac, relief flooding him when he saw Jac standing and moving, though she favored her left side. Turning from Jac, he followed the sounds of battle, heart pounding, a lump lodged in his throat as he watched Rene rush at two men racing up the incline.

He jerked his head away as Rene's sword tore into the throat of one of them, nearly taking his head off, and arrows landed in the throat and face of the other one. He closed his eyes, willed the contents of his stomach to remain there.

Knowing this sort of thing would happen and actually seeing it... Well, at least now he had seen it. Surely it would get easier with time. He opened his eyes, saw Wystie throw a woman off the mountain, and closed his eyes again.

Training. He could hear his mother's stern, loving

voice. He had endured endless, ruthless training so that it was there reflexively when he needed it. When in doubt, fall back on training. He was a prince of Gaulden, and High Consort Presumptive. He hadn't fallen apart when a man died in his arms; he hadn't fallen apart when he'd watched Rene and Lesto kill those prisoners. He would not fall apart in front of the people trusting him to be their silver tongue. When they reached Benta, any mistake he made would cost lives. If he was going to succeed then, he needed to succeed *now.*

Steeling himself, pushing back images of swords through chests and arrows through faces, he dragged his eyes opened and looked around.

All seemed to have quieted.

"Allen!" Rene strode toward him, pushed his horse out of the way, and wrapped a hand around his arm, the blood on his gloves smearing on Allen's sleeve. "Are you all right?"

"I'm fine. How are you and your people?"

"We're fine. Only injury is Jac, who is going to be put on horse duty for taking an arrow and falling off her horse." He turned his head to mock scowl at Jac. "What are you, Penance Gate?"

Jac grinned, though it looked strained as another Dragon treated her injury. "That's a little harsh, Captain. I prefer to think I took the arrow for our silver tongue."

Rene grunted and ruffled Jac's hair, gave her head a gentle shove.

"Are you sure you're all right?" Allen asked.

Jac smiled. "I've taken worse injury than this in practice drills. The armor did its job, never fear. Given it went all the way through *with* armor, I shudder to think what state my arm would be in if I hadn't been wearing it. Bastards were probably going for a headshot, but their marksmen thankfully aren't that good."

Allen nodded, then glanced toward Rene again, noting the anger and worry on his face. "What's wrong?"

Rene shook his head slightly, then motioned for Allen to follow him. Once they were somewhat apart from the rest of the group, he said, "Something was off with this attack. Whoever initially attacked us wanted us dead, but they abruptly broke off and pulled back. Like someone told them to stop. That's not how Carthians usually act. They're much happier killing people, especially Harkens. The scouts think a different group has been shadowing us since we broke camp. It was likely that group which told our attackers to stop."

"That seems strange, even to me," Allen replied. "Why would they want us alive? Do you think this has to do with our mission?"

"Yes," Rene said, eyes dark, mouth tight. "Normally with a compromised mission I would call it off and head home. But I get the feeling we're not going to be allowed to go home, not if they're keeping us alive. That means they need us for something, which means they won't let us leave any more than they'll let us die."

"So we continue on?"

Rene nodded. "Yes, we're going to fight our way through. Once we reach Benta and assume our disguises it'll be harder for anyone to get to us. Be extra careful, though. I cannot stress enough that you must do what I say, when I say, without question or hesitation."

"I will," Allen said. "I know I'm just a spoiled little noble, but I can follow orders and stay out of the way."

"You're the least spoiled noble I've ever met," Rene said, and clapped him on the shoulder. "Saddle up." He strode off calling out orders to the others.

Allen returned to his horse and swung into the saddle, fell into position alongside Jac as they continued on. His mind turned and tumbled with thoughts, but one thought stood out sharp and bright: If the mission was compromised, that meant someone had told the Carthians they were coming and why. Who had betrayed them?

Chapter Eight

"I am really getting sick of people vanishing," Sarrica said flatly. "If you don't stop coming in here to tell me some noble or another has run off, I am going to have you and everyone else banned."

"Empty threats," Lesto replied. "What do you want to do about it?"

Sarrica threw down the papers he'd been holding and scrubbed at his face. "First you're going to have to tell me why it's my problem that two spoiled brats decided to elope. Because to be perfectly frank, I don't care. It is a problem for their families to deal with, not me. I'd much rather continue dealing with these confounded contracts that nobody can seem to agree on. I've had six silver tongues look over them and about the only thing everyone can agree on is that they're a mess. I'm about to implement a policy of throwing people out the window whenever they make my life harder instead of easier."

"With greatest respect," Lesto drawled, "Your Majesty would have to pitch himself out first."

"No, I would go second, right after my esteemed High Commander," Sarrica retorted, jabbing a pen in his direction. "You've yet to tell me why I care that Lady Something and Lady Whomever have done a vanishing act. They've probably eloped because of true love and oh-so-evil parents and will come back thoroughly divorced in a few months. This sort of thing happens at least six times a year. People thought it would happen with me and Nyle. What is all the fuss about this particular pair of halfwits?"

Lesto dropped his arms where they'd been folded across his chest and rested them on his hips, probably in an effort not to throttle Sarrica. "The halfwits in question are Lady Laria Amorlay and Lady Quell Devren."

It took Sarrica a couple of minutes to sort the names. "Oh. I see. That is a bit of a problem." Lady Laria was the Duke of Emberton-Heights' youngest child. She was meant to be marrying the Nemrith Ambassador in a few more months. That was going to make certain negotiations decidedly difficult. The Queendom of Nemrith was quick and brutal to respond to insults, and the abrupt end of a marriage that had been in the works for six years...

Lady Quell was the daughter of the Earl of Mark, who provided a lot of the weaponry used by the imperial army and mercenary bands—weapons made from raw materials imported primarily from Nemrith. Now his damned daughter had run off with Emberton-Heights' daughter, mere days before the negotiations that would precede the renewal of contracts.

A little more than a week after a pair of brutal murders that were further straining already tense relations between Gaulden and Mesta. Nor did it help matters that Emberton-Heights and Mark despised each other.

"Is somebody seeding discord, or am I going mad?" Sarrica asked.

"Those aren't mutually exclusive," Lesto replied, but the tense set to his shoulders eased slightly. "If you see it too, perhaps we're not entirely crazy. It bothers me, especially on the heels of the murders—murders that remain unresolved, for all it seems clear at a glance that Vren is responsible for both deaths."

Sarrica shook his head. "Except, even pretending for a second that Vren is capable of killing coldly like that, which she's not to my understanding, she'd be better at it. She is the exact opposite of stupid. If she wanted them dead, she could have killed them with no one the wiser. She's not the sloppy, impatient type."

"Agreed, and she's one of the few generals I trust implicitly." Lesto sighed. "Though as to that, Faharm was the other one I trusted to that degree. So we have two lovers dead, and now two lovers missing. And the two events are only a little over a week apart. Both matters have increased hostilities amongst the council and in court—hostilities we really don't need right now when we are trying to convince them to cooperate for an enormous war against Benta."

"Let us hope Rene's having a better time of it than us." Sarrica sat back and scrubbed at his face again, silently willing away the headache he could feel building. The very last thing he needed was to be bedridden. "How long ago did they run off? Have we any chance of locating them?"

Lesto shook his head. "The problem is we only *noticed* they're missing two hours ago. Lady Laria was meant to be traveling to see a friend for a holiday before she returned to focus on the pending wedding and preparing to journey to Nemrith. She left the day of the mourning ceremonies for General Faharm and Lieutenant Bells. As to Lady Quell, she is always coming and going due to the work she does, so one took it amiss that they hadn't seen her for some time. Her family only realized she was missing a short time ago. She probably vanished the day of the mourning ceremony as well, though nobody can say for certain."

"Damn it," Sarrica said. "That was five days ago. They could be anywhere by now." It wasn't as though they were the isolated, delicate sort of noble. Both had been well-trained to move in the world. 'Anywhere' was not as much of an exaggeration as he would have liked. "I don't care what it takes, find them."

"I've already sent out every soldier who can possibly be made available and anyone else I could think of, and pulled Jader from his other duties to oversee the search. Their respective families have sent out plenty of their own people as well. Something will turn up. It just may come too late. I wish we were working with a couple of completely stupid kids instead of only slightly stupid ones." He pressed his thumbs to his temples. "The last time I was this strung out was when Nyle was pregnant and making everyone suffer with him."

Sarrica cast him a look but did not otherwise react. "I don't suppose there is new information regarding the murder of Lieutenant Bells?"

"If there was, you would have heard me singing hymns in the temple," Lesto replied.

"Sit down and have some wine before you burst into flame." Sarrica rose and stepped around his desk, shoved Lesto down into a chair. "If everything is already bound for the Penance Realms, you doing nothing for five minutes isn't going to make a bit of difference. Any reports from Rene?"'

Lesto shook his head. "No, but that's not strange given the nature of the mission. Thank you." He took the glass of pale, golden wine that Sarrica held out and took several sips. "You should probably go join the madness before the madness comes to you."

"I want to know the secret to keeping the madness away from me entirely."

A smile twitched at Lesto's mouth. "Marry Prince Allen."

Heaving a sigh and giving Lesto's head a shove, Sarrica left the sanctuary of his private office and returned to the contained chaos of his main office.

Myra looked at him in a way that suggested he was about two steps from submitting his resignation and running before Sarrica could talk him out of it. "The Duke of Emberton-Heights and the Earl of Mark are here to see you, Your Majesty. I told them you were busy, but they insist it's a matter of urgency."

"I've been apprised by Lesto. Send them in. Everyone else can leave until I recall you. Take a break, Myra. I've already got Lesto threatening to quit; I don't need both of you abandoning me. Who would I have to run my empire?"

"I would never do anything to hurt the empire, Your Majesty," Myra said. "Thank you."

Sarrica nodded, watching as Myra and the others in the office all left, leaving it strangely silent. He kicked everyone out at least twice a week, sometimes twice a day, but the silence never stopped being strange. The only thing as loud as his office in the middle of the day was the army preparing for war. Or the court during a sacred day, drunk on wine and brandy and three steps from an outright orgy.

Sitting down at his desk, Sarrica looked over all of the work he would not be getting done. That didn't include the piles that remained in his private office. If the gods were trying to drive home the point regarding Prince Allen, they had more than made it. A consort right then would have been worth his entire fortune twice over.

The door opened and two men strode in as though they were entitled to do so. Sarrica watched them until they caught his gaze and checked themselves. "Your Majesty," greeted Lord Celia Amorlay, Duke of Emberton-Heights and all that remained of the line that had once commanded an important territory in the Cartha Mountains. He had married at just seventeen to the last remaining heir of the Emberton-Heights line, a woman thirteen years his senior. It had not, by all accounts, been a happy marriage, but it had produced three children before illness and alcohol took Lady Brenna at age thirty-six. Celia had inherited everything, though many had thought he would be snubbed and everything given directly to his eldest child.

He was an austere, elegant man, with the faintest touches of silver to his ink-black hair and a thin mouth that Sarrica had seldom seen smile. He was nearly as thin at forty-three as Sarrica remembered him being as a youth, though his rough edges had smoothed out impressively.

By contrast, Lord Rhodes Devren, the Earl of Mark, seemed to be all sharp edges and cold impatience. The man made his fortune on war and had no qualms about it. He was just as elegant but with a derisive edge to it. His "Your Majesty" was spoken as if the words were a chore.

Sarrica stared him down until he held still and looked away. "You may sit, gentlemen."

The door opened and Lesto stepped inside. "Sarrica, I am going—" He stopped when he saw the other men in the room. "The guards didn't tell me you had company, my apologies." He closed the door and walked across the room to join them. "Your Grace, Your Lordship."

"Commander, I hope the day finds you well. I'm certain our family drama is not making your day any easier," Lord Celia said.

"Your day is more difficult by far, Your Grace," Lesto said.

Sarrica clapped his hands and rested back in his seat. "Commander Lesto has conveyed to me your troubles. I am sorry this has happened. I cannot image what I will do when my own children one day do something equally stupid. Have you learned anything new?"

"Possibly," Lord Rhodes said, tone sour, eyes on the cane he absently twisted back and forth in one hand. "My daughter was meant to do a favor for me the day of General Faharm's mourning ceremony. She begged a delay of a few hours because later that afternoon was the ceremony for the dead lieutenant Faharm was buggering. I told her no, but she insisted, said the man was the brother of a friend of hers."

"Bells," Lord Celia said, mouth set in unhappy lines. "Laria spoke of him on many occasions. They were both good friends with Gorden Bells. He seems a smart boy, a competent silver tongue and hard-working clerk, according to my investigations. Several people recall seeing the three of them together at the ceremony, and a few swore they saw them outside the palace a short time later, though they could not swear to it or say what they had been doing."

Bells again? That was peculiar, though stranger coincidences had crossed his path. Too impatient to order Lesto to do it, and frankly tired of sitting around listening to people yell and fret at him, Sarrica stood and crossed the room. He yanked the door open and bellowed, "Somebody locate Gorden Bells and drag him—" He broke off as a familiar face registered, splotchy from crying and wide-eyed with alarm. "Nevermind. I see he has managed to drag himself here. How convenient of you, Master Bells. In here now, please."

"Yes, Your Majesty," Bells mumbled.

Sarrica stepped aside so he could enter, and looked to the attendants guarding his door. "Tea for a small army, if you please."

"Yes, Your Majesty."

Sarrica thanked them, closed the door, and motioned for the anxious-looking Bells to follow him. He nudged Bells toward the remaining seat. "Sit, sit. Tell me everything you know about this situation, or I swear you will not like what happens to you."

Gorden, looking more than a little terrified to be sandwiched between Celia and Lesto, and across from Lord Rhodes, nodded jerkily, but it was still a moment before he finally started talking, looking at his hands throughout. "I told them not to do it. They've been... um, involved for a little less than two years now and have been talking more and more about eloping. I had so far persuaded them not to act so foolishly, but after the tragedy of my brother and General Faharm, they were terrified something much the same would happen to them. So they begged me to help, and they are my friends... Now they are gone, and I wish I had been a better friend and stood up to them. I'm eternally sorry, Your Majesty."

Celia leaned in and rested a hand on his shoulder, squeezing lightly. "Do not worry upon it. Whatever you did, you were going to upset someone. You did the best you could. At your age, in your circumstances, I cannot say I would have acted so different. I remember what it's like to be young and feel boxed in. Can you tell us anything about where they went? What they were going to do, exactly?"

"There's not many places they could get married quickly and without questions being asked or paperwork being demanded. Send people to those locations, catch them when they arrive," Rhodes said, bored and irritated.

Gorden shook his head. "They wouldn't tell me their plans; they said it was to protect me. I think they were planning to take a ship, though. Quell had friends amongst the sailors and either had already arranged something with them, or thought she'd be able to. That was all I could follow, I'm afraid."

"Damn," Celia said. "If they were planning to take a ship, it's probably long gone by now. If not, we'll never find them before they board and depart. There are simply too many ships and too few hours."

"The battle is not lost quite yet," Lesto replied. "They are adept at many things, but hiding their tracks, I suspect, is not one of them."

Sarrica looked at Gorden. "Anything else you can tell us? The smallest detail might be the key we need. What did they pack?"

"Practically nothing: just clothes in a couple of bags they could easily carry, money, and travel food they had me fetch from the kitchens."

That wasn't enough to travel for more than a day or two. It was the kind of packing someone did when they knew they had belongings at their destination. Sarrica shared a look with Lesto, who, by the grim set of his mouth, had reached the same conclusion.

Damn, they might be good at covering their tracks after all.

"So they aren't going by ship," Celia said thoughtfully. "Laria has no suitable holdings for them to run to. She only had a summer cottage that she sold last year since she'll no longer have need of it. She could not have moved that kind of money without my knowing. Lord Rhodes?"

"Quell could have purchased a house without my knowledge. She travels so frequently and deals with so much money, the funds would not have been remarked upon. It will take me some time to sort through the finances to find it."

"The truth must out somewhere, especially when land is sold and purchased," Sarrica said. Wars were fought over land, after all. People liked to be painfully clear about who owned it. "I'll put my secretaries on it. They have a particular talent for rooting out this kind of thing, probably because nobles like to be shifty about such matters."

"Shifty?" Rhodes repeated coolly.

Sarrica ignored him, because he'd meant exactly what Rhodes thought he meant, and focused again on Gorden. "Any other tidbits to offer up?"

"No, Your Majesty. I'm sorry I am not more useful to you, in either of the matters..." He swallowed and looked at his hands again, blinking rapidly against tears.

Poor bastard. Brother dead, friends lost... Sarrica gestured to Lesto, who rose and escorted Gorden from the room. Sarrica heard the door open, the familiar rattle of a teacart, and Lesto's low voice speaking briefly with whoever was bringing the cart in.

Sarrica ignored it all, focusing on his thoughts, the

nasty snarl right in the midst of his palace. Damn everything to the lowest Realms, he could not untangle the mess. Something was amiss, but what?

He watched, not really paying attention, as one of his assistants from the front room poured and prepared his tea. Sarrica stirred enough from his thoughts to thank her when she handed him the cup, made of delicate china painted in swirls of blue, red, and gold set on a small saucer featuring a blue and red checker pattern.

Black tea, spicy and fragrant. Sarrica sipped at his, smiling at the flavor, a small bit of pleasure in the middle of the frustrating mess he was untangling.

A familiar jangling stride drew his attention. "How is...?" he trailed off when he saw the figure standing next to Lesto: Jader Star, Deputy High Commander of the Imperial Army. He was slightly shorter than Lesto, and even thinner, with bone-white skin and ink-black hair cut close to his head. He wore the uniform of the imperial army, but his ears were full of holes where normally he'd be wearing the elaborate earrings and other piercings that were so important to Farlanders. Most people assumed he was from Gaulden or Rilien, tended not to realize until too late that despite his strange coloring he was essentially native to Farland.

Sarrica looked to Lesto, whose face gave nothing away to most, but to Sarrica, he looked about two steps from walking out and not stopping until he reached the ocean, and maybe not even then. "Your Majesty, I made Jader supervise the soldiers we sent into the city. Some of the Winter Dark believe they've located something we think is connected to Lady Laria and Lady Quell."

"What—" Rhodes snapped but stopped when

Sarrica shot him a warning look. "I would like to know if my daughter is well, with greatest respect, Your Majesty."

Sarrica looked to Jader, nodding for him to speak freely. Jader bowed. "Your Majesty, Your Grace, Your Lordship, I cannot confirm whether your daughters are well. Winter Dark found a carriage we believe they used to try and leave the city, or perhaps head to the harbor. At this stage it's hard to say. But one door and the inside were heavily covered in blood."

"How heavily?" Sarrica asked sharply.

Jader did not reply save to give one sharp, short shake of his head.

Rhodes stormed to his feet, clutching his cane so tightly it reddened his knuckles. Nearby, in his own chair, Celia seemed to pale and whither. Rhodes lunged toward Jader. "I want my daughter right now, tell me—" He broke off with a bellow as Lesto grabbed him and shoved back across the sitting area and into his chair.

"You will remain in that seat, my lord, or you will be removed."

"I want to know where my daughter is," Rhodes hissed. "Not even you, High Commander, will keep me from finding her."

Lesto rested one hand lightly on the pommel of his sword. "If you attempt to act violently in the vicinity of His Majesty again, I will see to it the only news you receive is what I choose to tell you while you cool that temper in the dankest cell available. Am I clear?"

Rhodes did not reply, but Sarrica supposed the absolute hatred on his face was answer enough. "Lesto, enough. If my children were missing I would be thrice as hostile. Jader, tell us everything you can."

"We found the carriage, marked with the crest of Emberton-Heights, about an hour ago behind the carriage house of Red Sparrow Inn."

Lesto's mouth cut into a sharp frown, and nearby Rhodes looked even less pleased. "I take it Red Sparrow Inn is a bad place?" Sarrica asked.

Rhodes struck the ground restlessly with his cane. "To say the least, Your Majesty. Despots and mongrels of every sort gather there to sell or buy things no place of even barest decency would dare. It is not a place they would go, even on the run as they were."

"Indeed," Celia said quietly. "We can probably all think of at least a few inns and travel houses that would be far more accommodating to a pair of eloping lovers. I don't understand why they picked the Red." He grimaced. "Their carriage was definitely behind it?"

"Yes," Jader replied with a nod. "A couple of stable boys were reluctant to talk but did admit they'd been told to take the carriage off and burn it the moment full dark fell. Of the passengers, they knew nothing, or at least would not speak of it. The innkeeper told us to, um, remove ourselves from the premises and not to come back without the proper paperwork."

Sarrica smiled. "Lesto, fetch the proper paperwork and a pen."

"Already being drawn up. Should be here shortly," Lesto replied.

Jader shook his head. "It may not be necessary. I don't have much patience with well-known criminals acting that way. We aren't allowed to enter premises without permission, but the man made himself available to being dragged off his stoop and into the street. After a brief discussion with the man regarding all the charges that could be levied against him, he decided to tell us what little he knew. Two women came into the bar last night and spoke with a man they were very obviously afraid of, who seemed to enjoy frightening them. They gave him something, left in a haste. Shortly after, the man grew angry and stormed out after them. Two hours later, the man returned and paid a large sum to our man to burn the carriage."

"That sounds more like the kind of tale a drunk tells to impress his friends, not something that actually happened. I almost don't believe it," Sarrica said, shaking his head, a knot of dread and resignation forming in his stomach. If the women were alive, it would be by the grace of the Pantheon alone. "Where is that damned paperwork?"

Lesto strode off but returned almost immediately with a stack of papers that he promptly handed to Sarrica.

Skimming through them quickly, Sarrica rose and went across the office to his desk and began to sign off at the bottom of them, then pulled out his imperial seal from around his neck and stamped the last page. "There. If our fine fellow wants to play precisely by the rules, then precisely we shall play."

"Majesty," Lesto said, bowing as he took the papers and beckoned to Jader. When he reached the door, he whipped around and jabbed a finger at Sarrica. "Remain in this office. Do you understand what will happen to you if you disobey me?"

"Perfectly," Sarrica said. Lesto gave him a parting warning look, then turned and stormed off, Jader on his heels.

A moment later a Fathoms Deep guard stepped inside. "High Commander bid me watch you or else."

Sarrica sighed and motioned for the man to sit. He

then turned his attention back to tea and distressed lords. "We will do our best to find them, I promise."

"You need not honey-coat it, Your Majesty," Rhodes said bitterly, cane across his lap, both hands wrapped around it. "That kind of blood, that neighborhood—"

"They're not dead until they're dead," Celia cut in, though his voice was ragged around the edges and his pinched, sad eyes indicated he agreed with Rhodes.

Sarrica wished he could argue, but Jader was a soldier. If he felt there was too much blood for anyone to have survived, Sarrica believed him. "I suggest you return to your families, my lords, and await further news. No good will come of stewing here. If—"

He broke off at the sound of bellowing and shattering porcelain that came from the front room and stormed to his feet when something large and heavy struck his door hard. "Stay here," he said to Rhodes and Celia as he stood and went to retrieve the sword he kept by his desk.

The Fathoms Deep guard surged to his feet. "Majesty, it's not safe—"

"Do not attempt to Lesto me," Sarrica said, not bothering to look at the guard as he spoke, intent on the door as something else slammed into it. He pulled the sheath off and cast it aside, then yanked the door open—

And barely jumped out of the way in time as two men tumbled in, one clearly intent on beating the other's face to pulp. Sarrica grabbed the man by the back of his collar, yanked him back, threw him to the floor and kept him there with a boot to his chest and a sword tip to his throat.

"I will fucking kill—" the man stopped, paled,

though Sarrica did not know if that was from having just threatened to kill the High King or registering the sword.

"Your Majesty!"

Sarrica ignored the Fathoms Deep guards that came running up, save to indicate the man with the battered face. Putting his attention back on the man at his feet, Sarrica pressed the tip of his sword so it just touched the man's skin. "What in the name of the Realms do you think you are doing?"

"He started it," the man muttered. Lord Riddell, Sarrica noted belatedly. He would wager his fortune the other man was Mestan, or closely associated with Mesta.

Removing the sword, Sarrica motioned for one of the hovering guards to get him up. He handed his sword off to another one to sheath and return to his desk. He looked between the two men now held securely by the guards. Behind Sarrica, Rhodes and Celia had risen from their seats and drawn a few steps closer. Sarrica looked again at Riddell. "You should be far more concerned that I am the one ending it, Lord Riddell. Somebody tell me what this is about because I promise, the longer it takes, the worse the punishment will be."

A woman stepped forward, unfamiliar but she wore a dark, yellow-gold ribbon around her throat embroidered with the ornate bird that was the crest of Gaulden. "Your Majesty, we apologize—"

"Skip the apologies and tell me what is going on," Sarrica snarled. "Now!"

She jumped, but then seemed to rally. "Mesta spoke grossly out of turn about General Faharm and Prince Allen. We told them to be quiet, but they refused to back down. I tried to keep my compatriots from reacting, but the matter grew out of hand. We should not have let it. I have no excuse."

"No, you do not," Sarrica said. "I do not feel like dealing with this right now. My hands are full with trying to resolve the murder for Gaulden and Mesta, and now I have missing, likely murdered, women. On top of a million other problems. I have neither the time nor the inclination to deal with people who choose to behave like children. All of you are confined to your rooms until I feel like letting you out, and you will pay a thousand crown fine for this behavior. *Each.*"

"That's not fair!" Lord Riddell snarled. "They—"

Sarrica looked at him. Lord Riddell snapped his mouth shut. "You can pay two thousand, maybe that will teach you to control your temper and your tongue." Turning sharply around, Sarrica looked to the Mestans. "Did you speak inappropriately about General Faharm and Prince Allen?"

The man at the front of the group bristled. He was similar in appearance to the man with the battered face. "It wasn't—"

"Yes or no," Sarrica cut in. "My patience is wearing extremely thin."

"Yes, Majesty," the man said reluctantly.

"Two thousand crowns apiece in fines. Get out of my office or you're all spending the night in prison."

They fled, moving with all the speed and enthusiasm of children who knew they'd just escaped a sound switching.

Turning to Celia and Rhodes, Sarrica said, "I will keep you both apprised as we gain new information. For now, please go." He motioned to the lingering Fathoms Deep guard assigned to watch him by Lesto to escort them. Though neither looked happy about the dismissal, they bowed and let the guard lead them out. Sarrica pressed his fingers to his temples as the familiar spikes of a crippling headache rose up. Of course, because blinding pain was the only thing his day was lacking. Damn everyone, could just one thing go right?

He looked up at the sound of footsteps, saw his secretaries had returned from the offices they used when he needed privacy. "So what am I facing next?"

"Taxes," Myra said. "Master Searidge and Lady Heathering are awaiting you and were informed the meeting would likely start late."

Emerella stepped forward. "Miss Emilia came down a few minutes ago to let you know that Bellen feels unwell and has a bit of fever. She says it's nothing to worry about, but Bellen has been asking for you."

"I'll go see Bellen now," Sarrica said. "Tell Searidge and Heathering I'll be there as soon as I can and move all my other appointments forward by at least an hour, or whatever you think is best. Bring the revised schedule to me as soon as it's ready—in the nursery or the meeting room."

"Yes, Your Majesty."

Sarrica strode off, motioning for two Fathoms Deep to follow him because the last thing he needed was Lesto being angry.

Stress, pain, and helplessness pressed down like a boulder on the verge of crushing him. More than that was the loneliness, a sharp, digging ache that hollowed him out and left him scraped raw.

And in the end, he had no one but himself to blame. He hadn't been reason enough for Nyle to stay, and he'd given Allen every reason to run away.

CHAPTER NINE

Allen definitely hated snow, and increasingly with every second that passed. He shivered in his cloak, tugged his hat more firmly down on his head, and pulled his hood up. "It was beautiful weather when we left."

"Welcome to the bitter, rancid asshole known as Cartha," Rene said and clapped him on the back. "Sit down. There's some brandy in your coffee. That should make things slightly more bearable. Or make you care less, which amounts to the same thing." He sat down on his bedroll, motioning for Allen to join him.

Taking the metal cup Mixx handed to him, Allen sat down. When he and Rene were as alone as it was possible to be in a small, crowded camp, he murmured, "You are worried."

"Yeah," Rene said. "The blunt truth is that we're fucked no matter what we do. We've taken every precaution, but every time I think we're getting ahead of the bastards we get attacked—herded, in fact."

"Herded?"

Rene nodded, mouth tightening. "Yeah. We should be well to the west by now and practically out of these Pantheon-damned mountains. Instead we're only a few hours from Amorlay fortress. The bastards could simply take us prisoner, but instead they're playing with us and biding their time. I should have called the whole thing off when I had the chance, but in the end

I'm still not sure it would have done a damned bit of good. Pressing on and hoping we can break free of them is still our best option. I don't like the odds, though."

Allen nodded and took several sips of hot, brandy-laced coffee. "I suppose at least I will not have to stand through a three-hour wedding ceremony. Or explain to my mother why the ceremony won't be happening at all."

Instead of laughing as he'd intended, Rene just looked more miserable. "I thought I did the right thing, saying no when Tara asked me to marry him. Right now, I'm not so sure."

"You've as much admitted you regretted ending matters," Allen said softly. "I might have been drunk but I remember what you said. For a man who claims he is not the settling type you look very much like you want to try. So why didn't you?"

Rene blew out a long sigh. "It's complicated, or it seemed so when I said no. In the safety of the palace, surrounded by people and life, it's easy for memory to dull the edges of those moments when you were afraid you were going to die." He stared into his own coffee before picking it up and gulping it down. "Right now, I am certain I will die, and Tara will never know I wished I had said yes."

"Perhaps I am just a clueless civilian, but you are not dead yet, and despairing about it won't get you very far," Allen said. "If I had kept my own pride and despair in check, I could still be at home getting into snippy little fights with His Majesty instead of sitting here wondering if it is sword, arrow, or snow that will get to me first."

"I will give my last breath to see you make it home

safe, Highness. It is one of the reasons I am considering abandoning the mission and returning to Harken."

Allen finished his coffee and poured more from the pot sitting close to the little fire in front of them. He was tempted to add more brandy, but a fuzzy head would not help anything. "If you think it is the barest bit safer to push on, then we should. I am important but not irreplaceable, if we are being brutally honest. They haven't killed us yet, at least. Surely that means something?"

"It means they're waiting on something," Rene said, staring at the ground like he wanted to stab it. "They either need us to be in a particular place, or they need someone in the group." His right hand curled into a fist. "Once they have or know what they need, there is no telling what will happen to us. I would like to get my hands around the throat of whoever sold us out."

"I hope someone does before a great deal more harm is done."

Rene grimaced. "I wouldn't even know where to start looking for the bastard, but that's always the way with traitors."

Allen drained his coffee a second time and set the cup aside. "I wish I could puzzle it out for you, but I am missing too many pieces. At least Morant is still safe for now."

Rene nodded, rubbed the backs of his fingers across his eyes and forehead. "I just wish I knew why Cartha is bothering to get involved. Cartha doesn't love Harken, but they don't love anyone else either. They've always been dangerous because they hate everyone equally and have no need of allies. What would convince Cartha to join up with Benta?"

"There's quite a few reasons, actually," Allen

replied. "Cartha has always been simultaneously strong and vulnerable, situated right between Harken and Benta as they are. They have close ties to Tricemore in terms of culture and history; it's always been a concern of the empire that Tricemore might rebel and side with Cartha, which would make them quite a force to be reckoned with. Cartha has historical ties to Benta as well, ties that Benta may have figured out how to exploit. There are other, more boring reasons centered on money, trade, and the like. There could also be a reason that we will not know until too late."

"Captain!" They both looked up as Hedge and Jac came striding toward them, stopping just short of where they were sitting. "Scouts have cleared a path, we're ready to move out at your command."

"Good," Rene said and pushed to his feet. "Gather everyone together—"

Hedge cut the words off with a derisive noise. "Captain, if you're going to blather on about the danger and how we're fucked no matter which way we go, you're wasting your time. What do you think we've been muttering about to each other? You brought along all the smart Dragons. We're not going back, not after coming this far. Too many people relying on us."

"It's become a fool's mission," Rene said flatly.

"Only fools do this job for the pay we get, anyway," Jac said with a laugh. "Anything is better than the stocks I was in when you found me." She knelt to pack away the cups and other miscellany Rene had dragged out.

Hedge laughed. "Stocks? For what? Working the wrong street? Because that is definitely the kind of stupid—"

Allen screamed and jerked back, head slamming into the tree behind him, unable to tear his eyes away from the sight of Hedge with an arrow sticking out of her throat, blood streaming down her torso, coating her lips and chin.

"Jac!" Rene bellowed, even as he drew his sword and rushed off toward the sounds of screams that abruptly filtered into Allen's awareness.

Allen scrambled to his feet, tried to run after Rene—and snarled when Jac grabbed him and dragged him into the woods. "No! We have to help—"

"The only thing you're doing is getting out of here," Jac said, and swore loudly and creatively as the sound of horses and angry voices came toward them.

A moment later the riders appeared, wearing black leather armor, swords and axes in hand, riding black horses draped with blood-red blankets beneath their black saddles. Jac shoved Allen to the ground, snarling at him to stay there as she drew something from a pouch at her waist and lobbed it at the riders.

It burst and splattered over the closest rider's face, a thick, red-brown liquid that made the woman scream in agony and lose control of her horse. As she fell, her horse kept running, screaming as it went, jerking and twisting as though trying to get something off its back.

In the next moment, the other rider was upon them, and Jac bellowed as she charged forward, dodging low and to the side, sword flashing as she sliced open the rider's leg. That drew a scream from the rider, who jerked his horse's reins and whirled around, made to charge Jac again.

Allen scrambled to his knees, grabbed the rock that had been digging into his side, and lobbed it at the man. It missed him and struck the horse instead, but it was all the distraction required as the horse jerked in surprise. Jac drew another one of her nasty little balls and threw it, then dashed forward and dragged the screaming man from his horse and slit his throat.

Screams and shouts came from the campsite. Jac turned to look at Allen, strode over to him, yanked him to his feet and threw him at the horse. "You have to get out of here, Highness."

Allen ignored her in favor of throwing open the saddlebags and yanking out everything inside, throwing objects to the ground one by one as they proved to be unhelpful. Jerky, useless. Water, useless. Folded papers. Too much to read at present but possibly useful. He shoved them into his belt. Cigarette leaf and cigarette papers, useless. Flask, use—

No. Allen sniffed. Tore the cap open and took another sniff. That was brandy. Cartha didn't make brandy, especially not brandy that smelled of *citrus.* He took a swallow, coughing as the alcohol burned.

"Highness, you must—"

"Leave me be!" Allen snarled and shoved the flask back into the saddlebag. "Make this horse hold still!"

Jac obeyed, giving him a wide-eyed, angry, worried look. "We can't linger, Highness. Whatever happens to the rest of us, you must get home safely."

"I won't leave the Three-headed Dragons to save myself," Allen said, most of his attention still on the saddlebags. "I wish that other horse was here, damn it." Abandoning the first bag, he went around to the other and dug through it—and froze as he pulled out a small sack of dried grapes. That was something else that Cartha did not have, and the flavor of them... Allen had once made himself sick eating the damned things as a boy when he'd been studying in Tricemore for six months. Tricemore was known for its wine almost as well as Gaulden, but they also produced grapes that were good for other things.

And the brandy was made by monks of the Twelve Voices Monastery. In Delfaste, right along the border and close to the place where the dried grapes were produced. Both were highly sought after by other kingdoms in the empire, and by nations abroad.

There were hundreds of people who could, in theory, trade such things to Cartha, even if trade with them was illegal—but only one family traded frequently at both ends of Tricemore and was affluent enough to send their son to study in Harken, a son who would be in the perfect position to spy and glean secrets, especially with his brother a lieutenant in Fathoms Deep.

Allen looked up at Jac. "You need to return to the palace."

Voices came, louder than ever, speaking in rough, urgent Carthian.

"No! You have to go!" Jac snarled. "I swore to keep you safe—"

Allen grabbed the front of her shirt, yanked her close and hissed, "I don't have time for noble gestures. I will never make it back alive on my own, and I would only slow us down if we tried to escape together. It is vitally important—" He broke off as the sound of people crashing through the underbrush drew close then turned back to Jac. "Return to the palace. Tell Sarrica that Gorden Bells is a traitor. If I'm right, and all of this is about Prince Morant, then they need someone who can identify him, and they think someone in this group can do that. They've been herding us toward Amorlay, so they're probably bringing the captured sailors there. Do whatever it takes to convey all that to Sarrica. Do you understand?"

"Yes, Highness." Jac gripped his shoulders tightly. "Dragon strength keep you. I'm sorry." She drew back, mounted the horse, and with a last, regretful look, raced off into the forest.

Only seconds later three soldiers came bursting through the trees and shrubs, bloody, disheveled, and angry. They saw Allen and rushed toward him, grabbing him roughly. One raised his sword—

And stopped when another cracked out a harsh, *"Civilian! Don't!"*

"Why not?" Demanded the man who had been about to kill him. *"Who cares?"*

"That is for the captain to decide. Bring him."

"How did he kill the others?"

"No horses. Someone else might have escaped. They won't get far. Bring him!"

The man who'd nearly gutted Allen grabbed his arm and dragged him along, snarling in rage and slapping him after Allen stumbled too many times. *"Help me,"* he snarled at the third man, who grabbed Allen's other arm, and together they dragged him back into camp.

Allen almost threw up as he took in what was left of the Three-headed Dragons. Tears stung his eyes, streamed down his cheeks. Hedge... Regena... Oh, god, Mixx's head— He looked away, swallowed the bile that burned in his throat.

Dead, every last one of them dead, and not killed kindly either. In the middle of the small clearing, Rene was on his knees, arms behind his back and bound in chains. He looked up at the sound of movement, eyes widening briefly before going dark and sad and defeated as he saw Allen.

The men dragging Allen shoved him to his knees beside Rene, and two more came up to jerk his arms back and wrap them in cold, heavy chain. One of them yanked the papers from his belt and handed them off to another man who came striding up.

"Who is you?" Barked the new man, who seemed to be in charge, judging by his arrogant demeanor and the way everyone deferred to or seemed afraid of him. Allen knew some of the Carthian marks of rank, but the man seemed to bear no marks at all. From the way they were dressed, in rough ordinary clothes, they were trying to avoid being identified, though the way they acted and some of what they said marked them as soldiers.

"My name is Allen Carter," Allen replied. "I'm a silver tongue, hired by the Three-headed Dragons."

The man narrowed his eyes. *"Silver tongue, that means you're a master of languages. Do you understand me?"*

"I understand you," Allen said. *"What is the meaning of this attack? Whatever Cartha's opinion of Harken, the treaty says we have permission to travel these mountains."*

The man laughed as he backhanded Allen so hard he tasted blood. He spat it out, glaring at the man as imperiously as he knew how. Chuckling, the man lazily slapped him again then motioned to the others. *"Secure them to horses. I want to be at the fortress before dark falls. Mind your words. That one understands everything we say."*

"Yes, Captain," the men chorused, and roughly

hauled Allen up and away. He was thrown over a horse and tied down so tightly he feared blood circulation would be cut off. Twisting and jerking, finally giving up when he ran out of breath, Allen squirmed until he could at least look around.

Allen's gaze fell on Rene, tears stinging his eyes. Rene's people lay dead in the field quickly vanishing behind them, and there was probably nothing any of them could have done to change that outcome. Allen was a master of words, but he could think of nothing to say. He let his head fall again, grimacing against the headache that quickly rose up as he banged against the side of the horse while they rode.

By the time they finally stopped moving, he was too exhausted and numb to do anything but collapse. He went without protest when they dragged him along, across rough, cold stone, into a fortress that smelled of smoke and unwashed people and burned meat.

They kept moving, dragging him through the hall, up a short flight of stairs, and down a dark hallway that smelled of piss and wet dog. One of the men pulled a key out and opened the door. The men threw him into a dark room that smelled mostly of dust, but with faint hints of spices that must have once been stored there. A couple of minutes later, Rene was dragged in as well.

The men undid their chains, dragged them over to the wall farthest from the door and secured them to manacles there. Allen's shoulders, already sore from being pulled back for hours, screamed in protest at being dragged up and secured that way.

One of the men kicked him hard when he was finished, laughed when Allen gasped in pain and tried to double over. *"Silver tongue. Not so very silver now, is it?*"

What had he done that they hated him so much? Allen kept his head down until they'd gone, hoping his fear didn't show, but suspecting from their mean laughter that they saw it clear as day.

The door slammed shut behind them, and fresh tears stung his eyes as he heard the door lock.

"I'm sorry," Rene said quietly. "I assigned Jac to protect you, to make sure that even if the rest of us died, you got safely home. I was sure she'd gotten you away soon enough."

Allen shook his head. "She did—got me away, killed our pursuers, secured a horse... But I found items in the saddlebags and made her go alone to relay to Sarrica who I believe the traitor to be. I could be wrong; I had only seconds and it was mostly guesswork, but I think I'm right. I never would have made it home though, and I would have been a hindrance to Jac."

"You're a fool," Rene whispered. "But I'm a bigger fool. We should have turned around the same day we were first attacked. They're all dead..." he closed his eyes, swallowed. "I think I'm the reason they're dead."

"Cartha is the reason they're dead," Allen said. "You did the best you could, but up against a cowardly traitor and heartless Carthians? We never stood a chance. I'm guessing you're alive because you're the one who can identify Prince Morant?"

Rene nodded. "Yes. He was visiting Harken in secret before finally journeying home when Korlow was overtaken by Benta. We hid him in Farland until he could return home to take back his country. It's been months in the preparing. We've also slowly smuggled in forces. The moment Morant gives the signal they'll be ready to move. All would have been fine and this whole stupid matter nearly over with if not for that fucking storm—" He took a deep breath, let it out slowly. "Anyway, I was assigned to take him to Farland. No one else aboard knew who he was; we mixed him in with a bunch of traders and such headed that way, and I went as his manservant. Three men from Fathoms Deep went by land and met us there. They remained as his protection until it was time to return home."

"Was one of them Lieutenant Bells?"

Rene shook his head. "No—" His head snapped up, eyes sharp, anger pushing out the despair. "But Bells *was* good friends with one of the guards assigned to Morant. Those men were not supposed to reveal why they were gone for months, but if one of them talked to a good friend they trusted..."

"And Lieutenant Bells in turn confided in the brother *he* trusted," Allen finished. "That means Gorden Bells knows exactly who in the palace knows what Prince Morant looks like. He somehow conveyed to Cartha that you would be in the mountains and that you knew Prince Morant. I don't know how he knew of your mission, though."

"It took you only looking at my requisition forms. I'm sure some other seemingly minor detail tipped him off. Or one of the Dragons ran their mouth when they shouldn't have. It doesn't matter how many times you say 'keep your mouth shut,' nobody gets how important that is until people die." He let his head thunk against the wall, eyes sliding shut. "I dread what comes next, especially for you. Those two harassed you like they did to rattle you. They want you scared, probably so you'll cooperate, but I'm not sure why.

There's no way they could know who are you, and I don't know why they would need a silver tongue."

"I don't know," Allen whispered. "I guess we'll find out. How long do you think we have before something else happens?"

"There's no way to know. They may come for us any moment; they may let us rot a while in hopes it will make more cooperative." Rene frowned. "Though as to that, I don't know if they'll take us to Morant, or bring Morant to us. It would be easier to move two captives than all the prisoners they took from the shipwreck, I'd think, but they may have a reason to drag all the prisoners here."

Allen was more afraid of why they'd decided to keep him alive. What would happen, how long they did they have until the Carthians decided they no longer needed their prisoners. "Do you think we'll—?"

"Don't ask that question, because you are not going to like my answer," Rene said, voice harsh. "I never should have let you come."

"I'm an adult. My choices and their consequences are mine alone. If we make it home alive, Sarrica owes me the most lavish wedding to ever grace the empire." Allen mustered a smile, fragile though it was. "I think he should pay for yours, too."

Rene let out a cracked, broken laugh. "I don't need a wedding. At this point I would settle for filing the paperwork and calling it done. You need to brace yourself as best you can, because if they are keeping you alive and trying to terrorize you into submission, that means they're going to ask you to do something you won't want to do. They need me alive to identify Morant, but they can still hurt me, and they will if it means you will cooperate. If hurting you doesn't work, which is what they'll do first. I'm sorry, I'm so fucking sorry."

"No, Captain, it is I who owe the apologies. Sarrica embarrassed me, and I let a bruised ego persuade me to precisely the kind of behavior I should know better than to indulge. When my mother finds out about this she will kill me herself." He closed his eyes, lost the battle against the tears that streamed down his cheek.

Damn it, he would not give in to terror and helplessness. He was Prince Allen Telmis of Gaulden and High Consort Presumptive. He would not fall apart now. He was going to figure out how to survive this, and when he got home he would shove this entire wretched affair in Sarrica's face and order the stubborn ass to marry him.

Though by the time Cartha and Benta were done with him, there might not be enough of him left to be worth marrying. Allen let out a fractured laugh.

"Allen," Rene said softly. "Don't think about it. The more you think about it, the worse it will all be."

"You sound experienced," Allen said. "I'm sorry for that."

"My body isn't any less scarred than yours," Rene said wryly. "You saw that well enough; the damage is just a bit more scattered. I was kidnapped by enemy soldiers once, back when I was still with Winter Dark. The bastards wanted to know where we were hiding a noble they'd been hired to kill. Beat the shit out of me, broke my leg, and left my throat so bruised I couldn't talk for days. If the others hadn't found me when they did, I wouldn't have lived to see morning." He winced. "That probably wasn't the best story to tell right now."

"I'm focusing on the part where you survived and seemed to recover—as much as anyone does, I suppose. I know war changes soldiers forever, in ways seen and unseen. I can handle pain, as you saw. Let's hope I can survive it long enough."

Rene looked at him, eyes full of such piercing intensity they seemed to burn like a bonfire in the dead of night. "If Sarrica doesn't get his head out of his ass and marry you, he deserves the misery in which he's wallowing. You want a distracting story? I have one for you: Nyle and Sarrica loved each other, deeply. But love isn't always enough. I think if my brother had lived, there would have been a divorce by the end of the year. They both changed too much as they got older, and I think everyone but them knew it was time to part ways and move on. Nyle would have admitted it first. I think he was working up to it by returning to active duty. Whatever Sarrica claims, he needs someone who's not Nyle. If you two do not work out, so be it, but I think you would do well together. At the very least, you're just as stubborn as him."

That drew another faint smile. "I'm not sure it's a quality he'll appreciate; he may just help my mother kill me and hide the body."

Rene laughed. "Well, for what it's worth, they'll be burying me alongside you."

"At least I'll have the company of a friend," Allen said quietly, more hesitance in the words than he wanted to admit.

"Yes," Rene said firmly.

"I've never really had those before," Allen said, looking at him and dredging up another smile. "I have scores of acquaintances, peers, allies... but no one I could call friend. All my tutoring and training did not leave time to forge friendships. I was hoping to change that once I became High Consort. You and Tara are the first friends I've ever had."

"Tara is a good friend to have," Rene replied, then smile wryly. "I cannot say the same for myself. I wish..." He fell silent at the sound of heavy footsteps followed a key turning in the lock.

The door swung open a moment later, and two unfamiliar men stepped in, unlocked Allen's manacles, and jerked him to his feet. *"Where are you taking me?"*

"Shut your fucking mouth," one of the men said and knocked him upside the head, reawakening the headache that had just tapered off. He fastened manacles around Allen's wrists; they were heavy and ice-cold, the edges digging into his skin.

"Be strong, Allen," Rene said as they dragged him away. "I'm so fucking sorry."

Allen looked over his shoulder, gave him one last smile, and then the door was pulled shut and they were dragging him off back down the stairs and into the hall he vaguely recalled from before.

It was nearly empty, all the tables save one cleared away, the floor swept clear of the filthy rushes that had covered it before. A large, heavy man with a pockmarked face and thin beard sat at the table, one meaty hand wrapped around a silver goblet, a plate piled with food nearby. *"You are a silver tongue,"* he said in Carthian.

"Yes," Allen replied.

"What languages do you know?"

"Harken. Carthian. Tricemorien."

The man grunted and smacked the table. "Sit." He motioned to the men holding Allen, who unlocked his manacles and shoved him forward.

Allen walked over to the table, resting his hands on it as he sat, grateful to have the weight of the manacles off his wrists for however long it lasted.

With another piggish grunt, the man slapped a stack of papers on the table. Not the same papers they'd taken from Allen, but he supposed they knew what those had been. At a glance the writing appeared to be gibberish, nonsensical informal Harken interspersed with other languages, like a student silver tongue had gotten bored and written an essay in as many different languages as he could manage, but gotten everything wrong.

Code, obviously. Papers taken from the ship survivors? Stolen from elsewhere? Whatever they were, the Carthians believed them important, and thought Allen could figure out what they said.

"This is gibberish," he finally said. *"I don't know most of these languages."*

"You will figure out what you can," the man said.

Allen looked down at them, skimmed over the papers again. *"I told you the languages I know, and there are at least six—no, seven—here. Even if I knew them, there's no way I could break a code like this. I'm not that skilled a silver tongue. My job is to translate Tricemorien contracts into Harken."*

The man grunted and gave a mean little smile. *"I think you lack motivation, and I can provide that."* He snapped his fingers. *"Take him to the yard. Ten will suffice for now. Then let him rest, and in the morning we'll see if he's changed his mind."*

"Ten what?" Allen asked, though he had a terrible, gut-twisting feeling he knew.

The two men who'd brought him downstairs stepped forward and dragged him to his feet, and around them the other Carthians laughed, low and mean, watching him go and idly betting on how long he would last.

As they dragged him across the hall to the door at the back, the distant crack of a whip confirmed his fears. At least it was cold; that would numb some of the pain, eventually. He already knew how to endure the rest.

But that didn't stop him from crying as they stripped him to the waist and chained him to the post.

CHAPTER TEN

Sarrica threw down his pen and buried his head in his hands, closed his eyes and silently begged any god that might be listening to please make his damned head stop hurting. The letters and numbers in front of him refused to hold still and make sense. His breakfast had wound up in the chamber pot and he'd given up any further thoughts of food. He had barely slept the past couple of days, between Bellen being sick and staying up late to tackle the work that had been neglected while he was with her.

He'd postponed more meetings than he cared to think about; half the palace wanted to kill him and the other half wanted to make him suffer first. The only person who greeted him with genuine friendliness was Tara. Even Lesto was so frayed at the edges he was probably contemplating murder. Or retirement.

And despite their efforts, Nyla was getting sick right alongside Bellen, who still hadn't recovered, which meant Sarrica was going to have two sick, cranky children in his rooms at all hours, crying for stories and needing to be soothed, and how could he possibly tell them he had work to do?

All he wanted was to take his powder and sleep for several hours, pretend that everything would be well when he woke up. Rene and Allen would be back, he could right his wrongs, marry the man before he had the sense to refuse, and have someone who could help him run the damned empire that suddenly seemed to be falling down around him.

Mercy of the Pantheon, he hoped Allen, Rene, and the others were doing well.

He jumped as the door slammed open, stared at Myra's pale face and wide, frightened eyes. "Come now."

Sarrica didn't waste time asking for an explanation. Abandoning his desk, he followed Myra out of the office, sparing a brief look for the wide-eyed, trembling soldier who must have brought Myra whatever news had him so shaken. They passed through the antechamber and into the hall.

Where they stopped short and watched as two guards approached practically carrying a woman wearing a blood-soaked Dragon tunic. Her face was a mess of cuts and bruises, and the rest of her was even worse. She was walking between the two guards holding her up, but only barely.

Fear set Sarrica's heart to pounding against his ribs. The sound of pounding feet briefly distracted him only because he recognized Lesto's tread as he came up from behind them and stopped as he reached Sarrica's side. "Jac!" Lesto burst out, surging forward as the guards and Jac reached them.

Jac looked up and drew a breath that looked painful. She met Sarrica's eyes, and in a cracked voice said, "Gorden Bells is a traitor. The Dragons have been slaughtered. I don't know if anyone survived. Allen—"

She passed out, sagging heavily between the guards still holding her up.

"Get her to the healing ward," Sarrica barked. "Lesto, bring me Gorden Bells *now.*"

Lesto was already running down the hall. "Fathoms Deep! All to me!" Along the length of the hallway, all the Fathoms Deep guards left their posts to take up position behind him. Lesto whipped around at the end of the hall. "Sarrica, get in your damned office and stay there." He pointed to two of the guards closest to him. "Guard His Majesty. No one enters his private office until I return."

"Yes, Commander." The guards walked quickly back down the hall to stand with Sarrica.

Hands clenched into tight fists, Sarrica returned to his private inner office. One guard stepped inside; the other remained outside, right in front of the door as it closed.

Sarrica's head throbbed worse than ever, but he ignored it in favor of focusing on his rage. Gorden Bells—the bastard who had seemed so helpful, had cried over his friends, his brother. Even Lesto had believed him, accepted the explanation as to why he had been so entangled in two distinct, but probably not unrelated events. *Damn* it. Damn him for being such a fucking fool.

A knock came at the door and Sarrica whipped around. The door opened a moment later and the guard outside motioned to him. Sarrica crossed to the door and saw Myra standing just outside.

"Majesty, Sergeant Jac is in the healing ward, and Master Bettelma says that while she will be some time recovering, she should recover. Master Bettelma will send more information once he has it and will notify you when Sergeant Jac is awake and strong enough to talk."

"Thank you, Myra," Sarrica replied and went back into his office, reluctantly sat down and stared at the piles of work on his desk.

He hated his stupid box of an office, the lack of

windows and natural light, the irritating glow of the many lamps required to keep the place from feeling like a tomb. Papers upon papers were piled on the desk, which was three times more crowded than usual. Even during the busiest times of the year he usually managed to stay a bit more in control of his work than this.

Heaving a sigh, Sarrica tried to focus. As before, though, nothing would make sense. His head was too strained, and now he had anger and fear drumming down upon it.

And if he dared to think about—

Too late.

Sarrica closed his eyes, splayed one hand over his face. Jac had said the Three-headed Dragons had been killed. She had no idea if there were other survivors. What had she tried to say about Allen? If they had marked Allen as a civilian, the Carthians might have spared him. There was no telling with Cartha. Their moods and whims were as changeable as the wind, if not more so.

He looked up when the door opened and stared at Lesto, who said, "We have him; he's awaiting us downstairs."

"Empty my office; lock it down."

"Already done," Lesto said as he motioned to the two guards. "Guard the main door. Nobody comes in. If they try, disable and detain them."

"Yes, Commander."

Lesto waited until they had gone, then pulled out his keys and led the way to the secret passage entrance.

Sarrica remained silent until they were in the passage and the door locked behind them. "Lesto, do you think Rene..."

"I don't know," Lesto said, voice breaking at the end. He closed his eyes, but tears escaped anyway. Sarrica stepped in close and hugged him tightly. After a moment, Lesto pulled away. "I think he may be alive, if I am right in some of my suppositions. But I don't dare hope I am correct, not until we've spoken with Bells. I can't believe that fucking *rat*—"

"We'll make him regret it," Sarrica said. "Let's go."

Nodding, Lesto turned and swept off down the passageway, murderous intent in every hard, jangling step.

They stepped out of the secret passage into an empty hallway. Torches flickered behind thick, heavy glass, struggling to cast more than dull, distorted light.

Sarrica hated the dungeons; they were dank and depressing. His mother had always believed that prisoners deserved better treatment, that improved quality of cells, food, and so forth given to them would make a world of difference. Sarrica's father and grandfather had always ignored her, but it was something he had taken to heart. His first step had been to institute the program that let convicted criminals work off their time in exchange for a full pardon. They were called pardon sentences, and there pardon sites all over the kingdom. One of the best was Fathoms Deep. Unfortunately, the pardon sentences were the only change he'd so far been able to implement. The rest of his plans kept waiting for him to find the time, one more thing on a very long list of items that he feared would never be completed.

He followed Lesto down the hall, where they turned left to go into the deeper parts of the dungeon, the ones that did not even get torches, just lanterns that the guards brought when they checked on the rare prisoner dangerous enough to merit what was typically called Shadow Row.

Two Fathoms Deep guards stood outside a door at the end of the hall, each of them nearly as big as the door. "Majesty, Commander," they greeted. "The prisoner has been quiet—almost too quiet."

"Hopefully that means he'll cooperate," Sarrica said and motioned for them to unlock the door.

Lesto picked up the lantern that was on the floor nearby, drew a dagger, and led the way into the cell. Gorden Bells had been chained to the far wall, strung up with his limbs so far apart and tightly secured that moving was near-impossible. The only thing that gave him respite was the small block that stuck out of the wall to give him someplace to rest his weight.

Not all prisoners were that lucky.

"I'll give you this," Sarrica said, staying against the far wall, folding his arms across his chest. "You're a superb liar."

"I don't know what you're talking about," Bells said, and he did look perfectly terrified, right down to tears falling down his cheeks. The guards had stripped him of all but his breeches, and even those hung loose on his hips where the guards had removed them to search for hidden pockets and put them back on sloppily.

Lesto stepped in close. "Let's have done with the theatrics. A Three-headed Dragon told us you are the traitor."

"Traitor? I'm just a clerk!" The words broke on a sob.

"Perhaps I'm not being clear," Lesto said coldly. "The Three-headed Dragons have been slaughtered, save the one woman who made it back alive to tell us about you. Among the dead is the silver tongue sent with them—Prince Allen Telmis, High Consort Presumptive."

That bled the color from Bells' cheeks. "What are you talking about? Prince Allen would never be permitted—"

"Funny thing is, he's near to being the second most powerful man in the empire," Sarrica replied. "He doesn't need anyone's permission to do as he pleases. Now, you can tell me everything, or we can extract the information bit by bit, and I may just let Rhodes and Amorlay have the first pieces."

Lesto stepped back, but he kept the dagger in his hand ready and easy to see. "Let's start with something simple: why did you send the Three-headed Dragons off to die?"

For a moment, Bells' face was set in lines of protest—but then he seemed to shatter like a dropped glass. "They weren't supposed to kill them. I told them Captain Arseni could identify Prince Morant. I thought they'd grab him and leave the others alone. If I had known about Prince Allen..."

The man was entirely too good at lying, but Sarrica thought the regret over Allen's death was actually genuine, even past the fact that it guaranteed Bells would be executed.

"You would have still betrayed everyone, but you would have saved him?" Lesto demanded. "Spare me. So you colluded with Cartha and Benta to bring down Korlow. Bells is a minor barony, and most of your money is made from your merchant ties. You own several warehouses, ships, and wagon trains from what I recall. So Benta must be offering you money, power? Hoping to get your hands clean of trade once and for all, get yourself a title? Is that it?"

"You don't know anything about it," Bells said bitterly.

Sarrica dropped his arms, braced his hands on his hips. "Is it just you? Or is your family tangled in this as well?"

"Just me."

"They're being arrested anyway," Lesto said. "You killed your brother, didn't you? What I don't understand is why you killed Lady Quell and Lady Laria."

That genuine regret flickered across Bells' face again, but it was gone in the next heartbeat. "My brother figured out what I was doing, so I killed him. But that caused other problems. I needed to deliver some papers to a contact, but I couldn't get out of the palace, not without drawing attention to myself. Quell and Laria had been muttering about running away for months. I just nudged them toward it, which wasn't hard in light of my brother's funeral. They agreed to deliver the papers for me. I played it like something I was doing to get one of my siblings out of trouble. It should have been a simple matter, I don't know what happened or why it went wrong. I don't!" He repeated, screaming the words when Lesto approached with the dagger, pressed it to his bare skin, and drew a thin trickle of blood. "That's all. They were meant to be the messenger. Nothing should have happened. I *liked* them, however stupid they could be."

"Where are they?" Lesto asked in a voice as soft as a sword sliding from its sheath.

"I don't know," Bells said. The dagger made another nick. "I mean it! I'm pretty sure they're dead.

If one of them survived, then they're not able to contact someone who can help them, which makes them as good as dead."

"What was in the papers?"

Bells shook his head. "They were encoded; I never figured out what they said. I'm a good silver tongue but not that good. I was ordered to hand them off to a runner in the city. That's all I know."

"Who gave the papers to you?"

"I don't know! I never see their faces. They were left in my room. I wasn't supposed to open them and look, but I did. It was all gibberish to me. Then I got stuck and had to convince Quell and Laria to take the papers. It should have been simple!"

Lesto snorted. "Espionage is never simple. It's tedious, which is why everyone makes mistakes. Do have further orders? Who gives them to you?"

"I have no orders right now. They come by way of envelopes delivered while I'm asleep or out of my room. The only direct interactions I have are when I hand the envelopes off to a contact in the city, and it's a different person every time."

"Someone had to convince you to do this," Lesto said. "Who convinced you to become a spy?"

"A man, heavy Carthian accent. I only met him a few times and never saw him again after I started taking orders." Bitterness slipped out with those words, and Sarrica wondered how much of those meetings had involved fucking. How much of convincing Bells to turn traitor had involved seducing him. "He gave a name, Keesho, but I doubt it's real."

Lesto grunted. "Now is the time to volunteer every remaining scrap of information in that head of yours."

"Will it spare my life?"

"No," Sarrica said. "You are directly responsible for the deaths of Prince Allen and several Three-headed Dragons, including my brother-in-law, since they will undoubtedly kill him once they have what they wanted. You are guilty of treason. You are also guilty of *murdering your own brother*, in case you've forgotten about that. It won't be hard to charge you with something regarding Lady Quell and Lady Laria, either. There are many ways you could die, and I will have the final say in which one is picked. There are also many things the law permits me to do to your remaining family." Not that he would hurt them if they innocent of treason, but he was happy to let Gorden worry about it. "We'll let you hang there and ponder it." He rapped on the door, and a moment later it swung open.

Once it was locked again, Sarrica looked at the guards. "No one comes down the hall save Lesto and I unless they come bearing a note from me. If they do not offer it, and insist on being here, incapacitate them and send for us. See that Bells doesn't do anything stupid."

"Yes, Your Majesty," the soldiers chorused.

Sarrica turned and walked off, electing at the last minute to go by way of the public halls rather than the secret passages. "Summon Rhodes and Amorlay. They deserve to know about this. Release General Vren and inform the Gaulden set of the real killer—but do not share more details than strictly necessary. I am going to the healing ward."

"I'll join you in a little while. After I take care of everything else, I want to speak to the Dragons myself," Lesto said. Out in the main hallway, he gestured sharply to three of the Fathoms Deep lining it. "He never leaves your sight. Sarrica, I mean it. Where there is one rat, there are many, and we clearly will not find them until too late. Stay close to Fathoms Deep."

"I will. Be careful, Lesto. I'm not the only one they'll come after."

"No, but one of us is wearing armor and hasn't gone soft," Lesto said as he walked away.

Sarrica rolled his eyes but smiled as the guards did a poor job of not laughing. "Come along, then. We're going to the healing ward." He turned back to the remaining guards. "Locate a servant. Send them to fetch Lord Tara to my office at once."

"Yes, Your Majesty."

People moved quickly out of Sarrica's way as they walked through the palace. Anyone not put off by the trio of guards took one look at his face and found something else to do. Whispers rose up in his wake; no doubt everyone had already heard of the Jac's dramatic arrival and the hostile arrest of Gorden Bells.

His head throbbed and stabbed hard enough he was feeling nauseous again, but Sarrica ignored it. He did not have time for a headache; it would have to wait its turn like everyone else.

The healing ward was unusually quiet when they arrived, though it was as crowded as ever. Sarrica looked around, but saw nothing unusual—except perhaps the wide-eyed looks everyone was giving him. Well, fair enough. The last time he'd been in the healing ward, it was to view his husband's body.

Unballing the fists his hands had unconsciously formed, Sarrica strode onward through the enormous main wing of the healing ward, continuing through the wide double doors at the back that led to the private rooms, with offices and the like up a flight of stairs.

"Majesty," an old but firm voice said.

Sarrica slowed, looked toward the source, and saw Master Healer Bettelma standing in a doorway.

"You have excellent timing, Your Majesty. I was just about to send someone to you. Sergeant Jac is awake and insists on seeing you."

"Thank you." Sarrica strode into the room, indicating with a gesture that everyone else was to get out. He sat down on the stool vacated by Bettelma and looked at Jac, who was propped up against the headboard, but by the tightness to her face and the sweat gleaming on her skin, the effort was costing her. "I'm glad you survived," Sarrica said softly. "Thank you for working so hard to get here."

Jac gave a shaky laugh and covered her face with one hand. "Those bastard Carthians nearly had me. I swear they get nastier every month. I hate to say it, Your Majesty, I hate it so much, but Prince Allen was right. If he'd been with me, we both would have died. I could not have kept him alive and beaten them off, and he would not have survived alone."

Sarrica's chest clenched. "Prince Allen is alive?"

"I don't know," Jac said, and the hope withered and died, leaving Sarrica more miserable than ever. At least Rene was still alive, but if Sarrica let himself feel that relief he would not focus. "He was when I fled, and I like to think even Carthians would not slaughter a helpless civilian, but I cannot trust to that. Rene ordered me to protect him at all costs, and I tried, Your Majesty, I swear. But Prince Allen ordered me to escape without him because it was more important the message reach you and he was afraid he'd hinder that."

Sarrica rested a hand gently on the general vicinity of Jac's good knee, could feel Jac's fever-warm skin through layers of blankets. "You did the best you could, I have every faith in that. Tell me exactly what happened."

Jac nodded, licked her lips. "We were breaking camp when they attacked. They killed Hedge first. I grabbed Allen and fled into the woods as I'd been ordered. Two riders came after us. I killed them with firebombs."

Sarrica stifled a grimace. Firebombs were used by many of the mercenaries, and occasionally by the army, but they were the hallmark of the Three-headed Dragons who'd invented them: balls filled with what looked like red paint but was in fact a potent mix of chemicals that amounted to liquid fire. He'd very rarely seen anyone survive them, and when they did there was usually heavy scarring and amputation involved.

"We could have escaped then but Prince Allen refused to flee. He was determined to look through the damned saddlebags. I don't know what he saw. He just looked at a flask and some papers, some stupid, uh—" She frowned, said a word in Tricemorien. Sarrica couldn't speak anything but Harken, nothing worth remarking upon, at least, but he knew a few words—including that one. Nyle had hated dried grapes. Sarrica enjoyed them baked or cooked in other foods but hated to eat them on their own. "That's when he told me to go on alone, to report back to you at all costs that Gorden Bells is the traitor. I obeyed. I wish I could have saved him. Any of them." She closed her eyes, dropped her head into her hands.

"You did the best you could, and you made it back

here to tell us what happened. Your comrades would be happy and proud to know that. Prince Allen would not have ordered you to leave him behind if he did not believe it was of utmost importance." Sarrica rested his hand on the back of Jac's neck, then rose and went to the door, beckoning Bettelma to return. "Take care of her; spare nothing." He motioned to the waiting guards and strode from the healing hall and back to his private office.

Lord Tara waited in the antechamber, standing like a man who was fighting an urge to pace. "Your Majesty, I heard—is Rene—?" His eyes were already red and raw, and fresh tears fell down his face. "Is it true Rene was killed?"

"I don't know," Sarrica said quietly. "We have reason to believe they may have taken him alive, but I cannot promise it. Come with me." As they strode into the main office, he beckoned to Myra. "Cancel my whole day. If anyone has the nerve to complain, put them at the bottom of the list of new appointments to make."

"Yes, Majesty," Myra said and spun away to start cracking out orders to the others.

Sarrica led Tara into his private office and motioned for him to sit. He went over to the cabinet against the far wall, beside and behind his desk, and poured a measure of brandy into one of the many glasses on a lower shelf. He carried the glass over to Tara. "Drink, because you're not going to like what I'm about to say."

Tara eyed him warily then tossed the brandy back like it was water and set the glass down on the desk with a hard clack. "All right, Your Majesty. Let's have it said."

"Prince Allen went with Rene and his Dragons. We have reason to believe Rene is alive, but Allen is very likely dead."

"Oh, no," Tara said, fresh tears falling. "He... I liked him. He was so kind. He said I was the first real friend he'd ever had. He seemed like he would do well here. I'm so sorry, Your Majesty."

Sarrica shook his head, shoved back emotions he could not yet afford to feel. "I am going to Cartha to rip those bastards into pieces. If Rene is alive, I will bring him back to you. While Lesto and I are gone, however, you must take care of everything here for me."

"What!" Tara jumped out of his seat. "You cannot—"

"Sit down," Sarrica said calmly.

Tara sat.

"We have found a traitor in a place we did not expect, and right now I cannot trust anyone else in this wretched place. But you—you I can trust, or at least I hope so, or Pantheon's mercy, we are all doomed."

"I'm not certain you should be trusting me with so much when I'm far from trained to it, but you can trust my loyalty, Your Majesty," Tara said quietly. "You've always been kind and tolerant of my eccentric behavior."

"You cause no harm and by all accounts are good to people, even when they do not return that kindness," Sarrica said and added more quietly, "Rene loves you. I trust his judgment even if I did not already trust you. Until I return, you are Acting High King. I will have Myra draw the papers up and sign them before I leave."

Tara stood again and bowed. "Yes, Majesty. I will...

go prepare, I suppose."

Sarrica removed one of the rings on his finger, a small signet that bore his personal crest. He tossed it to Tara. "There. Wear it. Let's see them gossip meanly about you now."

Smiling even as he still sniffled and cried, Tara slid the ring onto the first finger of his right hand.

Scrubbing at his face, Sarrica stood and strode out of the office, Tara close behind him. Beckoning to two of the Fathoms Deep standing nearby, Sarrica said, "Guard him as you would guard me. Fathoms Deep does not leave his side until I or Lesto commands otherwise."

"Yes, Your Majesty," the guards said.

Sarrica nodded and next called to Myra and Emerella, relating all they would need to know before he left and what was to be done and not done in his absence. By the time he was finished and had dismissed them along with everyone else in the room, Lesto's familiar tread warned of his arrival.

"Lord Tara," he greeted after closing the door. "I assume Sarrica told you Rene might be alive."

Tara's brows rose, mouth opening slightly. "I hadn't realized you..." He shook his head. "Pardon, Commander. Yes, His Majesty has informed me. I shall leave him to tell you what else he's done."

Lesto watched Tara and his bodyguards leave, and turned back to Sarrica when the door had closed. He narrowed his eyes. "You are not leaving this fucking palace, Sarrica. I'm not kidding. Do not give me that look."

"I'm the High King; I'll do whatever I want, including giving you looks and going to Cartha."

"Not if I drop your worthless carcass in the ocean,"

Lesto hissed. "You're too important and you know it, check your Pantheon-damned ego and stay here!"

"No," Sarrica said, shoving Lesto back when he got too close. "It's my fault Allen is dead. If I had—it doesn't matter, I can't undo what I did. I *will* go up there myself and do whatever it takes to put an end to this mess. It's the closest I can come to making amends. We'll bring Rene home and hopefully get Prince Morant to safety as well." He raked a hand through his hair. "This matter has spiraled out of control, and I have every right and reason to take care of it personally from here on out. I will drop *your* carcass in the ocean if you insist on arguing with me."

Lesto shoved him hard, sent him slamming into a nearby desk then strode past him to the bar on the far side of the room. "You better hope to the gods you come back alive, you worthless piece of shit."

"Fuck you," Sarrica replied. "What have you got to tell me?"

"We rooted out a servant who was likely involved, mostly by dumb luck. I went to see Seyn, who was able to figure out who we wanted. We found him in his room, throat slit, gambling slips conveniently piled on the floor next to him."

Sarrica grunted. "That's a thin cover."

"Even Seyn thought that seemed suspicious," Lesto said. "I'm still not certain what secrets were stolen, but if I had to guess, I would say it's the location of the troops lying in wait to help free Korlow, or the chain of spies we have to keep us apprised of goings on up north. Either way, it's not good if they break the code. Our encoders are good, but no code is absolutely unbreakable."

He took a sip of wine before continuing. "I've

ordered people to keep searching the city for Quell and Laria. I've arranged the troops going with us into Cartha, including the nastiest mercenaries on the premises. In addition to the imperial army and Fathoms Deep we'll be accompanied by Penance Gate, Blood Night, and Last Breath. You get to explain to Captain Chass of Penance Gate why his brother is in Cartha." He shook his head, stared into his wine, suddenly looking twice his age. "If I were you, I would not tell him that Prince Allen is probably already dead."

"I am clinging to a faint, stupid hope that he is not," Sarrica said. "If I believe anything else—" He curled his hand into a fist, slammed it on the desk. Pushing away from it, he jerked his head toward the door. "Come on, Commander. It's time to prepare for war. If the Three-headed Dragons demand to come along, permit it."

"Yes, Your Majesty." Lesto drained the few sips of wine left in his glass and followed Sarrica out of the office. "What did you need to tell me about Tara, by the way?"

"He is standing in for me while I'm gone."

Lesto groaned. "Why would you be that cruel? Rene will kill you."

"As long as he's alive to try, I don't care. Come on." Increasing his pace, Sarrica headed for his room, calling for someone to have his personal servants summoned and his armor brought from storage.

CHAPTER ELEVEN

Allen was in so much pain, he couldn't even feel the separate agonies. His whole body was one giant ball of misery. He lay face down on a mat on the floor, too exhausted to cry, too afraid to sleep, too wrung out to do more than lie there and drift in and out.

He could hear Rene's ragged breaths nearby, a cough that would turn deadly if it wasn't treated soon.

The door opened, and the healer came in to treat his back with fresh snow, murmuring in broken Carthian, but Allen did not have the energy to make sense of the words. Finally the man drifted away to cluck and mutter over Rene. Allen was fairly certain he heard something about fingers. Something had happened earlier, hadn't it? They'd broken one of Rene's hands, or part of it, or something.

Another form filled the doorway, though all Allen saw were the shadows they cast, part of a dark shape filling the doorway. "*Captain wants to know when he can talk,*" the man said in Carthian.

"*I don't know. He's lucky to be alive at the rate the captain is beating him. It needs to stop if he wants the man to be useful. If he enjoys whipping so much, he should hire some whore and stop breaking prisoners.*"

"*Shut up, old man. Finish treating them, tell us when that one can translate the papers.*"

"*Yeah, yeah. Go away and let me work.*"

The healer resumed muttering as he continued to treat Rene. This time Allen paid attention and managed to catch snippets that made the healer's opinion of the Captain and his thugs very clear. He tried to keep listening, but eventually drifted out again.

He stirred when a heavy but gentle hand rested on his head. "Here, you must lift up enough to drink," the healer said. "You are not supposed to have it, but I do not care anymore. Drink, drink. Little sips. There you go."

"Thank you," Allen whispered.

The man said something he didn't understand, and then left.

Rene groaned a few minutes later. "Doing all right?"

"As well as I can, I guess," Allen replied. "How is your hand?"

"Does it really matter?" Rene sighed. "It could be mostly fixed with the right care. Even if it's useless, I will still be better off than you."

Allen didn't reply. His back was a mess. Healing would take weeks, if not months. Assuming he was ever allowed to heal, which he doubted. If he didn't agree to translate the documents soon they would just kill him and find another silver tongue.

But he would hold out as long as he could, damn it. Give Jac time to get home and bring reinforcements. Allen assumed that was what would happen, anyway. He really didn't know. Would it be better to let them die and make new plans to get into Benta and get Prince Morant out? No, that wouldn't work. Since he and Rene were still at the fortress, that meant the Bentans were bringing the prisoners to them. So he had no idea what Sarrica would do if Jac made it back.

He should be able to figure it out, but the pain

made it almost impossible to concentrate on his thoughts long enough to untangle them.

"If we live, we'll have to get you a tattoo—assuming you want to endure further pain," Rene said quietly.

Allen dragged his eyes open, stared across the dim space at Rene, who looked as broken and ragged as him. It had only been two days. Three days? Possibly more, he had lost track. It felt like a month had passed. "Like the one on your thigh? The dragon?"

"Yeah."

"But I'm not a Dragon."

"You are."

Eyes too heavy to keep open, and stinging with sudden tears, Allen let his eyes fall shut again. "I think I could handle a tattoo."

Silence fell, and a warm, floating sensation curled through him, dulling the pain and pulling him into sleep. Whatever the healer had given him, Allen was eternally grateful.

The sound of shouting roused him some time later, pulling him out of a warm cocoon of oblivion into damp, rancid darkness laced with heavy grogginess.

Allen jerked slightly as the door was pulled open and someone strode inside. "Oh, my fucking gods!" Someone dropped down to kneel between them, and Allen noted the woman's blood red tunic, the black gashes embroidered across the front in a way that made it look like some beast had raked her chest open and found only darkness. The crest of Penance Gate. "Captain Rene! And this—!" The woman stood and turned. "Get the High King! Tell him Prince Allen and Captain Rene are alive! Do it now, run! And get me a healer, or I'll remove your balls. Go!"

The woman dropped to her knees again. "Prince Allen, can you hear me?"

"Yes," Allen whispered, licking blood from his cracked, dried lips. Had she really said High King? Sarrica had come? That was dangerous, though. He shouldn't be putting himself at risk.

"You're safe now. We've taken the fortress. All the Carthians are in custody. We'll take care of you, Highness."

Allen whispered an acknowledgement as the drugs pulled him back under.

Some unknown time later voices pulled him out of sleep once more. Familiar, that voice was familiar...

"I will tear those bastards to pieces with my bare hands," Sarrica growled. It really was him. Allen's breath hitched as he watched a large pair of boots moved closer. He forced his eyes to stay open, fighting a fresh wave of exhaustion as he watched Sarrica kneel, and managed to look up enough to stare into Sarrica's face. The fingertips of Sarrica's large, warm hand, still encased in supple leather, touched his cheek. It really was Sarrica. He'd come personally to rescue them. Allen tried to speak, but all that came out was a thin cough. Sarrica's voice was soft, surprisingly gentle, as he said, "Rest, Highness. All is well now. I'm sorry we took so long."

"You came..." Allen whispered, but sleep took him back before he could say anything else.

When he woke again, it was to a somewhat clearer head.

He could also feel sunlight on his skin, and the air was filled with the smell of fresh bread and roasting meat. He was lying on the softest bed he'd ever known. Allen slowly dragged his eyes open. His breath hitched when he saw Sarrica fast asleep in a large chair next to the bed, slumped over a stack of papers... Or what was left of them, the rest having spilled across the floor.

"Sa—" He broke off, voice coming out a thin, hoarse whisper. Allen licked his dry lips and tried to leverage himself up on his elbows, but the effort left him weak and shaky. His back hurt, but it was distant, like there was a thin wall between him and the pain. Now that he was awake, he could feel the fuzziness, the floating sensation. "Sarrica," he tried again, but the word came out barely audible, and Sarrica remained fast asleep.

Just as well. Even addled from pain and medication, Allen knew better than to act so familiar. He and Sarrica were a long way from being on a first name basis with each other. He looked away from Sarrica, spied a glass of water on the table by the bed. He reached out and tried to lift it. After a couple of attempts, he finally managed it, lifting the glass to his lips and taking a couple of tiny sips.

Setting it back on the table, however, proved more than he could manage. Allen cringed as it fell, shattering into pieces on the hard stone floor.

Sarrica jerked to his feet, crying out, hand going to his left hip—for his sword. Allen swallowed. "Sorry."

Whipping around, Sarrica stared. He relaxed, shoulders slumping, and dropped back in his seat. "You're awake. I was beginning to think the healer had been a little too generous with the dosage. We had to knock you out pretty heavily to properly treat your back."

His eyes looked bruised, like he'd barely slept, and he obviously had not trimmed his beard for a few days.

Hair hung in his eyes, messy and limp. Nothing at all like the sneering, dismissive king who had made it clear he saw nothing worthwhile when he looked at Allen.

Sarrica frowned. "Are you all right? Should I summon a healer?"

"N-no. I'm f-fine," Allen managed. "Rene?"

"Being treated across the hall. They spent hours on his hand, and he's sick enough he won't be out of bed anytime soon, but the healers say that with medicine and rest he'll be fine. They even think they can save his hand, at least mostly." He opened his mouth, hesitated, then finally closed it. Strange to see Sarrica so uncertain.

Allen swallowed and lay back down because staying propped on his elbows was simply too exhausting. "Jac?"

"Battered but recovering back in the palace," Sarrica replied. "Feel up to some broth?"

"Ugh, not broth," Allen said with a groan.

Warmth flushed through him as Sarrica laughed. He was finding it increasingly difficult to believe the man beside him was the same man who had thrown him out of court.

Sarrica pushed out of the chair and crouched on the floor to start cleaning up the pieces of shattered glass. "I once got sick as a child, was in bed for nearly a whole month. The only thing I was permitted was a thin broth and the occasional bits of waterlogged bread. It was months before I could stand the taste of bread or soup."

"I definitely prefer things that do not come in broth," Allen said.

Chuckling again, Sarrica stood up and carried the

broken glass over to a trash bin across the room. "You must have hated eating gruel."

"It wasn't as awful as I had feared," Allen admitted. "But I am glad I do not have to eat it regularly."

Sarrica smiled as he resumed his seat. "Good food is definitely something soldiers never get enough of. Speaking of food, *are* you up to eating? I will try to ensure the broth is not terrible, but I fear only so much can be done, and the healers insist you shouldn't be trying anything solid quite yet, with having to lie still and all the drugs that have been poured into you."

"Oh, I'm familiar with the delights of recovery," Allen said with a sigh.

"Yes, the healers brought that to my attention," Sarrica said quietly, tone and expression growing somber. "I will not pry into private matters, but I admit I am alarmed that this is not the first time you've been whipped."

Allen cringed. Of course they'd noticed, of course they'd told Sarrica. Why couldn't they have just left it alone? Hadn't he suffered enough? Sarrica's opinion of him was already low, and made worse by seeing him so weak and pathetic, but to dredge up Allen's past and compound it all? Sarrica was clearly being kind to him while he was bedridden, but how long after Allen was recovered would he return to being cold and derisive?

Or had his stupid, reckless, selfish plan succeeded? If so, it didn't feel anything like a victory. Allen would rather return to Sarrica hating him, where everyone was alive, his back wasn't in shreds, and Rene's hand wasn't broken. "It's over. That's all that matters."

Sarrica nodded. "I'll have some broth brought. Maybe some wine that you're not allowed to have."

He winked and stood, started to turn away but abruptly turned back. "I'm a fool because I nearly forgot to mention that if you'd like a friendly face, your brother Chass is here. He was ecstatic to know you're alive, and utterly furious about the state in which we found you. He's taken particular delight in overseeing the prisoners."

"What!" Allen couldn't bite back a cry when his jerk of surprise caused sharp pain to flare across his back. Tears stung his eyes but he wiped them angrily away with the blanket beneath him. Since when did his stupid, worthless brother give a damn about him? Probably he just wanted to look good in front of Sarrica.

Alarm cutting across his face, Sarrica sat down and reached out. This time, instead of pausing and withdrawing, he hesitantly rested his hand lightly on top of one of Allen's. "What's wrong?"

"Not—" Allen swallowed when the word came out rough, tried again. "Not Chass."

Sarrica's brow furrowed. "You do not want to see your brother? I thought family would..."

A bitter laugh slipped out even as old fears shivered through Allen and woke more pain. "You want to know why I bear the scars of previous whippings? Because growing up my brothers Chass and Manda thought I was a weak, lazy, selfish brat who sat around doing nothing all day. They took it upon themselves to give me 'real' lessons. My eldest brother eventually put an end to it, but not for several years. I want Chass nowhere near me, even if asking that makes me sound like a songbird."

Emotions flickered across Sarrica's face—anger, sadness, regret. He nodded. "I'll convey your desires.

I'm sorry for causing you distress. I'll return shortly, but if you need anything before then, ring that bell and someone will come. There are several Three-headed Dragons stationed in the hall who vehemently refuse to hand over guarding your room to anyone else and are instead taking all the shifts themselves."

"That seems strange. Why are they doing that?"

Sarrica laughed and winked again, then turned and strode from the room. The door closed softly on his calling out to people further down the hall, and Allen was left to brood in the quiet room.

Stupidly, he started to cry. Damn it. Whatever his original selfish motivations, he had truly wanted to help the Dragons rescue Prince Morant. He'd wanted to write their letters. Had promised to help them learn to write their names and other basics. Had secretly hoped that meant they would still talk to him when they were all back in Harken and no longer really needed him.

Instead he was bloody and broken and crying. The people he'd tentatively begun to regard as comrades, another thing he'd never had before, were dead. Regena. Hedge. Mixx and Handel. Wystie and Saral. He hadn't even gotten to tell them goodbye.

Pantheon be merciful, he could still see Hedge and the arrow punching through her throat if he closed his eyes for too long.

He wiped his tears on the soft blanket beneath his cheek and tried to think of something else. Like the fact that he really needed to piss, and he would quite literally rather die than have someone help him with that. If Sarrica offered, Allen was going to throw himself out a window.

Gritting his teeth, bracing for the pain, Allen slowly

shuffled and shifted his way to the edge of the bed. He carefully lowered his legs over the edge then rested a moment, ignoring the fresh tears, the burning agony breaking through the wall of potent drugs. He was probably due for a new dose, but he didn't want it almost as much as he did want it.

Taking a deep breath, bracing anew, Allen pushed himself upright. After the pain and nausea eased, he slowly let go of the bed completely. Turned around slowly. Took a tentative step. It wasn't fun, but it *was* manageable. Thankfully, the pisspot was close to the bed.

By the time he was finished with even that small task he was completely exhausted. Climbing back on the bed was nearly too difficult to manage.

At least he was back in place by the time the door opened again and a man in a Fathoms Deep tunic strode in. Allen didn't recognize him, though he did recognize the green and white armband that marked him as a healer. He carried a tray bearing a bowl, a cup, and a small glass bottle: broth, water, medicine. The sight was so familiar Allen wanted to sigh. Instead he stifled it and mustered a polite, "Thank you for tending me..."

"Trevail, Highness," Trevail replied with a smile as he set the tray on Sarrica's vacated chair. "This is probably a stupid question, but how are you feeling?"

Allen managed a faint smile. "I've felt better, but I have also felt worse. I would not object to more medicine if that's possible. I do not want to overuse it, given the side effects, but I've also found it's easier to sleep through the worst of the pain." He didn't care if admitting that made him sound weak. He could only endure so much pain to prove a stupid point, and he'd failed miserably at making it, so what did it really matter now?

"A small dose is certainly possible, Highness. It's good you seem familiar. So many are not and refuse to listen to my explanations and warnings, if you will pardon my saying so."

"Of course," Allen replied. "If you will help me sit up, I think I can manage that long enough to drink on my own."

Trevail frowned but gave a nod and slowly helped Allen to sit up. Wiping sweat from his brow, Allen accepted the bowl of broth Trevail held out and began to sip it. He gave it back after it was about half gone. "I do not think I should try more than that."

"You are a magnificent patient, Your Highness. I am going to use you as an example to shame everyone else into behaving."

Allen gave a soft huff of laughter. "I hope it helps."

A mischievous smile curved Trevail's mouth. "I think invoking your name may even convince the most difficult patient in the palace to cooperate from time to time."

"I would not count on that," Allen replied, "but you are the expert." He accepted the tiny medicine cup Trevail held out and quickly drank the thick, bitter tonic that filled it. He chased it with a few sips of water then gratefully lay down again. "Thank you."

"Thank *you*, Your Highness. Captain Rene has been speaking highly of you every chance he gets. Everyone is most impressed with what you've accomplished. Picked out a traitor because of a bag of dried grapes, and honestly, there are too many embellishments now for me to pick a favorite." His eyes were bright, crinkled at the edges. He winked and stood, gathering up the tray. "Get some more rest. In a few more days you should be able to walk around with minimal trouble. Ring the bell if you have need of anything." The mischievous smile returned. "I am surprised His Majesty has not returned; he's scarcely left your side since we found you. I suppose Commander Lesto was bound to abscond with him eventually. Pleasant dreams, Your Highness." He gave a graceful bow and left, closing the door quietly behind him.

Allen tried to stay awake, curiosity eating at him. What was Rene saying to everyone? Why had Sarrica clung so tightly to his side? Well, no, that was a stupid question. It would have caused Sarrica a world of trouble if Allen had died so soon after his arrival in Harken, killed in a place he never should have been.

Joining the Three-headed Dragons had been an exceptionally stupid thing to do, but he'd let wounded pride and foolish stubbornness convince him otherwise. If he'd died his parents would have been furious, outraged, and would have lashed out in brutal retaliation. Relations between Gaulden and the High Throne would have been tense for years, if not generations. His family would have lost the ties to the High Throne they had been anticipating, his kingdom the prestige of that connection—prestige they'd never had, being one of the southernmost kingdoms and easily ignored in favor of places like Tricemore and Selemea, which shared borders with Harken.

And there were so many other consequences that could have resulted from his death. All because he'd acted like a child, flounced off like a jilted lover. All the worse when the marriage was purely a matter of state. He should have remembered that and treated it like the business transaction it was instead of doing everything he was supposed to be smart enough not to do.

Sarrica must have been as aware of all of that as he had come personally to handle matters to minimize the fallout of what he must have believed was Allen's death. A smart move, really.

But though he was immensely relieved that he was alive and all those potential disasters would be avoided, mostly Allen felt only a heavy knot in the middle of his chest, pulling and twisting at his emotions, leaving him feeling thin and fragile. That moment when he'd believed Sarrica had come to his rescue was lodged in his memory, no matter how warped a memory it was. Sarrica had come to rescue Rene first and foremost, and to head off a political disaster if necessary. That's all Allen was in the end. Whatever he had hoped to accomplish with his stupid actions, he had most definitely failed.

He couldn't just give up, though. There had to be something he could do. Once he was well enough to move on his own he would work harder than ever to convince Sarrica that he was still worth marrying, could be a good High Consort despite his foolish actions.

Exhaustion washed over him like a tide, and Allen stopped fighting it, falling back into the sanctuary of drugged sleep.

When he woke again, it was dark save for the crackling fire. His back ached, but the medicine was still blocking the worst of the pain, which meant it was somewhat easier to slide out of bed to relieve himself. What time was it? How long had he slept?

"Is all well?" Came a rough, sleep-soaked voice that sent a brief hot tingle down Allen's spine that he should have been far too wounded and exhausted to feel. A large shadow came into view from the foot of the bed, a hand combing through tousled hair. "Are you all right?"

"F-fine," Allen stuttered, absently recalling he'd stuttered the same earlier. He was meant to be good with words, but around Sarrica his abilities seemed to fail him utterly. "Why—what—are you sleeping on the *floor?*"

"Yes?" Sarrica said. He cleared his throat, and the lovely roughness was gone when he added, "This is the only proper bed in the fortress, and I'm not sleeping in the hall where I have to listen to everyone snore and grunt and make obscene noises in their sleep. I am spoiled enough to avoid that whenever possible."

"You shouldn't be sleeping on the *floor,*" Allen replied.

Sarrica laughed and walked around the other side of the bed. The scratch and smell of a match filled the air, immediately followed by a small flicker of bright light. Sarrica lit the candle on the bedside table, and it was only then Allen recalled he was naked. Face hot, he crawled back into the bed as quickly as he could manage, which unfortunately was not quickly at all.

"You shouldn't be moving around alone," Sarrica said, smile fading into a frown.

"With greatest respect, Your Majesty, I am long accustomed to functioning on my own with a wounded back. The first few times, I did not even have the luxury of good medicine since I did not know how to ask for it without giving myself away."

"Why didn't you tell someone?"

"Tell someone?" Allen let out a single sharp, bitter laugh. "That would have just confirmed that I was as weak and pathetic as they thought. Just a stupid little songbird with no real value." That brought the weighted silence he'd anticipated, wanted, but victory didn't make him feel anything but miserable.

Finally Sarrica said, "I'm sorry. I wanted to say that when you were not lying in bed unable to go anywhere else, but I am. Even being High King doesn't excuse my behavior. For whatever little it is worth, I did not set out to be an ass every time we crossed paths. Even at the end, I meant to spare you having to side against your own people so soon after arriving in Harken. I conveyed that poorly."

Allen swallowed, taken aback. "I cannot say my behavior was any better, Your Majesty, especially at the last."

"Well, nobody else is having any trouble blaming me for everything," Sarrica said with a smile. "You may as well do the same. Are you up to enduring more broth? I tried to smuggle you wine, but Trevail and Lesto are being particularly stubborn, and I've not yet succeeded."

"That's probably for the best, though I admit I wouldn't mind the wine. The sooner the broth is drunk, the sooner it's gone."

Sarrica laughed and went to get it. Allen slowly sat up, pulling the blankets up to cover himself. "Here you are. I don't know if it's better or worse that it's gone cold. I can attempt to warm it over the fire if you like, but I fear you'll end up with no soup and an overcooked, irate High King." Allen laughed, and Sarrica grinned, looking like a pleased boy for a moment.

Damn it, this man was nothing at all like the High King back at the palace. This man acted like he didn't hate Allen, like marriage might still be a possibility. Allen was trying not to be stupid by getting his hopes up, but he had the sinking feeling that he was failing. "Speaking of irate, why are you so untroubled by sleeping on the floor? If somebody put my mother on the floor, they would beg to be sent to the Penance Realms to face punishment. I certainly did not enjoy sleeping on the damnable ground."

Sarrica shrugged and sat down in the chair by the bed that he'd been using when Allen first woke up. "I was a soldier for a long time, and I did not hold with enjoying every luxury while my men slept on cold, hard ground with not even campfires to warm them some nights. I joined the army when I was fifteen and joined Fathoms Deep a few years before my father grew ill and I had to resign. That is a lot of years spent sleeping on hard ground, in trees, against walls, or wherever else I was able to find a few minutes of rest..." Sarrica shrugged again, smiled briefly. "A floor in a warm, dry, well-made fortress is relatively comfortable by comparison."

Well no wonder he saw Allen as a songbird. Whatever Allen's strife, he'd always had a comfortable bed to retreat to at the end of the day. At worst, he'd spent a few days in a luxurious tent on the beach; even there he'd had a bed of sorts, far removed from the sand and rugs on which everyone else had slept. "It still feels wrong to be using your bed while you sleep on the floor, Your Majesty."

Sarrica's smile faded, replaced by hesitance. "You need not stand on such formality unless you insist upon it. I will, of course, happily respect your wishes, but you do have leave to call me Sarrica."

Maybe the engagement was still possible, after all.

Allen started to ask, but bit the question off. It wasn't the right time, in the dead of night, him so badly injured and Sarrica feeling guilty over it. He would not get what he wanted through such low means. He licked his lips, nodded. "Sarrica, then, and of course you can use my name. You were named for the High Queen, I assume?"

"Yes. My mother used to say that my father loved his great-great-grandmother more than her," Sarrica drawled. "I think she chose the name so he'd be forced to stop rhapsodizing about her, which he was."

Allen laughed. "In your father's defense, she was a wonderful High Queen."

"You should hear the stories not known to the public," Sarrica said with a snort. "Finish your broth, or I'll get yelled at in the morning and receive disappointed looks all day."

"Well, we can't have that," Allen said and finished the last few sips of broth. He started to ask more about what was happening in the fortress, but the words were overtaken by a yawn.

Sarrica chuckled. "May as well give in and sleep some more. We're lingering as long as we can to give you and Rene time to heal, but we must return to Harken in a few more days, and you will not be able to do much sleeping on the trip home."

"I believe you," Allen replied, unable to hide a wince. Shifting around carefully, he once more stretched out on the bed. His breath hitched when Sarrica fussed with the blankets and settled them more comfortably about his hips and legs.

"Sleep well," Sarrica said quietly. Before Allen could get his voice to cooperate, he vanished again to his place at the foot of the bed, leaving Allen with a pounding heart drumming in his ears, thoughts and emotions tumbling around in his head until exhaustion finally won out.

Chapter Twelve

"Is Prince Morant safe?" Allen asked. "I should have asked sooner..."

"I think you had enough on your mind." Sarrica looked up from the paperwork that had managed to find him even on top of a mountain when he knew very well he'd left it all behind in the palace. Sometimes he suspected people made up reports and lists and contracts just to aggravate him. "I do not know if he's safe, but we will be finding out shortly. Blood Night was sent out to locate the hostages and take them from the Bentans, and they returned last night. We are bringing up the Carthian captain now, letting him stew a bit. Under the watch of Penance Gate, who have a particular talent for being menacing." He made a face. "I'm sorry. I suppose you would know that better than anyone.

"Chass excels at being menacing, that is divine truth," Allen said. He lay stretched out on the bed, eyes closed. Though he'd been there the past few days, Sarrica still could not reconcile the quiet, fragile man on the bed with the sharp, frosty noble he'd thrown out of court.

Allen *should* still be that man: a politician safe at home playing courtly games that Sarrica would never have the patience to truly understand. It was Sarrica's fault he was here instead, too injured to leave his bed to do more than take a piss, crying quietly when he thought he was alone or that no one was paying attention. At least he would be on his feet soon, according to Trevail.

"If it gives you any satisfaction, the Carthians are going to be livid by the end of this meeting. I daresay their captain will be completely broken once the rage passes." Sarrica smiled as Allen opened his eyes. "Even I am capable of playing a game here and there."

"I wish I could bear witness," Allen said, "but I sense if I leave this bed Trevail will tie me to it."

Sarrica snorted and threw the paperwork aside, picked up the remarkably good mulled wine someone had managed to scrounge up. He had no idea where or how, but he knew when not to ask questions. "I know Lesto and Trevail like to boss the rest of us around, but you *are* High Consort Presumptive. If you want to be in attendance, even I cannot tell you otherwise."

Allen had closed his eyes again, and there was no smile or frown or anything else to indicate what he thought of the words. Sarrica was entirely too used to working with people he knew well, or who did not hide their emotions so expertly. Allen gave away precious little, leaving Sarrica flummoxed and frustrated.

When the seconds stretched on in silence, he gave up and returned to his paperwork. The topmost of the pile was a report in Lesto's neat hand detailing information about the prisoners, though it was precious little because if the Carthians spoke any Harken, they were stubbornly pretending otherwise, and the two silver tongues he'd brought along could not break them.

"I wouldn't mind attending, if I truly may," Allen said quietly.

"You may do as you like," Sarrica replied, looking

up. "I will see arrangements are made." He hesitated, looked at his papers. "You're a silver tongue of remarkable skill from what I hear."

"Yes..." Allen replied slowly. "Knowledge is power, and the person who understands every word in the room holds the most power. Or so my mother, father, and dame repeated to me a hundred thousand times."

Sarrica rose, keeping hold of the papers as he walked over to the bed. "Can you sit up?"

"Yes," Allen said. "Though if I am going to be working I would not mind some clothes."

"Hold these." Sarrica handed him the papers, then went to the wardrobe on the other side of the bed, exactly opposite the fireplace, and pulled out one of his own tunics. In their haste, they'd not considered that Allen would require clothes if he was alive. Clothes had since been obtained, but his back probably wasn't up to closer-fitted clothing. He carried the tunic back to the bed and held it out. "It will be far too large, but that's all to the good. After Trevail comes to fuss over you, we'll work out something better."

"Thank you." Allen grimaced and winced as he moved but stubbornly pulled the tunic up and over his head. Sarrica reached out to tug the folds away from his back.

"Would you like to sit at the table?"

"I'd like a bath," Allen said with a sigh. Sarrica extended a hand, and slowly Allen took it, letting Sarrica help him out of the bed and across the room to the table. His hand was small and pale, almost fragile-looking in Sarrica's larger, rougher, much uglier hand. But there was strength in it, more strength than Sarrica had ever expected to find. He sat down slowly, face paling but jaw set. Sarrica fetched the papers they'd left on the bed and resumed his own seat. Nudging the wine across the table, he said, "Do you know what other languages the Carthians speak?"

Allen nodded, eyes still on the papers. "At least one of them, the man in charge of the group that grabbed me, spoke poor, informal Harken. I would wager the captain speaks at least that, and if I had to guess blindly, I would say many of them speak Tricemorien. It would be strange if they did not, given Cartha's history with Tricemore. Do you have any Tricemorien soldiers, or some who speak it well enough to be mistaken as Tricemorien?"

"I have no idea, but I can find out." Standing, Sarrica strode to the door and yanked it open. "One of you go find—oh, good morning, Lesto. What excellent timing. Get in here."

"Yes, Your Majesty," Lesto drawled.

"No, wait. First I want you to do something about all these hovering Dragons. It does not require five men a shift to guard this room. Security isn't this stringent back home."

Lesto gave him a look and only signaled for the guards to stay where they were before striding past Sarrica into the room. Rolling his eyes when the soldiers did not even bother to hide their grins, Sarrica closed the doors and trailed after Lesto.

"You shouldn't be out of bed," Lesto said, stopping short a few steps from Allen and bracing his hands on his hips. "What is Sarrica wheedling you into doing for him?"

Sarrica lifted his eyes to the ceiling behind Lesto, grinning when that startled a laugh out of Allen. Strange how Allen almost looked surprised when he laughed, like it wasn't something he did a lot. Had he lived so serious a life in Gaulden? Surely not, the way he was raised, all his training.

Lesto whipped around, pulling Sarrica from his thoughts. He gave Lesto his best innocent look, but all it got him was a rude shove before Lesto stole his seat and what was left of his breakfast. "Everything is arranged and awaiting your presence, Your Majesty."

"They can keep waiting. We're working on something else. Who amongst our current troops is from Tricemore?"

"Quite a few, actually, though I don't have exact numbers stored to memory," Lesto replied, eyeing Sarrica warily. "Why do you care?"

"I don't—he does," Sarrica said, nodding at Allen over Lesto's shoulder.

Lesto's brows rose, and he turned back to Allen. "How can I help, Your Highness?"

Sarrica rolled his eyes a third time and leaned against the table, close to the fire and directly across from Allen. He picked up his wine and snatched up one of the remaining biscuits on the plate Lesto was rapidly emptying.

Allen leaned forward slightly in his seat as he said, "I think you should tell your men to gossip—the ones who speak Tricemorien, I mean. Where the prisoners can hear but not so it's obvious they're meant to be overheard. Have them talk about when the executions will take place: whether they should take place here, or if the prisoners should be dragged back to Harken to be made spectacles of. Whatever they can think of, as long as it's convincing enough to spook the prisoners that understand Tricemorien."

"That's so childish and simple I'm surprised you

didn't think of it, Sarrica," Lesto said.

"You've room to talk," Sarrica retorted. "Who still holds the records for most disciplinary laps around the city?"

Lesto ignored him, save to give Sarrica another shove as he stood. "Highness, I will see it done. Thank you for the suggestion. It should work, if I know soldiers."

"While you're busy issuing orders, see there is a place for Allen in the hall. He wants to be present."

Lesto glared at him in a way that usually sent new recruits running for their lives and had reduced several to tears. When Sarrica refused to bend, he shifted the glare to Allen, who managed to meet it without flinching. Lesto heaved a sigh. "Fine." He turned and strode off.

"Stop being so rude!" Sarrica called after him. "Prince Allen doesn't deserve it."

Lesto gestured crudely and slammed the door behind him. Sarrica chuckled and took his seat back.

Allen stared after him, eyes widening for the barest moment. He slowly turned to look at Sarrica again. "Commander Lesto is not what I expected. Not what he seemed the first few times I saw him."

"Lesto? He's all growl and bark, unless you're one of his soldiers and make the mistake of pissing him off. Or me, but he can't actually kill me because then he might get stuck running the empire." Sarrica gathered up the scattered papers, spying some of the trade agreements he knew for a fact he'd left on his desk back in Harken. He should have known it wouldn't be that easy. "I know I left these on my desk." He'd been sick of looking at them, trying to sort out translations of contracts and the many formal complaints that had accompanied them. There was also a depressing number of notes from the silver tongues trying to help him sort out the mess.

Such things would not normally be his problem, but the mess had spiraled out of control and involved four angry kingdoms, so there was no one else who could declare a final solution. He just wished they could all agree on what exactly the problem was and stick to one language when explaining it. Dropping the papers back on the pile to deal with later, Sarrica stood and walked across the room to the wardrobe. "I think it's time to get dressed. I believe your clothes are on that trunk there if you want to risk them, or I can call for Trevail now and you can dress after he's fussed over you."

"I'll wear them now," Allen said, but the words were spoken in the tone of someone who wasn't really paying attention to what was being said.

Sarrica turned as he reached the wardrobe and saw Allen bent over the papers Sarrica had thrown down in disgust. After a moment, he rifled through the scattered papers and other items on the table until he came up with blank paper, ink, and pen.

Leaving him to it, Sarrica stripped off the clothes he'd thrown on when he first woke and pulled formal attire out of the wardrobe. Much like paperwork, courtly wear seemed to find him wherever he went. He blamed Lesto. He pulled on black hose followed by loose, red breeches that were slit up the sides to show the black beneath. Those were followed by a long-sleeve black shirt, a red vest, and a black jacket with a short, stiff collar and red stripes of varying width across the bottom, chest, and cuffs.

He pulled a comb out and tidied his hair before

braiding it back, eschewing all jewelry except his imperial ring. Sitting on the bed, he slowly worked on high, black boots that required lacing.

Finished, he swung a heavy, fur-lined cloak over his shoulders and pinned it in place. His room was relatively warm, but the large, open great hall would be decidedly more frigid. He glanced to the table, where Allen was still bent over the paperwork, his face and the back of his neck flushed pink. "Do you need help dressing?" Sarrica asked.

"What?" Allen looked up. "Oh, no. I'll be slow about it, but I should be able to manage. My apologies, I should have dressed already, but I got distracted sorting out these contracts. The short explanation is that whoever drafted them for Delfaste and Mesta is not very good at their job, or more likely they are very new, because instead of using the High Court trade system values, they tried to use local forms. That skewed numbers heavily, so proper amounts were not being traded, but nobody noticed. When they tried to go back and fix the contracts, the errors started compounding. I wrote out a lengthier, more detailed explanation, though I'll need more time to translate it to other languages. The contracts will have to be redrafted and compensation made to the injured parties. I've started making notes on that as well, I can finish them after the meeting. Um." He set down the papers he was still holding and lifted a hand, then faltered and let it drop into his lap. "I hope I haven't overstepped."

Sarrica winced inwardly as he realized Allen had been reaching up to brush back a strand of hair that wasn't there. He returned to the table and picked up Allen's notes. It wasn't often something made him feel so completely stupid, but... "This is amazing," he conceded, unable to tear his eyes away. "I've been trying to untangle this mess for weeks, and you did it in minutes." He looked up to see a small, pleased smile right before Allen pulled it back and contained himself. Sarrica was coming to truly hate the way he did that. He much preferred when Allen forgot to contain himself, smiled and laughed more.

"It's what I'm trained to do."

"That doesn't mean it's not impressive," Sarrica said gruffly. "Even I know that. I'll see this is all sent on to the necessary parties and that the proper people draft these contracts in the future. Is it hard, knowing and working between so many languages at once?"

Allen looked up, surprise flickering across his face for the barest moment. Well, maybe Sarrica was chipping away at him. Any progress was better than none. "It can be tricky sometimes. The biggest problem is remembering to speak only one. If I'm not careful, I can slip between two or three in a single sentence. My mother does it as well. My father and dame teased us all the time." He braced his hands on the edge of the table and slowly pushed to his feet. He hung there a moment and then turned away and walked over to where two small stacks of clothes were set on top of a large trunk.

When Sarrica had arrived, the entire room had been cluttered with the trappings of a man who lived higher than he could actually afford. Sarrica had ordered most of it to be split out amongst the troops, or otherwise dealt with per Lesto's judgment. All he'd kept for himself was a small cask of Bentan bourbon that he would probably gift to Rene when the poor bastard was on his feet again.

He tried to keep his eyes on his paperwork, but still they strayed once or twice to Allen. Anger and shame curled through him at the sight of all that terrible scarring. If he thought it would accomplish anything, he would go find Captain Chass again and do a great deal more than leave him with a broken nose. Sarrica ran his fingers over the split knuckles of his right hand. Tried not to notice the bare finger where a ring used to be. Leaving it behind, putting it away once and for all, had been the right thing to do, but its absence was still as raw as his knuckles.

A sharp, pained intake of breath drew his attention, and he looked up to see Allen frozen with his undertunic pulled just halfway down, stuck just where he wouldn't be able to squirm and tug without hurting himself. Sarrica strode across the room and gently tugged the fabric down. He picked up the tunic, borrowed from the Three-headed Dragons, and helped Allen put that on as well.

"Thank you," Allen said, briefly meeting his gaze before skittering away, shoulders hunched, chin dipping.

"You should have seen me with a broken leg," Sarrica said. "It was only my third time in battle. Was down for six months. I swear Lesto stopped talking to me the last month."

Allen smiled briefly, ducking his head like he didn't want to be caught doing it. "I appreciate everything you've done for me."

"It's nothing," Sarrica demurred. He reached out as Allen turned away to pick up his cloak, started to rest his hand on Allen's shoulder, not certain what he intended from there—

And jerked away when someone pounded on the

door. "Come in!"

Lesto threw open the door and stepped inside. "Are you ready yet? Believe it or not, we have other things to do with our time."

"You're being breathtakingly rude today."

"You shouldn't keep making me sleep on floors," Lesto retorted. "Hurry up, or I'm not going to stop anyone when they get cranky and start rebelling."

Sarrica shrugged. "I'll arrive when I am ready to arrive." He turned back to Allen, helped pin his cloak in place, then knelt and helped him pull on the ankle boots that were slightly too big but lined with soft fur. Standing, he frowned at Allen's face, once more flushed pink. "Are you certain you feel up to this?"

"Yes," Allen said sharply. "Thank you again." He walked slowly toward the door, movements stiff and careful... Except with every step that faded off a bit, and by the time he reached Lesto, Allen walked as though he was perfectly hale and hearty. Only the paleness to his skin and the slightest tightness around his eyes and mouth gave away that all was not as well as it seemed.

Lesto looked past Allen and gave Sarrica a look that said they were going to be having a long talk later. Sarrica made a face but didn't argue. He had ways of avoiding Lesto when he really wanted. Stepping past both of them, Sarrica moved into the hallway and motioned for the Dragons to fall in around them. With Lesto in front of him and Allen at his side, they walked through the fortress down to the main hall where a small court had been arranged.

A group of perhaps thirty men, worn and haggard but still radiating relief from having been rescued by Harken, stood in the middle of the room. Nearby, chained and surrounded by four large, looming figures from Blood Night, was the Carthian captain responsible for killing Rene's team and torturing Rene and Allen. At the back of the room were arrayed the rest of the Carthians, to be taken care of after Sarrica had dealt with their leader. Once he was broken, the others could probably be persuaded to cooperate, especially if Allen's plan worked.

Several paces in front of the fireplace, close enough to keep them warm without overheating, benches had been pushed together and draped in cloth to form a large seat, with plenty of cushions and pillows piled around for comfort and support.

Sarrica took his seat and offered a hand to Allen, who after the barest hesitation, took it and let Sarrica help him sit. When he was settled, Sarrica finally turned his attention to the crowd, gesturing for them to bring the captain forward. "Do you know why you've been kept alive?"

The man replied in Carthian, sharp and rough and with an ugly grin. Before Sarrica could motion for the nearby silver tongue to translate, Allen leaned slightly forward and replied in even sharper tones. The man faltered, and Allen said something else that made him jerk forward—only to be knocked hard to the ground by two Blood Night soldiers, the sharp tips of their pikes pressed to his back and throat. Allen said something else, and the man's face flushed red.

Mouth quirking, Sarrica cast Allen a look and asked, "What delightful exchange am I missing?"

"He says whatever you do to him here, it's a lost cause because the prince you were hoping to protect will never make it home, there are too many others who will stop him," Allen replied. "I reminded him that though he is standing in the middle of Cartha, he'll never see home again either, and that for his failure he probably wouldn't even get a proper funeral."

"Succinctly put." Sarrica glanced at the nearby sailors. "Ask him what happened to the women who were aboard the ship. The captain and at least half the crew were women, but all I see here is men."

Allen asked the question in rapid fire Carthian, sounding as native to it as the man on the floor. The captain did not reply at first. Sarrica jerked his head at the men who had him pinned to the ground, and at the sharp jab of their pikes, he finally replied in a tone far less smug than the one used earlier.

"He says they were set free as the dead weight they were, left to fend for themselves, and are probably Bentan whores by now if they were not dead."

Sarrica laughed and laughed. That fucking storm might have caused him no end of trouble, but it hadn't ruined everything. "Tell him I'm eternally grateful to him for setting *Princess* Morant of Korlow free. It's not enough gratitude to spare his life, but it's sincere."

Allen looked at him, eyes going wide before he contained himself, but he did not entirely hide a pleased smile as he turned back to the captain and conveyed Sarrica's words.

On the ground, the captain went still—then began to thrash and bellow angrily, dark skin taking on a red flush, spittle coating his lips.

"Get rid of him. Tell me when he is dead," Sarrica said, and the guards dragged the man off, his screams cut off as the door to the yard slammed shut behind them. Sarrica looked at Allen. "Would you like to keep translating? I do have silver tongues here who can handle it. Do not overtax yourself on my account."

"I don't mind doing it," Allen said. "Unless they're adamant." He glanced at the silver tongues, who vehemently shook their heads and murmured platitudes and encouragements that Allen should, of course, feel free to do as he liked. Sarrica cast them an amused glance before looking at Allen, who seemed oblivious to the awe with which the silver tongues were regarding him.

"Very well," Sarrica finally said and motioned to the guards. "Bring the others forward. Dismiss the sailors. Highness, could you convey to them that they are to travel with us to Harken and will be free to go from there, provided with funds and passage as required."

"What do the sailors speak?" Allen asked.

"Outlander, mostly, I think," Lesto said. "Some speak Gaulden."

Allen nodded and repeated everything Sarrica had said, first in Outlander, then in Gaulden. A few sailors replied, smiling and gesturing. Allen nodded and continued talking to them for a few minutes before the sailors finally bowed and slowly left the hall.

The Carthian prisoners were brought forward and kicked to their knees, chains rattling and banging against the stone floor. "Is there a reason I shouldn't send you to hang with your captain?" Sarrica asked.

Allen repeated the question in Carthian, and they all remained stonily still and silent. Allen said something else, and two of them glared hatefully. A third said something, his low, mean tone perfectly clear even if the words weren't. Allen did not move, did not react in face or body save for a faint hitch of breath. As contained as Allen tended to be, it may as well have been a scream.

"What did he say?" Sarrica asked quietly.

"That he enjoyed whipping me," Allen replied. He looked at Sarrica, expression blank, but his voice was faintly puzzled when he said, "I don't understand why he would admit that. Even I didn't know who actually did the whipping. He must know admitting he's responsible is a death sentence."

Sarrica snorted softly, shared a look with Lesto, and tapped his right wrist with his left hand. Looking back at Allen, he replied, "That is what he was counting on. He is a prisoner, and even if he's released, Cartha will never trust him again. The problem with being a disconnected collection of clans with no real leader to pull them together is that they have their own plans and agendas most of the time and cooperate only in brief spurts—and so are never able to completely trust one another. He is trying to take the easy way out."

The man was hauled up and dragged away.

Allen watched. "You're not going to kill him, are you?"

"No," Sarrica said as Lesto strode off to convey his orders. "You may have noticed, I seldom do anything the easy way."

"What are you going to do?" Allen asked.

"If you really want to know, I'll tell you," Sarrica said. "But it makes little difference whether you know or not, and it's not pleasant."

Allen's mouth set in a stubborn line Sarrica already knew well. "He's being punished for what he did to me. I should know."

"As you wish. His hands are being removed," Sarrica said flatly. "If you will, remind these men that death is merely one possible punishment, and there are many others for me to choose from. That Cartha's treaty with Harken said that we could expect to travel safe and unharmed so long as we confined our activities to passing through the mountains—which we have always done. Cartha, however, has never upheld their end, instead choosing to kill us time and again. We have tolerated the treaty violations, the rampant violence and countless murders, long enough, and I am here to end the matter. We can do it peacefully or violently. I leave the choice to them."

Allen conveyed his message. The more Sarrica listened to his voice, the more he liked it—especially in those rare moments where Allen let down his guard, smiled and laughed, looked warm and soft instead of so stiff and cold. It had been shockingly difficult, the past few nights, to lie on his pallet on the floor and not succumb to the temptation to share the bed simply to be close to him.

He was more than a little distressed that more and more it was thoughts of Allen who filled his nights. Usually it was all the work he still had to do, his children, or memories of Nyle. Lately, though, he spent his nights spinning fancies about what he would do once they were back at Harken.

It was impossible to think amorously of a man in so much pain, so weak he could barely move, but Sarrica had no doubt those thoughts were merely biding their time. What did it say of him that he was so easily leaving Nyle behind, contemplating things he'd sworn he would never need nor want in his second marriage?

Though none of that mattered if Allen no longer wanted to be his consort, which Sarrica had serious doubts about. All his quiet nudges in that direction were met with silence, which was frustratingly unclear, and even he had enough decency and sense not to harass a man still recovering from serious injury.

But once they were back at Harken and Allen had fully recovered, Sarrica would do whatever it took to convince Allen to stay and marry him. If he hadn't already been set on that course, the current meeting would have convinced him. Normally such a meeting would take hours upon hours as silver tongues went back and forth to convey what everyone was saying. Allen could do all of it, and do it shockingly well. He'd mentioned once that sometimes he lost track and spoke multiple languages at once. Sarrica wanted to make him do that, drive him so wild—

And there were the amorous thoughts he should not be having.

Sarrica gave them a firm shove to the back of his mind as Allen fell silent. The prisoners responded with more stony silence. "They have until tomorrow morning to think on the matter. Perhaps seeing what has happened to their captain, and overhearing more rumors, will persuade them to be reasonable. Get them out of here."

Allen repeated the words, and as he finished, the guards hauled the prisoners away, leaving the hall empty save for the two of them, the Dragons serving as their bodyguards, and Lesto as he came striding back in. He looked at Allen, then Sarrica, and at Sarrica's nod said, "I had them remove one. He's being tended now, and understands that if he doesn't cooperate the second will go and after that we'll start on his feet. Are we leaving him or taking him?"

"Taking him," Sarrica replied. "We'll give him to a ship or put him on a farm; I've not yet decided yet."

"Yes, Majesty." Lesto turned to Allen as he drew

close to them. "If Your Highness is feeling strong enough to travel, I highly recommend we make ready tonight and leave tomorrow. The weather is looking to worsen, and we do not have the supplies to stay here much longer. Captain Rene says he is fit to travel; we fear only causing Your Highness further harm."

"I can handle it," Allen replied. "At worst, we can put me to sleep and strap me to something, right?"

"That is certainly what we've done with His Majesty a time or six," Lesto said with a toothy smile. "Majesty, are you amenable to leaving tomorrow?"

Sarrica flicked his fingers lazily. "Whatever you want, Commander. I'm just here to look pretty."

"You might want to keep practicing," Lesto retorted as he turned and strode off, sending the Dragons into a coughing fit.

"If you lot are done cackling at my expense," Sarrica drawled, "we'll return to our room now. Have an early lunch brought, and an early dinner, so the kitchen has plenty of time to pack up."

"Yes, Majesty," the Dragons chorused.

Sarrica rose and offered a hand to Allen, smiling when he took it. "Are you certain you're up to travel?"

"I'm ready to be home," Allen replied.

Sarrica's smile widened, and he gently squeezed Allen's fingers. "Then home we go."

He counted the faint smile he received in reply a victory.

CHAPTER THIRTEEN

Allen missed Gaulden. The familiar sights and sounds, rhythms and patterns. He knew where to go to get peace and quiet without hiding in his rooms. He knew how best to avoid people, or how to find them. Harkenesten Palace was still strange to him, and after several days trekking through woods and being whipped and beaten in a fortress at the top of a mountain, the ordinary bustle of palace life felt strange, like clothes that had been stretched out of shape. Nightmares chased him whenever he was not exhausted enough to sleep heavily. The few times he'd been out of his room, he had jumped at sounds he normally wouldn't have noticed, tensed when people came rushing up behind him, flinched at voices that seemed too loud or too rough. Rene had said all of that would ease with time, but Allen wished 'with time' would come a bit faster.

At least he felt well enough to try to get back to a normal routine, venture farther than the sitting room at the end of the hall. After returning to Harken, he'd been so exhausted and in pain he'd fallen into bed for two days and done very little else since then. Allen had not seen anyone except the servants tending him, the guards in the hall, and Master Healer Bettelma. He should not let that bother him, but telling himself that didn't help. The days kept passing and he'd not received so much as a short note from Sarrica, Rene, or even Tara. It was like they'd all forgotten about him.

He could send a note to *them*, but he did not want to push himself on anyone. This was not his home. Yet, anyway—or so he still stubbornly hoped. He had thought he and Sarrica were doing so well in Amorlay Fortress, learning to get along and how they might act as a team, but perhaps he'd only seen what he desperately wanted to see. Now they were home, Sarrica probably had better things to do with his time, had remembered all the reasons he didn't like Allen.

Not unexpected, but Allen had stupidly hoped...

But sitting in bed sulking was not going to help anything. The sun was barely up but he was wide awake, thanks to lingering nightmares. He was determined to make the most of the day... even if he had no idea what he would do.

Perhaps finally manage to speak with Seneschal Seyn and Chamberlain Anesta, if they had not given up on him entirely.

He pushed his blankets aside and climbed out of bed, shrugging into the soft, pale blue robe that hung on a hook right by the bed. He reached up—and stopped as he remembered for the hundredth time that his hair was not there. Wincing inwardly, still afraid to look in the full-length mirror on the other side of the room, Allen walked out to the sitting room and sat at the table by the window.

A servant had already come and gone with a light breakfast—black tea, toast with butter and honey. Allen's stomach had not been willing to deal with much else after days of gruel followed by nothing followed by only broth.

He ate slowly, mentally going through ideas for how to spend his day. He didn't get very far in his endeavors, however, his mind more interested in contriving and discarding a thousand thin excuses to visit Sarrica in his office, feel out if he wanted anything to do with Allen still, or if the hours they'd passed together in the fortress were not meant to lead to more. Sarrica had kept acting like they were still going to be married, but... but *songbird* still echoed in Allen's head. Now they were back in Harken, would he go back to being a songbird in Sarrica's eyes?

Figuring that out could wait a few hours, which was both a frustration and relief. First he wanted to see Rene and Jac, pay his respects to the Dragons.

Finished with breakfast, he returned to the bedroom and over to the wardrobe. He pulled it open and stared indecisively at the contents. He wanted to present himself as strong, capable, not weak and recovering. Subdued, serious, but nothing that tipped into somber and boring.

After choosing and discarding several options, he finally settled on an outfit and spread most of it out on the bed before stripping off his robe. He picked up his underclothes, hesitated, then set them down and slowly went over to the mirror. The scars on his back were as awful and ugly as he'd expected. He'd already been worried about the older scars, silently planning to keep his back to Sarrica as much as possible if they ever reached a point of intimacy. The fresh scars were uglier by far; he could barely stand to look at them. Nobody who saw them would continue to find him appealing. Allen swallowed against the lump in his throat, curled his trembling hands into fists.

It didn't matter. He could still do the job he'd been brought there to do. Whatever Allen had secretly hoped for their marriage was irrelevant. Also foolish since it had always been made clear to him it would only be a business arrangement.

Even if his hopes had stood a chance of becoming reality before they were certainly futile now. Not only had he proven himself to be a selfish, reckless brat. Not only had he proven to be weak and useless outside a songbird setting... his beautiful hair was gone, he looked as pale and stretched thin as he felt, and once the clothes came off, he was a truly unpleasant sight. If Sarrica hadn't found him appealing when he'd been pretty, what chance did Allen stand in drawing his notice now?

He angrily wiped away the tears on his cheeks, scrubbed at his eyes until they stopped falling. Damn it. How much more pathetic was he going to get? But as much as he hated to admit it, Allen very much wanted to appeal to Sarrica. To the kind, irreverent, and compelling man who'd come to his rescue and attended him personally at Amorlay. The man he'd gotten to know during the two weeks they'd spent there.

The man who'd not spoken to him, had not even sent a note, since their return. Sarrica had already forgotten him, but why had Allen expected otherwise? Sarrica must have hundreds of matters demanding his attention. There was no time for songbirds, especially one he'd never wanted in the first place. Allen should be grateful for all that Sarrica had done and call himself content.

He looked at his back again. The man who whipped him had not been considerate. It churned Allen's stomach to realize that his brothers *had* been considerate, keeping to a strict portion of his back, spacing everything out, usually bruising more than cutting. Well, Chass had been considerate. Whenever

Manda had gotten the whip, blood had spilled. It was Manda, in fact, who went too far that last night. Even Chass had been angry, though Allen hadn't cared at the time.

The Carthians hadn't been interested in anything but humiliation and pain. The whip had cut all over, from his shoulders clear down to the top of his ass, had wrapped around his sides to his front in several places. It wasn't fair. The scars on Sarrica's face didn't detract from his appearance at all. If anything, they enhanced Sarrica's strength and beauty.

While Allen's scars made him look... Well, he wouldn't be in a rush to fuck him. Maybe the scars would look better over time. It sounded like a feeble hope even in his own head. At least his hair would grow back, though he doubted he'd ever get it back to the length it had been. He ran his fingers through it. There was still barely anything there, but it was soft again after the bath he'd insisted on before sleeping for the better part of two days. Maybe he could use some of his special powders, add a light gold or silver sheen to it. Something, anything.

Allen sighed. He had hoped the mirror would reveal that all was not as bad as he feared. Instead, it had proven to be worse.

It didn't matter. Once his clothes were on and his hair grew out a bit, he would be plenty good enough to hold his own in court, and he didn't need beauty to translate contracts and facilitate conversations. He was fretting over nothing because Sarrica would never see him as a potential lover.

Tearing away from the mirror with a rough, broken noise, Allen focused on his clothes. Pulling on underclothes, he sat on the edge of the bed and pulled on black and red clocked stockings, then black breeches with gold ivy patterning and four gold buttons running up the outside of the bottom of each leg. A dark gold shirt followed, and over all of it went a long jacket that stopped just a few fingers from the floor, dark red and heavily embroidered around the edges with gold flowers. It was open on both sides to show off the breeches and the gold-heeled black shoes he pulled on.

He added the barest dusting of gold powder to his hair to give it some life. Ruby-studded hoops for his ears, ruby and gold rings and bracelets, and as a finishing touch a gold choker set close to the base of his throat to hide the small scars on the sides.

Dressed, he almost looked like his normal self. Only his hair had changed, and it didn't look *awful.* He hoped. It was entirely possible he was only fooling himself and in reality looked terrible. Only one way to find out.

Taking a deep breath, Allen left his bedroom and crossed to the main chamber door. He pulled it open—

And froze in surprise as two men rose from their relaxed stances to stand at attention. "Highness! Good morning. How do you feel? We're happy to see you up and about."

"Good morning," Allen said, nodding to each man, disconcerted at the way they grinned back. "Why are two soldiers from the Three-headed Dragons troubling themselves to guard my door?"

"We told Commander Lesto you were ours, and he hasn't countermanded us yet," said the second man, short and wide, with a blunt nose, freckles, and bright brown-gold eyes. "Uh, that is, His Majesty said you were to be issued bodyguards, and Lord Rene said the

Three-headed Dragons would take up the duty."

Allen tilted his head. "That is not the first time I've heard everyone say 'Lord Rene' instead of 'Captain Rene'. Am I correct in assuming he has resigned from the Three-headed Dragons?"

"He's still in the process of withdrawing, but yes, Highness, he has resigned." The two men shared grins. "Not that he has much choice as he's scarcely been allowed out of Lord Tara's sight since his return."

"I wish I'd been awake to see their reunion," Allen said, smiling faintly. "It makes me happy to know they're doing well."

The taller man, with dark red-brown skin and heavy, dark red dreadlocks hanging almost to his waist, grinned. "They're the talk of the palace, mostly because people are mad there was a wonderful bit of gossip right beneath their noses and not a soul ever figured it out. I wouldn't be leaving my room either." He winked. "His Majesty says that if you are feeling well enough, and inclined to indulge him, he invites you to join him for lunch in the white garden at half past two."

Allen heartbeat sped up, and he curled his fingers into his lace cuffs to resist reaching up to fuss with his hair at thoughts of seeing Sarrica. Who had invited him to lunch. "Of course, I'd be honored."

"We'll find someone to deliver the message," the first man said.

"Thank you...?"

"Oh!" They bowed and babbled apologies. The taller man said, "I'm Rickley, Highness, and this is Barrow. We're assigned to day duty for the next four days, and you'll have three other sets to switch off day and night duties. I don't remember who is on the roster, but I'm sure Lord Rene will drag us all in to meet you properly, so you know your bodyguards."

Allen smiled. "Thank you. I'm honored to be guarded by the Dragons. I don't suppose you can tell me where the white garden is, so I do not try to find it later and wind up lost?"

"We'd be taking you there anyway," Barrow said with a laugh. "But we can take you there now so you're at least familiar with the route later. You also have requests for an audience from..." He pulled a list from his belt. "Master Seyn and Mistress Anesta. The Gaulden delegates have invited you to dine with them when you are well again. They wanted to leave notes, but His Majesty gave orders you weren't to be drowned in correspondence before you could even get out of bed. He says if there's anything you need or want, tell Myra—that's his head secretary—and it will be taken care of."

Allen nodded as he fell into step between them. He tried not to get his hopes up, but Sarrica would not be so generous if he was still opposed to their marriage, right? Damn it, he was supposed to be good at this sort of thing. Instead Allen felt like it was his first day of lessons with a terrifying instructor. "How is Jac? I was hoping to see her today, if that was possible."

"She returned to the barracks yesterday," Barrow said. "Healers told her to take it slowly for a couple more weeks, but I'm pretty certain she's already back in the yards. We can go see her after we show you the white garden, if you want, Highness."

"Thank you, I'd like that," Allen said. At some point he would have to send notes to Seyn and Anesta, but it could wait a little while.

The white garden proved to be a beautiful little

place, a large white-stoned patio covered by a white pergola. All manner of plants and flowers spilled over the edges and through the holes, a colorful hanging garden adding a sweet scent to the air. In the middle of the patio was a water fountain shaped like women in flowing dresses dancing and playing, flowers tumbling from the baskets they carried.

Beyond the patio was an open field framed in more flowers with a large tree from which hung a swing. Allen had not seen one of those since he'd been a boy, and he'd only played on it once. Too many lessons, too little time, and he'd gotten only enough time outside to remain healthy as a child. He'd also made the mistake of playing where his brothers could see. After that day, Chass and Manda had made certain the swing was never free.

He would have loved running around this field as a boy before being dragged back to the table by his tutors to recite verbs and adjectives and a thousand other words and forms.

"It's lovely."

"It was designed by—" Rickley broke off with a pained grunt, and Allen turned to see him clutching his stomach and glaring at Barrow. At a sharp jerk of the head, Rickley slunk away into the hallway, where Allen could hear him call to a servant.

Well, even a halfwit could figure out what Rickley had almost said. High Consort Nyle had designed the garden? Why had Sarrica invited him to a private lunch here? That was... hopelessly confusing as signals went. Why had he ever thought Sarrica was easy to read? Was Sarrica trying to welcome him by dining in such a personal space? Or was he using it to make clear that there would always be firm lines between personal and imperial matters? "I'm not going to be distressed knowing High Consort Nyle designed the garden." Not visibly, anyway. "It really is beautiful. High Consort Nyle must have had true skill for such things."

"His hobby, from what I understand, though I'm only a soldier who overhears things," Barrow said with a shrug. "We can take you to Jac now, if you like."

Allen nodded and once more fell in with them as they wended through the palace. They told him stories and tidbits of history they knew, interspersed with the occasional jest or comment regarding one noble or another. By the time they reached the barracks, Allen was flushed from laughing.

The laughter faded as silence fell across the yard. He recognized it vaguely from the day when he'd rejected Sarrica by turning and walking out. The day General Faharm had died. Allen had been so wrapped up in his own petty squabble he'd never given that tragedy the attention it deserved.

First, though, he needed to figure out why the entire yard was staring at him even as they went back to work. "Should I not be here? Everyone is staring."

Barrow and Rickley looked at him like he'd lost his mind. "Why shouldn't you be here? Ignore that lot. They have to wait their turn, you belong to the Dragons so it's the Dragons who get to see you first." They ushered him into a large, cool building that smelled like leather and steel and sweat.

"Prince Allen!" Came Jac's voice, and after a moment, Allen saw her standing in a doorway off to the left. Grief cut through Allen like leather across his back. Before he could say a word, Jac had crossed the room and was hugging him tightly.

That broke all manner of protocol, but Allen did

not care. He hugged Jac tightly back and whispered, "I'm sorry for your friends, that we could not save them."

Jac nodded as she drew back. "Welcome home, Highness. Come in. The other Dragons have been wanting to meet you. I mean, if you want."

"Of course I do," Allen replied.

"Is it true you figured out the whole scheme because Rene requisitioned sugar?" A woman's voice came from the back right corner.

Allen laughed. "I surmised only where he was headed."

"What about the brandy and dried grapes told you who the traitor here was?"

"Combined with other things," Allen replied, and he went along as they practically dragged him further into what seemed to be a central hall of sorts.

The imperial army had its own armory and barracks to the northeast of the palace grounds. The mercenaries, at least those who maintained palace quarters, occupied a series of halls along the north edge of the grounds, connected to the imperial army by way of the massive practice yard.

Allen sat on the stool they nudged him to and accepted a cup of dark stout someone handed him. "Thank you. I was told Rene resigned. Who is replacing him?"

"Captain Sheva, but she's off busting heads somewhere. She'll bust our heads when she finds out she wasn't here to greet you all proper." The Dragons grinned and sprawled out around him. "Silver tongues don't usually do what you do."

"Get captured?" Allen asked wryly. "Most silver tongues aren't sheltered princes."

The Dragons laughed, loud and open and carefree. "Let themselves get caught," Jac said as it faded. "Most silver tongues stay in their tents and gripe whenever we make them come out. It takes them much longer to thaw and adjust to camp life than you did. How did you learn all those languages? I still don't understand what the dried grapes had to do with anything."

"If I told you that an archer hitting a target nearly dead center was amazing, he'd scoff because he knows the practice and effort behind it, that he could have done better if he had done this or that. Much the same with any of the tasks all of you are trained to do. Languages are no different. I was trained and trained and trained."

"That doesn't explain the sugar and dried grapes," said a man on the far side of the room.

Allen took a sip of beer then began to explain both to them, repeating everything in Tricemorien and Delfastien every couple of sentences when he noticed people trying to follow along but not getting everything. When he ran out of his first beer, it was replaced.

He was surprised his stomach was handling it, especially given the early hour, but he wasn't complaining. Delfaste claimed there was a beer for every ailment, and he'd drunk just about every kind while he studied there, right at the border with Selemea and Rilen so he could study in all three countries practically at once. Some days, the beer had been the only thing to get him through nine months of intense, exhausting training.

One of the Dragons closest to him leaned in, face bright with curiosity, eagerness. "So what—?"

"Why in the Realms is every last bloody Dragon

sitting on their worthless—" The sharp voice cut off as the source of it, a large, towering woman with dark skin and bright red tattoos covering most of it, stepped into the room. She pushed and nudged Dragons out of the way as she crossed the room. Captain Sheva, by the markings on her jacket. "Barrow, Rickley, you're supposed to *guard* Prince Allen, not fucking kidnap him."

"We didn't!" Rickley replied, drawing himself up, one hand resting on the hilt of his sword.

"Does he look kidnapped to you, Captain?" Barrow said, not bothering to move from where he was leaning against the wall, arms crossed over his chest.

"Yes, obviously," Sheva replied. "Your Highness, it's good to see you up and about. I hope these worthless layabouts haven't caused you too much trouble."

Allen shook his head, smiled. "It's an honor to be here, Captain."

"Don't tell them that, they'll never leave you alone," came Rene's voice, gruff and amused.

Looking up, Allen set his beer aside and rose as Rene crossed the room. Rene embraced him as tightly as Jac had. It was strange, to be treated so casually. Even with his parents, with his dame, there had always been a certain amount of formality that was never breached. He was growing rather fond of the casual treatment. "How is your hand?"

"Still useless for the moment, and it itches to distraction. I have been tempted this whole damned day to cut it off." Rene grinned. "How are you, Highness?"

"Very well, especially given the hour. How are all of you so lively when the sun has been up only a couple of hours? I had to do it my whole life, and I never was anything but grouchy."

The Dragons all laughed. "You didn't see us the first hour, Highness," one of them said. "We drink tea and run drills until we act more human than dragon."

"Or sneak away to sleep more—don't think you were fooling anyone," Sheva replied. The man she'd spoken to groaned. She smiled. "Speak to me later about your punishment."

He tossed her a flippant salute. "Yes, Captain. I'd say all the new authority is going to your head, but—"

"But you probably don't want additional disciplinary measures taken for insubordination, do you?" Sheva asked.

The man grinned. "That would be correct, Captain."

She gave him an unimpressed look then turned back to Allen. "Thank you for indulging the Dragons, Your Highness, but I believe they will have to let you go now, as Lord Rene was hoping for your time if you are willing to part with it."

"Lord Rene can speak for himself," Rene said, giving Sheva a shove. "Go Captain something. Your Highness?"

Allen bid farewell to the others, shook hands with Jac, and followed Rene out of the building and fell in alongside him as they headed back to the palace proper, Rickley and Barrow walking a few paces behind them. "I was told Lord Tara was not letting you out of his sight."

"He had to fall asleep sometime." Rene winked. "Also, his father demanded his attention *or else*. His family is not very amused with me right now, as they had a rather fine marriage already arranged, but they cannot exactly be mad about it since I am theoretically an excellent prospect, and they dare not risk Sarrica's wrath by forbidding it. I think they're almost more offended that we didn't tell them before we told everyone else so they could use it to their advantage in some way that eludes me."

"They wanted to look clever and like they managed to arrange it, knew from the start their eccentric son was good enough to capture the attention of one of the infamous Arseni brothers. Everyone likes to look three steps ahead of the game, but rarely does anyone manage to be so."

Rene grinned. "I suspect you're usually at least five steps ahead of everyone."

"Even I barely manage to stay two steps ahead most days," Allen replied. "People can only be predicted so far, especially in an environment such as this."

"I don't believe you."

They passed through a wide pair of doors, back into the cool, muted light of the imperial palace, the guards at the doors bowing as they pulled them shut. "I'm certainly hopelessly behind right now," Allen said. "Though now I am walking again and the medicine is completely gone from my body, I hope to fix that. Where are you taking me?"

"I wanted to see if you still wanted to get a tattoo so that I could arrange it, and Lesto and Sarrica are so buried in work they left the matter of your office to me."

Allen's brow furrowed slightly; he smoothed it out. "Yes, I still want to get the tattoo. What do you mean, my office?"

Rene tossed him a half-grin as they climbed stairs

up to what proved to be a beautiful hallway decorated in green, cream, brown, and gold. Crystal chandeliers hung from the ceiling, scattering rainbows across every surface as the sun struck them through the windows and skylights scattered along the hallway.

Far at the opposite end, where it widened into a large foyer, two Fathoms Deep guarded a set of double doors. They were ornately carved, but Allen could not make out the design. The guards bowed their heads slightly when they saw them. Rene lifted a hand in greeting but didn't call out.

Instead, he stopped in front of another door, plain except for a large, rectangular, stained glass window set in the top center of it depicting a man reading a book. Signaling the bodyguards to stay in the hall, Rene pulled a key out of his pocket and unlocked the door. He pressed the key into Allen's hand before lightly rapping a knuckle on the stained glass. "That was just finished yesterday." He led the way into the room, then turned and held his good arm out in a flourish. "What do you think?"

"It's a handsome room," Allen said, resting his fingers lightly on the desk, smiling tentatively. It was an unusual gift, to be sure, but Sarrica seemed like the type to give practical gifts rather than fanciful. And really, any gift at all was a good sign. The desk was a third as wide as the room, set close to the back wall so Allen would be able to see whoever entered. There was a cabinet behind it that had everything from supplies to a tray with wine and brandy. Gaulden wine, even. Another table close to the door had plants bearing colorful Harken orchids and a couple of flowers Allen didn't recognize, as well as a salver for correspondence. "What did I do to merit an office?"

Rene's mouth curved in a mischievous little smirk. He leaned against the desk, bracing his good hand against the edge. "He's planning to speak to you at lunch today, assuming his secretaries and all those squawking nobles let him leave, but he is exactly as enamored of your skills as everyone except him knew he would be. He's hoping to put you to work, start acclimating you to your duties as High Consort. Bits and pieces at a time, of course, so that by the time you realize what you're truly in for it'll be too late."

So Sarrica *did* want to go through with the marriage. That was certainly a victory to feel good about. He was going to be High Consort. Sarrica was certain enough of it to let him start taking on some of those duties.

But it was disappointment, rather than elation, that rushed through Allen. Despite the mixed signals he had clung to the hope that the private lunch meant something rather more personal. That Sarrica had chosen it so they could be assured of a quiet place to talk undisturbed. Still...if Sarrica was simply planning to put him to work, then they could have met anywhere at all. Why choose the garden created by his late husband?

All the training in the world could not puzzle out what Sarrica meant by inviting him to such a meaningful location for their first meal together. Allen refused to count anything in Amorlay, where he'd been too drugged and in pain to do much more than sip broth and go back to bed.

The best assumption was that Sarrica was drawing a firm line. He'd arranged lunch in a highly personal location so he was surrounded by memories of Nyle while he explained all the things Allen would never be.

Stupid, so stupid, to feel hurt. When was he going to learn to stop getting his hopes up? He had a long way to go before he was truly the intelligent, capable, controlled ruler his mother had trained him to be. Sarrica's behavior in the fortress had been the result of guilt and duty. Now they were home again, it was back to business as usual.

Fine. Business it was. Lifting his chin slightly, tucking away foolish, empty hope and useless emotions, Allen said, "I've known what to expect for years. I'm looking forward to the challenge. Hopefully I will prove to be of use."

Rene's mouth and brow pulled down. "Is something wrong?"

"Not at all," Allen said with a shake of his head. "Given my initial reception, and my foolish behavior, I am honored to still be considered worthy of the position of High Consort."

Rene's frown didn't ease, but he only pushed to his feet and said, "Tara should be finished meeting with his parents about now. Would you like to come have tea with us before your lunch with Sarrica?"

"Why do I sense that I am the very last to know about my lunch with Sarrica?"

"Nothing Sarrica frets himself to death over ever stays a secret long," Rene replied with a grin. "Tea?"

"Tea sounds delightful," Allen replied. "You can tell me what you plan to do now that you've retired from the Dragons. I was surprised to hear that."

Rene shrugged, gestured to his hand, which was secured against his torso so he would not accidently hurt it. "My hand is never going to be the same. The healers say I'll be able to use it, but not well enough to hold a sword reliably, or anything else strenuous or requiring long periods of time. Much better than I hoped for, and if I insisted on staying in the Dragons I'd have support, but I'm done pushing my luck. As to what I'll be doing instead, I've no idea yet. Shall we?"

They left the office, and Rene led the way through the halls, showing Allen portions of the palace he'd not yet seen, explaining the various halls and rooms as they went. Between Rene, Rickley, and Barrow, Allen would know the whole of the palace by the end of the day.

Eventually they reached the great hall where Tara had once tried to begin a tour of the palace for Allen. He smiled as Tara and Rene greeted each other with a brief, soft kiss. Tara then turned to Allen, and he was treated to his third embrace of the day, this one nearly squeezing the breath right out of him. "I have a present for you!" Tara said as he finally drew back. He reached into a pocket of his brilliant purple and blue, floor-length jacket and pulled out a small, dark green jewelry box.

Allen accepted it and, at Tara's eager look, went ahead and opened it. His mouth opened slightly at the contents, and then gave in and laughed. "You did not."

"Oh, I did," Tara said.

The earrings in the box were made of pink Bentan rubies and Carthian onyx, the jewels forming alternate petals of a Harken orchid. As subtle bragging of his recent victory over them, it was well done. Not the kind of game Allen would normally play, but at the smile on Tara's face, he could not refuse. "They're beautiful. If you'll hold this..." He placed the box in Tara's hands then removed the studs he was currently wearing and put the new earrings in their place. "There."

Tara hugged him again and kissed both his cheeks. "Are you joining us for tea before you go to lunch?"

Allen sighed. "I *really* am the last to know about my own lunch."

"I was helping Sarrica catch up on work yesterday. All he did was worry about it while trying to pretend he wasn't worrying about it," Tara said with a snicker and began to regale Allen with court gossip and other goings-on as they headed off to tea.

CHAPTER FOURTEEN

Sarrica shrugged into a green jacket he was relatively certain he hadn't owned two days ago, and picked up the book the Master Librarian had delivered to him only a couple of hours ago. He tucked it into the front pocket of the jacket, then left his room and headed for the white garden.

He couldn't remember the last time he'd been in the white garden. The space had once belonged to Sarrica's mother, but after her death it had fallen largely into disuse. When Nyle had asked if he might use it, Sarrica had acquiesced happily. Even if he'd wanted to refuse, how could he when Nyle had said he wanted a place just for them and the children?

What was Allen's opinion on children? The extensive file on him had not covered that. Probably because it was a moot point in the eyes of the council. But Sarrica was not going to marry someone who disliked children. He did not expect Allen to raise the children with him, but he didn't want him avoiding them either.

That was a problem for another day, though. It was not a question that needed to be answered if he could not convince Allen to still marry him.

"Sarrica!"

Biting back a groan, but not bothering to hide the scowl, Sarrica turned to face Lesto. "What?"

"Oh, stop it. I'm not impeding your lunch, just following orders. The scouts have returned with no luck. We're still combing the city, but so far we've had no luck finding Quell and Laria. I hate to say it—"

"Then don't," Sarrica snapped. "I'm not giving up until we dredge the damned bodies from the river or find them washed up on shore, if that's what it comes down to."

"They're probably dead and their bodies could literally be anywhere, and that's assuming they weren't killed by someone smart enough to cut the bodies up before dumping them," Lesto said flatly. "You know finding them alive at this point is a fool's hope."

Sarrica shrugged irritably. "I don't care. There is very little that rat in our basement says that I believe, but I think he was upset about what happened to the friends he betrayed. They might barely be more than kids, but they are well trained and resourceful. There's a chance one of them is alive, at the very least. If they are hiding in the city, which still seems their likeliest action, someone, somewhere, saw something. I don't care if we have to start arresting half the city, find me a clue."

"Fine," Lesto said, jangling loudly as he turned sharply and stormed off back the way he'd come.

Leaving Sarrica battling the knife edge between anger and misery. Damn it, should he cancel his lunch and help Lesto?

No, Lesto didn't need his help. No one needed him directly involved right now. It would do no harm to keep his lunch, and canceling it would likely do irreparable harm to his already-tenuous relationship with Allen.

He cut briskly through the palace to the little garden—and paused at the threshold, caught up admiring Allen, who sat at a well-appointed table and was speaking quietly with the servant pouring wine and fussing over the food. She laughed, said something as she bowed her head. The words drifted over the air, just loud enough Sarrica registered she was speaking Gearthish. Allen responded in kind, making her laugh again.

The way he'd already so effortlessly enthralled the Dragons and half the palace staff, Sarrica almost couldn't wait to set him loose on the High Court. Allen would have the arrogant lot of them begging to eat from his palm inside of a month.

He was dressed in a long, dark red jacket, one of those that was so popular at present, but Sarrica didn't think it was just bias that made him think Allen wore it better than most. His beautiful hair was gone, but that just left his neck bare above the short collar, a patch of skin meant to be stroked and teased by eager fingers before they slid...

Sarrica jerked away from the thought, feeling the worst sort of lech. Allen had no such interest in him, and that was no way to repair the damage he had caused upon Allen's arrival. Allen also needed adequate time to recover from travails he never should have endured. Later, much later, he might be able to consider approaching Allen with amorous intent.

He finally stepped forward, making certain his steps made plenty of noise as he walked across the white stones. "Good day, Allen."

The servant bowed then hastily finished pouring Sarrica's wine before bustling away. Allen smiled, but there was a stiffness to it. Had he not wanted to do lunch? Was something else wrong? On the heels of

Lesto's bad news, it was more than a little disheartening. So much for a promising day. "Good day, Sarrica. Thank you for inviting me to lunch."

"Thank you for joining me." Sarrica pulled the book from his pocket as he sat down and held it out. "I brought you something. The Master Librarian was pleased to have located it; I do not think he actually wanted to part with it. But I'm High King and it was my money that paid for it, so part with it he must." He winked and sat back, picked up the first of six different glasses of wine set out.

Allen's face lit up in a way Sarrica had never seen before as he turned the small book over and over in his hands. "This is written in Pemfrost."

"So I was told, though it looks vaguely like mangled Gaulden to me," Sarrica said with a smile. He took a sip of wine, set the glass down, and pulled out a piece of warm flat bread from the basket above his plate, dipping it in the spicy sauce covering the grilled chicken and vegetables on his place. "A journal, if I recall correctly."

"The private journal of a rather famous woman of the Pemfrost court. I've seen *copies* of this journal, but I did not know the real one was still around and in such good condition."

"I don't think the Master Librarian did, either." Even Sarrica's considerable wealth had felt the sizeable hole left behind by its purchase, but the look on Allen's face as he continued to pet the little book made it worth it. "You will probably have to ask to store it in the special archives, or I fear he may cry inconsolably forever."

Allen laughed as he gently set the book aside and looked up. "I will speak to him. I'd been hoping to house my own collection there."

"Well, certainly feel free to do so, they are at your disposal. Whatever you like. I hope you found the office to your satisfaction? I thought you might like a space to call your own for a time before you are forcibly dragged by my fire-breathing secretaries into the main office. They caught sight of those contracts you sorted out, and now they will not stop piling more things on me with pointed notes about what I should do with them."

That got him another laugh, and some of the tension that had been in Allen's stance washed away. "Rene warned me you had plans to put me to work, though he said you were going to move slowly so I would not run away."

"Running away just attracts the notice of the secretaries. Like wolves. Stand and fight or hide, but do not run. They like the chase." Sarrica beamed when more laughter spilled across the table. "Surely your own secretaries back home were much the same."

Allen shook his head, took a sip of wine. "No, I only had one since I had little in the way of work and correspondence outside of what I did to help my parents. Especially these past two years, I've focused heavily on training for my role here. We were considering several marriage prospects when the council's men came to visit." He looked at his wine glass. "It was not a proposition we were expecting. Youngest sons do not generally marry High Kings. My mother was... There was no containing her. She got *drunk*. She's never done that for as long as I've known her. My father and dame wouldn't stop making fun of her for two weeks. If she finds out I've told you that story she will murder me, and she'll do it very slowly."

Sarrica grinned. "Wait until I inflict a court dinner on you. I meant to the night of your arrival, but that was when everything concerning Prince Morant went wrong, and I lost track of time. From what I am told, everyone is quite impatient to meet you and mad I keep failing to bring you along. They rarely are sober at the beginning of the meal, and by the end of it, half of them are either passed out in their wine, making fools of themselves, or have the sense to let the servants cart them away. It's exhausting. Although those nights are better than the sniping and dagger-thrusting of the past few nights."

"Oh? Why so much tension?" Allen asked, gaze sharpening, taking on a thoughtful, almost eager look.

"Because Gorden Bells is from Delfaste, and we still cannot find Lady Laria or Lady Quell, which is bringing tension from those quarters, and Gaulden is still not appeased despite Bells' capture and the apologies that have been issued. And with Lady Laria missing, Nemrith is angry with us. That is just the start of the mess."

"Lady Laria and Lady Quell? What happened?" Allen asked. "What do you mean you cannot find them?"

"I'm sorry, I do not know how we managed not to tell you that part of the tale," Sarrica said, draining his nearest wine glass of its last few sips. "Bells used them to deliver some stolen papers for him, but something went wrong. All that we've found is their carriage and a great deal of blood. They were running away to get married and were meant to deliver the papers before vanishing. We've no idea where they are, and so far combing the city has turned up no clues."

"I see," Allen said, a frown cutting deep lines into

his face. "I hope they are found."

"As do I," Sarrica replied with a sigh. "I meant this to be a pleasant lunch for us. Though I am also surprised you were not dragged away by the Dragons or Gaulden. They've all been most adamant to see you. If the Dragons had not claimed victory in the matter of guarding you, I have no doubt the lot of them would currently be camping in your hallway until they did get their way."

"I don't know what I've done, but they were quite happy to see me. I spent the morning with them and some of the afternoon with Rene and Tara."

"Ah, yes, Lord Tara. I owe him many favors, though I am trying to repay some of them by scowling heavily at his parents whenever I see them. I know they're mad their wedding plans have been ruined, but they'll have to accept defeat." He took a sip of his next glass of wine and then began finally to eat more than bread. "I hope the food is adequate? This will be the first time I've had a chance to taste anything I've eaten since we returned. I've barely been allowed to leave my desk. How are you feeling?"

"Very well, and the food is delicious. I was afraid my stomach would protest after all that broth, but it seems to be cooperating today."

Sarrica smiled. "Good."

Allen took a bite of his own chicken, another sip of wine, and chased that with bread. "So what work did your secretaries have in mind for me?"

Shrugging, swallowing his food, Sarrica replied. "I've no idea, past more mangled contracts. If you're amenable, I may also borrow you to speak with some people and sort out issues in the court sessions I attend once or twice a week. Those can be arduous, however, so do not bother with that until you're back to full strength."

"I'm ready whenever you need me," Allen said.

And oh, there were such lovely interpretations to those words that Sarrica wished he could enjoy. "Do not be in too much of a hurry. Once you take up the duties, no one will let you free of them, and it will only get worse when you're High Consort." He winked, finished the last few bites on his plate. "Do you like the garden? I have not been here in months, but it seemed a good location for our lunch. No one else comes here except my children on occasion. Ny—it was made for them." Sarrica swore inwardly and went for his wine. He was thirty-seven years old; he should have enough sense not to mention his dead husband and their children during his first truly private meal with his new fiancé.

"It's beautiful," Allen said with a smile, but there was a trace of... not sadness, precisely. Defeat? But that seemed absurd. "Tara mentioned your children had been sick. Are they feeling better now?"

Sarrica nodded. "Bellen is well, and Nyla is on the end of it. He should be fine in a couple more days." He hesitated, fiddled with his wine. Well, why not? Maybe it was better to know now rather than later. "I can introduce you to them, once he is well again, if you like."

Surprise flickered for the barest moment across Allen's face. "You want to introduce me to your children?"

"Of course. I don't want you to be strangers," Sarrica said. "We are going to be spending a lot of time together, after all."

He hadn't realized just how much pleasure had

filled Allen's face until it was gone. "Of course. I would be honored."

What had he said wrong? Sarrica could not entirely contain a frown as he moved on to the next glass of wine, meant to accompany the plate of cheese and fruit that he began to methodically empty.

An unhappy silence hung between them, and for the life of him Sarrica did not know why. Perhaps he should just have done with it, once and for all, instead of dragging them through all this poking and prodding, all the cautious nonsense of getting to know each other. "Being blunt has gotten me into trouble more often than it has not, but I think maybe it would be best right now."

Allen set down the wine he'd just picked up, some of the color bleeding from his skin, mouth twisting and pinching before he respectfully lowered his head. "I understand, Your Majesty."

"My initial behavior regarding you was wrong, and I have been trying to apologize and make amends, but I understand if that and the abuse you suffered at Amorlay has put you off marrying me, and I will not think less of you or your family if you prefer to call the marriage off."

Allen's head jerked up. "Call—Majesty—I have no wish to call the marriage off. *You* are the one who has never wanted to marry me. I thought perhaps I had proven myself useful enough to retain, but..." He shrugged. "I was not certain. At times you seem to want to move forward with it; other times it feels like you want to end it. I know my behavior was reckless and stupid, not at all how a High Consort should behave."

"I have no business telling anybody not to be

reckless or foolish," Sarrica said dryly. "Nor do I wish to call off the marriage. I have been trying all this time to convince you to go through with it despite having every reason not to."

"I do not give up so easily," Allen replied, chin tilting slightly. "I came here for a purpose, and I still would like to fulfill that purpose."

Damn it, he really need to curb his inappropriate thoughts, but the problem with inappropriate thoughts was that it only took one and then the floodgates were open. Sarrica tried to ignore them. If the marriage was still a very real possibility, there was time enough for that later. If he repeated that a hundred more times maybe he'd start to listen to himself. "Know that for my part, I still plan to see this marriage through. It will not be called off unless you insist upon it. And stop calling me 'Majesty'. I thought we were past that."

"My apologies, it's instinctive to fall back on formalities, especially when I'm certain I'm about to be thrown out." He didn't say *again*, but Sarrica heard it well enough.

He smiled. "I have an official ring for you, but I did not bring it because I was not yet certain you would accept it. I think there is a better occasion for which I should be saving it anyway."

"Better occasion?"

Sarrica's cautious smile turned into a grin. "Now, that would be telling. Speaking of making everything formal, there is a dinner of some importance that I cannot avoid in a couple of weeks. If you would care to join me, you may get a true taste of what you're in for. In the meantime, it's been made clear to the court that you're welcome, so I am certain you'll be plenty busy with other dinners and lunches and whatever else they can drag you into. My only request, if you will indulge me, is that you not leave the palace without letting me or Lesto know, and always in the company of your bodyguards."

"Of course," Allen said. "Although..."

Sarrica's brows lifted.

"Rene is taking me to get a tattoo sometime next week. I'll have to leave the palace for that, though I believe he said he would work it out with Lesto."

"That's fine. I'm not trying to hold you prisoner or anything, but life as High Consort is even more dangerous than life as a prince. Especially right now, when we've angered Cartha and Benta and have yet to hear from Korlow."

"Well, I'm in no rush to get myself into further trouble." Allen smiled wryly. "Anyway, I have plenty to keep me occupied here in the palace. I'm dining with Lord Seyn and Lady Anesta tonight to finally speak with them of a project I had in mind before... everything went wrong."

"That sounds vastly more interesting than the piles of paperwork attempting to drown me," Sarrica replied, pushing away the empty cheese plate and foraging the table for the sweets.

He'd just started working on a sticky honey-nut pastry when he heard a familiar jangle in the distance that rapidly drew closer. Sarrica sighed and dropped the pastry, licking honey from his fingers just as Lesto blew into the room like a hurricane. With a black eye. Sarrica jerked upright in his seat. "Lesto! Are you all right? What happened?"

Lesto grimaced, reached up to lightly touch the bruise with the tips of one gloved hand. "Some prisoners were dragged in, a particularly rowdy set of pirates. One of them took issue with me telling them to shut up or else. He has an impressive swing, I will grant that. He hits almost as hard as you. Has quite a mouth on him, too. I didn't understand a word he said, but the tone carried. I'm probably better off not knowing what 'larshara sese' means anyway."

Allen sputtered and choked, nearly spilling his wine as he hastily set the glass aside before picking up his napkin to muffle a coughing fit. His face was flushed red by the time he stopped, though whether it was from the coughing or what Lesto had said, Sarrica couldn't tell. "Do you mean *laoshaara sesee*, perhaps?"

"Yes, that sounds exactly it," Lesto said. "What did he do, tell me to go fuck a dolphin or that my face resembles the ass end of a goat?" He shrugged. "I get such insults fifty times a week."

"Um, no," Allen said, looking torn between horror and amusement.

Sarrica grinned. "Now you have to tell us."

Allen winced ever so slightly. "He called you a mother fucker, but with Farlander, the way you decline a word lends additional negativity or positivity. He said you fuck your mother and that you enjoy it with particular enthusiasm."

Lesto lifted his eyes to the sky. "Pirates."

"You—" Sarrica broke off when it proved too difficult to talk around his laughter. He only laughed harder when Lesto kicked his shin. "I'm going to remember that one.'"

"I doubt it," Lesto said sourly. "You can't even remember how to count to ten in Tricemorien."

Sarrica shrugged because it was true, and he

wasn't going to bluster in front of a man who knew every language in the empire and a few spares. "Why are you interrupting my lunch to tell me about how pirates punched you in the face and accused you of enthusiastically practicing incest? Not that I mind, exactly. I always enjoy a story about you being humiliated. It could have waited until dinner, though."

Pinching the bridge of his nose, Lesto said, "The moment you are married, I am killing you."

"Well, I respect your honesty."

Lesto dropped his hand. "Shut up. I came to get you because the cargo we unloaded from the pirates' ship contained hidden caches of stolen weapons. Nasty ones, like the Dragons' firebombs, stuff unique to Harken that we do not trade. Much of what they're smuggling could only have come from the Earl of Mark's facilities. Given the tensions there lately..."

Sarrica shook his head. If it wasn't one problem, it was another. At least smugglers were a relatively easy one. "Fine." Draining the last glass of wine, Sarrica rose. Allen rose with them, and Sarrica gave him a slight bow. "I apologize our meal must be cut short. Apparently pirates cannot wait. Enjoy the book. I'll send round to see when you're free again. Perhaps we can attempt another lunch later in the week."

Allen smiled, clutching the book close to his stomach. "I would enjoy that. Thank you for dining with me today. Good luck with the pirates. If there is any assistance I can offer..."

"I'll send for you, never doubt it. But you should not begin your time here by putting the Earl of Mark on your bad side. Especially right now, when he is resigned to his daughter being dead and stricken with grief." Allen nodded, and Sarrica bid him farewell, then turned and followed Lesto from the room. He waved off his bodyguards, who fell back several paces.

Lesto gave him a look. "Your lunch seemed to be going well."

"You needn't sound so surprised."

"I really think I do need," Lesto retorted. "So is he still willing to marry you, do you think?"

"He is, yes," Sarrica replied. "Things... started to fall apart, so I stated the matter bluntly. Barring further disasters, the marriage will take place."

"Mmm," Lesto said thoughtfully, casting Sarrica a look that he didn't like at all. "How long will it take you to stop fighting with yourself and fuck him?"

Sarrica made a face. "I have no intention of fucking him, and it's none of your business anyway."

Lesto made a frustrated noise low in his throat. "You cannot still be feeling guilty—"

"Of course I feel guilty," Sarrica said. "Why shouldn't I? Nevermind Allen is still recovering, and probably does not like me much."

"Those last two reasons are so stupid they're not worth addressing. As to feeling guilty, do you want me to list all the reasons?" Lesto came to a stop, gesturing sharply for the bodyguards to vanish completely. "We've had this discussion numerous times already, but fine, let's have it once more. One, my brother is dead. We loved him, all of us, and it still hurts to think about him. But he's dead. It's been four years, and he would never want you to waste away from guilt and grief like this. Two, it is long past time for you to stop hiding from the fact the marriage was dying anyway."

"It wasn't—"

"Shut up," Lesto said. "Just shut up. You were ignoring it then, and you're ignoring it now, but that doesn't mean it's not there. Three, Prince Allen is beautiful and smart and bizarrely willing to put up with you. Only a stupid, stubborn fool would not try to build something more than a perfunctory marriage with him. Stop letting Nyle's ghost control your life, Sarrica. If you make me rehash this discussion one more time, I will throw you in the ocean."

"Fine," Sarrica said. "Can we go deal with the pirates now?"

"You brought it on yourself," Lesto replied but resumed walking. "I mean it, Sarrica. Put Nyle in his grave once and for all before you lose the chance to build something new."

Sarrica sighed. "All of this presumes Allen wants more than a perfunctory marriage."

"You're a fool," Lesto said. "I don't know why anyone lets you rule an empire."

"Shut up."

Lesto grunted and remained silent, but only because they'd reached the iron doors that led down into the dungeons.

It didn't really make a difference. Lesto's earlier words still rang loudly in his head—louder than they ever had before, when Sarrica had always been able to shut them out with little to no effort. Probably because it had never mattered all those other times, when he'd just wanted to be left alone and was certain alone was all he would ever be.

There was no shutting them out this time, and worse, they came almost as something of a relief. Like maybe it really would be all right to let Nyle go. His chest still ached at the thought, but it wasn't as sharp-edged as it had always been.

He still thought Lesto was seeing something that

wasn't there, and wasting his time encouraging Sarrica to make more of the marriage than it was ever intended to be. Allen would take the court by storm, and all sorts of beautiful, fascinating people would fall at his feet. He could have his pick of lovers, and owed Sarrica nothing in that respect. Why would he choose Sarrica when there so many other, better, options available?

High King he might be, but that didn't mean much behind closed doors. Despite his best efforts, and with years of history and love behind him, he hadn't been good enough reason for Nyle to stay. Why would he be enough for a young, beautiful prince who had the whole of Harkenesten Palace to choose from? A prince nine years his junior, new to the court, and primed to finally enjoy the life he'd already spent so many years training for? Who'd just survived a terrible ordeal that Sarrica's behavior had driven him toward, and was probably more eager than ever for the chance to enjoy the High Court and all it offered.

Why would a man like that settle for an aging, mercurial man with two children and a dead husband already to his name?

CHAPTER FIFTEEN

A soft knock came at Allen's office door. He looked up from the letters he was reading through as the door opened and Rickley stuck his head in. "Jac is here to see you, Highness."

"Send her in," Allen said with a smile.

Jac stepped inside a moment later, the door closing with a click behind her. She was dressed in civilian clothes, looking strange but handsome in a dark blue jacket that flared out slightly and fell to her thighs over dark brown pants and boots. "Good afternoon, Highness."

"Jac," Allen greeted, setting aside his papers and leaning back in his seat. "Would you like some wine or tea?"

"No, thank you," Jac said. "I wanted to, uh, ask you something."

Allen nodded and motioned for Jac to pull up a seat. "Ask, please."

"The Dragons are being shipped out to help Penance Gate take care of a ring of smugglers and pirates. All Dragons will be necessary for the mission, which means pulling your bodyguards. Commander Lesto and Captain Sheva said that, subject to your approval, I could stay behind and serve as your bodyguard as needed. They, um... Captain Sheva said they had someone else in mind, but I insisted—only if you approve, of course."

"I'm not eager to approve that anyone put their life

at risk for mine, but if I am going to have a semi-permanent shadow, then of course I'd like it to be somebody I already know and trust. Who else did they want?"

Jac shrugged. "Miana, because she's done it before and can read and stuff." She looked down, embarrassment and shame flushing her skin, drawing her shoulders tight. "I'm just a soldier."

"A soldier who saved my life, Rene's life, and the lives of everyone up north," Allen said quietly. "You won't block a sword or arrow by reading a book, even I know that much. If my approval is all that is wanting, consider it granted. And if being able to read means that much to you, I don't see why you can't be taught."

Jac's head jerked up, pale amber eyes wide. "Really? How? I should be guarding you, not getting fancy schooling."

"Most of my time is going to be spent precisely like this," Allen said, waving an arm over his desk at the neat stacks of paper, the rows of ink and wax and pens off to one side. "The higher the title, the higher the stacks of paper. Since I'll be in the office, surrounded by known faces that have permission to be there, with scores of guards between us and the rest of the palace, there will be hours where you'll have nothing to do. I see no reason you cannot spend that time studying. I can tutor you personally or see a tutor is hired. The latter might be better, given my time constraints, but we'll work it out if you prefer I handle it."

Shaking her head furiously back and forth, Jac said, "Oh, no, Highness. I would never presume upon your time like that. Not really another fellow in camp, reading Wystie's bawdy letters anymore, are you?" She smiled sadly. "I appreciate the offer, though."

"I'll see something is arranged. When do the Dragons depart?"

"Six days. Penance Gate is resupplying, and transport is still being arranged."

Allen nodded. "That should be time enough to see everything is properly arranged. I assume you've plenty to do before you begin following me around everywhere. Do you have papers for me to sign so you can start drawing the proper pay?"

"Oh! Right." Jac smiled sheepishly and unbuttoned her jacket, pulling out a set of papers folded in half inside a protective leather cover that had been loosely knotted closed. She handed them across the desk.

Opening them, Allen smoothed the papers out and carefully read through them, signing the bottom of several and putting his seal to the very last page. Once it had dried, he handed them back with a smile. "That is that."

"Thank you, Highness."

"You may as well go back to Allen. Assuming Lesto and Sarrica are the example we're to go by, I never hear Lesto use 'Majesty' unless he's mad at Sarrica or they're in a formal situation."

Jac grinned, the last of her anxiety fading away as she tucked the papers away again. "As you like, Silver Tongue. Though I think Golden Tongue is starting to catch on."

"It had better not be," Allen said, casting her a quelling look. "If I start hearing that, I will blame you and punish accordingly."

Jac laughed as she stood and bowed. "I'll be off to see to my affairs, then. I'll start tonight, so I have a few days to learn and settle before the Dragons depart, and Barrow and Rickley have time to pack up."

Allen smiled. "Very well, I'll see you tonight." When she'd gone, Allen drew out a small piece of paper and wrote a quick note. When it had dried, he folded it in half and went to the door. He opened it, holding the note out to Barrow when he turned. "Would you locate a servant and see this is delivered to the butler."

"Yes, Highness."

"Thank you." Allen returned to his desk and resumed his work, translating the letter written in Outlander easily into Harken and adding it to the stack of papers to be taken back to Sarrica's office when he was done.

He worked until another knock came at his door and Barrow popped in to tell him it was nearly time for his lunch meeting with some of the nobles from Gaulden. "Good, because I'm hungry." He gathered up the papers he'd worked on all morning and stepped out into the hall. "Anything exciting happen while I was shut away?"

"I think the housecleaners are having a bit of a tiff," Barrow said thoughtfully. "Two of them walked into that empty office down the hall. One came out with a split lip and wounded pride; the other looked mad enough to go another round."

Rickley grinned. "Lesto has stormed up and down the hall six times, jangling louder with each go, so I think His Most Holy Majesty will soon be given a most unholy demise."

Allen tried to smother a laugh, but in the end lost the battle. So much for courtly decorum at all times; he was finding that increasingly difficult to do and feeling less and less sorry about it. "I see."

The Fathoms Deep guarding Sarrica's doors smiled in greeting and pulled them open, bowing and murmuring, "Good day, Your Highness," as he passed them.

He smiled and nodded in return, then stepped into the perpetual contained-chaos of Sarrica's offices. The antechamber was crowded with people awaiting an audience, delivering or retrieving paperwork, or some other errand, all of them managed by the receiving staff settled behind enormous, high set desks. Scattered about the perimeter of the room were more huge and looming guards from Fathoms Deep.

The door to the inner chambers was pulled open by one of them, another smile and greeting as Allen walked by. Behind him, Rickley and Barrow hung back, already chatting with some of the guards.

The inner offices were even busier than the antechamber, all of Sarrica's secretaries and their assistants bent over their desks, speaking with people crowded in front of them, or flitting about the office fetching and delivering. Allen glanced fleetingly at the large, empty desk that sat directly across from the one Sarrica used when he wasn't hiding in his private office. It was presumptuous to think Allen would ever be invited to use it, but he kept working and trying, always hopeful.

The only person not at their desk was Myra, who stood in the doorway to Sarrica's private office. Something must have caught his eye, because Myra turned his head slightly and smiled briefly when he saw Allen. He turned back as Sarrica's voice grew louder. "Yes, Majesty." Withdrawing, Myra sent one of his assistants running to fetch something then returned to his desk and bowed to Allen. "Your Highness, I should be eternally grateful if you would distract His Majesty for a little while so I can get some work done."

Allen set the papers he'd brought down on Myra's desk. Distract Sarrica? Him? He wished. That was a task better suited to Lesto, who was seldom far from Sarrica's side and knew every trick for getting Sarrica to do or not do something. For all they spent most of their time bickering and sniping, they were so obviously brothers in all but blood. Allen wished he could converse even half as easily with Sarrica as Lesto did. Talking was supposed to be one of his greatest skills, but with Sarrica he struggled to form every sentence.

In the week since their interrupted lunch they'd not managed a second, but he saw Sarrica every day when he dropped off whatever work he'd completed. Papers he could easily have a servant deliver, but he kept hoping doing it personally might persuade Sarrica to... something. Give him the empty desk? Be hopelessly distracted by his presence? Invite him to another private meal? Pantheon, he would settle for being asked to go for a walk.

But whatever he hoped to accomplish, it never seemed to work. Patience was the key, and normally he excelled at patience, but Sarrica destroyed that like he seemed to destroy all of Allen's other strengths.

"I will see what I can do, but I promise nothing."

Myra beamed and made shooing motions. Having no other choice, Allen ventured into Sarrica's office, but stayed by the door, wary of intruding. Sarrica was bent over his desk, head in one hand, a pen in the other poised over the document he was reading. Lamplight flickered all over the room, drawing out the hints of red in his hair, lending a rich gold tone to his skin. He didn't bother to look up as he said, "If you are not holding the records I need then get out."

Cautiously stepping further into the office, Allen said, "I do not have records, but I am under orders to distract you, and I fear for my livelihood if I do not."

Sarrica jerked up, pen dropping from his fingers and leaving a smear of ink on the paper he'd been reading. "By all means, distract. I am damned tired of all this work." He pushed away from his desk and moved around it to join Allen. "Do you have immediate plans?"

"I'm supposed to be meeting the Gaulden delegates for lunch in the gold room." Until that very moment, he'd been looking forward to it, but he desperately wished right then he was available for whatever Sarrica had in mind.

Sarrica smiled. "I'll walk you there. That should be distraction enough that Myra will let you live." He motioned for Allen to precede him out of the office. "Stop threatening my fiancé, Myra."

Myra didn't say anything, but his mouth tipped up in a faint smirk as he continued reading the papers spread out in front of him.

As they stepped out of the offices into the hallway, Sarrica said, "Speaking of dining with nobles, that important dinner I warned you about is the day after tomorrow. Still willing to join me?"

Allen laughed. "Yes, of course. After all you've said about it, I think I will be disappointed if it's not as challenging as you've warned."

"You will not be disappointed, only sorry you agreed to come." Sarrica smiled down at him—then suddenly frowned as they turned a corner. He reached out, grabbed Allen's arm, and drew him in close as they came to a sudden halt.

Allen stumbled slightly, catching himself by bracing one hand on Sarrica's chest. His heart jumped into his throat, tongue coming out to touch his top lip as he looked up. "Sa—" He broke off as a nearby set of doors flew open and a rowdy group of soldiers and students spilled out and tumbled past them in a careless wave.

Oh. Sarrica had pulled him close to keep him from being run into. Disappointment and humiliation rushed through Allen, setting his face aflame. He turned away and tried to resume walking.

Only to realize Sarrica had never let go of his arm. He looked at Sarrica's hand then reluctantly up to his face, breath catching at the pensive look on Sarrica's face, the sharpness to his pretty green eyes. "Sarrica..."

"Watch your step," Sarrica said softly and slowly withdrew his fingers. He offered his arm, smiling faintly, hesitantly.

Allen wasn't giving him a chance to withdraw the offer. Returning the smile tentatively, he wrapped his hand around Sarrica's arm, careful to hold firmly but not cling as they continued on their way. Sarrica was nearly too tall for it to work comfortably, but Allen wouldn't have cared if it had been.

It wasn't the kiss he'd been so stupidly certain of a moment ago, but it was still a victory of sorts. Friendship was his goal, after all, not... What, romance? Nonsense. He didn't need a romance from Sarrica no matter what sort of fanciful notions tried to overtake his thoughts. The marriage would happen, that was the important part. The friendship they seemed to be cautiously building was a pleasant bonus. Anything else was irrelevant.

And hopeless, so he'd do well to stop hoping for

things like stolen kisses in hallways.

They continued on in silence. Allen could feel the heavy weight of it despite the drumming of his heart in his ears, but more than two decades of tutoring were not enough to tell him how to break the tension strung between them. Short of things that would end in polite rejection and abject humiliation.

In the past week he'd been dragged through the art galleries for one pretentious discussion after another, and one of those trips had included the gallery of imperial portraits—which included High Consort Nyle. He'd been stunning, even more beautiful than his brothers, who were nothing to dismiss.

If Allen was a songbird, then High Consort Nyle had been a breathtaking hawk. Any fanciful notions of Sarrica being on the verge of kissing him in the hallway had been precisely that: fanciful notions. Even at his very best, before running off with the Dragons, Allen would never have been able to compete. Nobody who loved a hawk would be drawn to a songbird, especially not a damaged one.

The murmur of conversation grew steadily louder, familiar voices speaking Gaulden, laughing and jesting, something about a fall in a garden that set them all into fresh peals of laughter.

The chatter lapsed as Allen and Sarrica turned the corner and saw them: Lady Naurren, Lady Meyer, Lord Riddell, and Lady Harmonia, the four nobles appointed by his mother to represent Gaulden at the High Court. Typically referred to as the Gaulden set. Though he'd seen them at meals a few times, this would be his first time dining with only them.

It would be the first time since his arrival that he'd

spoken Gaulden for more than a sentence or two at a time.

But for the moment, they all switched back to Harken and bowed in greeting to Sarrica. "Your Majesty, this is a happy surprise. Are you joining us for lunch?"

Sarrica laughed. "I would never deprive you of the chance to tell stories about me to my fiancé. If I vanish for too long, my secretaries will come seeking my head." He pulled Allen's hand from his arm and lifted it to bow over it. "Enjoy your lunch." Squeezing his hand, Sarrica slowly let it go. "Good luck with this afternoon."

"Thank you," Allen said, and he could not help but watch Sarrica go until he was out of sight.

Soft laughter drew him back to the others. Lady Harmonia tossed the long fall of numerous braids into which her dark hair had been woven and switched back to Gaulden. "We are happy to see you are doing so well, Your Highness, after your less than propitious beginning."

"I'm certain that in His Majesty's position, I would not have been any better," Allen replied. "There is no goodbye quite as firm as saying hello to someone else." The group made soft noises of agreement, but he could read the continued dissatisfaction in their eyes and movements. "With respect, my friends, it is not your grudge to hold, and I do not wish you to hold it on my behalf. His Majesty might not have greeted me as graciously as he could have, but he also did not need to personally rescue me from Amorlay Fortress. If you cannot let go of anger over a situation that does not concern you, this lunch is at an end."

They blanched at his words and bowed their

heads. "Apologies, Your Highness," Lady Naurren said. "I hope you will forgive that we are protective of our own, especially you. Everyone knows how deeply your mother dotes upon you, how hard you've worked, and we're fiercely proud to have seen you come so far. We are ecstatic to see His Majesty has changed his mind regarding the marriage."

Allen nodded. "I am honored by your devotion."

"Is there anything we can do to help you continue to settle in, Your Highness?" Lord Riddell asked.

"Find me a decent glass of wine," Allen said, provoking laughter. "Does no one in this palace drink *good* wine? His Majesty saw to it there were some put in my office, but I do not yet have a regular supplier to harass at my leisure."

"They do tend to prefer it..." Lady Meyer pursed her lips. "Sweeter and less robust in this corner of the empire. My first few weeks here I could scarcely drink the stuff they call wine. I have a reliable merchant who brings it up from Gaulden. I'll send you her information, Highness."

"Thank you."

Servants came in bearing lunch on three carts, accompanied by enough wine to put a tavern to sleep. By the time he excused himself to go change and meet with Rene, Allen's head was floating.

Rene grinned as he saw him, reaching out to steady him when Allen stumbled slightly. He waved off Allen's bodyguards, who left snickering. "A little drunk, Highness? If I recall correctly, this is how you got into trouble the last time."

"I was sober by the time I made that very, very stupid decision," Allen replied. "Unless you're talking about the *other* thing I did when I was drunk, in which case, feel free to call yourself a bad decision."

"You've been spending too much time around Sarrica and Lesto, to give retorts like that." Snickering, Rene turned them around and let Allen go as they began walking. "Rumor has it you've taken Jac on as your bodyguard."

"That would be true."

"Rumor also has it His Majesty is more than a touch smitten with his fiancé."

"That is *not* true," Allen said, ignoring the look Rene gave him. "Any other rumors I should know about?"

"Not presently, but I think by tomorrow they will be saying the smitten-ness goes both ways."

"Also not true," Allen muttered. "If they do start to say that, I know where to find you and how to make your life miserable."

Rene snorted but let the matter drop. "Have you decided where you want the tattoo?"

"I was thinking my abdomen. Maybe. I've honestly no idea. I've never done anything like this. Which you obviously know." He sighed. "My mother would screech if she knew what I was about."

"The High Court corrupts everyone," Rene replied with a grin. "You were bound to fall eventually. At least it's a tattoo and not running about naked."

Allen cast him a look. "You're joking."

"Get the High Court drunk some night—not a hard thing to do, as I'm sure you already know—and get them to tell you tales of Lord Haster and Lady Mirriath. Naked as the day they were born, and I will not spoil the fun for you. Suffice to say that Lady Mirriath weathered the scandal, but Lord Haster fled to his country home and has not been seen since."

"Nudity is not so strange in Farland, but anywhere else... and the High Court of all places."

Rene snorted again and then grinned, a touch of mischief in it. "Your fiancé has a few tales of scandal in his past, too."

Allen's mood immediately soured, but he managed to keep his tone idle when he replied, "So I have heard." Right around the time he had seen the portraits of High Consort Nyle. He didn't know if the people telling the stories were being spiteful or simply hadn't been thinking, but he could have done without hearing about the several occasions Sarrica and Nyle had been caught in intimate behavior by servants and friends and random nobles.

"I don't mean *those* stories, I'm not— I wouldn't do that." Rene's hand fell on Allen's shoulder, forcing him to a halt. Rene dragged him to the side of the busy street they'd been walking along. "I'm sorry."

"I'm fine," Allen replied, shrugging the hand off. "Just a little drunk and bracing for pain." And desperately trying to convince himself he was not completely and utterly crushed that Sarrica had not wanted to kiss him. How stupid and pathetic must he have looked? He certainly hadn't been smart enough to hide his thoughts. Sarrica had been kind about it, but he must have been cringing inside, trying to figure out how best to tactfully convey his disinterest without ruining their tenuous friendship.

Rene sighed but did not say anything, merely guided them back into the flow of foot traffic and resumed walking. Allen followed him—and cried out when someone knocked into him, sending him sprawling on the street, the wrap he'd pulled around his head coming loose and falling in the dirt and dust.

"Apologies," the man said gruffly, never slowing his step as he continued on and vanished into the crowd.

Allen scowled after him, grimaced at his scraped hands before slowly pushing to his feet. Rene offered him a hand, but Allen waved it off. On his feet again, he bent and retrieved the dropped scarf, grimacing as he shook it out. "This was my favorite one."

"Pout like that at Sarrica and you'll find a hundred of them in your room tomorrow."

Allen transferred his scowl to Rene. "I'm starting to appreciate why Sarrica is always telling you and Lesto to shut up, and in a very particular tone."

That only got him an unrepentant grin as they continued on their way, pausing only when Rene got thirsty and stopped at a stall to buy some cheap wine. "Not that you need more, but you may as well enjoy being out of the palace this time." Rene's grin changed, skipping right past mischievous and going straight on to evil. "Once your tattoo is healed, I will give you my entire fortune if you walk up to Sarrica in the middle of a crowded room and ask him if he wants to see it."

"I don't need your fortune, and even if I did, I would not do something so crass," Allen said.

"Everyone can be bribed. I'll find your weakness."

Allen lifted his chin and very pointedly ignored him, earning a soft chuckle in reply. He gave Rene a look. "You are welcome to—" He went stumbling back, but this time, thankfully, did not fall, as a small girl crashed into him.

"Sorry, my lord!" the girl said over her shoulder as she bolted off.

"Am I in the way? Do I have a mark on me?" Allen

demanded, righting his mussed clothes.

"Wealth is enough of a mark," Rene replied. "Best check your pockets."

Allen shifted just so to feel the pouches of money against his skin. "My pockets should be empty." He pushed his hands into his pockets anyway but felt nothing but a piece of folded paper. When had that gotten there? With him there was no telling. Probably it was a note from his mother given to him several months ago. "All seems well."

"Good. Try not to get toppled a third time, Highness."

"I shall do my best." Allen shook his head as they continued on their way. "I am damnably tired of being knocked over."

"Well, we've arrived, so that should spare you for a time," Rene said and pointed to a modest-looking white and brown building at the end of the little street they'd turned onto."

Allen swallowed, some of the lingering warmth and buzz from the wine abruptly fading off, replaced by anxiety and the memory of pain. He *really* hated pain... but the tattoo was important, and he was as fond of the Dragons as they seemed to be of him. He never would have thought he would build a camaraderie with soldiers, but there it was all the same. Rene had said he should get the tattoo, so he would get it.

He let Rene guide him into the building, tensing against the faint smell of blood that lingered on the air. The man inside was old, kind, with dark skin and bright blue eyes that seemed to see far more than most. By the time Allen lay down so the man could begin work, some of his anxiety had faded.

When it ended hours and hours later, Allen was grateful it was over, but not so terrified by the process and the pain that he was opposed to getting another someday should there be reason.

He bid Rene goodnight at his bedroom door and nodded sleepily to Jac, stationed in the hall as she'd promised she would be. His stomach growled as the smell of food struck his nose. Pantheon thank whoever had left a meal to be waiting for him. First, however, he wanted to clean up.

Walking through the sitting room into his bedroom, he almost moaned aloud at the sight of the small bath waiting for him in front of the fireplace, where a fire was already crackling. He stripped off his clothes and left them in a pile, stepped into the small tub, and scrubbed himself clean, carefully avoiding the fresh tattoo on his abdomen. His fingers hovered over it, but he didn't touch it.

A few weeks and it would be healed. Allen couldn't wait. Tattoos were something most often associated with Farlanders, sailors, and soldiers. They weren't often tolerated by his class, the same people who would sneer and scream at his scarred back. But unlike his back, which left him despondent, the tattoo felt like a badge of honor. A mark of belonging.

His fingers reached from habit to his back, feeling out the lurid scars there, tracing the ones that wrapped around his side, a few reaching as far as his torso. Had High Consort Nyle had scars? Tattoos? Surely Sarrica must have plenty of battle scars—but if so, he probably wore them as beautifully as the ones on his face. Certainly no one ever seemed to look down on him for having scars.

Letting his hands drop, Allen climbed out of the tub

and shrugged into a robe, then bent to retrieve his hastily discarded clothes. He dug through the pockets by habit, paused when his fingers found the piece of paper he had already forgotten about.

He pulled it out, dropped the clothes in a wash basket for the servants to take away, and finally unfolded a small piece of cheap, water-stained paper.

Prince Allen,

We need your help. I don't know who else to trust. Please, please, come and help us. Tell no one else. If you can, come to the Inn of the Orange Blossoms tonight, no later than tenth bell. Third floor, room seventeen.

Laria

The note was written in Selemean. Damn it. What was he supposed to do? Time, what was the time? The tenth bell was twenty-three minutes away. Damn. Allen bolted to his wardrobe and hastily pulled on clothes, yanked on boots, and snatched up a jacket, cap, and the note as he headed out of his chambers into the hall. "Jac, we have to go."

Jac's eyes widened, but she obediently fell into step alongside him. "Yes, Highness."

Allen removed his royal signet and tucked it into an inner pocket of his jacket.

Jac cast him a worried look. "What's wrong?"

Allen quickly explained the note. "I don't like

rushing off like this, but there's no time."

Jac opened her mouth, closed it. After another moment, she hesitantly said, "Beg pardon, Your Highness, but the curfew laws hardly apply to you, and that's surely why they gave the time limit."

"I am more concerned that, having revealed their location, when I do not arrive, they will go somewhere else rather than risk someone else figuring out where they are. If we lose them this time, there is no telling if or when we'll find them again. They may not be willing to trust me a second time if I fail them the first." Allen made a face. "Believe me, I'm in no rush to go flouncing off by myself again."

Jac grimaced. "Fair enough, but it's not safe to go with just you and me, and His Majesty and Commander Lesto will string us up. Orange Blossom isn't the worst place to be this time of night, but it's not the best either. We should at least take some of the guards at the gatehouse with us."

"If we delay or bring too many people, they will run away or do something else drastic. Am I wrong?"

"No," Jac conceded slowly.

"Then let us go. All they want to know is that they are safe. Once we've assured them of that, we can summon guards easily enough."

Jac nodded, still clearly reluctant. "All right, but do as I say, Highness."

"I will," Allen said quietly. "If there was time to do anything else, I would. Let's hurry. We've not much time left."

Jac led the way outside, speaking in low tones with the guards at the gate before they continued on. "This way," she murmured, leading Allen down the road to the city, where she spoke with the city guards as well.

A couple of minutes later, they were through the gates and walking along unfamiliar streets, chilly night air washing over them. Allen shivered and pulled on his jacket and the close-fitting cap he'd obtained from the Dragons a few days ago, having been inordinately fond of the one they'd given him while in Cartha. It was certainly proving to have its uses.

"I hope the people waiting for us are who you think," Jac said.

"Who else could it possibly be? Someone hoping to kidnap me? Surely there would be easier ways to do that. I was walking through the city with only Rene; they could have taken me then. Why all this? And there was no guarantee I would read the note or obey the plea to come. I don't think this is a scheme, only the desperate act of scared youths. They're barely more than children."

"You're not that much older than them."

"Neither are you, but I bet you still feel worlds apart."

Jac nodded and they lapsed into silence.

"It's so quiet," Allen said softly a few minutes later. "I do not think I've ever walked a city when it's this still. The earliest I've been out is when the markets are just opening up. It's a good time to practice my skills without getting in their way by lingering overlong. It's peaceful."

"Creepy is what it is," Jac muttered. "I hate when it's like this. Bad things happen in the dark."

"Bad things happen in the light, too," Allen replied. "Where is this Orange Blossom place we're going?"

Jac lifted a hand and waved it vaguely toward the northeast side of town. "It's right on the edge of the, um, leisure district. A street or two away, if I'm remembering correctly. It's one of those inns people will stay in so everyone thinks they're going shopping and to the plays and all that, when really they're sneaking off to the brothels. It's the kind of secret everyone knows. Orange Blossom is cheap but still fairly safe. There's a few that are better but obviously more expensive, and a whole lot that are much, much worse. If we were going to one of those, we wouldn't be going at all without a heavily armed escort."

"I am fairly certain that after this I am going to be stuck with one of those anyway," Allen said with a sigh. "Sarrica is never going to forgive me for disregarding his request not to leave the palace without letting him or Lesto know."

"Ha!" Jac clapped a hand over her mouth. More quietly she said, "He's got a lot of nerve. Everyone knows how often he used to sneak out to do things he shouldn't be doing. The fights between him and his father are almost legend. Why do you think Lesto is always having to yell at him to take bodyguards? His Majesty plays at being responsible, but if he ever figures out a way to dodge his bodyguards completely, he won't hesitate to do it. High Consort Nyle used to get mad at him, too. Guess His Majesty is starting to get a taste of what it's like from the other side, being the one worried sick about someone he cares about."

Allen was fairly certain it had less to do with Sarrica caring and being worried about him and more to do with Sarrica not being in a hurry to accidentally start another war by getting Allen killed. He liked the idea of Sarrica caring about him too much to correct the misassumption, however.

They turned off the street they were on and headed down a narrower, much darker one. That led to an even darker street, where Jac actually paused long enough to steal one of the cheap torches shoved into a broken post at the street corner. She came to a stop in front of an old but well-cared for building. A sign above it displayed a trio of flowering orange trees.

Jac dropped the torch in a bucket of water, plunging them into darkness broken only by moonlight and the lantern hanging over the inn door. She turned to Allen. "If I tell you to run, hide, whatever, do it."

"I know," Allen said. "I will. One Cartha was enough for me. I am sorry I've dragged you into this."

"That's what I'm here for." Jac opened the door and stepped inside, shoving back the hood of her jacket and loosening her sword in its sheath. A single woman sat at the high desk off to one side. Jac made a sharp motion, and she nodded and went back to her knitting.

Beckoning to Allen, Jac led the way up the stairs, all the way to the third floor and down the hall to a room close to the end. She jerked her head at the door, and Allen stepped forward and rapped quietly. A few seconds later it cracked open, and Laria's pale, scared face filled the small space. "H-Highness. Y-you came."

"Of course, I came," Allen replied. "It's only me and my bodyguard. Let us in."

She nodded and closed the door. Allen heard a rattle and clink and then the door opened wide. He stepped forward—only to be jerked back. Jac gave him an admonishing look. "Wait here." She slipped into the room and vanished. A few long minutes later, she returned. "All right, Highness."

"Thank you," Allen murmured. The room smelled of sweat and blood, faintly of oranges and the remains of a meal that still sat on a tray by a sad, little fire. Laria stood off to the side, looking even younger than seventeen years in a too-large, cheap homespun tunic and breeches, threadbare, flat slippers on her feet.

There was only one bed, its occupant fast asleep, bare from the waist up and covered heavily in bandages. "What happened?"

Laria sat on the edge of the bed and fussed with Quell's bandages. "Gorden—do you remember him, Highness?" When he nodded, Laria continued. "He asked us to do him a favor. Only Quell looked at the papers even though Gorden said we shouldn't. She realized they were encoded military orders, so she... she switched them out with fakes, destroyed the real ones. We handed the fake papers off, hoping that was enough to stop whatever was going on without getting hurt, but the man found out they were fake somehow and came after us..."

Her hands trembled and she fisted them in her lap. "I've never seen so much blood... I didn't think Quell would survive. A kind young woman helped us; without her we'd be dead." She pulled a thin little blanket up over Quell and stood. "I was out buying fresh bandages and medicine and I saw you, Highness. Kiri was the one who passed the message on to you. I feel a bit silly, but I didn't know what else to do. My father is going to kill me, and I don't know who else might be working with Bells, and I was afraid they already believed us to be traitors... But I saw you, and you were kind to us, and I didn't think you could be one of the conspirators since you're new to the palace..."

"You were wise to be cautious," Allen said, "but rest assured that Bells has been caught and is currently sitting in the dungeons. Your fathers have been worried sick about you, and His Majesty and Commander Lesto are personally overseeing the search for you. What is wrong with Quell? Her wounds should be better healed by now, surely."

"She was, Highness," Laria said. "That nasty little rat we gave the papers to sliced her up pretty badly, chest and shoulder. A healer comes every day to look her over, but it's a slow process, and I'm afraid to move her until the wounds are better healed. I don't know why they aren't healing faster."

Jac grunted and went to the bed, gently peeled away the bandages covering Quell's shoulder. A sharp, faintly metallic smell filled the air. Jac swore softly. "Someone is keeping the wounds from healing up as fast as they should. Old trick used by some healers to bleed money from customers. We need to get her a real healer." She hesitated. "I should go back to the palace, but I can't leave you here."

"I'll be fine," Allen said. "We'll lock the door and not open it to anyone but you. It won't take you very long to return to the palace and fetch help. Rene, maybe?"

Jac shook her head. "I'll have to go to Fathoms Deep."

Which meant Lesto, which meant Sarrica, which meant Allen could count his remaining lifespan in minutes. Ah, well. At least they'd found Laria and Quell. "Very well. Go quickly."

Looking supremely unhappy with the decision, Jac nodded and departed. Allen moved to the fire and threw a few more small pieces of wood on it.

"So we could have come home all this time?" Laria asked.

"That's hard to say," Allen said. "I've only been back a week myself, after being taken prisoner by Carthians. We've rooted out Gorden Bells, but given the smuggling problems and the Earl of Mark's involvement... There is still quite a snarl to untangle, so I feel caution was a wise decision on your part. But now we've gotten to you before any threat could, all should be well."

Laria nodded and moved to sit across from him. "Thank you for coming, Highness. I know it was presumptuous to ask such a thing of you when it put you at such great personal risk."

"I'm honored you trusted me." He reached out and covered her folded hands with one of his own. "We'll get you and Lady Quell home safe, I promise." He withdrew his hand, fussed with the fire some more until a stronger flame was flickering and lending additional warmth to the warm.

They lapsed into silence for several minutes, broken only by soft snores from the bed and the occasional yawn from Laria. Allen was just beginning to fall asleep himself when someone pounded on the door. "Allen!"

Standing and crossing to the door, Allen pulled it open slightly. He saw Jac's face, scowled at the split in her lip and the shadows of a bruise forming on her jaw. "Who hit you?"

"It's nothing, Highness. Open the door. I've brought reinforcements."

Scowling, Allen closed the door, jerked the chain away, and pulled the door open. Jac stepped into the room, followed closely by several Fathoms Deep— including Lesto, who looked like a thunderstorm ready to break. "Highness," he said with deadly calm. "There is a horse waiting for you outside."

Allen ignored the order. "Who struck Jac?"

"It's nothing you need to worr—"

"I damn well *will* worry about someone hitting my bodyguard," Allen snarled.

"She—"

"It's not your place!" Allen bellowed. "She works for *me*. She follows *my* orders. I do not care that you are High Commander of the Imperial Army. I do not care if you're Sarrica's best friend. If you or anyone else strikes Jac again, for any reason, I will make certain you regret it. I don't tolerate violence amongst comrades. Violence done *for someone's own good*. Do you understand me?"

Lesto stared at him, and any other time Allen might have been pleased to see the respect on his face, but right then he was far too angry. "Understood, Your Highness. Now please return to the palace before Sarrica does something drastic. I have enough trouble keeping him safe, I really don't need you making my life more difficult."

"Fine." Allen turned to Laria and bid her farewell, not remotely surprised when she hugged him. It must be a Harken thing because his own mother had not hugged him as often his whole life as random people in Harken had in a single week. "You're safe now. Commander Lesto will not let anything happen to you." He shot Lesto another look then turned sharply away, motioning for Jac to follow.

A horse and six Fathoms Deep soldiers were waiting on the street in front of the inn. Allen mounted his horse, pulled Jac up behind him, and they returned to the palace in silence.

Chapter Sixteen

Sarrica glared at the wine glass on the large, round receiving table in front of him but didn't pick it up. If he picked it up, he would throw it, and the servants shouldn't have to clean up after his temper tantrums. He'd done that to them enough as a smug, know-it-all youth.

And he wanted to save his energy for his foolish, reckless fiancé. He was going to wrap his fingers around that long, pretty throat and strangle the man until he saw sense. What in the name of all of the Pantheon had Allen been thinking?

Brisk, rapid knocking came at the door, and Sarrica snarled for them to enter. He didn't turn around as they did so, however, trying to keep his temper reined in. "Have you heard from Lesto?"

"More like Lesto heard from me," came Allen's quiet voice.

Sarrica whipped around. "You're about to hear from me, you fucking fool."

Anger flashed in Allen's eyes. "I made the best choice I could given the circumstances. You don't even know the whole of the tale."

"There is no excuse for traipsing off into the city in the dead of night with only a soldier barely fit to be a bodyguard for protection!" Sarrica bellowed. "You know better—"

"Laria was scared," Allen cut in. "She didn't know who to trust, but she saw me and decided to take the risk. I didn't read the note until almost too late, so I had to act quickly. We were cautious, took no risk that wasn't strictly necessary. You would have done the very same in my position, so don't stand there barking at me like you've the right."

Sarrica balled his hands into fists to keep from knocking something off the table like a petulant child. "I'm High King—"

"I'm High Consort Presumptive," Allen cut in, voice level but full of so much anger he may as well have shouted. "Do not speak to me as though I'm not your equal."

"I'll speak to you like the reckless ninny you are," Sarrica snapped. "What if it had been a trap? What would we have done if you had been kidnapped or worse?"

Emotions filled Allen's face, gone as quickly as they'd come, but it was more emotion all at once than Sarrica had ever really seen from him—bitterness, hurt, frustration, anger. Come to that, he'd never seen Allen lose his temper. Provoking it didn't feel much like a victory. "You would have told my parents that keeping a reckless halfwit alive proved to be too difficult and then told your council to find you a better consort." His blue eyes blazed as fierce as any fire. "I did the right thing, no matter how dangerous it was." He turned away and stormed back toward the door.

"Oh, no, you don't," Sarrica muttered and went after him, reaching Allen just as he pulled the door open. Ignoring the gawking guards, Sarrica yanked him back and slammed the door shut—then shoved Allen up against it. "We're not done here."

"What more is there to say? You yelled exactly as predicted, refused to listen *exactly as predicted.*"

Sarrica grabbed his shoulders and shook him so hard Allen's head knocked lightly against the door. "I'm allowed to be worried about you. Jac told us what had transpired, and all I could think about was the five thousand times I almost got myself killed running around the city at this hour. Why do you think I instituted the curfew? It has made the city safer, forced smugglers and the rest to confine their work to hours where we can better catch them, allows people to sleep a little bit easier." He gave Allen another shake. "I know personally how much danger still lingers there, and I do not want to find you hurt again, or worse, dead."

"If you don't want me hurt, then kindly stop shaking me before my teeth fall out," Allen snapped. "If you are worried that my death might provoke a war—I told you, even my mother would respect that there is only so much you can do to curb a *reckless halfwit.*"

"What?" Sarrica let go of him. "What does war have to do with this conversation? What are you talking about?"

Allen slipped out from between him and the door. Sarrica stepped away before he pulled him right back, still able to feel the press of Allen's body against his. "That's why you came to find me, right? Or more likely, came to find my body. Why you're angry now. If I die, Gaulden would have every right to be furious with you—"

"I don't fucking care about the politics!" Sarrica bellowed, loud enough they probably heard every word of it in the hallway. Well, it wasn't the first time half the palace had been privy to his marital spats. He could practically hear Lesto's admonishment to act his age, like a man who had been married before—and for over a decade—but the only clear thought in Sarrica's head was knocking sense into the stubborn, confounding, absolutely infuriating fool in front of him.

"I know," Allen said, and the bitterness, the defeat, in his tone fractured Sarrica's anger. "You don't care about politics, you don't care about court, you don't care about any of the things that make me who I am. You wanted a soldier. Someone you would no doubt trust to go to Cartha or into the city without yelling at them like a child. Someone still beau—" He broke off, looking for the barest moment like he might cry. But in the next moment it turned into a glare and then he turned away. "I think we've said all there is to say, Majesty. I am returning to my room."

"We're still not done here," Sarrica said, speaking softly, every thought fleeing his mind save one: a flame-bright memory of that moment in the hallway when he'd pulled Allen in close and had barely kept from kissing him breathless. At the time he'd thought he'd imagined the look on Allen's face that said he wanted Sarrica to do precisely that.

But now... now he suspected that Lesto, damn him, had been right all along.

He prowled toward Allen, for once not fighting the *want* that stirred to life whenever Allen was in the room, whenever Sarrica so much as thought about him. Allen took a step back, then another, disbelief popping his eyes wide in the moment before Sarrica descended.

Sarrica grabbed his shoulders and firmly pushed until Allen collided with the table, practically wound up sitting on it. Pinning him there, Sarrica dipped his head and finally got a taste of that distracting, infuriating mouth.

Allen tasted of the dry, heavy wines that Gaulden fawned over for reasons beyond Sarrica's comprehension. Beneath that, his mouth was faintly sweet, and surprise had rendered him deliciously pliant. A hard shudder ran through Allen's body and then he was kissing Sarrica back in a way that proved his too-clever mouth had all sorts of skills.

Letting go of the hands he'd pinned to the table, Sarrica lifted Allen up onto it and wrapped one hand around the back of Allen's neck, tilted his head just so, and pushed deeper into his mouth, tongue sweeping, exploring, tasting. A groan tore out of his chest, encouraged by the long, surprisingly strong fingers that dug into his shirt, Allen's nails long enough he could just feel the bite of them.

He wanted to spread Allen out on the table and fuck him until he screamed. Which was *not* the right way to go about this. Not so soon. Bad enough his plans for something romantic to initiate this element of their relationship had gone straight to the Penance Realms. He tucked the thought away for another time.

Reluctantly tearing away from Allen's mouth, Sarrica attempted to gather his thoroughly scattered thoughts, panting quietly. When he trusted himself to form coherent sentences, Sarrica repeated, "I don't care about the politics." He let go of the back of Allen's neck, fingers falling slowly away. "I care about *you.* Please stop trying to get yourself killed. I've had quite enough of people who matter to me going off and dying."

Allen's face went white. "That's not—I didn't—I'm sorry."

"As you said, you did what seemed best. What probably *was* best," Sarrica said gruffly. "I—" He broke off when Lesto's knock came at his door, and yanked Allen from the table right before the door swung open and Lesto stepped inside, followed by Jac and Rene.

Lesto and Rene looked at them. "Ha!" Lesto said and held out a hand. Grumbling, Rene reached into the pocket of his jacket and slapped several coins into Lesto's palm.

Sarrica rolled his eyes. "Don't we have more important things to focus on?"

"Clearly *you* don't," Rene retorted. "If I'm going to be pulled away from *my* lover, I may as well make crass bets on you and yours."

Pinching the bridge of his nose, Sarrica said, "Could I get a report on matters, please?"

"Lady Laria and Lady Quell have been returned to their families," Lesto said with a smile. "Who are most ecstatic to have them home. The Master Healer is tending Lady Quell and thinks she will make a full recovery now she's being properly treated. In the morning I'll find someone to track down the corrupt healer and see his license is revoked." That was said to Allen, who nodded.

Sarrica made a note to ask later. "Did they say anything about Bells or anyone else who may be involved?"

Lesto shook his head. "Nothing we didn't already know, but they were scared and exhausted. Give them a day or so to rest, and I'll see they're interviewed."

"Fine. What of the guards who attacked Jac?"

"In stocks until I remember they exist," Lesto said.

"Guards—" Allen's face flushed. "My apologies, Commander."

Lesto's mouth curved in a half-grin. "No apology necessary, Your Highness. It was an easy misunderstanding, and I would have acted the same in your place."

Sarrica frowned, looking between them. "What happened?"

"I thought he punched Jac, and I got mad," Allen said, looking like he wanted to crawl under the table and hide there forever.

Sarrica's jaw dropped. "You—did you *yell* at Lesto?" He looked at Lesto. "He yelled at you?"

"Threatened to kill me," Lesto said, almost sounding cheerful about it.

"I feel I should issue some reward. That's remarkable." He grinned at Allen. "Well done."

Allen's skin went a darker red. "It's not *funny.*"

Sarrica laughed so hard he had to brace one hand on the table. "It's hysterical, you've no idea. Most of this palace is wary of me but *terrified* of Lesto, but you told him off and threatened to kill him."

"I didn't threaten to *kill* him," Allen said, pressing his fingers to his temples.

"To be fair, his actual words were that he'd make me regret it," Lesto added.

Sarrica's laughter grew louder.

Rene rolled his eyes. "I threaten to kill and maim him all the time, and nobody gives me a reward."

"Siblings don't count," Sarrica said as his laughter faded off. "Now all of you get out of my room, unless you have something further to report."

Lesto snorted, but at the look Sarrica gave him, kept his mouth shut and herded the others out. The door closed with a click, and Sarrica turned back to Allen. "Are you *certain* you want to marry into this lot?"

"I—it's not precisely what I was trained to expect..." Allen said, eyes lowering, looking almost shy, which was the strangest thing to see on a man who knew he could charm a room and had no qualms about doing so. He looked up slowly. "I think I'm growing accustomed. I did get a tattoo, and have snuck out of the palace twice now."

"Do not remind me," Sarrica said. "Wait here." He turned and slipped into his bedroom to pick up the small box sitting atop his bureau. He took the ring out of it and returned to the front room where Allen had not moved from his spot by the table. "I did not mean for this," he gestured between them, "to happen this way. I had plans for a nice dinner, outings... as always, my plans go awry."

"That's not always a bad thing," Allen said quietly. "At least, for my part, there are no complaints."

Sarrica put a mental mark by his long-term plans to fuck Allen on the table. He took Allen's right hand and slid the engagement ring on his second finger. "If it does not suit, I'll have another made, but let this be *my* formal request: would you marry me?"

"Yes," Allen said softly, eyes on the ring, throat working. "It's beautiful." Sarrica paid little mind to most jewelry, but even he had been particularly pleased with the jeweler's work: a white gold band set with ten sapphires arranged in pairs, fading from a deep, almost-black blue to a blue so delicate it was nearly white. Finally looking up, Allen added, "It would be an honor to marry you."

"That I'm not so sure of, but the sentiment is appreciated," Sarrica replied and finally gave in to the need to once again curl his fingers around the back of

Allen's neck, feel the faint thrum of his pulse, the warmth of his skin, and the soft brush of his hair. He tugged gently, and Allen obligingly stepped in close, leaning up on his toes to meet Sarrica's soft, lingering kiss. It didn't have the anger-spawned heat of the first, but it burned just as fiercely.

Allen was nothing like Nyle at all, who'd always had edges to him, an impatience that never seemed to ease. Everything was a battle to Nyle, even playing and fucking. Sarrica had thought—worried—the differences would be harder to adjust to, but it was easier than it maybe should have been to tuck lingering thoughts of Nyle away and focus entirely on Allen. On the present.

Pulling away was more difficult than he cared to admit. "You should probably go before I drag you to bed. I'm not letting you undo *all* of my plans."

"If you insist," Allen replied, but Sarrica was slowly getting better at reading all the little tells that gave away what he was really thinking. If there was one thing he'd noticed during their moments together, it was that Allen liked to be fussed over. He looked at his ring again and smiled at Sarrica. "Goodnight then, Sarrica. I'll see you tomorrow."

"Yes," Sarrica said and put his own hands on the table so he did not promptly make himself a liar by dragging Allen back in and carrying him off to bed.

But he still did not draw proper breath until Allen was gone. He sat down, finally drank the wine he'd poured when he'd first heard that Allen had run off to the city.

The night had certainly ended far better than he could have hoped. So much better. Perhaps he wasn't too old and used up for a young, pretty prince to find interesting after all. Draining the wine, he put out the lamps and headed into his bedroom.

He stopped when he reached his bureau and picked up the ring box. There was a second ring in the box, a simple, white-gold band with a single line of small sapphires set within it, on the same gradient as the larger ones on Allen's ring. It still felt strange not to be wearing his wedding ring, but that would change in a year or so. He slid the engagement ring in place, admiring blue where once he'd always seen green and yellow.

Stripping off his clothes, Sarrica crawled into bed and lay staring up at the ceiling. When had he gone from feeling lonely because Nyle was gone to feeling lonely because he had to tell Allen goodnight? When had he started anticipating the day he'd once more sleep beside someone instead of dreading it?

In a damp, dark fortress where he'd watched a stubborn prince show more strength that anyone Sarrica had ever met. And throughout Allen had acted like enduring alone and without complaint was expected of him instead of realizing that should never be expected of anyone. Sarrica had never heard anything about Allen's mother that wasn't good, or obviously skewed gossip best ignored, but sometimes he wanted to ask the woman a few strongly-worded questions.

He rolled over, buried his head in his pillow, and tried to sleep. If he didn't get some sort of rest his head would take that as permission to start hurting, and he could not afford to be laid low by one of his damned headaches. Allen would think he'd changed his mind and was avoiding him, or something equally ridiculous.

Of course, thoughts of Allen immediately stirred

images of him sitting on the table, clothes mussed, his mouth red and wet from use. Sarrica couldn't wait to see what other uses he could put that mouth to. He wanted to hear Allen gasp and moan, wanted to make him beg for it. Wanted to see those pretty lips wrapped around his cock, blue eyes locked on his face, wanted to see how much of that lovely skin he could get to flush pink. Allen would make quite the sight with all those princely trappings stripped away, leaving behind only a man eager to indulge in every pleasure they could find the time for.

Sarrica pushed the blankets away, wrapped a hand around his cock, and brought himself off hard and fast.

When was the last time he'd done that? Sarrica preferred not to remember. He climbed out of bed and cleaned himself off, then slid back beneath the blankets and settled in. Minutes later, he was fast asleep.

Lesto's voice dragged him into wakefulness, and Sarrica groaned. "Go away."

"No."

"I outrank you, and I don't countenance disobedience," Sarrica groused, dragging his pillow over his head. He'd been asleep, damn it. The first time he could remember sleeping so soundly in longer than he cared to think about.

The pillow was yanked away, and Sarrica cast Lesto a look that promised violence.

Dropping the pillow on the floor, Lesto said, "We've just gotten a message from Korlow."

"What—" Sarrica jerked up, swinging his legs over the side of the bed. "Why didn't you *say* that?" He scrubbed his face, palm scraping over bristle. "Send someone to wake Allen. If I am to deal with Benta once and for all..." He frowned at Lesto's amused look. "What?"

"You should probably start with 'what time is it?'," Lesto replied.

Sarrica stared blankly at him then looked around the room, belatedly noted the sunlight spilling in. His room was never so bright early in the morning. "What time is it?" he asked slowly.

"Not quite midday."

"What in the Pantheon—" Sarrica bellowed. "Why am I still sleeping in the middle of the damned day?"

Lesto's attempt not to smile finally failed and an amused grin overtook his face. "You wouldn't wake when your servants came, kept grumbling to be left alone. When they couldn't find me they took the problem to Allen, who said to let you rest. He's been in your office all day, doing his best to tend matters while you slept. It's all over the palace that's he's got that flashy new ring." The grin widened, turning a bit more smirking than Sarrica liked. "And that he was in your rooms last night. *Late* last night."

"Who was there to see that except my personal guard? Aren't you supposed to have Fathoms Deep terrified enough not to gossip like they're out on market day?"

"Ha!" Lesto rolled his eyes. "Sarrica, there is nothing in the world that will keep soldiers from gossiping. I don't prevent it; I merely attempt to manage it. Now, get up and get dressed, please. Not everybody wants to stare at your damned dick and there is a war requiring your attention."

Sarrica retrieved the stolen pillow and threw it at Lesto as he left, ignoring the threat Lesto issued in response. His servants came in a moment later, and

Sarrica obediently stood still while they prepared him for his day.

When they finally set him free, he joined Lesto at his table and took the missive he held out. "Princess Morant is in place, and her troops are poised to move. They plan to launch their counters in three weeks. Can we be ready to move that quickly?"

"Yes, though it won't be pleasant fighting our way through Cartha first."

"I don't care if I have to burn those damned mountains down," Sarrica said. "I'm going to speak with Allen."

"Giving him the keys to the empire?" Lesto asked. "Are you certain that's a good idea?"

Sarrica nodded. "Yes, and it's not as though I have much choice, anyway. I am going to be gone for months, and someone needs to be in charge. You're the one who's been reminding me since the day he arrived that he's been trained for this."

Smiling faintly, Lesto replied, "You misunderstand. I meant that he might realize he doesn't need your sorry ass while you're gone."

"Shut up. Have the council summoned to the amber room and go do what you do best, Commander."

"Yes, Majesty," Lesto said and stole Sarrica's breakfast bun on the way out.

Sarrica scowled after him and scooped up his teacup, carrying it with him as he left his room. Three bodyguards fell into step around him as he stepped into the hall. "We're headed for the office," he told them.

But when they reached it, Allen wasn't there.

"He went to meet with some of the council and

several others for lunch, Your Majesty," Myra said. "The ivy room."

Sarrica nodded and started to turn away—but paused when he noticed the desk across from his was still empty and unused. "I thought Allen had been working in here all day."

"He was borrowing your desk out here," Myra replied. "He didn't want to use that one without express permission from you."

"Get his belongings moved," Sarrica said. "See the office down the hall is kept for him should he want it for something else, but I want him settled comfortably in here by end of day. Everyone will be answering to him until I return."

Myra's eyes widened, but he'd worked for Sarrica long enough not to bother asking questions. "Yes, Majesty."

"Thank you, Myra." Sarrica set his teacup down then strode off, bodyguards in tow, headed across the palace to the ivy room.

Despite the urgency of his quest, he still lingered just outside the ivy room's doorway, caught up in the simple pleasure of watching Allen work, the way everyone else in the room seemed almost enchanted. Sarrica was fairly certain the council had never listened so raptly to anyone else.

Of course, part of it might have been the way Allen switched between languages as he spoke Harken to the general room but switched to Outlander and Gearthish on occasion for the sake of the guests on either side of him. Sarrica had always been selfishly content to speak Harken and expect others to conform to him or hunt down a silver tongue. Watching Allen work made language interesting, made him envious he could not do that... reminded him he still wanted to see if he could make Allen lose track of his languages.

But that lovely thought was for another time. Sarrica motioned for his bodyguards to stay where they were and stepped into the room, immediately drawing all eyes toward him. "Councilors, your presence is required in the amber room. Everyone else, please remove yourselves. I require a private word with His Highness."

He stepped to the side as people rose from their tables and slowly filtered from the room, ignoring the curious looks cast his way and keeping his own gaze on Allen. When the room was finally empty and the door shut, he closed the space between them in a few long strides and dipped his head to drop a hard kiss on Allen's mouth. Drawing back, enjoying the pleased surprise on his face, Sarrica said, "One ring and half a day and you've apparently taken over my palace. Very neatly done, I must admit."

Allen laughed. "I am not so skilled as that, nor am I that ambitious. I've overheard, and been told, that you have trouble sleeping. When they said you were fast asleep and refusing to wake up... Well, I hope I did not overstep. I assumed Lesto would inform me if I had."

"Not at all," Sarrica replied. "I'll never be allowed to forget it, but there are already many things on that list. Did Lesto tell you of the missive that came?"

"Yes," Allen said, happiness fading from his face. "Korlow is ready to attack. Lesto didn't say it, but it wasn't hard to interpret that you'll be going to lead the fight from our side."

Sarrica bobbed his head from side to side. "Nothing so direct. Lesto will be doing all the hard work, I am merely going to supervise from a safe distance and be on hand when it's time to negotiate and sign treaties, other such High King things." He hesitated a moment, then said, "If Nyle were alive, he would have leapt at the chance to do this, and I would have let him. To be honest, you and that well-trained tongue of yours would be well-suited, but I'd rather have you here." He lifted a hand to brush the back of it against Allen's cheek. "I'm obstinate, but I do finally have sense enough to know I can leave Harken in your capable hands." Allen's face went pink, though Sarrica couldn't tell if it was the touch or the words that provoked it. One day, when he returned, he would happily spend hours figuring it out. "I have to deal with the council and put a war in motion, but I thought first we could do a handfast so that you have full authority in my absence. It's not the way I would prefer to do this, but the council had terrible timing when they sent you here. They usually have terrible timing."

"Uh—" Allen stared, unable to force words out. That was likely not something that happened often. Sarrica tucked it away in memory. "If you wish, certainly, but I do not think such a measure is necessary. I'm sure many here would say you should not be handing so much power over to me so hastily."

"You've been running my palace all morning and assisting me for the past many days. Even the council is already under your sway. If you're amenable, then you can arrange the ceremony while I run one last vital errand."

Allen nodded. "As you wish."

"Good." Sarrica hesitated, then said to the Realms with it and bent to take another kiss. Allen leaned up into him, fingers twining into Sarrica's hair. Sarrica spanned his hands across Allen's back and gently slid them down, wary of causing harm if any of his wounds lingered. The fingers in his hair tightened, and Sarrica was more than happy to take that as an invitation to prolong the kiss. He withdrew only when his lungs burned with protest and the distant chime of a clock reminded him there was a lot to do and precious little time to do it.

Making himself step away, he said, "I'll see you and the witnesses in my private temple as soon as you can be there."

Allen nodded, smiling as he slipped away to arrange the handfast—an informal marriage that carried nearly the full weight of a formal marriage. Handfasts were used precisely for circumstances like this, though generally on a smaller scale. He would be gone for months, though, and did not want to leave Allen without the authority he would need to rule Harken in Sarrica's absence.

Leaving the ivy room, shadowed by his guards, Sarrica turned down the hallway headed south, then down a short set of stairs, another hallway and finally to the tightly spiraled staircase that led down to the imperial treasury. The clerk watching the antechamber gawked and didn't remember to stand up and bow until Sarrica was well past him. Leaving the bodyguards in the hall, Sarrica threw open the door to the Master Treasurer's office.

"Your Majesty," the old man at the desk greeted.

"Harrio," Sarrica replied. He reached beneath his shirt and pulled out the heavy chain on which he kept his imperial signet. "I need the other."

The slight widening of his eyes was Harrio's only reaction. He stood up slowly and unlocked a drawer, pulling out a ring of keys that he used to unlock the enormous, heavy door to the imperial treasury. Sarrica helped him pull it open, then led the way inside and through the many shelves and special locked rooms until they reached the one at the back. He pulled out his own ring of keys and unlocked the first of two locks. Harrio unlocked the second and pulled open the door to a room that contained approximately a hundred items ranging in value from priceless to the empire to priceless purely for sentimental reasons.

Going to the furthest set of shelves, Sarrica pulled down a large gold box. With the smallest key on the heavy key ring fastened to his belt, he unlocked the box and threw back the lid. The last time he'd opened this box, it was to put away the ring Nyle had worn from the day of their wedding until the day he'd died. It had been returned to Sarrica by Nyle's bodyguard, a woman who'd resigned shortly thereafter and returned to her family's home in Outland.

He gripped the ring tightly in his fist, let grief wash over him one last time, then closed the box and put it back on the shelf.

Once everything was locked up again, he quickly made his way back through the palace to the small, private temple on the far end of the hall where his private chambers were located. He glanced over the witnesses Allen had chosen: Tara, Lord Celia, Lady Naurren, and Lord Rhodes. They all gave deep, formal bows as he approached, and Sarrica returned them with a nod and murmured thanks, but his eyes flitted almost immediately away.

His heart gave a lurch when he saw Rene and Lesto standing off to one side, the bittersweet expressions on their faces echoing his own roiling emotions.

Sarrica crossed over to them, glaring at Lesto. "Aren't you supposed to be putting my army to work?" Lesto rolled his eyes, and Sarrica turned to Rene. "What do you even do anymore? Let the fiancé who is entirely too good for you keep you like a pet?"

"Shut up," the brothers chorused, then each hugged him tightly.

"Thank you," Sarrica said as he drew back, and he tried to say something more, but the words stuck in his throat.

"Go," Lesto said gruffly and shoved him to where Allen was waiting with the head priest of the private imperial temple, clerks with paperwork waiting patiently off to the left.

Sarrica climbed the steps to join them, extended a hand that Allen immediately took. "You work quickly."

"Me?" Allen laughed. "Last night you told me we'd be having dinner, not handfasting."

"I have yet to make a single plan that did not change on me a hundred times," Sarrica replied. "We should get this done before something happens, as a matter of fact." He signaled the priest forward and held tightly to Allen's hand as the ceremony began.

CHAPTER SEVENTEEN

Allen sat in the window seat of his sitting room, rolling a glass of brandy back and forth in his hands. Not much brandy, he had entirely too much work to do, but he needed *something* to soothe his tightly-strung nerves. Even the days he'd spent lying in bed in unbelievable pain had not seemed as long and difficult as this one, though the reasons were completely different.

Why did important things always happen so quickly? He crawled and crawled to reach a certain point, and when he reached it, the moment was there and gone in the snap of his fingers. He had arrived at the palace anticipating a months-long courtship that bore closer resemblance to forging a business relationship. Instead he'd spent several days hiking through mountains and later being whipped and beaten.

After they'd returned to Harken, he hadn't known what to expect, and after weeks of dancing around each other, he'd gone from a shouting match to scorching kisses to handfasted. He'd spent his morning gazing like a halfwit at his engagement ring, and now he wore the imperial signet.

Which had barely been put on his finger before his husband had departed to go to war, Fathoms Deep and part of the imperial army moving out ahead of the rest to begin laying everything in place. Allen's wedding night had been a kiss that even the burn of good brandy could not banish and a clawing dread that something would go wrong and Sarrica would not return.

Watching his brothers go off to fight had never been this agonizing. His brothers, however, had always been more like strangers than family. Sarrica...

Allen pressed the cool glass to his overwarm forehead then took another sip of brandy before letting the glass rest in his lap again. Leaning his head against the window, he stared unseeing at the darkening city in the distance. His right hand felt heavy, awkward, still unused to the weight of not one but two rings—the beautiful engagement ring he still wore on his second finger, and the imperial signet currently on his first finger because it was too big to fit on his third. Even on his first finger it was still a touch too big. He would probably just imitate Sarrica and keep it about his neck.

Allen took another sip of brandy, savored the sharp, faintly sweet flavor, the burn as it slid down his throat. He would have to return to the rest of the world soon, especially with dinner looming—an important dinner he could not miss since Sarrica was no longer there. A dinner where he had been meant to make his official debut as High Consort Presumptive... Now it was High Consort, and just that morning his only thought had been whether it would be a little too obvious to wear a blue jacket that matched the sapphires in his new ring.

He drained his glass and stared indecisively at the decanter on the nearby table. Before he could make up his mind, however, a series of brisk knocks came at the door. He started to get up to open it then remembered hasty admonishments from Rene that it was a security risk. It was something he remembered being told back in Gaulden, but it was also one of those things they generally ignored, given the risk of attack was almost negligible there. "Come in."

Rene stepped into the room, followed by a handful of servants. "I know you wanted to be left in peace for a time, Majesty, but we wanted to get you moved before it got much later."

"Moved? Oh." Allen shook his head and stood, setting the glass beside the decanter. "I hadn't even thought of that, how silly of me."

Grinning, Rene signaled to the guards. "Come along, Majesty. I'll take you to inspect your quarters while your belongings are packed, see if there's anything you'd like moved or otherwise changed."

"Stop calling me that," Allen muttered, which did nothing to diminish Rene's grin. Allen thanked the servants before following Rene out of the room. Though he'd been called 'Majesty' many times since the ceremony, it still sounded strange. It was what he'd wanted, what he'd come here for, but hearing himself called 'Majesty' would still take some getting used to.

As they turned onto an empty hallway, Rene snickered and reached into his pocket, holding out a small ring of keys. "These are for you. Sarrica had them in his jewelry box, forgot about them until the last moment. They're keys to various little things no one but the high king, the high consort, and one or two of their bodyguards should know about." He smirked, then dropped his voice and said, "Like the secret passages."

"The what—" Allen faltered, stopped, and when Rene laughed again, resumed walking. "You're joking."

"I'm perfectly serious. I technically shouldn't know about them, but Lesto's had me fill in for him often enough it became necessary. I'll show them to you some night when it's quiet. Sarrica and Lesto don't use them often, but they come in handy every now and again."

Allen bit back all the questions he wanted to ask as it wouldn't be wise for anyone to overhear. He tucked the small ring of keys away in his pocket. "I need a chain, for my signet and these keys."

"That's an easy matter to fix," Rene replied. "Steal one from Sarrica's jewelry case. I'm pretty certain he has like fifty of the damned things, and even if he noticed one or two were missing, he wouldn't care." Rene smirked. "Especially if it was missing because you were wearing it, I'd wager."

Helping himself to Sarrica's belongings seemed more than a little forward, but the idea sparked heat in Allen's gut that unfurled slowly and warmed him clear through. A heat that didn't ease as they reached Sarrica's suite. It had only been a couple of kisses, but Allen would never look at that table the same way again. He could remember the edge of it digging into his back, the way it had warmed quickly after Sarrica had lifted him onto it. He'd wanted Sarrica to push him down on top of it, strip his clothes away, and spread him open.

Allen had invited several lovers to his bed over the years, but none of them had affected him quite the way Sarrica's kisses had. He tore his eyes away from the table and followed Rene. At the back of the enormous front room were two doors, each leading to a bedroom. The one on the left he knew to be Sarrica's, which meant the one on the right must be his.

Nyle's former room. It showed, somewhat, in the military banners, shields, and various weapons that decorated the space. The room was free of dust, a faint soapy, lemon smell indicating the room had been recently cleaned. The color scheme was handsome, at least, browns and blues with touches of dark gold.

There was an enormous bed on a raised dais in the back right corner, drapes hanging from the wall to surround the whole dais rather than just the bed. The floor was dark gold wood, polished to a shine and scattered with ornate, colorful rugs. There was also a writing desk, bureau, several empty bookshelves that looked much newer than everything else in the room, a large chest at the foot of the bed covered with several neatly folded blankets, and a little sitting area around an immense fireplace.

Two modest crystal chandeliers hung from the ceiling, and four candelabra were scattered about the room, with a pretty stained-glass lamp on the desk and another on a table beside the bed.

"Suitable, Majesty?"

"More than," Allen replied. "Though would it be too much trouble to have the war paraphernalia taken away?"

"Not at all. Anything else?"

Allen shook his head. "Not at the moment. Completely redesigning it can wait until everything has quieted down and everyone is back home. Unless you think it's a problem it still looks like..."

"Nyle's room?" Rene finished. Allen nodded. "I wouldn't worry too much about it. I'll tell them to take down the weapons and shields, put in, what, paintings? And lighten the place up a bit. That should do it." He pointed to a door not far from the bed. "That door leads to your dressing room and washroom." He pointed to the two doors on the opposite wall. "That first door is a room shared between suites, but Sarrica is working on something for you so stay out of it for now."

"He's working on a *room* for me?" Allen asked, excitement overcoming anxiety. Why had he ever thought Sarrica was the type to give practical gifts? "What is it?"

Rene lifted his eyes to the ceiling. "That would be telling. That last door leads to Sarrica's room. The keys for the bedroom doors, the suite door, and that connecting door are all on the ring I gave you. I will leave you to get acclimated, Your Majesty."

"Quit it!"

Rene's laughter lingered in his wake as he strode off.

Pulling out the keys Rene had given him, Allen walked across the room to the connecting door and, after trying several keys, unlocked the door. He rested his hand on the handle, drew a deep breath, and slowly released it before finally pulling the door open.

It definitely felt illicit to be in Sarrica's room without invitation, without Sarrica. But he wanted a chain for his ring and keys, and this was the most expedient way to obtain it. Hopefully Rene was correct in that Sarrica wouldn't mind.

The jewelry case was on top of Sarrica's bureau, against the same wall as the door to the main room. Allen glanced at the door then rolled his eyes at himself. Pulling the case closer, he threw back the lid.

He wasn't entirely surprised to see the contents were a mess. It reminded him of Sarrica's desk: chaos at a glance, but the disorder probably made sense to Sarrica. No doubt Sarrica would be hopelessly confused and frustrated if someone sorted the mess out.

Allen rifled through the topmost portions then pulled open the drawers set in the bottom half of it. The last one proved to be unusually tidy, filled with carefully coiled chains in silver and gold. He picked up one of the larger gold ones, heavy enough it was probably, in fact, gold laid over a sturdier metal.

It was a little longer than he preferred, but that was probably for the best if it was going to be under his clothes all the time. Pulling out his keys again, removing the ring from his finger, Allen strung them on the chain and fastened it around his neck.

Taking another deep breath, he returned to his own room—just in time to see a line of servants come in bearing his belongings, including those recently arrived from Gaulden. He retreated to the main suite to leave them to their work, since nobody would enjoy him standing over them and fussing over every little thing. A carafe of wine and a light snack had been set on the table. Allen walked over to it, rested his hand on the tabletop, and tried to think of anything but sitting right there while Sarrica had kissed him like it was the only thing on his mind.

"Your Majesty."

"Yes?" Allen turned, looked at the woman with the marks of a head footman on her left shoulder.

"All your belongings have been moved, and we've taken away those objects you requested be removed. Is there anything else you require?"

He shook his head. "No, thank you very much."

The woman bowed and led the other servants out

of the room, closing the door quietly behind her.

Allen glanced at the clock on the far wall and sighed. Time to get to work. Sarrica was off to war, and he had his own battles. He returned to his bedroom and stripped off his clothes, then went into the changing room where his clothes had already been hung up. What to wear...?

He picked through his options carefully, discarding several immediately, dithering on others, before finally settling on a long, moss green jacket with crisscrossing bands of silver and gold and mother of pearl buttons. Since the jacket was solid all the way around, he opted for hose and green shoes with silver heels and gold flowers along the top. Gold hoops for his ears and a heavy necklace with emeralds set in squares of gold, and he was ready to soothe ruffled feathers and hopefully negotiate a new marriage contract or two.

Allen was determined to have the High Court behaving and getting along again by the time Sarrica returned, and hopefully he'd be able to address several other problems as well. He would do whatever it took to prove Sarrica's trust was not misplaced.

He was fussing with the black lace trim of his cuffs when he heard the main door open and close.

"Majesty?" A familiar voice called.

Allen smiled and strode out into the main room. "Hello, Jac. I've been wondering where you were."

"I was busy running some last errands since I'm being put to work a bit sooner than anyone expected," Jac replied with a grin. "Settling in?"

"Slowly. Shall we go to dinner?"

"Yes, Majesty," Jac said, snickering when Allen rolled his eyes.

They walked side by side through the halls of the palace. Allen tried not to notice the stares and whispers that were definitely more prevalent than usual. He supposed it wasn't every day the High King woke up late, handfasted his fiancé, and promptly went off to war. Pantheon knew Allen was still dizzy from the tumultuous afternoon.

As they drew ever closer to the grand dining room, however, the discombobulation fell away, replaced by a calm confidence built by years of training. He might not be fit for climbing mountains and facing down enemy soldiers, but there was more than one kind of battlefield.

And this—hundreds of nobles, opulent and spoiled and sharp-edged, with needs and weaknesses, willing to do most anything for a price—was his battlefield. Espionage and combat were beyond his abilities, but he thrived on conversations where every word spoken stood for five not spoken, and what went unsaid was vastly more important than what was.

The guards at the huge, open doors bowed low at his approach, and the herald just inside cried his arrival. A hush swept over the room, hung there a moment, and then was brushed away by the scrape of chairs and the swish of fabric as everyone rose to bow to the High Consort. As Allen passed by them, applause and cheers and congratulations rose up, nearly loud enough to bring down the colorfully painted ceiling high above.

Allen took his seat at the high table, motioning for everyone else in the room to resume their places.

Feeding everyone who lived there was one of the most expensive parts of Harkenesten Palace, even with residents of a certain income required to contribute funds toward room and board. One of the most expensive meals was dinner, held every night for all the nobles and their family and guests. They sat scattered across various large, round tables, speaking every language in Harken and several foreign languages. Though all guests could sit wherever they liked, many tables were informally reserved for certain parties, often broken up by kingdom, region, and family. Other tables were much more a mix. Not a bit of it was random.

The only table under absolute control was the high table, where only Sarrica, Allen, Rene, and Lesto were allowed to sit. Everyone else must be invited by Sarrica or Allen, though Sarrica had already granted Tara permanent place.

Jac fell back to stand with the other guards behind the table, and Allen took Sarrica's seat. He looked around the table, mentally marking off everyone he had invited. Other than Rene and Tara, there sat: Lord Celia, the Duke of Emberton-Heights, from Selemea; Lord Rhodes, the Earl of Mark, from Harken; Lady Jetehl, Ambassador of Selemea, who had to deal with not only the cancellation of Lady Laria's marriage to the Nemrith Ambassador, but also the cancellation of Lord Tara's marriage to Prince Bann; Lord Eseera, Ambassador of Nemrith; Lady Byre, Ambassador of Delfaste, being quietly but pointedly ignored by the others, punishment for the betrayal of the Bells family while they and a great many others connected to them were further investigated; and finally, Lady Naurren from Gaulden and Lord Fellmont from Mesta, stiffly ignoring each other save for the occasional glare when one thought the other was not looking.

The quiet conversations had lapsed as he sat,

everyone waiting for him to speak and set the games in motion. Allen gave a last, quick glance around the table before finally coming to rest on Lady Byre, who tried to smile but only looked sad, lonely, and resigned to a terrible fate. "Lady Byre, the Three-headed Dragons are returning from their mission soon. I know from personal experience they all have a Delfastien love of beer. I wanted to have several barrels waiting as a welcome home gift, but I'm new enough I'm not sure where best to obtain good beer."

Byre's face brightened slightly, and this time her smile managed to take hold. "I keep a generous private stock, Your Majesty. You'll find no better, not without waiting to have it hauled in. The palace doesn't keep the same stock since not many here favor the stouts and porters we prefer in Delfaste. If you'll tell me the number of barrels you want, I'll see they're delivered to the Dragons' quarters tomorrow."

"That is too generous by far," Allen replied.

"Not at all, Majesty. Please, I would be honored."

Allen gave a single, slow nod. "Twenty barrels of good stout then, and send the invoice to my office."

Byre shook her head, and the smile now held a note of triumph. "Majesty, I would be honored if you would consider them a wedding present."

Allen smiled and gave her the barest nod. The others would be hard-pressed to continue snubbing her when Allen had made clear the high throne held no grudge against Delfaste, *and* she was giving him such a handsome gift, as twenty barrels of good Delfastien stout were nowhere close to cheap. They were now forced to match her generosity, and bring her back into the fold, or they risked looking rude and defiant.

Taking a sip of pale, rose wine, Allen shifted the conversation to more idle chatter of coming fetes, the looming winter, slowly bringing it around to the subject of travel, where, as he'd hoped, Lord Celia began to talk of traveling to his family seat in Selemea to celebrate the end of year holidays with his family— and take Lady Laria out of court for a time.

Now it was time to resolve another problem. He turned to the Nemrith ambassador. "Have you ever been to Selemea, Lord Eseera?"

Eseera looked up from where he'd been half-heartedly eating the dark, spicy soup the servants had just brought. "No, Majesty. I've been privileged to visit Tricemore on two occasions, but not Selemea."

"That's a pity, I think you would like it. The capital there is as lively as Harkenesten, without being as big and overwhelming. I believe it has a small but growing population of Nemrithian immigrants, sailors and the like, a result of the long history of trade relations between Nemrith and Selemea; Harken relies heavily upon them."

"Yes, Majesty," Eseera said politely but with a stiff undercurrent.

"I'm surprised you've never been, given those close ties."

Eseera lifted one shoulder, accent thickening slightly when he replied, "My duty is here, Your Majesty, and I enjoy Harken. We are much more austere at home."

Allen smiled faintly. "My home is quite stiff, too. Gaulden has always made a practice of strict upbringing and proper behavior at all times. It was always a little strange, and a bit of a struggle when I traveled to places where people are not so strict. So you've not been to Selemea. Have you met any of the royal family when they've traveled here?"

"No, Your Majesty, I've regretfully not had that honor. I had hoped to meet them when I married and before we returned to Nemrith..."

The Selemean Ambassador, Lady Jetehl, cast Allen a brief, thoughtful look before turning her full attention on Eseera. "The palace will be quieting down with so many families traveling to their respective homes for winter festivities. I'll be returning to the Selemea palace myself. We'd be most honored to have you join us if you are inclined to come. Prince Bann especially would love a new face about the place."

Eseera regarded her pensively. "I admit it sounds tempting, my lady."

"Well, do be tempted," she replied. "It does seem a travesty that with the close ties between our countries, you've never been to visit us."

"I have always thought it unfortunate," Eseera said. "Very well, my lady, I would be honored to join you when you return home."

She beamed at him before glancing at Allen. "I hope you enjoy the journey," Allen murmured. "It does seem the place to be this winter. Lord Rhodes, are you not headed there as well?"

"Yes," Rhodes said in his curt way. Allen was fairly certain the man did not know how to unbend, though in all fairness, his daughter was still bedridden, her recovery slow and difficult. "Once they return and resupply, I am departing with Your Majesty's Dragons to investigate matters at my warehouses there since I do not hold with pirates or smugglers or that my name has been besmirched by them."

"Pirating sounds like too much risk for too little

reward for you, Lord Rhodes," Eseera said hesitantly. "Smuggling is slightly more profitable, from what I know of it, but you seem hardly in need. Are you traveling with the Dragons? Or merely departing alongside?"

"With, unfortunately," Rhodes replied cautiously. "I had not planned on leaving Harken any time soon and so all my ships are elsewhere. It will be easiest to travel with the mercenaries."

Eseera shrugged, motioning with one hand. "I will not be needing the ship I was going to use to travel to Selemea as I am now departing later and in the company of Lady Jetehl, but I will need it to be waiting for me when my visit there concludes. You are welcome to make use of it, and of course, if any of our people there are of use in your investigation, you may rely upon them. I'll send a letter with you."

"That... would be most gracious of you, my lord," Rhodes said slowly, some of the tension in his shoulders easing as he realized Eseera—and thus Nemrith—was not going to hold a grudge about the canceled marriage.

Allen beckoned to a servant to carry away the soup course and bring the next. Only when they'd made it to the dessert course did he finally turn his attention to Gaulden and Mesta, whom he'd largely ignored throughout the meal. "Lady Naurren, Lord Fellmont."

"Your Majesty..." they said together, regarding him warily.

"I am slowly going through a lot of the projects that His Majesty has not had time to put in motion, and I came across one that I think should be given into your capable hands—that is, I want the two of you to work on it together."

Though both had years of experience in containing themselves, there was no hiding the displeasure that flared in their eyes at his pronouncement. Allen ignored it. "His Majesty has long wanted to improve the way prisoners are treated. He was able to start the project, but has never had the time to finish. Given the hours that he currently spends—and that I will spend sorting through the many, many cases the court systems are incapable of handling—I agree problems are only getting worse and the changes need to be made. I think you are both well-suited to the project, given your legal backgrounds and the long problems Gaulden and Mesta have had regarding treatment of prisoners."

It was, in fact, one of the things that had first created hostilities between their countries. Hostilities his mother had eased somewhat but could never completely end. But Allen had the weight of the High Throne, and neither Naurren nor Fellmont were in a position strong enough to defy him.

"As you wish, Majesty," Naurren replied, the words polite, but her eyes full of betrayal. Opposite her, Fellmont seemed equally resigned but not as hostile.

Allen allowed the table to remain on idle matters after that, slowly pulling himself away from conversations until the clocks chimed midnight. A few minutes later, he drained the last of his wine and rose, nodding politely as the table rose and bowed. Jac stepped away from the rest of the guards, and they left the hall by way of a back door.

"I don't know much about politics," Jac said into the silence, "but even I can tell that last bit was a little mean."

"They've had long enough to learn to play nice, and I have always agreed with my mother: Begin strong, remain strong. Begin weak, remain weak."

Jac shot him a look. "Was beginning strong running off with the Dragons?"

"That was beginning foolish, I admit," Allen replied. "I am grateful no one seems to be holding it against me."

They stopped outside his room. "You're welcome to go to bed, Jac. I won't be going anywhere else tonight save my own bed."

Jac gave a lazy salute and nodded to the Fathoms Deep standing guard. "As you like, Majesty. See you in the morning. Sleep well."

"And you." Allen slipped into his chambers, yawning hard enough his eyes watered.

The soft sound of someone singing drew him up short. Allen frowned as he noticed candlelight coming from the open door of Sarrica's room, and padded across the room to it.

Oh. He froze and drew back slightly when he saw a woman sitting by the side of Sarrica's bed, singing to the two small children fast asleep *in* the bed. So she must be Emilia, their nurse. Allen started to withdraw entirely, but Emilia saw him and stopped singing. She glanced at the children, then gathered up her skirts and stepped out of the room, bowing low as she reached him. "Good evening, Your Majesty. I'm sorry, I thought I would get a chance to speak with you before they did this." She smiled faintly, looking briefly over her shoulder back toward the bedroom.

Allen shook his head. "I hardly think I've anything to do with this. Are they all right?"

"Oh, they're quite well, Your Majesty." She smiled,

eyes bright and cheerful, if a little tired at the edges. "They simply miss their father, especially since he's gone off to war, and that is how they lost their sire. I can remove them to their beds if you prefer."

"It makes no difference to me. They should stay where they're comfortable and happy." Allen glanced at them again. "May I?"

Emilia bowed her head. "Of course, Your Majesty. I promise at this point there is no waking them. Getting them to sleep is a trick, but once they are, they sleep like the dead."

Allen laughed softly as he stepped into the room and up to the foot of the bed. Sarrica had meant to introduce Allen to his children, but they'd never had the opportunity. Doing so at the same time he bid his children farewell was hardly appropriate.

They were beautiful children, but that wasn't surprising given their parents. The younger one looked exactly like Sarrica, and Allen could see traces of Nyle in the older one. "They look like their parents."

"Yes," Emilia said softly. "His Majesty hated carrying them, but he adored them once they were born." She glanced up at Allen, chuckling at whatever she saw on his face. "Would Your Majesty like to meet them tomorrow?" She laughed again. "Though as to that, you may not have a choice. I turn my back for one minute and they're off like cats. You may wake up to uninvited guests unless you lock your door."

Allen smiled, looking at them one last time before turning away to leave them to their rest. "They're always welcome." And those times when children definitely were definitely not permitted, the door would be firmly locked. "Goodnight."

"Goodnight, Majesty." Emilia returned to her seat

and resumed her knitting and soft singing.

Allen went to his own room and swiftly undressed, putting his jewels away and leaving the clothes for the servants to tend in the morning. He settled beneath the heavy blankets, which still smelled of the sachets they used in storage closets, and fell quickly asleep.

Chapter Eighteen

Sarrica winced and swore as Trevail stitched up his arm. A soldier stepped into the tent carrying an already opened bottle of wine and a cup. When she reached him, Sarrica took the bottle and waved off the cup. He drank several large sips, grateful to have something wet on his dried lips and parched throat. He'd prefer a good cup of tea, but that had run out days ago. He'd thought they'd run out of wine as well, but if more had been procured he wasn't going to ask for details.

"You did a fine job of slicing yourself up, Majesty," Trevail said, not pausing in his stitching as he gave Sarrica a reproving look.

Sarrica made a face. Thankfully the bastard who'd done the slicing had wound up soundly dead. The whole incident still left Sarrica feeling sick. Their last location should have been secure, but those fucking Carthians were as crafty and relentless as wharf rats.

Unfortunately for them, making a last, desperate attempt to assassinate the High King of the Harken Empire was only a good idea if it worked. Executing that lot finally sent the remaining rats scurrying for their nests.

"Just the leg left to stitch, Majesty, and then you should be all patched up."

Sarrica nodded and took another swig of wine before he gingerly stretched out his left leg so the healer could reach his hastily bandaged thigh. That particular injury had been a little too close for comfort. Cut someone correctly on the thigh and the blood drained too fast for anyone to do anything about it.

He leaned back in his seat, resting his head against the improvised pillow the healer had made. Cold metal chinked against his skin. Sarrica shifted the bottle to his other hand, then reached up with his right hand to curl his fingers around the rings lying on his chest, acutely aware of the still strange weight of his engagement ring lying next to his imperial signet.

Letters from Harken had been few and far between, mostly filled with need to know things that were carefully encoded. Scattered infrequently were snippets of home: that his children were doing well, that Allen was playing with the High Court like a musician with his instrument. From Allen himself, gentle teases that Sarrica had left just in time to leave Allen to deal with some particularly difficult tariff negotiations, and that he often woke up to find curious little eyes peering over the edge of his bed. Which always made Sarrica's heart give a hard lurch.

He wanted to be home. How had he preferred a life of war for so long? He remembered how much he had, but the memories were faded, distant. Save for precious memories of time with Lesto and Rene, and later Nyle, he could recall nothing remarkable about life as a soldier.

Right then, Sarrica would rather have his gigantic, soft bed, and his consort to help warm it. Realms, he'd settle for his office and stacks of paperwork so high he couldn't see over them.

Instead, he drank more wine and hid a wince as Trevail stitched up his thigh. The sight of the black healer's thread against his skin turned his stomach. He could grit his teeth and endure such things now, but it had taken him years of fleeing and throwing up as a youth to turn battle-hardened. His only consolation had been Lesto, who'd had an even more difficult time of it. Rene's stomach had always been made of iron, which had been a mixed blessing for the poor bastard.

"All right, Majesty," Trevail finally said as he finished treating the wound, smoothing his fingers feather-light over the fresh bandages. "I know this is going to be a futile request, but please do not exert yourself. Give the wounds a chance to heal. If you tear that leg open, I cannot promise it will cooperate with me a second time. You are lucky we are in such a good camp. I've had to take legs off when they couldn't be saved because some stupid soldier couldn't learn to hold still for a few days."

"I'm no young man with something to prove," Sarrica replied, offering him a tired but sincere smile. "All I want is to go home in more or less one piece."

Trevail grunted and clapped his shoulder. "Behave and you just might, Majesty. Summon me at once if anything begins to hurt in a way it shouldn't. I've left some pain draughts on the table. You know how to take them."

"Yes, and thank you," Sarrica said. "Would you tell one of the guards out there to find Lesto?"

"Of course. Goodnight, Majesty." Trevail bowed and left.

Sarrica stared across the tent at the work waiting for him, all the packing that needed to be done before they moved to the town Lesto's forces were securing in preparation for the negotiations that would hopefully take place soon, though it all depended on Morant being victorious now. Which she should, but

Sarrica did not count his triumphs until he had the surrender in hand. Getting up suddenly seemed too difficult. He closed his eyes instead, savored the still, quiet moment that likely would be the last one he'd enjoy until he was home again.

"You wanted me?" Lesto's voice came quietly.

Sarrica dragged his eyes open, held out the wine. "Have I ever mentioned how irritating it is that you look good no matter what happens to you? How's life with one eye?"

Taking the bottle and downing a long swallow, Lesto dropped onto Trevail's abandoned stool. "Shut up. It's not like you haven't gotten offers just because of those pretty scars on your face." He lightly touched the heavy bandages over his right eye. "Strange but manageable. I'll be happier when I can get rid of all of this."

The tense set of his shoulders and the tight lines around his mouth and good eye belied his dismissive tone, but Sarrica didn't say anything. Lesto didn't need the same sorts of verbal beatings he frequently gave Sarrica; more often than not, he just needed time. When that wasn't enough, Sarrica resorted to working him to death or making him angry, until he finally broke. "I'll get you a nice, tasteful eye patch. Lots of diamonds and gilding."

Lesto lifted two fingers in a crude gesture and drank more wine. "How are you? If your aim was to get some new scars so Allen would fuss over you, I suspect you've succeeded, though I hate to encourage such irresponsible behavior."

Sarrica rolled his eyes and stole the wine back. "Are we almost done here?"

"We should hear from Morant by tomorrow, day

after at the worst, but hopefully sooner rather than later. I've no reason to think that battle won't go to our favor, but I've been proven wrong before."

"Are we going to get any more visits from the Carthians?" Sarrica asked sourly. "Because I'm not sure your pretty face can take another surprise."

Lesto managed a laugh, though it sounded a bit frayed at the edges. "The Carthians don't keep me apprised of their surprise parties, but Solid Hollow volunteered to take care of them once and for all. I granted approval and didn't ask questions."

Sarrica grunted. He didn't keep the mercenaries around because he was a *nice* High King. International treaties on war kept the imperial army from certain behaviors and actions, but independent mercenary units were different. Harken wasn't the only one who made liberal use of loopholes, but they were the best at it. "Who do I have to kill to get some food around here?"

"No one," Lesto said. "I ordered it be brought before I came to see you. We should be ready to move tomorrow, and the town we're bound for has stores enough we should be able to get real food."

"Good. I've been in my cozy palace for so long, I'd forgotten how impossible it is to get decent food and sleep out here, even for a spoiled brat like me." He looked around his tent, the largest in camp and well-appointed, though not at his command. He could sleep on the ground with just his coat for a blanket as well as anyone. But Fathoms Deep did what Fathoms Deep wanted, and keeping him well was always one of their most important duties. "I would gladly trade one of my own eyes for both right now."

Lesto's gaze fell on the gleaming rings resting

against Sarrica's bare chest. "I think if you had to trade your eye, there is something else you'd want more."

Sarrica smiled faintly, reaching up to touch the rings again. "Maybe. I'd rather just add that to the pile."

"Have I mentioned how entertaining it is to see you so soppy? Especially given how much you hated him initially."

"One of these days you are going to fall in love, Lesto, and I will have revenge on all these years of harassment."

Lesto gave a single, sharp laugh and reclaimed the wine, draining the last measure of it. He started to speak, but a request to enter came from the tent entrance.

Sarrica granted permission, and a soldier came in bearing a tray of food and drink. "Dinner, Majesty."

"Thank you." When the woman had left, Sarrica picked up one of the bowls of thin stew and started eating. It tasted exactly as flavorless as it looked, but something was always better than nothing.

Halfway through the meal the air finally grew too cold for him to ignore. Gritting his teeth, Sarrica used his good arm and leg to leverage out of his chair. He walked slowly, stiffly across the tent to the trunk that held his clothes to pull out a linen shirt and a wool jacket that fell to his thighs and was just loose enough it wouldn't cause problems with the bandaging around his arm. Getting rid of what remained of his breeches, he pulled on a new pair, also slightly too big because war seldom sent men home overweight.

"I'm the one with the missing eye, but I still feel better than you look," Lesto said.

"I accept your apology for failing to keep me from

getting my ass kicked by a bunch of wharf rat Carthians."

Lesto laughed. "Wharf rats, how apt. Surprised I haven't heard that sooner. As to keeping you from getting your ass kicked, next time I tell you to stay in your damned tent, *do it*. Because if I have to report back to your pretty golden tongue that you're dead, I'll resurrect you so I can kill you again with my own hands."

"My what?"

"You should pay more attention to camp gossip."

Sarrica made a face. "I would rather surrender my throne than ever make that mistake again. What in the world is a golden tongue?" He lifted his eyes to the sky as realized he was a moron. "Allen. My golden tongue, is it? I admit it suits perfectly." Beautiful, rare, and worth an empire. He smiled.

"Quite," Lesto agreed with a smirk. "Pretty, expensive, and too good for you."

Sarrica rolled his eyes. "If I had the energy to kick you, I would."

"With that leg? You won't be kicking anything for a long time." He heaved to his feet with a groan. "Speaking of kicking, I need to get back to glaring and threatening if we're going to be ready to move out as soon as we get word from Morant. Try to stay out of trouble."

"I have no plans to do anything but sleep," Sarrica replied.

"Good." Lesto finished off the vile concoction that filled their mugs. Bark of some sort, if Sarrica recalled correctly. They'd been made to drink far too much of it as youths. It had tasted disgusting then, and it tasted disgusting now, but it was supposed to be strengthening. "I'll see you in a few hours."

Sarrica squeezed his forearm, looked up into Lesto's tired, battered, bandaged face. "Stop getting hurt. You're not allowed to look more dashingly injured than the High King."

Lesto smiled and cuffed him lightly. "The ass end of a horse looks better than you. Go to bed, Sarrica. I'll pass the order you're to be left alone."

Forcing down the rest of his food and the vile drink, Sarrica limped step-by-slow-step over to his cot and lowered himself onto it. He'd just gotten relatively comfortable and started to drift off when Lesto's voice came again. "Sarrica!"

Jerking up, immediately regretting it, Sarrica swore as he turned and lowered his legs more carefully over the edge of the cot as Lesto blew into his tent— holding a letter marked with Morant's personal crest. "Delivered by way of your falcon."

Sarrica broke the seal and read. *Bentan King dead. Crown Prince has surrendered. Rendezvous location remains unchanged. The moon sleeps in the sea.*

He stared at the last sentence, code between him and Morant that the words were in fact hers. If the words weren't there, the message was false. "We're still to meet them at Hallakanmark." Sarrica handed the letter to him.

"Good," Lesto said. "If they'd changed the location this late, I was going to kill them all."

Sarrica sighed and gave up any hope of sleep. "We're headed there at first light."

"Damn it," Lesto said. "Some of us had hoped to *sleep* tonight, you know."

"Well, some of us shouldn't have become High Commander, then," Sarrica replied. "Help me put on my boots. I can stand around looking threatening as well as anyone. I doubt I'll go back to sleep at this point, anyway."

Lesto nodded before turning sharply around to fetch Sarrica's boots from the other side of the tent. Sarrica called for one of his guards and ordered him to fetch the generals. Whatever Benta said about surrender, Sarrica wasn't going to relax until he was home.

~~*

Sarrica made himself hold still, save to move as he was bid to assist in the process, while soldiers dressed him. After four months of stiff, filthy uniforms spattered with mud and blood, it felt strange to don the sort of elaborate clothing he normally only endured for imperial functions.

He shrugged his shoulders to more comfortably settle his heavy, dark green jacket. Winter was slowly coming to an end, but it still clung tightly enough to put a bite in the air. The jacket was trimmed in gold, the buttons polished to a shine, and there were short bits of gold lace at the cuffs. His breeches and boots were black, the latter as well-polished as the buttons. They'd finally managed to trim his hair and shave his face, for which he was grateful.

And for once, his imperial ring was on his finger instead of hidden away. Next to it rested his engagement ring. Sarrica ran his thumb over it, admiring the sapphires. They'd dulled over the past few months and were sorely in need of a proper cleaning, but they still reminded him of fierce blue eyes that could freeze or melt a man with a single glance.

The soldiers fussed a few minutes more, adding accoutrements of state to his jacket. Where in the Realms had they gotten them? Who thought to pack stupid medals and ribbons and other such nonsense? He wished they'd packed more tea instead.

When he finally couldn't take it anymore, Sarrica thanked the soldiers and dismissed them. Leaving his room, which along with the rest of the house had been borrowed from the town mayor, he fell in with the half-dozen Fathoms Deep playing bodyguard and went downstairs to meet Lesto.

"I was right," Sarrica said as he stepped into the front room and saw Lesto standing by the fireplace. He was dressed in full High Commander regalia and quite possibly had more baubles on his chest than even Sarrica. The bandages covering his head and face had been removed, and in their place, a dark blue patch covered his right eye. Above and beneath it were still-healing marks from the dagger that had sliced open part of his face, destroying Lesto's eye in the process. "You look all dark and mysterious and dashing. They're going to fawn over you ridiculously when we get home. It's going to be unbearable. You probably won't even enjoy it because you're a bastard like that."

"What's to like about being crowded and touched and harangued to death?" Lesto asked irritably, but Sarrica didn't miss the way his hand started to lift to touch the patch. "I look like a criminal."

"You look like one of your ancestors, or some long lost tragic prince. Plenty of people will be happy to take up the role of true love should you slow the slightest interest. So shut up." Sarrica clapped him soundly on the back. "Are we ready?"

Lesto nodded. "Ready for things to go well, and more than ready for everything to go wrong."

"Let us hope the precautions prove unnecessary. Move out."

"As you command, Majesty." Lesto walked briskly out of the room, calling orders as he did so, barking more when they stepped outside into the chilly morning air. The sun had barely risen, the light still dull and flat. Sarrica's breath misted as he thanked a private who came scurrying up bearing cloak and gloves. Pulling them on, Sarrica swung into the saddle of the enormous stallion that was brought forward.

Fathoms Deep mounted up and closed in around him, Lesto at his side. At Lesto's signal, more soldiers fell into line on all sides. Scattered through the village, awaiting emergency signals, were imperial soldiers and mercenaries, each with their own set of orders about what to do if anything went wrong.

But as they traveled through town to the square where the meeting was to take place, everything remained mercifully quiet.

Morant and Desmond, the newly crowned King of Benta, were already waiting, each to their own end of the large, rounded square that made up the heart of the town. Benta was a strange place: all dark, hard edges and gloomy colors, and everything smelled like wood and smoke. Pantheon grant him mercy, but Sarrica was tired of their damned cold. Back home in Harken the approaching spring would already be warming the air, the lingering chill brisk and pleasant, little more than a good excuse to cuddle up close to someone and linger in bed a few minutes more.

Sarrica lifted a hand in greeting before going to his own section of the town square to consult with his silver tongues and negotiators. Across the way, Morant lifted her hand in reply. She was a handsome woman, big enough to throw around most men Sarrica knew. Get her mad enough, and she could probably throw *him* across the yard, and he had a few stone on her.

By contrast, Desmond was remarkably small and slender, a veritable waif half-lost among the much larger men protecting him.

Under his own canopy, Sarrica stepped up to the table and looked around at the gathered men. Lesto appeared at his left side, and one of the three silver tongues came to stand at his right, the others a few steps away. A sharp, deep ache sliced through Sarrica, a loneliness and need he tried to shove to the back of his mind and ignore. He wanted Allen, his children; he wanted to be home. "I want this done as quickly as possible, and not just because we will all freeze to death if this drags on for days. It's long past time we were home, and if it carries on too long, Benta may change their mind and go back to warring."

Lesto grunted. "I'd like to see them try when they are outnumbered two to one."

"We've beaten those odds ourselves more times than I care to recall," Sarrica replied, then turned to the silver tongues, the best he'd had available when setting out. All of them were extremely talented, as far as he could tell, but not a one was Allen. "Are we ready?"

"Yes, Majesty," said the most senior of the silver tongues. "We finished writing everything out last night, translations included." He motioned to the large pieces of paper laid out on the square table in front of them—all of Harken's demands, in Harken, Korlowan, and Bentan. Some of them were negotiable, and others most definitely were not.

He already knew Morant's requests matched or otherwise aligned with his. All they needed to see was what Benta had to say, though given they were the losing party, Sarrica cared only so far. "Let us begin." He lifted a hand, signaling the crier, who blew a horn.

Flanked by Lesto, surrounded by bodyguards, Sarrica walked to the center of the square where another canopy had been set up over a large, round table. Taking his seat, thanking the young woman who came bearing mulled wine and a plate of sausage, cheese, and bread, Sarrica waited while the others took their places.

Desmond did not smile, but neither did he scowl or otherwise act untoward. Not that Sarrica would have blamed him, or punished him in any way. In Desmond's position, he would be quite unbearable without someone to knock sense into him.

If anything, Desmond looked barely old enough to be considered an adult, like some runt of the litter forced to do work for which he was not intended. A scholar, rather than a soldier, and he lacked the courtly shine that Allen possessed. Ah, that was what caught Sarrica's attention. Desmond reminded him of an unpolished Allen. Peculiar, and not at all what a crown prince should be. Beside him sat a man who bore a passing resemblance, perhaps a cousin or something. On his other side was an older woman who definitely looked like a politician; it was all in the eyes, the confidence, the way she moved: precise and sharp, like a weighted dagger waiting to be thrown.

Morant looked tired but determined, her red hair loose for once instead of bound back. Strange to see her dressed like a princess, instead of in disguise—a disguise she had maintained all her life, right up until she'd finally returned home. How she'd made it home was a story Sarrica still had not heard, though he didn't much care. That she'd managed it was all that mattered.

When everyone was settled and basic introductions had been made, Sarrica said, "Shall we skip the pointless pleasantries and go straight to business?" They nodded, and Sarrica started to motion his people forward, but a strange look of disappointment flickered across Desmond's face. "Is something wrong, Your Highness?"

"No, Your Majesty," Desmond replied, his Harken... actually quite perfect. If Sarrica had not known better, he would have believed Desmond to be native. "I was only hoping, after all I have heard about him, that your Golden Tongue would be present."

"High Consort Allen?" Surprise rippled through Sarrica, along with a small measure of alarm. Why would Desmond know and care about Allen? "No, he is back in Harken. I would not bring him all the way out here, thought I won't deny his skills would be more than a little useful right now. How do you know of my consort?"

Desmond gave the barest smile. "Soldiers talk, even when all logic says they shouldn't know half of what they do. More than that, though, translators are a small community, especially at High Consort Allen's level—my level, in fact. I know ten languages. I believe His Majesty knows even more than that. Whatever greater problems and grudges exist here, I had looked forward to meeting your esteemed consort."

Pride and pleasure replaced Sarrica's wariness. "I

will convey your disappoint to him. Forgive me, but you seem misplaced here."

Waving the words aside, Desmond replied, "You are not wrong. It's not common knowledge, but I did have brothers, once. Older brothers. One was beaten to death by my father; the other killed himself. That was several years ago. I'm alive because I spent most of my life confined to a monastery, and the past few years in chains. I do not share my father's ambitions, but until he died and I was released from the prison he put me in, there was little I could do about it."

Morant frowned. "We have never heard a word of any of this."

Desmond's smile that time was razor sharp, and his eyes carried shadows that Sarrica had missed behind the glasses and waifish appearance. "Benta can keep secrets as well as any Korlowan princess. I'm sure the two of you keep plenty of secrets."

"Fair enough," Sarrica said. "I'm not here to discuss secrets. I'm here to negotiate the terms of peace. Shall we begin?" Morant and Desmond nodded. They signaled their people to distribute papers, and the arguing began.

It took them eight hours of arguing the first day, and four more on the second, but by the afternoon of the third, the papers were at last signed: Benta would withdraw from all the countries they had taken over and surrender control of Shalmoor Pass to Harken, who would retain it for a period of twenty-five years. They were to sever alliances with Cartha and keep their military to a restricted number for a period of fifty years.

Sarrica had stayed out of the marriage negotiations between Korlow and Benta and did not envy the children who would someday have to fulfill the terms of those contracts. Such was royal life, but he was grateful he would be able to give his own children the luxury of choice.

It was dark by the time everything was signed and sealed and stamped. After that official copies had to be drafted and those likewise signed, etc. Sarrica was somewhat impressed his hand did not fall off somewhere in the midst of the proceedings. How the clerks and silver tongues managed all the writing and rewriting that came with their job, he did not know.

By the time they were finished, he was more than happy to dismiss the notion of some banquet, and no one else bothered to hide their relief. Bidding them farewell, Sarrica motioned for his people to pack up before mounting his horse and riding back to the mayor's house, Lesto as ever at his side.

He dropped into the nearest chair the moment they were inside, groaning as he toed off his boots and stuck his feet as close to the fire as he dared. Frankly, he wouldn't care if they did burst into flame. At least they'd be warm. "I was beginning to think this would never end. Being banished to the Penance Realms would not be as miserable as these past days have been."

"You had best hope you never have to find out," Lesto said, taking the seat beside him but keeping his boots on. "Another month, month and a half at worst, and we'll be home."

That would make a total of nearly six months away. Once upon a time, that had seemed a trivial length. A lark, barely enough to prove to—or remind—the world just how wonderful a soldier he was. Pantheon, how had nobody strangled him as a youth?

"What has you smiling?" Lesto asked, brow quirked.

Sarrica shook his head. "I was remembering when we thought this sort of thing a grand adventure and were determined to prove how wonderful we were. I'm amazed that nobody killed me while I slept."

"You're mostly not unlikeable," Lesto drawled. "I am definitely unlikeable, but if they'd killed me, somebody else would have been forced to babysit you."

Sarrica laughed. "I may have to find someone else now. How useful can a one-eyed bodyguard possibly be? I think it's time to put you out to graze, find you a nice spouse. See how *you* like a surprise fiancé showing up in court out of nowhere."

"It wouldn't have been a surprise if you'd paid more attention to the matter," Lesto retorted. "I am fairly certain you have no real complaints. If you attempt to meddle in my affairs, I will turn you into cattle feed. I mean it."

Lifting his hands in defeat, Sarrica said, "I would never force a marriage upon you and you know that. It will be vastly more entertaining to see what poor fool stumbles into your path and stops you cold." And he kept hoping it would happen, if only because Lesto deserved better than all the conniving fortune hunters who'd made him miserable in the past.

Lesto kicked him then climbed to his feet with a jaw-cracking yawn. "Go to bed. Tomorrow we begin the journey home, and you can officially start counting down the days until you're once again a boring little High King moldering in his office." He smirked. "Or a smitten High King looking for any chance to sneak off with his beloved."

"I'm High King. I don't have to sneak anywhere," Sarrica muttered.

"Ha!" Lesto kicked his ankle again and dodged swiftly out of range of retaliation. "Goodnight, Your Majesty."

"Goodnight, Commander. Sleep well."

CHAPTER NINETEEN

"Next," Allen called, and the guards brought forward a man accused of theft and murdering the local sheriff, the vendor he'd stolen from, the vendor's son, and the daughter of the dead sheriff. Allen pulled out the notes from his folder, noting the crime had happened in Gearth, but the vendor and his son spoke Harken, and the thief spoke Farlander and a little Outlander. Allen glanced up at the man, quietly assessing his trembling, his downcast, red-rimmed eyes, and the way he hunched in on himself. "Proceed."

When the bailiff had finished recounting the case, Allen said, "I'm still not clear on *why* this man killed the local sheriff. There is a distinct lack of explanation there." He looked at the thief, who stared back, expression warring between resignation and hope. Taking a sip of tea, Allen said in Farlander, *"Tell me what happened."*

The man stared at him in shock and started crying as he haltingly explained, *"My name is Tima, Your Majesty. I went to market to buy some food. I haggled for three loaves of bread and two bits of dried meat, but when I handed over my coin and picked out my choices, suddenly they were screaming at me. I do not know much of other languages, but they spoke Outlander briefly, and I realized they were accusing me of stealing. I told them no, I negotiated fairly, but they threw me in a shed and left me there for two days until the Sheriff came by on his rounds. Then they—"* He pointed at the vendors and started shaking harder, more tears falling down his cheeks. *"They gave him money, put me in irons. They were going to put me on a ship again! I already did that, for seven years. I've earned my freedom. I don't want to be pressed back into that. I tried to run. They drew swords. I attempted to fight them off, but what am I to do in chains? I don't know—everything went quite mad. It was the vendor who stabbed the sheriff, not I, though I cannot prove it. I beg your leniency, Your Majesty."*

Allen smiled gently. *"I promise this matter will be addressed fairly. You need not be afraid."*

The man cried harder, nodding when he could not manage to speak.

Allen turned to the vendor, his son, and the sheriff's daughter and recounted what the thief had said. By the time he'd finished, they'd all visibly paled. "It sounds to me, sir, like you were bribing the sheriff. Explain to me why you were doing so, why not a single one of you attempted to find someone to help you communicate with this man."

"He's just an island rat—" The vendor snarled, but stopped at the look on Allen's face.

Turning to the vendor's son, who had gone as pale and trembling as the Farlander, Allen said, "If you have anything to confess, I suggest you do so."

"We didn't—" Again the vendor cut off, but this time because his son rested a hand on his arm.

Stepping forward, the son said, "It's as the man said, though in my father's defense, he did not mean to kill the sheriff."

"Why was this not admitted to at the time?"

"Fear, Your Majesty, and foolish decisions."

Allen turned to the daughter. "Are you satisfied with the explanation it was an accident, or would you like the matter further investigated?"

"I believe he is telling the truth," she replied. "No further investigation required for my part, Your Majesty."

"Very well. Bailiff, take them away. Restitution will be made to the Farlander, and the vendor's family owes the woman living funds denied her by the death of her father. They will pay those funds for the next ten years. As it was an accident, you are sentenced to five years in the shipyards and ten years serving the temples to atone for your sins, to be served concurrently. Lady, have you further demands?"

"No, Your Majesty," the woman said quietly. "Thank you. If I may beg the favor, would you convey to the wrongly accused man my deepest apologies?"

"Of course." Allen did so, and the man nodded at the woman in reply. Allen signaled to the bailiff, who had guards lead them all away again.

Allen looked down at his stack of papers, each one a case he needed to hear. It was called 'executioner's court' because that was what it had been in its inception. A last chance for those sentenced to execution to plead their cases to the crown and possibly be granted mercy. It had long since become much more convoluted than that and had a different, formal name, but the old one stuck.

Setting the papers aside, he signaled for a break and picked up his tea. After several soothing sips, he pulled his ledger close and refreshed himself on his schedule for the rest of the day: executioner's court for three more hours, followed by a meeting with the council that would probably last until dinner, then he had to attend dinner to start working on more delicate negotiations with Drymore. That aside, he'd promised Rene he would have dinner with him and Tara. He hadn't seen either of them in days and he was looking forward to hearing Tara's plans for their wedding.

After that, he had some smaller, late night meetings because there was no other place to schedule them that wasn't at least half a month out. Somewhere in the mess he had to start looking at and approving various things for his own wedding.

It seemed poor form to plan a wedding when a vital piece was still missing, but as he was oft reminded, it couldn't wait forever. The handfasting was all well and good, but the real, formal marriage needed to take place, and the sooner the better, given the vital roles Allen had already assumed.

Hopefully Sarrica would be home soon. Allen hadn't heard from anyone in nearly a month. Not so strange as they were probably traveling hard and fast, but he would have liked some estimate as to when to expect them. Days? Weeks? Another month? It had already been six.

More than enough time for everything to change again. What if Sarrica's time away had reminded him why he'd wanted a soldier for a spouse? Did he still think of Allen at all, or had his ardor cooled? They'd gone from antagonistic to cautious to married in the draw of a breath, followed by months apart. Allen's feelings had not changed, but what about Sarrica's?

There was no way to know until Sarrica returned, which meant he had to keep waiting. Which meant staying busy to keep from driving himself mad. At least staying busy was easy enough. Finishing his tea, Allen signaled for court to resume and pulled his papers close, looking over the next case. A baby left abandoned at a temple and two sets of parents who each insisted the child belonged to them and had been stolen.

He'd gotten no further than securing an adequate temporary home for the child when the air filled with the sound of the palace trumpets—played only upon the return of the High King. Allen's heart jumped into his throat. He surged to his feet, snatched up and slammed down the gavel. "Court is done for the day and will reconvene tomorrow."

He did not wait for a reply, lingered only long enough for Jac to fall into step beside him before practically running through the halls of the palace. Allen was outside on the grand stairs just as the imperial army came riding through the gates, rapidly filling the pavilion.

The sound of pounding feet came from behind him, and Allen half-turned as Rene and Tara came to join him, and shortly after them came a cluster of twenty or so other people. In balconies and windows and even along the walls of the palace gate, more people clustered and started cheering until it was impossible to hear anything, even Rene's words shouted in his ear.

Not that Allen was paying attention anyway as the crowded pavilion shifted and parted, making room for the imperial procession, led by Lesto and several soldiers from Fathoms Deep. Lesto, who had a patch over one eye and managed to look all dark and mysterious with it.

"Mercy of the Pantheon," Rene muttered. "I'm going to kill him."

Allen laughed and started to speak, but Lesto and

the guards moved aside and Sarrica came into view. He looked tired, dirty from traveling, clothes rumpled, hair overlong and face scruffy... But still just as beautiful as the first time Allen had seen him, as breathtaking as the man who'd come to his rescue and stayed with him throughout his recovery in Amorlay.

Dismounting, pushing through the crowds that tried to press in to greet him in their eagerness to see him safely returned, Sarrica swiftly mounted the stairs. Allen smiled as he drew close. "Welcome—" Was all he managed to say before Sarrica's mouth dropped over his, arms wrapping tightly around his waist. Allen flailed momentarily but managed to get his hands fastened around Sarrica's well-muscled arms. Then he kissed Sarrica back, matching the heat and fervor, shivering when Sarrica bit his lip and barely holding back a moan far too unseemly for public hearing. Not that the kiss itself was modest, but there were lines.

He was panting softly when Sarrica finally drew away. Allen licked his lips. "As I was saying: Welcome home."

The words were mostly lost in the renewed din of cheering and screaming and teasing, but Sarrica smiled all the same. He tilted Allen's chin up and kissed him more softly, not needing words to convey that it was good to be home.

Drawing back, Allen signaled to the arrayed guards, who managed to calm the crowd down enough that Sarrica was able to announce the victory and that there would be no further wars with the countries to the north.

By the time they were able to step into the palace, Sarrica's children had arrived. They screamed when they saw him and ran at him hard enough that when he knelt to meet them, they nearly knocked him over. Allen stood off to the side, smiling so hard it nearly hurt.

Movement caught his eye, and he turned to greet Lesto. "Did Sarrica do that?"

Lesto laughed and touched the edge of the dark blue patch covering his eye. "No, it was done by one of the Carthian assassins who attacked our camp. We were better prepared for such an attack than they liked, but they still got in some nasty blows."

"Assassins?" Allen said, and by the looks several people gave him, he'd said that a touch too loud. He snapped his mouth shut for the sake of the children but glared at Lesto.

"Sarrica still glares better than you," Lesto drawled. Nearby, Rene, Jac, and Tara snickered and smiled.

Allen could not bring himself to be amused. He turned away, heart thudding. Stupid to be scared and relieved at the same time, but if Lesto had been so terribly injured, how bad an attack had it been? Had Sarrica been wounded? He didn't move like he had been, unless the stiffness Allen had attributed to countless hours of riding was actually the result of injury.

A hand fell heavy on his shoulder; he looked up at Rene, who smiled reassuringly and gave his shoulder a gentle shake. "They're home safe. Do not drive yourself mad with what could have happened."

"I'll try," Allen said.

Sarrica slowly stood, Nyla braced on one arm, his free hand wrapped around one of Bellen's. He grinned at Allen. "Don't think I haven't noticed that Bellen has gone from her pretty little gowns to dressing like a miniature silver tongue."

Ignoring the sudden burn to his cheeks, Allen said, "I had nothing to do with it. She was outgrowing her old clothes, and her nurse said that was what she wanted." He had no intention of admitting she might have been influenced by her near-nightly demands that he teach her new words instead of reading a bedtime story.

Chuckling, Sarrica leaned in and kissed him briefly. "I'm going to take them back upstairs, steal some time before the rest of this place comes clamoring for attention. Did you want to join us?"

Swallowing the rock in his throat, Allen shook his head. "Tempting, but I'm sure they'd like to have you all to themselves and I need to do a few things to clear my schedule for the rest of the day. Go rest, enjoy."

The smile Sarrica gave him made a sweet, sharp ache bloom in Allen's chest. "I will see you again at dinner then, and after that, I don't intend to let you out of my sight."

Allen's mouth tipped up at one corner, and he gladly returned one last soft, fleeting kiss before drawing back. "Yes, Majesty."

Sarrica departed, their nurse trailing behind, Bellen and Nyla talking too fast to follow as they fell over themselves trying to tell Sarrica about everything he'd missed.

"How has everything been here?" Lesto asked.

"Busy," Allen said. "I received confirmation today from Selemea that they've agreed to a betrothal between Prince Bann and Lord Eseera."

Lesto shook his head and let out a soft huff, smiling. "How did you manage that?"

"Eseera doesn't really want to return home, so I

gave him and Nemrith a good reason for him to stay, and Selemea a marriage prospect far better than Lord Tara, as marvelous as Tara is."

Tara laughed. "I'd have made terrible royalty." He twined an arm through Rene's, smiling at Lesto. "You look like quite the dashing war hero."

Lesto heaved a sigh. "I had a feeling you would all be as intolerable as Sarrica. What happened to giving a man sympathy?"

"Too handsome, don't deserve it," Tara replied.

Lesto gave him a shove as he strode by. "I'm going to find a bath and my bed, and nobody had better make me work until tomorrow. My wine had better be at the banquet table!"

Allen lifted a hand to acknowledge the words. Tara snickered. "As if we wouldn't make certain to have his wine out."

"I hope he's all right," Allen said. "For all the jesting, that must be a difficult adjustment."

Rene shrugged. "Lesto is very self-contained. He wouldn't want anyone to fuss." He dropped a quick kiss on Tara's cheek. "I'm going to go help contend with the returning army. I'll see you both at the banquet."

Once he was gone, Tara said, "I believe that leaves me with the banquet while you go handle the secretaries already fluttering impatiently behind you."

Allen stifled a groan, made a face as Tara laughed at him. "Go away." Waving, Tara strode off, signaling to the hovering seneschal, who fell into step beside him and bent his head close as they set to work.

With Jac on his heels, Allen finally allowed his secretaries to drag him back to work. Even pushing himself as hard as he could, it took hours before he had every pressing matter dealt with, and his schedule for the next few days rearranged because he wasn't stupid—Sarrica was going to be distracting, and Allen had every intention of letting himself be distracted. Especially when even hours of grueling work could not erase the feel of Sarrica's kisses, or cool the hot rush of that enthusiastic homecoming. Clearly his fears had been for naught.

He slipped from the office with barely enough time to go to his room to change for dinner. "I did not think they would ever let me go."

Jac chuckled. "You are High Consort—you *can* tell them to go away. If I recall correctly, Sarrica does it all the time."

"The work must get done before the playing can begin," Allen replied and paused outside his door. "Speaking of playing—I believe the general guards will suffice for protection. Tonight is for revelry, Jac, and you should join in with that. You can resume your duties again tomorrow and be as hungover and miserable as the rest of us."

"I'm not going to argue with you," Jac said and with a wink and bow, eagerly departed.

Allen hurried into his room—and drew to a halt when he spied a dark wooden box resting on his bed. Next to it, his manservant had kindly laid out his clothes for the evening. Allen stripped off the clothes he was already wearing and went into his dressing room. Ignoring the chest that held the underclothes he usually wore he threw open a smaller chest tucked below all the shelves. Rifling through the contents, considering his options and all the different possible reactions, he finally made a choice and pulled the drawers on.

Returning to the main room, he succumbed to curiosity and examined the waiting box. It was marked with the imperial griffon, and though someone had cleaned it, there were still traces of dust at the hinges. Allen flipped the box open then simply stared for a moment. He was accustomed to costly jewelry, had been wearing it from the moment he was old enough to attend formal gatherings, but still, the diadem nestled in black velvet was beautiful. It was made of silver and gold, shaped like ivy and woven together in intricate knots. Set in the very center was a beautiful star sapphire, and on either side of it was a line of three pale blue diamonds.

His manservant must have known, or else had peeked, because he'd set out Allen's midnight blue jacket with the silver lining and silver and gold flower embroidery, gray breeches, and the dark blue shoes with silver and diamond flowers. Unlike most of his jackets, this one stopped at mid-thigh and flared slightly.

Allen dressed quickly and combed out his hair. It was still shorter than he'd like, but at least there was enough of it to comb. Or grab. Shoving *those* thoughts forcefully away, he quickly finished dressing, adding sapphire earrings, diamond and sapphire rings, and a heavy diamond necklace, resting at the base of his throat, that sparkled where the light caught it, the collar of his stiff shirt open to show it off. He settled the diadem in place last and smiled happily in the mirror.

If he was still anxious about what Sarrica would think when the clothes were gone... Well, those fears were going to be ignored as long as possible.

Nodding to his reflection, he spun away and

headed back out of the room—just as Sarrica came out of his, handsome in black, green, and gold. Sarrica broke into a wide smile as his eyes fell on the diadem. "Do you like it?"

"Yes," Allen said. "Thank you."

Sarrica closed the space between them, cupped Allen's shoulders, and bent to kiss him. "It belonged to my mother, and it seemed a shame to let something like that continue to collect dust when I knew it would suit you."

"I suspect you like putting me in sapphires," Allen said, voice a touch breathless.

"I picked them for the ring because they match your eyes," Sarrica replied, "but I admit I'm developing a fondness." He brushed Allen's cheek with the back of his hand, eyes so dark and intent, full of affection that Allen had never thought he would see there. Just like the one other time Sarrica had done it, the gesture warmed his face, made it hard to draw breath. "Have you been well? I neglected to ask that before."

Allen smiled softly, turned into Sarrica's hand, and let his eyes fall shut, savoring the warmth and scent and closeness of this man he'd missed more than seemed reasonable or fair. "I'm fine. I wasn't the one fighting for my life—the one nearly assassinated, don't think I've forgotten about that."

"I'm going to kill Lesto," Sarrica muttered. He turned his hand, danced his fingers over Allen's lips before tracing the lines of his face. "I'm fine, and happier still that you've been well in my absence. From what I have heard, I think you've rendered me superfluous. You are even charming away my children, or did you think I wouldn't find out little Bellen has decided she's going to be a silver tongue?" He smiled.

"I didn't—she just likes to learn new words at night." Allen's cheeks burned. "She hadn't mentioned she intends to be a silver tongue. I'm sure she'll change her mind again in a month."

Sarrica laughed. "I wouldn't be so sure of that. Nyla says you're an excellent story reader." He slid his hand back to curl his fingers into the hair at Allen's nape. "I'm glad you're getting along, even if it means I have been rendered entirely useless."

Heart thudding in his chest, Allen curled his fingers into the fabric of Sarrica's jacket and replied, "I think there's still one or two things for which you might be useful." His breath caught at the way Sarrica's eyes flared; he couldn't recall ever making someone burn quite like that.

Sarrica's mouth dropped over his, hard and hot and heady, claiming it like a conqueror, leaving Allen breathless and aching for more. Allen licked his lips, not at all sorry for the soft growl that got him, the faint tug on his hair. "We have a banquet to attend, Majesty. If we don't go soon we'll be late."

"I am fairly certain it's impossible to arrive late to my own party," Sarrica replied, but he let Allen go after another hard kiss. "Let's go before I surrender to irresponsible impulses." He offered his hand and Allen took it.

Outside, Lesto was leaning against a wall, recounting some story to Jac and the Fathoms Deep gathered around them. He paused when he saw them and pushed away from the wall, clapping the nearest soldiers on the shoulder. "I was starting to think the two of you would make us late."

"You could have gone without us," Sarrica said.

Lesto shrugged. "When have I ever been in a hurry

to attend a party?"

Allen could not remember ever seeing Lesto in anything but his uniform, and it was as strange as it had been with Rene for the first few weeks. He was always impressive in his uniform, but cut an even more handsome figure in civilian clothes. His jacket was dark teal and silvery gray trimmed in black, and there was a choker of black pearls set with a single large black diamond around his neck. The blue patch had been exchanged for a black one. "You don't like parties?"

"I'm a soldier, Majesty, and have been for a long time. We lose our ability to be pleasant and sociable, as I'm sure you've noticed." He winked, then turned and strode off down the hallway, lifting a hand in farewell to the Fathoms Deep guards.

Jac fell into step just behind them, also handsomely dressed in civilian clothing, though her breeches and dark pink, ruffled jacket were a good deal less ornate than what the rest of them wore. Though she tried to hide it, smiling brightly when Allen glanced at her, she didn't quite manage to stifle her discomfort. Well, it wouldn't be an issue for long, not with what Jac was getting paid to serve as personal bodyguard to the High Consort.

The banquet hall was packed to overflowing when they arrived, and by the time the cheering had died down Allen's ears were ringing. He lifted his glass with everyone else as Sarrica gave a toast to the fallen and signaled for the musicians to begin as the solemn moment passed.

Sarrica took a sip of pale pink wine then gave Allen a slow smile. "I've not had a chance to tell you that Prince Desmond of Benta was disappointed he did not get to meet you."

"Why would he care about meeting me?" Allen asked.

"Something about translators being small in number and hearing many great things about my golden tongue," Sarrica replied.

Allen lifted his eyes to the ceiling as everyone around them laughed. "I am not a *golden* tongue."

"Oh, I think you are," Tara commented over the rim of his wine glass. "I hear it everywhere I go. I'm not even remotely surprised our soldiers carried it all the way to the north. Nobody gossips better than a soldier."

Lesto made a face. "There is entirely too much truth in that statement." He lifted his glass to Allen. "It's true your name came up several times. The Dragons and the rest of the mercenaries have built you into quite the legend. The imperial army is happy to spread it, and onward it goes. Nevermind the way you helped Lady Laria and Lady Quell. I dread to see what will happen if we let you out of the palace a third time, Golden Tongue."

"I don't think Sarrica's secretaries will permit it. No one loves Allen more, except maybe His Majesty," Tara said with a smile.

Sarrica rolled his eyes and muttered, "There is no maybe about it."

Allen sucked in a sharp breath, wine glass freezing right as it touched his lips. His chest felt like someone was squeezing it too-tight. He looked up and saw Sarrica watching him warily, as though he had only belatedly realized what he'd said and wasn't certain how Allen would take it. Allen dropped his free hand down over Sarrica's where it lay on his armrest and gripped it tightly.

The tension in Sarrica's shoulders bled away, and he lifted Allen's hands to kiss the knuckles. Ignoring the looks and laughs around them, Allen finally paid proper attention to the excellent wine in front of him.

"Sarrica, you still have not apologized to me for being so mad about the fiancé we chose for you," Lesto drawled. "The council and I worked hard to find someone suitable, you know."

"I think I have well admitted my mistakes and made it clear I'm more than happy with the golden tongue at my side."

Allen shook his head, but happiness won out over exasperation. "There's no such thing as a golden tongue."

"Ha!" Tara surged to his feet, tapping his glass with his spoon until the noise in the overcrowded room subsided. "A moment of gratitude for the fine man who has kept the palace in one piece while our High King was off winning a war. Cheers for the High King's Golden Tongue!"

Allen startled at the noise that rose up, nearly spilling the glass of wine he'd just set down. "Tara!"

Grinning unrepentantly, Tara resumed his seat and drained his glass. "I told you so."

"I'm not even certain what it is you think you told me," Allen said with a huff, fighting against a smile and losing. "Don't do that again."

Tara ignored him in favor of finishing his wine before dragging Rene to his feet. "Let's go dance."

"Dance?" Allen echoed and turned to where the dancing had, in fact, started up. He hadn't danced in longer than he could remember. His mother's birthday, maybe?

"Would you like to dance, Majesty?" Lesto asked.

Allen looked at him. "I would love to."

Lesto rose, offered a hand to Allen, and led him out to the dance floor, falling easily into the movements as the strains of a new piece started up. "I am not at all surprised you dance well."

"Thank you," Allen said. "I am sorry about your eye."

"No apology necessary, but thank you," Lesto said with a smile. "I'm glad all has turned out well for you. I was not looking forward to your mother's wrath if it had not. I only met her once, but once was all that was required."

Allen laughed hard enough he nearly missed a step. "She's not as terrifying as she can seem, and I do not think even she would kill the High King's closest friend—especially when that friend is one of the oldest and most powerful titles in Harken."

Lesto gave a soft, amused huff. "I have been High Commander so long, I tend to forget I'm also the Duke of something or other."

"Something or other," Allen repeated with another laugh and bowed playfully as the dance concluded. Rene and Tara appeared at their side, and before he could scarcely draw breath, Rene had whisked him off into the next dance. "So are you adjusting to being a lazy noble, my lord?"

"Slowly," Rene said. "Though I do not think I would be here at all if not for you."

"I do not think me and my reckless behavior have anything to do with it."

Rene didn't reply, save to smile, and bowed low as the dance came to an end. The smile widened to a grin when he rose and looked at something behind Allen. "I think someone is getting petulant."

"Oh?" Allen asked lightly and turned to face Sarrica, who was indeed scowling a bit. "Stop frowning."

Sarrica grunted and held out a hand. "Would you like to dance?"

"Yes, but I don't think you do," Allen said, accepting his hand all the same. Over Sarrica's shoulder he saw Rene and Tara both smirking, and beyond them, Lesto rolled his eyes as he said something to Jac, with whom he'd begun dancing.

After a few turns around the dance floor, Allen was the one scowling. "You dance remarkably well for someone who does not like to do it."

"It's less a matter of dislike and more a matter of abusing my knees in several incidents of youthful stupidity," Sarrica replied. "They've never quite forgiven me, and combined with the headaches that come from being in all this noise for too long..." He shrugged his broad shoulders, which should not have been so distracting, but Allen was most definitely distracted all the same.

Then the words registered. "Headaches?"

Sarrica shrugged again, but the hesitation and wariness on his face pulled at Allen more. "The healers call them crippling headaches; my father didn't get them, but they do run in the family. There are days I can barely crawl out of bed."

"Ah," Allen said. "One of my tutors got them. My mother would have dismissed her if she'd known how often the woman couldn't get out of bed, but I found other ways to further those studies. I'm sorry you suffer them."

"Small price to pay in the end," Sarrica said. As the dance came to an end, instead of bowing, he drew

Allen's hands up and kissed them, then said, "Come with me."

Anticipation warmed Allen's skin, raced up his spine and made him shiver. "As you wish."

Sarrica's mouth curved in a slow, hot smile before he turned and, holding fast to Allen's hand, wove and shoved and maneuvered through the crowded room. He ignored all attempts to speak with them except to nod politely as they passed, until they finally ducked through a side door and down a couple of hallways.

A short distance down the second one, Sarrica pushed open the door to what proved to be a sitting room. It was dark, save for the moonlight slipping between the curtains, and slightly chilly. Sarrica closed the door, then pressed Allen up against it and took his mouth like a man too long deprived of food and water. Allen moaned and threw his arms around Sarrica's neck, holding him close as he matched the artless, ravenous kiss.

"I both admire the skill it takes to put together such an excellent banquet so quickly with such short notice," Sarrica said, getting the words out between sharp, biting, hungry kisses that left Allen's lips throbbing, "and resent wholly that my staff possesses said skills. I should have surrendered to impulse upstairs because I am going mad from the need to touch you."

"Touch all you like," Allen said and surrendered to an impulse himself, putting his mouth to Sarrica's throat, sucking up a mark right where his pulse beat. The rough, pleased noises that fell from Sarrica's lips seared into his memory, became something vital that he needed to hear every day.

Sarrica kissed him again, tongue plunging deep,

fucking his mouth. It was as torturous as it was satisfying. Allen moaned, hands clinging tightly to the sleeves of Sarrica's jacket. Pulling away to put his own mark on Allen's throat—high up his throat, since his necklace was still in the way—Sarrica loosened his arms to slide his hands down and cup Allen's ass, fingers digging in, drawing out a long, stuttering groan that spilled into Sarrica's mouth.

Drawing back, nipping at his jaw, Sarrica said, "I can't wait to hear the noises you make when I have your cock down my throat."

Allen groaned again, grinding against him, whining when Sarrica drew back and deprived him of pressure. Sarrica's deft fingers unfastened the buttons of Allen's long coat and pushed it open before undoing the fastenings on his breeches. He slid those large, hot hands inside—and stopped. His fingers slid back and forth over Allen's ass as heat flushed Allen's cheeks. "What in the Pantheon are you wearing?" he asked, voice gone rough in that spine-tingling way Allen had never forgotten.

He couldn't quite keep all the smugness from his voice as he replied with a soft laugh, "Lace. Has no one ever worn lace undergarments for you, Majesty?"

Sarrica's reply was a deep, growly noise followed by a hard, hungry kiss. He closed the breeches and jacket he'd just opened, kissed Allen's nose when he complained. "I've had quite enough. I'm High King. I can abandon my own banquet if I want. What say you, High Consort? Shall we retire early?"

"Yes," Allen said, mostly because the bastard chose that moment to fondle him, rubbing and squeezing in a way that ruined the possibility of any other answer. Not that Allen had planned on more than a token protest, if that.

Kissing him again, Sarrica then tore away and hastily snuck them back down the hall, past the banquet hall, and up a set of back stairs.

CHAPTER TWENTY

Sarrica closed the door to his—their—chambers and leaned against it, drew Allen up against him, and went back to devouring that delectable mouth, sinking his hands into all the soft hair that had grown out while he was gone. "I did not like finally repairing matters between us only to be torn away for months. If someone tries to make me leave again, I'm throwing everyone in the dungeons."

"I don't think your dungeons have that much space," Allen replied with a breathy laugh.

Sliding his hands down Allen's back to cup his truly marvelous ass again, Sarrica drew him back in to resume the kissing, determined to leave Allen's lips so well-used Allen would be able to think of little else for days.

"Delightful as this is," Allen said, slowly pulling away just enough to speak, "you are craning my neck, and there is a bed close by." He frowned thoughtfully. "Mine or yours?"

"Mine," Sarrica said, grateful when that elicited a tolerant smile as he took one last kiss before dragging Allen across the room and into his bedroom.

He was gentle only with the diadem still on Allen's forehead, carefully setting it aside before he went to work on everything else Allen wore with a good deal less patience. Finally he was able to get a good look at what he'd only felt before: the delicate black lace drawers that were barely long enough to contain

Allen's cock and practically painted on his skin. They were the most decadent thing Sarrica had ever seen. "I need to make a law that you never wear anything but these ever again."

"That—" Allen groaned as Sarrica knelt and pressed his mouth to the hard cock still barely confined by lace that was already damp in spots. His fingers tangled in Sarrica's hair. "What was I saying?"

"Nothing important," Sarrica said, grinning up at him briefly. He brushed his mouth over the tattoo that rested low on Allen's abdomen: a black three-headed dragon, crouched with its heads fanned out. "I hope you realize this means the Dragons think they have marked you as their property."

Allen gave a short, breathy laugh. "I'd think you'd take issue with that."

"I did say they *think*," Sarrica replied with a smirk before going back to mouthing Allen's cock through the soft lace, slipping his fingers beneath the edges of it to tease him elsewhere, his own need growing hotter with every hungry, desperate noise that fell from Allen's lips.

Allen protested when Sarrica briefly pulled away. "Honestly, you're acting like I did the first time I saw a lover in lace."

"I don't exactly have countless lovers to my name," Sarrica said, pulling away and standing, herding him over to the bed, and pushing him down on it. "You do not fully appreciate how focused I was on soldiering. I had two lovers while in school and training, neither of whom lasted more than a few weeks. Then Lesto—"

Allen jerked at that. *"Lesto?"*

Sarrica shrugged out of his jacket and threw it aside, then began to fight with the irritatingly small buttons of his shirt, vastly more interested in the beautiful man stretched out on his bed, decadent and a touch bewitching against Sarrica's red coverlet, his skin a warm, delicate gold in the lamplight. "We tried it for... oh, I hardly recall. Maybe a month? Not even that long, I suspect. Realized we were much happier as friends."

"Rene and I..." Allen trailed off, eyeing him uncertainly. "Only the one night, before I left with him to go to Cartha. We were both rather despondent."

Sarrica gave a soft snort. "I think it was my mother who said that Arseni men are impossible to ignore and hard to resist. I'd be jealous, but even I know there is no cause for concern. I was probably responsible for that despondence. I'm sure Lesto would be vastly amused, somehow. Nobody laughed harder than him when I fell for Nyle." He made a face. "That is not who I should be talking about to my new husband on our very belated wedding night."

"I don't mind," Allen said softly. "You loved him."

Drawing a breath, giving up on his stupid buttons, Sarrica said, "I love you. I did not mean to say that so gracelessly downstairs."

Allen rose to his knees and moved to the edge of the bed, long, slender fingers easily defeating the buttons. "I have no complaints. I love you, too." He pushed Sarrica's shirt from his shoulders, a hungry look returning. Most days Sarrica felt every bit of his age, but he felt it a good deal less when Allen looked at him like that.

Until he scowled, fingers reaching out to touch the scar that remained from the Carthian attack. "You didn't have this one before."

Sarrica opened his mouth, then closed it. "How

would you know that? You've never seen me without my clothes, not that I recall."

Allen's face went pink. "I—it looks new?"

"Try again," Sarrica said, mouth curving.

The pink turned red as Allen conceded defeat by admitting, "I saw you change a few times in the fortress."

Sarrica laughed. "I always thought you were flushed from exertion, but the whole time you were being naughty."

Allen tried to bat away Sarrica's hands as they grabbed hold. "You're not distracting me from the fact that scar is new, and it looks like it was a bad wound."

"It looks worse than it was, I promise. Lesto took the real injuries from the fight," Sarrica replied, capturing Allen's hand and drawing it to his shoulder, mentally smirking at the way those fingers fluttered before firmly gripping. "There's another on my thigh, but I was never in danger. The worst I suffered was the miserable itching of healing wounds." He dragged Allen's other hand up to rest on his shoulder then slid his own hands around—

He stopped in surprise when Allen paled and jerked away. Wincing inwardly, Sarrica said, "I'm sorry, is there still some injury—"

"N-no," Allen said, but all the pleasure had fled his demeanor. "I just... My back is not a pleasant sight. I'd managed to forget about it, but unless you want to turn your stomach—"

Sarrica cut that nonsense off by the most expedient and effective means at his disposal, not breaking the kiss until Allen clung to him once more and his own lips felt bruised. Pulling back, he flipped Allen over and pinned him to the bed.

"Don't—" The words cut off when Sarrica dragged his lips over one of the more lurid scars on Allen's back, then the soft skin between two marks. "Sarrica..."

"If you think you're anything but beautiful, you're mistaken," Sarrica said. "You take my breath away."

"Sarrica—" Allen repeated, and this time sounded near to tears. Which was not at all what Sarrica wanted.

He turned Allen back around and kissed those well-used lips, the corners of his eyes, then slowly worked his way down to the cock once more hardening beneath wicked black lace. "I meant it when I said I'm instituting a new law. You are not allowed to wear anything but these, ever."

"These specifically?" Allen asked, voice dry as dust, though there was a slight hitch to it. "Because I have several other colors and different fab—" He gasped as Sarrica kissed him hard, and only when he was trembling and moaning did Sarrica finally pull back. Allen licked his lips, panting softly. "So you want to see the other colors then?"

"You are far more evil than I credited," Sarrica replied, and kissed his way back down Allen's body.

Allen laughed huskily, but it turned into a moan when Sarrica pulled the lace away and put his mouth to that hard, heavy, wet-tipped cock.

His own cock was hard enough it practically hurt, and he would probably never be able to think clearly again. Allen had quite neatly ruined that ability by filling his head with lovely, lovely images. Sarrica pinned Allen's hips to the mattress and went to work in earnest, drawing Allen deep into his mouth, cheeks hollowing as he sucked, tongue working the underside. When the body beneath his hands tensed, and he could feel the trembling in Allen's thighs, he drew back, left Allen swearing and panting.

It took him only a moment to find the oil in his drawer—oil he hadn't put there, hadn't needed in years, but he did not pay his servants good money because they were stupid or modest. Returning to Allen, Sarrica finally removed the lace underwear and cast it aside, spread Allen's thighs wide with slick fingers, leaving gleaming trails on his pale skin. "I want badly to leave you incapable of walking, so I know exactly where to find you all of tomorrow."

Allen laughed, lazily drawing his arms up to rest above his head, one curling around a wooden rail of Sarrica's headboard. Wasn't that inspiring of lovely ideas of bound wrists, a pretty consort completely at his mercy. Sarrica tucked that thought away right under the one about fucking Allen while he was spread out on the table. For the present, he teased at Allen's hole, slicking the edges, pushing with the barest fingertip before withdrawing to tease some more, not relenting until Allen started begging in a remarkably imperious tone for Sarrica to cease with the tormenting.

"As you command," Sarrica said and pushed one slick finger into him, drunk on the way Allen writhed and pushed for more, moaning his name so it filled the room.

Sarrica bent to lightly kiss his abused mouth, nibbled at his jaw and the long, elegant line of his throat as he steadily worked in a second finger, and after several minutes, a third. When they were both strung so taut he felt ready to snap, Sarrica finally withdrew his fingers and lined up his cock. He didn't even try to hold back his groan as he slid into that tight, hot heat.

Allen's nails bit into his shoulders, a pleasant sting mingling with the scent of sweat and sex and lingering cologne, the warmth of their bodies, the feel of Allen's soft, sweat-slick skin as Sarrica began to fuck him. The sounds of slapping skin filled the room, joined by soft moans and gasps and desperate pleas for more.

Pleas Sarrica was more than happy to indulge. Shuddering with the effort to hold himself back, he pulled out of Allen's body and flipped him back around, pulled him close and spread him wide, then thrust back inside. He managed a few more quick, hard and deep strokes, then plastered himself to Allen's back as he finally came. Beneath him, Allen moaned Sarrica's name, shaking hard as he almost immediately followed, spilling across the dark red coverlet.

Sarrica gently pulled out of Allen's body and made himself move enough to get them comfortably under the blankets. He buried his nose in Allen's hair, a soft, sweet warmth rushing through him when Allen pressed closer and settled heavily against him, tangling their legs together. Sarrica had always liked having a lover close when he slept, though he'd never minded that Nyle preferred his space. "It's good to be home."

"It's good to have you home," Allen said quietly, then gave a soft laugh. "It seems silly I was afraid that all those months away would have changed your mind."

Kissing the soft skin behind his ear, Sarrica said, "Well, I feared the same, so at least we're equally silly." A yawn cut him off before he could say more, and by the time he stopped, he'd forgotten what he'd wanted to say. He settled for nuzzling against Allen again and listening as his breathing evened out and turned into soft snores.

A smile on his face, Sarrica finally succumbed to sleep himself.

He woke to a soft knock on the door and a voice calling, "Breakfast, Majesties." He heard the servant walk away and gave half a thought to getting out of bed, but decided he'd much rather go back to sleep. He'd just returned from war. He had earned the right to be a bit lazy.

His mind was abruptly changed when long, deft fingers wrapped around his cock. He'd barely gotten his eyes open when the blankets were thrown back and Allen climbed atop him, straddled his thighs, and rubbed back against Sarrica's cock, which was far more awake than he.

But he didn't need to be completely awake to appreciate the decadent beauty shamelessly splayed across him. He curled his hands around Allen's hips, holding him steady as Allen wasted no time in taking exactly what he wanted, sinking down on Sarrica's cock, barely pausing to adjust to it before riding him like a man on a mission.

As ways to wake up went, Sarrica had no complaints. His hands tightened on Allen's hips as he thrust up in time to match Allen's movements, driving in deep, eliciting those sharp, hungry little gasps he already craved.

It didn't take long for either of them to come, cries muffled by a wet, messy kiss as Allen's release spilled across Sarrica's skin. Letting go of Allen's hips, Sarrica lazily petted him. "If that is how you wake up every morning, you may well be the death of me. I cannot find it in myself to be distraught about the matter."

Laughing, the sound faintly husky, Allen pulled off his softening cock and rolled out of bed. "Not every morning, but I admit I am feeling particularly energized *this* morning. Did I hear correctly that breakfast is waiting?"

"Yes." Sarrica sprawled across the bed, perfectly content to stay where he was and enjoy the view.

Allen looked over his shoulder. "Let's go eat."

"I'd rather lie here and admire your ass."

"My ass has had enough admiration for now," Allen said with a laugh. "Get up. I'll make it worth your while later."

Sarrica huffed but smiled and relented, going over to his dressing room and pulling on one of his dressing robes. When he came out again, Allen had vanished, but wandering out into the main room, Sarrica saw him already seated at the table. He wore a silk dressing robe of red and green, and it clung in a way that really shouldn't be allowed. Sarrica needed badly to know if he was wearing anything underneath it, eager to see more of the promised lace, but he was content to enjoy the anticipation while they ate breakfast.

Looking up over the rim of his teacup, Allen smiled. "Good morning, my king."

Warmth unfurled in Sarrica's chest as he took his seat at the table. He glanced at the folders and papers piled neatly to one side. "It looks like they're wasting no time in putting us back to work." He poured himself a cup of tea and took a sip, then reached for the nearest stack. "At least there are two of us to do it."

Allen's smile widened. He started to reach for the stack closest to him but froze. "Oh, I nearly forgot. The Master Librarian left a note for you." He pulled it from his robes and handed it across the table.

Abandoning his teacup, Sarrica took the note and opened it, breaking into an eager grin when he read exactly what he'd been hoping. "Come on. My gift for you is finally finished."

Allen's face lit up. "I finally get to see what it is?"

Chuckling, Sarrica offered a hand and pulled Allen from his seat. He lingered long enough to skate his hand down the slender body pressed against his, feeling that there was indeed lace beneath the sumptuous silk robe. "Come along, before I let you distract me."

He paused in his bedroom to fetch his keys then led Allen to the locked door. Pulling it open, he bowed Allen inside. And preened more than a little bit at the delighted cry as Allen stepped into the private library Sarrica had requested be built.

All of Allen's books were there, as well as some new additions the Master Librarian had worked hard to obtain for him. There was also a desk for cataloguing and other library-type work that Sarrica knew nothing about. It was stocked with the finest inks and papers an empire could provide, tools for maintaining and repairing books, and the rest he was completely clueless on.

From the look on Allen's face, every bit of it was as perfect as Sarrica had hoped.

He oofed slightly when Allen threw himself into Sarrica's arms, but was more than happy to go along with the eager, hungry kiss Allen gave him. Drawing back, Allen said, "You keep giving me things, and I've yet to give you anything."

"I think I have yet to match all that you *have* given me," Sarrica said, bending to kiss him softly. Pulling away a moment later, his smile turned into a teasing grin, hands dropping to the knot of Allen's robe. "Although if you're offering—" He broke off when he heard someone calling for them, sighed as he registered Lesto's voice. "If you're offering," he repeated dryly. "I'm in desperate need of free time in which to do filthy things to my consort."

Chuckling softly as he pulled away, tangling their fingers together as they headed back to the main room, Allen said, "I think I can help with that. I'm told I have a talent for helping kings."

Sarrica drew him back in to steal a last kiss. "That you do, golden tongue. That you do."

FIN

Coming Summer 2016 – *The Pirate of Fathom's Deep*

High Commander Lesto Arseni is the most feared man in the Harken Empire. None but the High King dares risk his wrath—and a pirate who once punched him in the middle of the imperial pavilion. A pirate who later snuck away with Lesto to an empty room, touched him in ways far more memorable. And then immediately bolted like a man who'd gotten what he wanted.

Shemal just wants to live a normal life, leave his pirating days behind him and prove that he's respectable now. The last thing he needs is the two idiots who show up wanting his help with the noble they've kidnapped—the very man Shemal had been hoping to prove himself to, the man he hasn't forgotten since Shemal punched him a year and a half ago.

About the Author

Megan is a long time resident of LGBTQ romance, and keeps herself busy reading, writing, and publishing it. She is often accused of fluff and nonsense. When she's not involved in writing, she likes to cook, harass her cats, or watch movies. She loves to hear from readers, and can be found all over the internet.

maderr.com
maderr.tumblr.com
meganaderr.blogspot.com
facebook.com/meganaprilderr
meganaderr@gmail.com
@amasour